"Your

table.

"What are you doing?" she asked nervously.

"This." He bent down and lightly touched his lips to hers.

Shocked, dazed, even frightened by this unexpectedly intimate contact, Fiona didn't respond. Her mind was skittering wildly, even as her heart thumped hard. Which Fiona *was* she right now? Oh God, which one?

He pulled away a little, and gravely said, "Do you not want me to?"

She shrugged, hanging onto her composure for dear life. "You can. If you want to."

"I do," he answered with that same gravity. He kissed her again.

By Lisa Berne

The Penhallow Dynasty
THE LAIRD TAKES A BRIDE
YOU MAY KISS THE BRIDE

Coming Soon
THE BRIDE TAKES A GROOM

LISA BERNE

THE LAIRD TAKES A BRIDE

THE PENHALLOW DYNASTY

AVONBOOKS

An Imprint of HarperCollinsPublishers

This is a work of fiction. Names, characters, places, and incidents are products of the author's imagination or are used fictitiously and are not to be construed as real. Any resemblance to actual events, locales, organizations, or persons, living or dead, is entirely coincidental.

Excerpt from *The Bride Takes a Groom* copyright © 2018 by Lisa Berne.

First Avon Books mass market printing: September 2017

Print Edition ISBN: 978-0-06-245181-1
Digital Edition ISBN: 978-0-06-245180-4

Cover illustration by Anna Kmet

Avon, Avon & logo, and Avon Books & logo are registered trademarks of HarperCollins Publishers in the United States of America and other countries.
HarperCollins is a registered trademark of HarperCollins Publishers in the United States of America and other countries.

FIRST EDITION

17 18 19 20 21   QGM   10 9 8 7 6 5 4 3 2 1

For Lucia Macro

Acknowledgments

With deepest gratitude to Cheryl Pientka, Sarah Weston, Katelyn Detweiler, and Sophie Jordan.

Chapter 1

The stronghold of clan Douglass
Near Wick Bay, Scotland
1811

It was Fiona Douglass's seventy-first wedding.

To be precise, it was her seventy-first time *attending* a wedding.

When you belonged to a large and thriving clan, there were naturally a lot of weddings to go to and the total number was bound to be high, especially if you weren't a giddy girl any longer, but — to put it politely — a lady of considerable maturity.

So: seventy-one weddings for Fiona.

The details had long begun to blur, of course, but there were certain ceremonies that stood out in her mind.

Today would be memorable because her youngest sister, Rossalyn, was getting married.

Two years ago, in this very church, a spectacular brawl had erupted at the altar when the bridegroom's twin brother (already roaring drunk) had lunged forward, seized the hapless bride, and tried to carry her off. A wild melee ensued as several other men (also already drunk) had, with joyful shouts, joined in. Forty-five minutes later, the combatants subdued by brute force and the bride's veil hastily repaired, the ceremony had proceeded without further incident, the chastened, bloodied twin the very first to warmly shake his brother's hand.

It was also in this church that three years ago Fiona had attended the wedding of her younger sister Dallis.

Seven years ago, old Mrs. Gibbs, aged ninety-eight and heartily disliked by nearly everyone in the entire clan, had loudly expired just before the vows were spoken. The general agreement was that she'd done it deliberately in a last triumphant bid for attention, and that she was likely chuckling up in heaven (or down below in the other place) because afterwards, as her corpse was being removed, her pet ferret had crawled out from a pocket in her skirt and dashed up the towering headdress of a haughty dowager from Glasgow, from which vantage point it had leaped gracefully onto the shoulder of Fiona's own mother, who had screamed and then fainted, sending the bride into hysterics and several small boys into paroxysms of noisy laughter, thereby provoking Fiona's father, the mighty chieftain of clan Douglass, into a fury so awful that the wedding was quietly called off and no one dared to partake of the gargantuan feast laid out in the Great Hall, resulting, of course, in a great deal of secret rejoicing in the servants' hall for at least three days after that. The ferret was never seen again.

Eight years ago, it had rained so hard during the wedding of Fiona's cousin Christie that the church had begun to leak in (Fiona had counted) fourteen places and quite a few hats had been ruined.

And nine years ago — why, nine years ago Fiona had watched as her younger sister Nairna had married the love of her life.

The love of *Fiona's* life.

Fiona had never told Nairna that. She knew that seventeen-year-old Nairna was madly in love with Logan Munro, and as for Logan, who could fault him for preferring sweet Nairna Douglass, as soft and playful as a kitten, petite and rounded in all the right places and with masses of dark curls that framed her piquant little face most fetchingly? Who *wouldn't* prefer Nairna to Fiona, at eighteen painfully thin and gawky and oversensitive, who blurted things out and tripped over her own feet? Especially since, at that moment in time, Nairna's dowry had been substantially greater than Fiona's.

It all made total sense.

Even back then, in the darkest period of her devastation, Fiona hadn't been able to summon resentment or hostility toward Nairna, whom she had loved — still loved — with the fierce, protective devotion of an oldest sister for her younger siblings.

To be sure, there was a secret part of her, a sad and cowardly part, that would have driven her far from home on this lovely summer's day, where she wouldn't be forced to look upon Logan Munro's handsome face, but to this desire she hadn't succumbed; wild horses couldn't have kept her from attending Rossalyn's wedding. She had, though, slid inconspicuously into the very last pew. She did this also as a kindness to her fellow guests. Even with her hair twisted into smooth braids, all coiled together and set low on her nape, she was so tall that she could easily block the view of others behind her. Nonetheless, and thanks to her accursed height, she could plainly see Logan where he sat, several pews away, next to Nairna.

Logan's hair was still black as a raven's wing, still thick. His shoulders were still broad and heavily muscled beneath the fine mulberry-colored fabric of his fashionable coat.

And, Fiona realized, a heart could still physically hurt, could ache painfully within one's breast, even after nine long years.

She made herself look away from Logan.

Instead she gazed down at her hands, loosely clasped in her lap. Hands that weren't white as they ought to be, fingers that were a little coarsened by riding without gloves, by long hours working in her garden.

Around her slim — the less charitable might even have said bony — wrist was looped the silken cord of her reticule.

Surreptitiously Fiona loosened the opening of the reticule and pulled out a small piece of paper, quietly unfolding it. On it she had written her latest list.

Ask Dallis — when new baby due?
Avoid Logan
5 sheep with bloody scours, 2 with rupturing
   blisters — why?
Help Aunt Bethia find her spectacles
   (bedchamber? solarium?)
Avoid Logan
Avoid Cousin Isobel, too
Mother's birthday next Saturday
Tell Burns — STOP cutting roses too early
Avoid Logan
Avoid Logan

Fiona withdrew a small pencil from her reticule and added another item.

Stop thinking about Logan

She also wrote:

Make sure maid packed Rossalyn's warmest
 wraps & tartans
Northern cow pasture — fence fixed?
Osla Tod — toothache — better or worse?
Stop thinking about Logan

Then she carefully folded the little piece of paper in two, slid it and her pencil back into her reticule, and looked toward the front of the church, ensuring that her gaze was firmly fixed on Rossalyn and her bridegroom, Jamie MacComhainn.

How exquisite was Rossalyn's gown, all shimmery silk and delicate lace, and how beautiful she looked in it. Jamie, in his turn, was a bonny young man. Fiona eyed him — the back of him — speculatively. Perhaps even a little bit suspiciously. He was amiable and intelligent, and from a good family. Father had approved his suit readily enough and had even, in a sentimental spasm, doubled Rossalyn's dowry, and so here she was, not quite seventeen, a bride.

Fiona watched as Rossalyn and Jamie turned to each other and smiled. Oh, she hoped that all would be well. She wished that she knew Jamie better, that she trusted him more.

But thanks to handsome, charming, winsome Logan Munro, Fiona tended to view men with a certain skepticism.

A certain reserve.

She thought back to that dark time when she was eighteen, when Logan had come to Wick Bay to visit. Nothing formal had been declared between them, but enough had transpired, previously, in Edinburgh, to make Fiona feel confident that she'd soon be betrothed. Instead, with stunning speed Logan had transferred his affections to Nairna, gone to Father to request her hand in marriage, and been — to everyone's amazement — accepted on the spot, quite possibly because Nairna, among all her sisters, held the softest spot in the hard and erratic heart of Bruce Douglass.

Even though Fiona had confided in her mother about her hopes, Mother had, without missing a beat, continued to smile and flutter around Logan, petting and praising her future son-in-law. Fiona had long considered her mother — warm and affectionate, plump and still pretty in middle age — as soft and yielding and altogether as comfortable as a child's stuffed toy, but still, her behavior did seem a trifle callous.

Privately, Fiona had said to her, hating the little tremble in her voice:

"Mother, why are you so *friendly* toward Logan? After what he did to me?"

"Oh, my darling child, I know how hard it is for you, truly I do," said her mother, her large dark eyes filling with tears. "I remember how dreadful I felt when I discovered that your father had married me for my fortune — I really had thought it was a love match. It all happened during that terrible famine of the eighties, and people were starving. I was an heiress, you know. And only seventeen, like dear Nairna! But," she had added, smiling through her tears, "I was considered quite beautiful in my day! Even your father said so! And he used my dowry so cleverly — within a few years he brought the clan back into prosperity!"

Earnestly Mother had leaned forward to pat Fiona's hand. "Thanks to your father we all live so comfortably, Fiona dear! Our gowns and jewels! Everything of the finest quality! So you see, everything always works out for the best. I'm sure that Nairna and Logan will be very happy together — such a *handsome* couple, and he simply *dotes* upon her! —

and that another suitor will come along for you — someone you'll like even better."

Fiona had brushed that aside. "You don't regret marrying Father?"

"Regret?" Mother's dark eyes had shown nothing but bewilderment. "What a foolish notion, Fiona, to be sure! Besides, by the time I met your father I had, luckily, very nearly recovered from my stupid infatuation for my second cousin Ludovic — or was he my *third* cousin? So confusing! — it would never have done, you know, for the very next year he went to America and was killed. And your father so tall and so strong, and so handsome! Like a Viking warrior, everyone said!" Mother had fidgeted with the soft fringe of her shawl, then smiled again and with every appearance of sincerity went on: "I've been very happy these twenty years. Your father has taken such good care of us, and I'm just sorry that I haven't been able to do my duty by him."

She meant, Fiona knew, that she had not been able to produce a living son, despite miscarriages (the total number of which she didn't divulge), two stillbirths, and four healthy baby girls. Of this sad fact everyone in the Douglass keep was fully aware, for periodically Father would erupt into one of his angry outbursts, quite often in the Great Hall with dozens of people present.

You've failed me, madam! he would roar, pounding his silver goblet on the table, denting it in a way that would have been comical if it wasn't all so unpleasant. *Other men have ten sons — a dozen sons — and I have none!*

Or: *I had my pick of maidens, and 'twas my misfortune to choose you, madam. They told me you were fertile! Fertile for sons, that is,* he might add, with a contemptuous glance toward his daughters.

Or: *I've managed to save this clan from extinction, and what have you done all these years? Nothing!*

Mother would sit quietly, passively, but Fiona — watchful, observant, even as a child — would see the quiver of her tender mouth, the quick rise and fall of her chest as she gave a deep silent sigh, her shoulders held tensely high.

And then Father might fling his tankard out into the Hall, striking an unwary soul, or abruptly stand up and shove back his chair, toppling it, or stalk off, aiming kicks at the dogs who, fortunately, had learned to be preternaturally nimble when their master's voice was raised. Fiona would look around and see the tears in Mother's eyes, and in her sisters' eyes, too. Not hers, though: her eyes were dry and her heart would feel all stony and angry.

"Mother," she would hiss, "he's *awful*."

And then Mother would pull herself together, and drop her shoulders, and smile. "Oh no, Fiona dear, it's just that he's had so much on his mind. Didn't you hear him say there's a wolf after his sheep, and the Talbots are feuding again and setting fires? It's not easy being chieftain, you know. Here — won't you have another slice of mutton? I vow, you've somehow gotten thinner since breakfast!"

And grumblingly Fiona would accept the mutton, being, in fact, still hungry.

The human storm that was Father would just as easily shift into good humor, and then there was no one in the world more delightful to be around. But you could never trust that he'd *stay* cheerful. His expression could darken in an instant, his fists would clench, and things might fly across the room. You always felt a little wary around Bruce Douglass.

Eventually, he seemed to accept his fate as the father of only daughters. There was, at least, a crumb of comfort for him in this unfortunate debacle: the wealth he'd amassed made the Douglass girls highly desirable matrimonial quarry.

Father had therefore had quite a bit of fun by decreasing his daughters' dowries on a whim, or suddenly increasing them to astronomical sums, thus keeping his lawyers in a continual anxious flurry of documents destroyed and rewritten. Fiona's case was a little different. When, in his opinion, she'd been particularly annoying by — for example — forcefully disputing something he'd said, or disappearing all day on her horse, Father would retaliate by eliminating her dowry entirely. But not forever. The sun would shine, Father would change his mind, and eventually restore it, quite possibly to a radically different amount.

Over the years, suitors for the Douglass girls came and went, thronged and melted away, and Father watched, welcomed, interrogated, feinted, scorned, rejected, laughed, and allowed himself to be shamelessly flattered by them all. One by one, his daughters wed.

All except Fiona, who had never, somehow, found someone she liked enough to accept, and Father, rather surprisingly, had only nine or ten times threatened to lock her in her bedchamber until she said yes.

And so the time had passed, on the whole not unpleasantly. Fiona had kept herself busy. There was always so much to do.

But weddings tend to resurrect old issues, old emotions; new ideas, new possibilities.

As if on cue, Fiona was distracted from gazing steadfastly (if a little absently) at Rossalyn and Jamie when, from his seat four pews away, Niall Birk turned and smiled at her, showing all his teeth and this, in the context of a rather long face with large damp eyes, reminding Fiona forcibly of a horse.

Niall Birk hadn't given her the time of day for quite

a while, which probably meant that Father had, in a last-ditch effort to get his remaining daughter off his hands, taken advantage of the massive clan gathering at the keep to make it known that Fiona was not only dowered again, but — judging by the breadth of Niall Birk's grin — very generously as well.

Fiona's suspicion was confirmed when, as soon as the ceremony was over, not only was she swiftly approached by Niall, but Ross Stratton and Walraig Tevis came crowding up around her, eagerly soliciting her hand for the dancing that was to follow the enormous meal awaiting them in the Great Hall.

Fiona looked at them thoughtfully. She was twenty-seven. Since Logan, she'd never met a man who had caught her interest, or made her laugh, or inspired her blood to run a little hotter.

Perhaps that was all behind her now.

Perhaps she was incapable of falling in love again.

Still, marriage had its benefits, didn't it? She would be mistress of her own household. Maybe there would be children. And she'd no longer be subject to the unpredictable, tempestuous swings of Father's moods — that in itself was appealing.

Walraig Tevis, a great lumbering fellow nearly as wide as he was tall, pushed spindly Ross Stratton to one side. "You're daft, Stratton, to think you've got a chance with Fiona," he said, his heavy face alight with malicious humor. "She's a full head over you, you wee mousie, you'd be the laughingstock of the clan!" He jabbed a beefy elbow into Ross's chest with such force that the smaller man reeled backwards and nearly fell over, but with surprising dexterity he whipped from his boot a nasty-looking dagger and only the quick intervention of the scandalized minister prevented what promised to be a vicious altercation, and possibly a murder or two, from occurring a mere twenty paces from the church.

Yes, as a married woman she'd be free of Father, Fiona thought, but she'd also be putting herself in the power of a husband who would have the indisputable right to do anything he liked with her.

To her.

And yet . . . and yet if *any* of them were to give the slightest sign that they really liked her, she might be tempted to seize the opportunity provided her by Father's momentary generosity. Niall, for example, wasn't bad-looking (especially since she liked horses). He wasn't completely stupid. And he had a decent estate not far from where Rossalyn would be living with her husband Jamie MacComhainn; she could visit them often.

Experimentally, Fiona stepped a little closer to Niall. She caught a whiff of stale sweat, alcohol, onions, and even — her nose wrinkled — a faint, flat, rank scent of blood. She flashed a quick glance over him and saw a reddish clump of matted hair near one temple.

He grinned. "Bad, eh? You should see Dougal Gow. Poor lad couldn't rise from his bed to come to the wedding. He'll miss the feast *and* the dancing. So, you'll give me the first two reels, lass?"

Fiona had a sudden image of Niall, stinking of blood and onions, saying casually to Rossalyn at some future gathering: *Fiona couldn't come, for the poor lass is in bed — fell down the stairs and she's all black and blue.*

She took a step back, abruptly reminded of something that happened during last year's sheep-shearing festival, when she had allowed Niall to kiss her behind a shed (she'd had a dowry then). Pressing his mouth on hers, he'd bent her neck back too far, while at the same time he squeezed her breast so roughly she'd thought for a bad, a very bad moment she would pass out.

She answered coolly: "No. I'm not dancing."

"Your loss."

"I'll try to bear it."

His arm shot out and he took a hard grip on her upper arm. "I don't care for your tone. You're to be a good girl and choose a husband from among the three of us. It's your father's decree."

"A fine way to woo, Niall Birk, grabbing at a woman and scowling at her. Let go of me."

His fingers tightened painfully for a moment before he released her. "You're thinking I'm a bad bargain, no doubt, but at least I'm not a great lump like Walraig Tevis, who'd crush you under him like a bug, or Ross Stratton, who'd as soon garrote you as kiss you."

A cold chill shivered up Fiona's spine, but she only said, lightly, "You may be right. Would you excuse me, please? My mother needs me." And she flitted off to where Mother did, in fact, require help untangling herself from the enormous plaid shawl she had wound about herself in so convoluted a fashion she was in danger of — curiously enough — falling down the church steps.

"Oh, thank you, dear!" Mother said breathlessly. "It was a lovely ceremony, wasn't it? I cried just like a baby! But I always do at weddings. I cried at my own! Isn't our Rossalyn the bonniest bride you've ever seen? Although Dallis, of course, was *just* as pretty, and so was Nairna! Your Aunt Bethia quite agrees with me! And oh! Bethia shared with me the most astounding piece of news! She had it from her sister-in-law Sorcha who is, I'm sure, *most* reliable. Apparently Alasdair Penhallow has been scandalizing the Eight Clans for years with his disgraceful behavior, and not just on special occasions but every day! Consuming spirits to excess, presiding over debaucheries, and so on! A monster of irresponsibility! And he the great laird of Castle Tadgh!"

"Well, Mother, so what? Besides, if he's been doing

this sort of thing for years, it's hardly news," said Fiona, guiding her overexcited parent down the uneven stone steps and at the same time keeping a sharp eye out for Logan Munro.

"No, no, you mistake me! According to Bethia, Alasdair Penhallow, on a dare, recently rode his horse all throughout his castle, and without a stitch of clothes on!"

"Did the horse have a saddle?" inquired Fiona, now a little interested.

"Bethia didn't say. I'll have to ask her. But isn't it an atrocious tale?" Mother made a tsk-tsk sound, but whether it was because of the enormous pile of dog manure blocking her path or her feelings about the shocking Alasdair Penhallow, Fiona didn't bother to ask. Her flicker of interest had already waned. And she had more important things to think about.

Nairna — is she expecting too??
Make plan: must get rid of Niall, Walraig
    & Ross
STOP THINKING ABOUT LOGAN
    MUNRO

Throughout the feast, Fiona was irritated to find that her three would-be suitors had decided to all sit next to her, two on one side and one on the other, altogether giving her a disagreeable sense of claustrophobia. It quite took away one's own appetite, which made her even more resentful.

Nonetheless, as the evening wore on, seemingly interminably, she not only managed to avoid the dancing, she also went here and there and got a great deal accomplished.

She found Aunt Bethia's spectacles, which were, in fact, in the stillroom, although they had inexplicably been placed in the bowl of a large wooden mortar otherwise used for crushing herbs.

She dashed up to Rossalyn's room, spoke with her maid, approved the packing of the trunks.

She neatly avoided speaking with Cousin Isobel, against whom she still bore a grudge after nine long years, for her role in the Logan Munro disaster —

But no. She *wasn't* thinking about him.

She went on.

She learned that her sister Dallis, three years married and with a little one at home just taking his first wobbly steps, was looking forward to the birth of her second child in six months or so.

She enjoyed a fascinating and productive discussion with old Clyde Keddy about rupturing blisters and the various possibilities for treatment, although he confessed he was stumped about the bloody scours.

She drew Nairna aside, into a private alcove, and clasped her hands in her own. She looked down into her sister's lovely heart-shaped face; it was thinner and paler than she remembered, although Nairna looked decidedly plumper in her midsection. "Are you quite well, my dearie?"

Nairna smiled radiantly. "I've never been happier! Oh, Fiona, it's happened at last!"

"You're increasing?"

"Yes! Finally!"

"I'm so glad for you!" said Fiona, meaning it, and warmly hugged Nairna, already thinking, in the back of her mind, about sewing some adorable little garments for the baby in addition to the ones she'd already planned for Dallis's.

"Logan's been so patient all these years," Nairna said, blushing. "It's not been for lack of trying. But three months ago, my courses ceased, and I'm already showing! And it's all thanks to Tavia Craig!"

"Who is that, my dearie?"

"She's a wisewoman, and so awfully kind! She cured Logan's mother of the warts on her hands — they've been plaguing her for *months* — and knew exactly what to do to make his sister's cough go away!"

"Yes, but —" Fiona hesitated. Wasn't there a vast difference between warts and coughs, and difficulty in conceiving a baby? "What does Mother say?"

"Mother said she wished *she'd* consulted a wise-woman, for very likely she would have had boys instead of girls."

Fiona refrained from commenting that Mother's regret implied a desire to negate her daughters' very existence, then immediately was ashamed of this sour thought, for she knew that Mother loved them all. "Well, it's wonderful news to be sure, my dearie!" she said instead.

"Yes, and Tavia is *certain* it's a boy! Logan is so excited!"

"So excited about what?" came a familiar voice, and at the sound of it Fiona felt as if her stomach dropped like a boulder to her toes. She took a breath, and tilted her head toward Logan Munro. She was considered very tall for a woman, but Logan was even taller. Once upon a time, she had loved that about him, loved gazing *up* into his deep, dark eyes.

"Excited about the baby, Logan!" said Nairna breathlessly, her pretty face lighting up as it always did when she saw him. "I've just been telling Fiona all about it — about *him!*"

"Yes," Logan replied, smiling, "it's wonderful news, my beautiful one."

Nairna blushed all over again, then said, "Oh! I have another question for Dallis about the lying-in!

Stay, darling, and talk to Fiona! Doesn't she look lovely in that blue gown?"

"Indeed she does." Logan watched as his wife hurried away.

With that crest of thick black hair and juttingly straight nose, his profile was magnificent. And how often, how very often, had he called her, Fiona, *my beautiful one* . . . Fiona tamped down a treacherous rush of sweet memories as Logan turned to her again. Behind them, along the stone corridor, tramped a raucous horde of guests, singing "At the Auld Trysting Tree" at the top of their lungs and banging — God in heaven, where had they gotten pots and pans? — on the walls. Yet Logan never took his eyes from her. It was another one of his attractions: he always made her feel as if she was the only one in any room, at any gathering . . .

Fiona almost felt as if she was melting in the delicious warmth of Logan's proximity. The years seemed to suddenly dissolve between them — she was once again a romantic, dazzled eighteen-year-old, and she found herself leaning a little closer to him, her lips parting expectantly, her limbs all at once feeling wonderfully heavy. Then, with a kind of inner gasp, she thought in horror: *You fool! Nairna! Your sister!*

She drew herself up to her full height, said coolly, "My congratulations to you both," and briskly walked past Logan Munro, away from him, ignoring the fact that in his expression, his half-smile, was a sympathetic sort of understanding, as if a little secret bond, unshakable, unbreakable, drew them together.

A night and a day later, the celebrations were finally over. Her sisters had left with their husbands. Nearly all the guests had gone, too, and the weary servants were hard at work cleaning up the keep — no small task given the broken dishes, the spilled food, the toppled bottles of spirits, the rushes in the common areas sodden and bad-smelling, and everywhere discarded items of clothing which made Fiona frown as she made her way up to the solarium where Mother spent much of her time. Here, at least, was order and cleanliness. Well, actually, to be honest there was more cleanliness than order, for Mother, as dear and delightful as she was, wasn't known for her organizational abilities.

Still, as afternoon sunlight poured in through the long bank of narrow windows that had once served as arrow-loops, the solarium was a pleasant chamber, with the scattered piles of fabric, the great loom in the corner, Mother's harp, old copies of *La Belle Assemblée,* shawls and ribbons and colorful spools of thread all combining in a scene of familiar and cheerful disarray.

"Hello," said Fiona cautiously, standing at the threshold.

Mother looked up from the escritoire at which she sat and put aside her quill, her face brightening in welcome, then promptly clouding. "Oh, Fiona *dear,*" she said uneasily.

Fiona came in and threw herself into a chair by the fire, stretching out her long legs to warm her toes in their tall boots. "What's done is done, Mother," she replied, unable to keep a slight note of defiance from her voice.

"Yes, but to challenge Niall Birk and Walraig Tevis to an arm-wrestling match?" said Mother with plaintive dismay. "And then to beat them both!"

"I can't brag about it, Mother, for they were both so drunk they could hardly sit up."

"Brag about it? Oh my goodness, why would you? So unmaidenly! And then to dare Ross Stratton to compete with you in a footrace!"

"It wasn't a fair match either. He was drunk *and* for some reason he had on someone else's shoes, and they were far too small for him."

Mother gave a little moan. "Oh, Fiona, this is dreadful!"

"Yes, but Mother, I *had* to get rid of them, don't you see? Everyone mocked them so badly that they left before dawn, without trying to propose to me again. And now Father can't pressure me into accepting them. Wasn't it clever of me?"

"Well, yes, of course it was, darling, you've always been so terribly clever, but now . . ." Mother looked nervously toward the doorway. She lowered her voice and went on: "But now your father is *furious* with you, and he's completely taken away your dowry again."

"I don't care about the dowry, but —" Fiona felt a frisson of anxiety on Mother's behalf. "— he's not angry at you, is he?"

"Oh no, dear, it's all you, I'm afraid. But without a dowry, and for who knows how long, what is going to happen to you? Who will want to marry you?"

Fiona knew that Mother didn't mean to be hurtful. But still it did hurt, a little, in some obscure, unprotected area of her heart. "Why, I'll go on living here forever," she said lightly. "When Father isn't angry at me, he finds me quite useful to have around. In fact, when he's in a pleasant state of mind, or is a little inebriated, he's often said I'm nearly as good as a son — such a way as I have with the crops and the animals."

Mother brightened again. "That's true. And you're *such* a help in the keep! Speaking of which, Cousin Isobel would like to switch bedchambers. She's worried her room is overlarge and requires too much wood to keep warm. I've tried to dissuade her — we've wood enough for an army! — but she insists! Please could you talk to Mrs. Abercrombie about it?"

"Cousin Isobel is still here? Ugh. Why?"

"Yes, dear, she's come for a nice long visit. You ought not to scowl so. You'll get wrinkles before your time, and that won't help matters! I invited her to stay on because she's suffered some financial reverses. She's had to give up her house in Edinburgh, you know, the poor thing. Where are you going?" Mother added, as her firstborn stood and shook out her skirts.

"Riding." Fiona glanced down at Mother's cluttered escritoire. "Your quill needs mending. Would you like me to do that?"

"No, thank you, darling, I've quite finished my letters. *Six* thank-you notes, and I even managed to write to Henrietta Penhallow — I've owed her a letter for these many ages."

Penhallow. That name again. How odd. "Who is she, Mother?"

"A distant connection in England, whom I met in London many years ago."

"Oh," said Fiona, losing interest. Not only did she want to avoid Cousin Isobel, she'd prefer to get out of the keep without encountering Father if possible, while his temper was running high. "Well, I'm off to see Osla Tod, and bring her a tincture for her toothache. You know she lives beyond the bogs, so don't expect me for dinner."

"Oh dear, *must* you stay out past sunset? You'll take a groom, won't you?"

"No." Fiona spoke without rancor. Mother knew she'd left off having a groom accompany her on her rides for many years now, but still she faithfully

asked, in the same sweet and hopeful way. Fiona
dropped a kiss on Mother's smooth white forehead
and quickly left the solarium, her boot-heels clicking
sharply on the cold flagstone flooring. She spoke with
the housekeeper Mrs. Abercrombie about accommo-
dating Cousin Isobel's request, and it was with relief
that some half an hour later she was on her stallion
Gealag and riding fast — away from the keep, away
from Father, away from them all. Sleep had not come
to her last night and now she was fatigued to her very
bones, but at least she could, for these few snatched
hours, be free.

She loved the feel of the cool afternoon air ruf-
fling her hair and her skirts, loved the vibrant green
of summer all around her and the great blue sky
above. Loved gripping the leather reins in her bare
hands and how willingly her big white horse carried
her along. It was almost like flying. Her tired mind
calmed, quieted; slowly, slowly, almost without real-
izing it, she drifted into a pleasant daydream.

Herself. In a lovely blue gown. Dancing, swirling
circles on a polished wood floor, her lacy hem fluttering around her ankles. Held in strong arms. Her heart
beating hard. Looking up. Looking up into dark eyes,
alight with passion . . .

No.

Fiona snapped out of it. Gripped Gealag's reins
more tightly. And fiercely summoned a new image into
her mind.

A small piece of paper.

Rheumatism — Mrs. Abercrombie —
    chamomile? Cat's claw?
Order new parcel of books
Sheep & rupturing blisters — research. Cause,
    treatment?

Visit northern cow pasture tomorrow
Gift for Mother's birthday?
Start sewing baby things
Gealag — to be shoed next week
NEW RUSHES brought in tomorrow
    WITHOUT FAIL

And so it went. Today she would visit old Osla Tod. Tomorrow she would cross off as many items as she could from her list. The next day, she would do the same. And the day after that as well. There was, after all, a kind of comfort in knowing what the weeks and months ahead would bring.

But Fiona was wrong.

Five days later, the letter came — the letter that would change everything.

Chapter 2

Castle Tadgh, Scotland
Three weeks earlier . . .

Pain. So much pain. His head felt as if it were clamped in the devil's own vise, and his temples throbbed with fiendish intensity, as steady and relentless as his own heartbeat. His limbs were stiff and cramped. His mouth was dry and his closed eyelids were but a feeble shield against the stabbing brightness assaulting them.

Alasdair Penhallow groaned softly.

Slowly, reluctantly, he opened his eyes.

Various items of note swam sluggishly up to the surface of his dazed consciousness.

He was sitting (more or less) in the laird's throne-like chair of beautifully carved wood, in his own Great Hall. Squeezed next to him was a voluptuous black-haired lass, dressed only in her chemise, deeply and peacefully asleep, with her head lolled back and a gentle snore issuing from between cherry-red lips. Late-morning sun illuminated the Hall with a cheery intensity that seemed, in his current pained state, to be more than a little incongruous, and possibly even slightly jeering.

All around the Hall — on the floor, in chairs, even atop the long tables — were men and women, sleeping, stretched out, curled up, flat on their backs, sometimes intertwined. Bottles, dishes and goblets, clothing and hats, candles burned down to their wicks, lutes and pipes and drums, all lay scattered without rhyme or reason. Someone — dear God, hopefully not himself — had knocked over one of the massive suits of armor which now lay sprawled by the fireplace in a very undignified way, with a spangled slipper sticking out of the visor.

Alasdair frowned and with an effort turned his aching eyes to the woman with whom he was sharing the laird's seat. Who in the hell *was* she? He had no idea. Uncle Duff had invited a lot of people to the celebration he'd organized in honor of his nephew's thirty-fifth birthday, and *they'd* brought a lot of people, and by midnight the Great Hall had been literally packed with guests.

Alasdair smiled faintly as the memories came flooding back. A good time had been had by all. The feasting, the singing, the dancing, and more . . .

So now he was thirty-five. He wondered if he should feel a little different. But why would he? A birthday merely represented, in an arbitrary way, the passage of time. Here he was, in the vigorous prime of his life, healthy as a horse, strong as an ox, rich as a king — enjoying an uninterrupted spate of years in which he did exactly as he pleased, whenever and wherever he liked.

Yes, life was good.

Just then, something cold and wet nudged his bare ankle.

Wondering where his shoes had gone, Alasdair

looked down to see his wolfhound Cuilean at his feet. Intelligent dark eyes were looking up at him inquiringly, shaggy ears were pricked: a hint, Alasdair knew, that breakfast was long overdue. He reached down a hand to caress that rough head, and as he did so Cuilean sharply turned it, toward an archway leading off toward the kitchens.

Fervently did Alasdair hope it was a servant, bearing a refreshing tankard of ale (or even a silver pot filled to the brim with blisteringly hot coffee), but no, it was Dame Margery, quite possibly the oldest member of the clan, hunched over her gnarled stick and stumping into the Hall. Trailing behind was her little granddaughter Sheila, who viewed the dissolute scene before her with blasé indifference, her expression, distinguished by eyes which seemed to gaze in two different directions at once, seeming more focused on something immaterial and inward — and for that Alasdair could only be thankful, as uneasily he wondered if a seven-year-old really ought to be in the Great Hall at this particular moment.

As Dame Margery drew near, she noisily banged her stick on the marble floor, causing people nearby to stir, moan, rouse. She passed by Uncle Duff, insensate, draped sideways on a chair and his long beard dangling perpendicularly, and muttered audibly, "Ach, the old wastrel!" before turning her piercing and unblinking stare to Alasdair. Finally she stopped before the dais on which the two great chairs — one for the laird, one (long unoccupied) for his lady — stood. Her silence, Alasdair noticed, had a heavy, expectant, rather ominous sort of quality, and he groaned under his breath. He wasn't in the mood for drama. Still, he *was* the laird, and one must be polite, so he cleared his throat and said:

"Good day to you, madam."

"And to you, laird," she answered with an awful, punctilious politeness. "May I tender my congratulations to you on your birthday."

"I thank you."

"I believe I am correct, laird, that as of yesterday you turned thirty-five?"

"Aye, madam."

"Not thirty-four, laird?"

"Nay, thirty-five, madam."

"Not married, are you, laird?"

Alasdair looked narrowly at Dame Margery. Had she gone soft in her aged head? Everyone knew he was unmarried and, in fact, happily so. But courteously he replied: "Nay, madam, I'm not."

"Well then, laird, perhaps you are not aware of the ancient clan decree which dictates that any chieftain of Castle Tadgh who remains unmarried by his thirty-fifth birthday must immediately invite the eligible highborn maidens of the Eight Clans of Killaly to stay within the castle, and within thirty-five days choose one to be his bride?"

Dame Margery issued this disconcerting pronouncement in stentorian tones and with a single breath, leaving her gasping a little by the end. She breathed in deeply, then added sternly:

"The wedding to follow within thirty-five days."

A sufficient number of people had woken up by now to create a stunned, openmouthed audience for Dame Margery, who seemed well satisfied by the effect of her words. Alasdair sat upright, jostling the black-haired lass who let out a choked snore but remained blissfully asleep. He stared balefully at her and then at Dame Margery as the unpleasant import of her proclamation sank in.

"And if I don't obey?" he said, losing a little of his earlier politeness.

"Death to you, I fear," the old crone replied with annoying promptitude. "Hanged and quartered, laird, and your head displayed in the courtyard as a warning to all who leave off their sacred duty to the clan."

"To be picked clean by crows?" he said sarcastically.

"Nay, laird, according to clan law it's to remain on a pike for thirty-five days before being buried along with the rest of you. Depending on the weather, the crows might not have time to pick your head clean."

Thirty-five, thirty-five. It was, evidently, a theme, and Dame Margery seemed to be enjoying her role in this farce a little too much. Alasdair scowled fiercely. To do her justice, however, the old lady had been renowned for decades for her comprehensive knowledge of clan affairs.

If you wanted to secretly find out a person's birthday, you went to Dame Margery.

If you were grappling with some particularly tangled lines of relationship extending back a decade, a generation, or a century, Dame Margery could likely help you sort it out.

If you were curious about an event in clan history your great-uncle had once described to you but you'd since gotten fuzzy about — like that time a boulder had rolled down Ben Macdui and crushed three cottages, or was it a spring flood that had carried them away? — well, there was a good chance that Dame Margery would recall it.

Still, Alasdair wasn't about to go under without a fight.

"Bring out the Tome!" he roared, which only made his throbbing headache worse.

Someone scuttled to obey, and in the meantime Alasdair noticed that little Sheila was studying him with that odd wall-eyed way she had. *"What?"* he snapped.

"A room with a door, a door with a lock," she said, dreamily. "An egg that won't hatch, a bird that can't fly . . ."

"Hush, sweeting, hush," Dame Margery interrupted. "The laird has a great deal on his mind just now."

"Oh, but Granny, the laird's path will be hard for him."

"Hush now. We each have our own path to follow. You do, I do, the laird does. You're not to presume about the path of others."

Sheila nodded, vaguely, and then, seeming to dismiss the subject entirely, began poking about a nearby table for interesting leftovers.

While Alasdair waited, he sent for some ale, dislodged the lass from his chair, found his shoes, and watched with profound irritation as Uncle Duff finally woke up, yawned, stretched his arms, scratched at his beard, and finally, serenely, brought himself to an upright position and glanced around the Hall with the complacent expression of one who has engineered a highly successful party.

When Alasdair enlightened him as to the developments of the last fifteen minutes, Uncle Duff was suitably outraged.

"What, being forced to marry because old Margery says so?" he said scornfully. "Ridiculous, lad! Ah, ale!" he added happily, and snatched the mug from a tray a servant had been carrying toward Alasdair.

"To your health, Uncle," said Alasdair grimly.

"Thankee, lad!" cheerfully replied Duff, oblivious, his mustache already doused with foam.

By the time a servant returned lugging the enormous old Tome, and blown off most of the dust and cobwebs in which it was encased, Alasdair had managed to safely receive (and down in one long gulp) his own mug of ale, and set in motion general cleanup

of the Hall and breakfast to be served. The Tome —
the hoary and irrefutable compendium of clan law
— was set at the head of the high table and he began
leafing through it, with Duff hanging over his shoulder and his beard continually getting in the way, forcing Alasdair to testily bat it aside several times.

After some twenty minutes of fruitless searching,
Dame Margery, who had remained standing there,
leaning on her stick, issued a noise suspiciously close
to a cackle and said, "Page three hundred and twenty-
eight, laird."

Alasdair favored her with a hard glance, then turned
to page 328. There it was, in plain black and white.

He was indeed thirty-five and unmarried.

But, apparently, not unmarried for long.

Unless he wanted to die, and that he most certainly
did not. He was having far too good a time for that.

Besides, if he died without a son, everything that
he owned and cherished — his title, his authority,
his vast holdings — would be inherited by (according to the delightful vagaries of clan law) his distant
English cousin Gabriel Penhallow, rumored to be
an obnoxious, unintelligent, generally unappealing
fellow. Second in line was *his* cousin, a man named
Hugo Penhallow, of whom Alasdair knew nothing
save for the fact that he was English.

Alasdair felt his lip curling. He *would* die before
he left everything to a bloody Sassenach, left his clan
in such repulsive hands. He couldn't do that to them.

His fate, therefore, was sealed.

Alasdair looked again at Dame Margery. "I suppose, madam," he said coolly, "you already know
which eligible maidens I am to invite."

"Aye, laird." She pulled from her skirt pocket a
crisp piece of paper. "I've the list right here. Miss
Mairi MacIntyre, from the Western Isles. Miss Janet

Reid, from the Lowlands. Miss Fiona Douglass, from the Northern Highlands. And Miss Wynda Ramsay, from the Uplands. All the other highborn damsels being already married, widowed, too old, or too young."

"You are a marvel of efficiency, madam."

"Thank you, laird." She smiled — was it ironically? — and held out the paper to him. "For future reference."

Alasdair eyed it as he might view (or smell) a rotting carcass. "Take it, Uncle. You're to write to the lasses, and right away, for the sword of Damocles hangs above my head."

Uncle Duff laughed. "Ha, you're a funny one, lad," he said, and took the paper from Dame Margery. "I'll have Lister do it. What's a steward for, after all? And here comes breakfast, not a moment too soon, for I'm about to perish from hunger!" With maddening casualness he stuffed the list that spelled Alasdair's doom into his own pocket, and plumped himself into his seat at the high table, just at Alasdair's left. Gloomily Alasdair shoved aside the Tome and sat down, to be promptly served a plate heaped high with fried eggs, bacon, sausage, and hot fragrant tattie scones. At this he only gazed morosely, but he did accept a cup of coffee.

As slowly he drank it he observed Uncle Duff consuming with relish — bordering on outright avarice — his own delicious breakfast. When finally Duff paused to reach for a fresh mug of ale, he glanced over at Alasdair's plate.

"Not hungry, lad? I'll take that bacon if you don't want it."

"Why? So you can have *more* bits of bacon decorating your beard?"

Duff looked down, plucked a few little shards free and unrepentantly popped them into his mouth. In

other circumstances Alasdair might have been amused
by his insouciance, but today was a — well, today was
a special day.

"You're a pig, Uncle," he said sourly.

"Eh, you are what you eat, lad," replied Duff, and
reached for Alasdair's bacon, neatly scooping the
strips onto his plate.

Alasdair nodded his thanks to the servant who
had just refilled his cup, and ran a hand through his
close-cropped hair. His headache was finally receding, and for that he was grateful, but what was that
small benefit compared to everything else that was
happening?

With a frown he pushed his plate away.

"What in the name of heaven ails you, nephew?
You look as if your best horse just died. I'll just take
those scones, shall I, since you're not wanting them."

"What ails me?" Alasdair repeated irritably. "What
ails me, Uncle, is that I'm soon to be wed against my
will."

"So?"

"So? Are you daft, man? The life we've led is about
to come to a crashing halt."

"Why?" thickly said Duff through a mouthful of
heavily buttered scone.

Alasdair stared at him, and put down his cup with
a thump that sent coffee splashing over the rim. It
was after the simultaneous deaths, on that memorable day fifteen years ago, of his parents, his older
brother, and the others (he would not think of the
others) in that ill-fated sailing party, that Uncle Duff,
his mother's younger brother, had become his boon
companion. It was Duff — irrepressibly lively and
larky and carefree — who had come to Castle Tadgh
for the funerals and simply stayed on. He had res-
cued Alasdair from bone-crushing grief and gradually, patiently, lured him back into life. Or at least his

own version of a merry nonstop hurly-burly involving wine, women, and song. And food. And dancing. And gaming. And whatever other pleasurable pursuit occurred to him.

Duff had never married, oft declaring bachelorhood to be the most desirable state known to man, and somehow, gradually, without really thinking about it, Alasdair adopted this same attitude. Not for a moment had he neglected his obligations as laird, but still there had been plenty of time for — why, for fun.

Just the way he liked it.

"You'll excuse me for not exactly loving the idea of giving up my freedom," he now said to his uncle.

"*You're* the one who's daft, lad. What is a wife but a brood mare? You'll pick one of the lasses, get her with child as many times as it takes to produce a son or two, and that's the sum of it. Nothing else will change." Duff very generously put Alasdair's bacon (all but one strip) back on his plate and slid it toward him. "And we'll have a grand time once the lasses arrive! Feasts, dances, picnics, riding expeditions, tours of the castle, excursions to the Keep o' the Mòr, boating on the loch —" He stopped himself, then hastily added, "No, no sailing! But we'll be as gladsome as the day is long, you can be sure of that. It's the Penhallow way!"

Thoughtfully Alasdair picked up a strip of bacon and bit into it.

It was true, after all, that as laird he *did* owe it to the clan to produce an heir.

But Duff had a point.

There was no need to get all worked up about the whole thing. Nowhere was it written that he had to permit a wife to cling to him, bother him, get in his way, make demands on him.

Nobody was talking about a love-match.

And love — as a word, as a concept — wasn't something which he spent much time dwelling upon. Was his life diminished because of it? Not a bit of it; he'd gone on very happily, thank you very much, these past years.

All at once, like the dark clouds of night giving way to a clear new day, everything seemed wonderfully simple again, wonderfully safe, and Alasdair felt his mood lifting.

He took another bite of bacon.

It was fragrant and crunchy, with a delicious little ribbon of fat on one side.

He chewed, enjoyed, swallowed, reached for another piece, and as he did so he realized that Duff was leaning back in his chair, watching him, his hands folded across his ample middle and his eyes twinkling.

"That's more like it, lad! We'll seize the day as we always do! Once I've given the list to Lister with his instructions — ha! The list to Lister! — shall we head down to the river for some fishing?"

Alasdair smiled, really smiled, for the first time that day. Normalcy, like a fine, familiar mantle, seemed to wrap itself all about him, warm and comforting. It was all going to be just fine.

"Aye," he said cheerfully, and found himself thinking about that delectable black-haired lass again, she of the voluptuous figure and the cherry-red lips. Perhaps later on today or tonight, if she was still around, he could get to know her just a little bit better.

When Miss Mairi MacIntyre, of the Western Isles, received and read the letter summoning her forthwith to Castle Tadgh, she gave a soft gasp, felt a trifle lightheaded, and promptly sat down on the nearest sofa, grateful that her maid was quick to bring her vinaigrette and wave it gently underneath her nose, and that dear little Pug kept trying to lick her chin, as if he wanted to help, too.

This was *just* like the *Cendrillon* story, which she had read countless times as a little girl. The prince — in this case, Laird Alasdair Penhallow, who really was a kind of prince among the Eight Clans of Killaly — had invited the young ladies of the land to his beautiful castle, in order to select one to be his bride! Only there would be just four candidates, which did improve the odds tremendously. And, of course, she herself wasn't a servant girl forced to do a horrid amount of housework, dress in nasty tatters, and sleep among the cinders to keep warm.

Instead she lived a very nice life in a luxurious mansion, with fond parents who doted upon her and kept her under anxious watch as her constitution was, unfortunately, rather delicate.

On the other hand, there were so many similarities that it nearly took one's breath away. For example, how often did Mama and Papa call her their little princess? Every day! Too, she had a wonderful godmother, a dear friend of Mama's, who was so very kind and was always sending the most delightful gifts. And, like Cendrillon, Mairi loved to dance. At all the local assemblies she was *quite* sought-after. Everyone said that she had the tiniest waist, the prettiest little feet, and a laugh like the tinkling of fairy bells. People were so nice, weren't they?

Mairi picked up Pug and cradled him in her arms. "Oh, I *do* hope there will be a ball, Puggie! If I'm well enough, and Mama and Papa let me, I'll stay up *long* after midnight!"

Pug gave a short, sharp bark.

"You want to know if you can go too, Puggie? Of

course you can! I'll dress you up in your very best collar, too! We'll make absolutely sure it matches my gown." Mairi smiled and held him close.

When Miss Janet Reid, of the Lowlands, got her letter, she had only an hour before returned from a stroll in the manicured gardens to the back of her house, and in the company of a young man who had for the past months been courting her most ardently. (Her governess, Miss Sad Shovel as she liked to call her, had been discreetly trailing behind, her face just as dreary and spade-like as ever.) Janet had been inclined to encourage this young man over her other suitors, for he was terribly good-looking, came from a fine family, and stood to inherit a handsome fortune from his father. Oh, and she liked him well enough.

But having read the letter, she changed her mind. And she laughed, and clapped her hands with joy.

A marriage to the laird of Castle Tadgh would be a far better arrangement — quite a coup, in fact. Besides, she'd heard a few things about Alasdair Penhallow, and he *did* sound like fun. And she was quite partial to fun herself. Not for her the staid life of your average miss, always sitting around sewing samplers, or plucking dolefully at harps, or poring over dull books. No, *she* was cut from a very different sort of cloth. Which reminded her. She went with her light tread to the drawing-room, and announced:

"I'm going to Castle Tadgh. We need Miss Cowden to come in right away, and bring all her assistants, and plan to stay as long as necessary. I need a new wardrobe, and we haven't much time."

Her mother — seated across from Parson Tidwell, who had no doubt come on behalf of his tedious orphanage or his seemingly endless supply of poor people — at once lost her look of thinly disguised boredom and turned to Janet in astonishment. "You're going to Castle Tadgh? Why?"

"So I can marry Alasdair Penhallow, of course."

"The *Penhallow*? He's *offered* for you?"

Janet Reid smiled. "No. But he will."

Instantly her mother grasped the salient facts. "I'll send a note to Miss Cowden right away," she said, and with a nod to Parson Tidwell she rose, indicating that his presence was now, well, more than a little onerous.

Miss Wynda Ramsay's home was in the Uplands, but she was not there to personally receive the letter. She was in Glasgow, where she was in her final weeks at Miss Eglinstone's Finishing School for Young Ladies, at which esteemed establishment she had over the years received a superior education in all the necessary subjects including dancing, French, needlework, watercolors, music, penmanship, and use of the globes.

However, an express had swiftly been sent from home, and Wynda was to wait at Miss Eglinstone's until her parents could arrive and sweep her directly off to Castle Tadgh. Wynda used the time very productively to graciously share the good news with her schoolfellows (was it her imagination, or did they seem to turn an unattractive shade of green?), as well as to consult her guidebook which described all the best estates, castles, and monuments in Great Britain.

Castle Tadgh, it turned out, figured importantly as one of the most magnificent dwellings in Scotland.

It had been completely modernized by the present owner's father, while still preserving the essential and historical qualities of its centuries-long existence. The grounds, said the guidebook, were extensive, with a breathtaking view of Ben Macdui, the towering mountain considered by many to be the area's distinguishing geological feature.

Wynda pondered this, then tossed the guidebook aside and turned to her tall stack of London newspapers, magazines, and Court announcements. Alasdair Penhallow was related to the *English* Penhallows, which was far more interesting. And Mrs. Henrietta Penhallow, the celebrated matriarch of the family, had recently been occupying their palatial townhouse in Berkeley Square during the Season, where she had been seen at receptions at St. James's Palace (hobnobbing with *Royalty!*), at Almack's, balls, routs, assemblies, Venetian breakfasts, concerts, fashionable galleries, and everywhere else the *haut ton* went.

Who cared about fusty old castles when Society beckoned?

Surely, thought Wynda, the Scottish Penhallows would be invited to join their English relations on a long, long visit, and who would provide the requisite *entrée* into the most exclusive circles.

And surely she — with her beauty, her charm, her many accomplishments, her deep knowledge of both the Peerage and social etiquette — would shine as one of the most dazzling ornaments among the *beau monde*.

Her parents had stupidly believed she would be content to return home to Dumfries. That provincial backwater! Filled with nobodies!

But now, Wynda's ambitions suddenly seemed within her grasp.

Marry Alasdair Penhallow, and then . . . London.

Glittering, sophisticated London. It was waiting for her.

Sitting in the solarium with Mother and, unfortunately, Cousin Isobel, Fiona had just finished sewing a handsome little baby smock and was deciding whether to start on a new one, or to pick up her book, or to (reluctantly) help Cousin Isobel with a ludicrously tangled mass of yarn with which she was ineffectually wrestling, when Father came striding in, his muddy boots leaving a damp, malodorous trail behind him. In one hand he held an opened letter which he tossed at Fiona.

"You're off to Castle Tadgh, girl," he said.

"What? Why?" she demanded.

"Clan decree."

Frowning, Fiona picked up the paper from the floor at her feet and scanned both sides. "This is addressed to me."

Father shrugged, and Mother said in a high, excited voice, "What on earth is going on?"

"Alasdair Penhallow's to choose a bride from among the eligible lasses of the Eight Clans, that's what's going on. I suppose I'll have to reinstate her dowry. Although those drains in the turnip fields *are* clogging in a bad way."

Penhallow, thought Fiona, her brain spinning frantically. Penhallow again! Then she seized upon one pertinent element. "I'm sure I'm too old for this, Father!"

He only gave her a wolfish smile. "Read the letter."

She did. And glared at Father. "It says here that if I were *twenty-eight,* I'd be past the age of eligibility. This is ridiculous! Demeaning! I'd rather die than traipse off to Castle Tadgh to be displayed like a sheep before some reprobate!"

"Keep reading."

In a disbelieving voice Fiona read out loud: "'The consequence for failing to abide by sacred clan law is death. Said female to be weighted with stones and flung into the nearest loch known to have a depth greater than twenty feet. Bagpipe accompaniment optional.'"

"How romantic!" put in Cousin Isobel, wreathed in smiles. "Fiona, dear, what a wonderful opportunity for you!"

Fiona glared at her, too, wishing she could hang a millstone around that dame's plump neck and shove *her* into the closest body of water.

"You're to leave tomorrow," said Father.

"Tomorrow?" Mother exclaimed. "But I couldn't possibly be ready to leave by then!"

"Oh, you're not going," Father told her, then looked over at Fiona, his eyes twinkling maliciously. "I'm sending Isobel as her chaperone."

There was a stunned silence.

"*No!*" said Fiona with revulsion, even as Cousin Isobel gave a little shriek of delight and said:

"My dear Bruce! What an honor! You can be sure I'll take very, very good care of dear Fiona!"

Fiona shot her a malevolent glance. *Yes, just as you did in Edinburgh nine years ago, you old bat, when I came for a nice long visit. Encouraging Logan Munro's advances to me. Leaving us alone together, when you knew it was wrong. And look what happened. I fell head over heels in love with him, and expected to marry him. Only it didn't quite turn out that way, did it?*

Mother faltered, "But surely I ought to go . . . I simply assumed —"

"My mind's made up, madam. We'll have no further discussion on the topic. Besides, they won't be gone long. Penhallow will take one look at her and I reckon that'll be that."

A soft, incomprehensible murmur of distress came from Mother but she didn't dare to actually say anything, and Fiona responded, with a politeness that imperfectly concealed deep irony, "Why, thank you, Father. Everyone says I take after you, after all."

He scowled. "Will you never curb that sharp tongue of yours, girl? It's lucky for you that you're the spitting image of myself, else I'd have sworn your mother played me false."

"And you'd have left me as a babe on the shores of the bay to die?"

Another murmur from Mother; a growl from Father who curtly said to Isobel, "Make ready, for you both leave at dawn," and stalked out of the solarium. Gone but not forgotten, thought Fiona, as he'd left the foul stink of his boots behind him. Furiously she jumped to her feet and thrust the letter into the fire, and with a satisfaction she knew was foolish, she watched it burn to cinders.

She did not turn around when she heard Cousin Isobel exclaim happily, "Well! This is going to be so much *fun!*" Because otherwise she might have been tempted to say — or do — something which later, it was just possible she might regret.

Chapter 3

Castle Tadgh, Scotland
One week later . . .

This dinner, thought Alasdair Penhallow, was bizarre. During it, as one course succeeded another, he'd been stared at by his guests as if he were a puzzle to be worked out, a celestial visitation, an exotic and possibly dangerous wild beast, or a meal for a starving person.

He took a sip of wine and glanced around the high table. How odd to think that sitting here before him was the young lady who would become his wife. He wondered how long it would take for him to make his selection. Would he decide right away, or wait until the last minute? Luckily, no one could expect him to make a decision tonight, so he could, at least, look at them without raising expectations too high.

One thing was already obvious: they were four very different women.

Miss Mairi MacIntyre was a wee dainty lass, pretty as a princess, even to the sparkly tiara set in golden locks. She sat to his immediate right, and shared her chair (and much of her food) with her asthmatic pug-dog, a friendly little beast whose overtures to Cuilean had been met with regal indifference.

Next to Mairi was Miss Janet Reid, whose emerald-green eyes shone and white teeth flashed. Attractive and vivacious, she seemed entirely at her ease, matching him glass for glass of wine, and exchanging endless jokes and banter across the table with Uncle Duff, who roared with laughter and sent speaking glances of approval to Alasdair.

To Duff's left had been placed Miss Wynda Ramsay, clad in a daringly low-cut gown which flaunted a stupendous décolleté. She ignored Janet Reid's spirited attempts to bring her into the conversation, saying, in a clear, carrying voice to *her* neighbor, "So *vulgaire* to *parlay-voo sur la table! Il ne foo passie,* don't you agree, *mein sherry* Mademoiselle Douglass?"

Miss Fiona Douglass, the fourth candidate, seemed to jump at the sound of her surname, then turned to Wynda and said a little absently (in flawless French, unlike that of Wynda):

"*Ce sont des circonstances extraordinaires, alors peut-être beaucoup plus doit être pardonné.*"

These are extraordinary circumstances, so perhaps much must be forgiven. Alasdair repressed a sardonic snort of laughter as Wynda smiled and replied, with kindly condescension, "You speak French *oossie! Trez bean! Quel bonheer!*"

Janet Reid was less circumspect and *did* laugh heartily, although Wynda seemed oblivious as to the reason why. Alasdair directed his gaze again to Fiona Douglass. She was a striking woman — he supposed that could, at least, be said about her. She was unusually tall, and very slim, with thick straight hair of so pale a blonde that it seemed almost to have a silvery shimmer to it. Her eyes, big in her slender face and framed by long dark lashes, also defied simple classification, for they seemed to change color, much like a stormy sea or a sky roiled by strong winds. Just now they were a mysterious gray-blue, remote, aloof, as if she were — or rather wished herself to be — a thousand miles away.

She alone among the four gave the appearance of utter disinterest . . . in him? In the competition for his favor? Alasdair studied her curiously. She wasn't his type at all. He preferred shorter, rounder lasses, with dark hair and laughing eyes, who were lively and sportive. *Not* ice maidens who looked at you, through you, like you didn't even exist. That, he thought wryly, was an unusual experience for him.

Well, what did he care?

Fortunately, there were three other lasses who seemed to find him quite appealing.

Still, as he bent his head to courteously attend to a remark little Mairi was making, something about dancing and a ball (was she actually talking about glass slippers?), he wondered, just for a moment, exactly what it was that Miss Fiona Douglass was thinking about.

In her mind, Fiona was composing the letter she planned to write to Mother later that evening.

Today we arrived safely after six straight days of travel. I am deeply grateful I was riding Gealag as it spared me the necessity of talking to Cousin Isobel for much of the time. She was very distressed by the extravagance of our accommodations and insisted on, for her part, sleeping in less expensive bedchambers and so by the time we arrived at Castle Tadgh she was covered in fleas and the carriage is infested. I

will look into remedying that as soon as pos-
sible. The carriage, I mean. Cousin Isobel is on
her own.

The castle itself was a surprise. I've only seen
a little of it, but apparently it has been exten-
sively renovated. My rooms — yes, rooms —
include a capacious dressing-room with its very
own bathtub, with hot water cleverly conveyed
into it by means of a cylinder and pipe. Cousin
Isobel was scandalized when she saw it and de-
clared I must take my baths in a tub before the
fire, with hot water brought up by maids, as is
customary, but there she is wrong (yet again). I
am going to take a long, hot bath TONIGHT.

I'm very sorry to have missed your birthday,
Mother, but I send you my felicitations and
love. This stupid event here cannot, according
to its own arcane rules, last beyond thirty-five
days, but with luck I'll be home before then and
I will finish your gift as soon as possible. Please
can you send Nairna the little smock I made?
Also, I'm afraid that tooth of Osla Tod's will
have to be pulled — could you have Ranald
Keddy out to do that? He will be gentle, I know.

By the way, at the inn in Dornoch I had a
nice talk with a farmer (a very gentlemanly
fellow, no matter what Cousin Isobel may ur-
gently write you as she threatened) who sug-
gested warm oat and burdock poultices for
sheep suffering from rupturing blisters. Perhaps
you could mention that to Father.

In this fashion Fiona passed the time agreeably
enough, although as she was contemplating adding a
border of crimson to the shawl she'd been knitting for
Mother, and wondering if tomorrow she could start

on a baby smock for Dallis, she became aware of a creeping sensation of being watched. She blinked, and realized that at her side was standing a thin, rather scrawny child of perhaps seven or eight years of age, whose pale blue eyes, with faint, almost transparent lashes, were fixed simultaneously upon herself and some other unknown object.

Fiona smiled. "Hello."

"You face in the wrong direction, lady, you stare at the moon, ever changing," intoned the little girl in a solemn voice.

Perplexed, Fiona caught at her small, grubby hand and clasped it in her own. "I understand you not, hinny."

"You look but you do not see. Turn about, lady, turn about."

From across the table Janet Reid gave another jolly laugh — reminding Fiona irritably of a braying donkey — and cried:

"We have a wee poetess among us! How charming! How inscrutable!"

The girl freed her hand from Fiona's, and slowly twisted toward Janet. After an interval of silent observation, she said, "You leap, but should not. You go, but you ought not."

Janet only laughed again, and Alasdair Penhallow said, "Away with you, little Sheila, for you disturb my guests. Return to your place at your table, and you'll see that ices are shortly to be served."

Suddenly Sheila looked like every other child who craves dessert. "Oh, laird, 'tis my very favorite," she exclaimed, and hurried away at once.

"Ices," Wynda Ramsay informed Fiona in a knowledgeable tone, "are the most fashionable *goorman-dooze* in London. The *trez charmeent* Prince Regent is said to be particularly fond of pistachio ice."

"I see," said Fiona politely (although in fact she could not have cared less), then looked at her pretty, gold-rimmed plate as if seeing it for the first time. She had to admit — in another surprise — that dinner had been a most elegant experience, quite surpassing even the most formal meals served at home, where one could count on mutton being served every day: boiled, broiled, braised, baked, fried, stewed, and, occasionally, fricasseed. She had enjoyed every bite of her cold pheasant pie, and the *poulets aux champignons,* garnished with a delicate watercress sauce, also were delicious. Perhaps she could get the recipe from the cook. Something else to do tomorrow. She added it to her mental list.

When at last dinner was over, the annoyingly jocund old man with the preposterous beard, Duff MacDermott, uncle to Alasdair Penhallow and apparently in charge of herding them around like farm animals, announced that each of the young ladies was to have time to privately converse with the laird — with himself and at least one chaperone, of course, at a discreet remove.

"Oh! A *teet-à-teet! C'est amoosing!*" gaily said Wynda Ramsay, and Mairi MacIntyre asked, in her soft, sweet voice, if both her parents might sit by as chaperones, and could she bring along darling Pug?

"As you wish, my dear," Duff MacDermott answered jovially. He shook the crumbs from his beard and glanced speculatively around the high table. "Miss Fiona, may I escort you, the laird, and Miss Isobel to the Great Drawing-room?"

Yes, get the least likely candidate over with first, thought Fiona cynically, and, placing her linen napkin next to her plate, stood up without haste. She resisted the temptation to paraphrase the famous line from *Macbeth* and say, *Lay on, MacDermott,* and

merely nodded. As their little group — preceded by
servants bearing candelabra — made their way along
a long gallery whose walls were hung with dozens
and dozens of portraits, Fiona glanced left and right
at them, aware, to her chagrin, that she and Cousin
Isobel surely made a comically odd pair: herself so tall
and thin, Isobel so short and plump. Nor did Isobel
improve things by the manner in which she was discreetly, but continually, scratching at her flea-bites
which, by the look of things, covered her from head
to toe.

When at length their party entered the drawing-
room Fiona had to suppress a gasp of further astonishment: never in her life had she seen such an
elegant, such an exquisite chamber, from the handsome array of sofas, chairs, and tables, all arranged
so as to encourage easy conversation among small
groups, to the luxurious tasseled window-hangings
of dark green velvet and the many works of art, both
paintings and sculptures, in sizes large and small,
that were placed everywhere about to best advantage.

Briefly she envisioned the saloon at home that served
as their drawing-room — darkly wainscoted, low-
ceilinged, incurably draughty, roastingly hot when one
sat near the fire, and frigidly cold when one stepped
ten paces back — and she couldn't help but contrast it
unfavorably to this warm, gracious, light-filled room.

And yet . . . and yet there was something about
it which baffled her, though she could not, at the
moment, specify what exactly it was.

"You stare, Miss Fiona, and why not?" said Duff
MacDermott. "Here you see the hand of the laird's
mother — my sister, God rest her soul. According to
common report, it was his father — my brother-in-
law, may he also rest in peace — who undertook the
renovations you'll see everywhere, but it was really

Gormelia. Never happier than when she was having old curtains ripped down and new ones put up, and fancy new dishes brought in by the hundreds!" He chuckled, which made his beard ripple in an undeniably fascinating way. "She's probably redecorating heaven as we speak, and telling Saint Peter he needs a modish new desk at the Pearly Gates! I suppose," he added thoughtfully, "she did so much here in the castle, during her day, there'll be little for the laird's new wife to do, beyond producing offspring, of course."

"Of course," echoed Fiona, sardonically. "And I'm sure the castle practically runs itself."

"Now, now, don't trouble your head with domestic affairs, my dear," he said with an avuncular condescension that made Fiona's teeth grit. "Come! The laird's waiting for you."

With what struck her as overdone courtliness, Mac-Dermott proceeded to usher her to a tasteful little sofa near the cozily crackling fire, and drew Cousin Isobel away to a seat on the opposite side of the room. Fiona sat, and, opposite her, so did Alasdair Penhallow. Stubbornly she gazed at the leaping flames within the hearth. Here she was, just as she'd angrily remarked last week to Father, on display like some poor dumb animal before a reprobate.

Even though — she now realized — she'd mixed up her metaphors, it *was* a ridiculous situation. And a demeaning one.

She sat very straight. Set her lips firmly together. Thought of other things.

> *Go to stables tomorrow — all well with*
> *Gealag? Our other horses?*
> *Check on carriage also. Fleas. How to treat?*
> *Cook re: recipes*

Find something to read. Library here?
Write to Dallis & Rossalyn

"We ought, perhaps, to have some conversation."
His voice was deep, calm, pleasant.

Unwillingly, Fiona was jolted back into the present moment. She tore her gaze away from the fire.

So here, sitting across from her, was the infamous laird of Castle Tadgh.

He was tall (but not as tall as Logan Munro), and his shoulders were, she supposed, broad enough (though not as broad as Logan's). Altogether he had a big, lean, active sort of look about him, and wore with casual distinction the traditional evening wear of black coat, black breeches, and black stockings, with the usual white waistcoat and a white cravat, tied gracefully and without ostentation. But goodness, that dark red hair, clipped very short, and those ordinary brown eyes!

Oh, well, perhaps not completely ordinary: they did seem rather brilliantly alive, with an unusual kind of yellow-gold gleam to them, and he had nice dark eyelashes and strongly marked dark eyebrows. Still, what was red hair to black hair, brown eyes to deep dark ones? He really wasn't her type at all.

Nonetheless, Fiona had a sudden, unexpected pang of self-conscious regret over the gown she had deliberately worn, a severely cut, rather high-necked, somewhat dated dress of a nondescript blue color. Then again, what did it matter? Composedly she folded her hands in her lap. "Conversation, laird?" she replied coolly. "To what end?"

His expression of polite interest gave way to one of mild surprise. "Why, so we might get to know one another a little better."

"With respect, laird, I've no desire to know you

better. All I ask is that you make your choice as soon as possible, so that I might return home."

"You do not wish to be my wife?"

"No."

He lifted one dark eyebrow, and said lazily, easily, in his deep voice, "You do not find my person comely?"

Fiona found herself leaning back, as if retreating from what felt like a wave of pure masculine charm, warm and seductive. She'd had her fill of that from Logan. "Not particularly."

"You are blunt."

"I beg your pardon. Would you prefer the social lie?"

Instead of answering her question, he posed one of his own. "What sort of man *do* you find attractive?"

An all-too-familiar image flashed into her head and just as quickly she banished it. "It's not relevant."

He said nothing, only eyed her appraisingly for several deliberate moments. "You are twenty-seven, I believe, Miss Douglass?"

"Yes."

"And unmarried. Why?"

"It's none of your business."

"You also have three younger sisters who all are married."

She gave him a challenging glance. "How came you to know that?"

"We have a resident authority on such matters. No doubt you'll meet her by and bye."

"I'd rather be gone before that happens." Fiona sat up straight again and spoke with a new earnestness. "See here, laird. We both know you don't want me, and that I don't want you. Let's spare each other all these false courtship rituals. I'll bide my time, and you can have fun watching the other three jump through your hoops."

"Yes, you're very blunt. What makes you think I don't want you?"

Fiona smiled at him humorlessly. "Do you?" She watched as he shifted in his seat, as those dark brows drew together. Finally he leaned against the cushions of the sofa on which he sat, and crossed one leg over the other, his expression now one of relaxed alertness.

She thought of a cat, playing with a mouse, and firmly set her jaw.

"Your father, so I've heard, is a hard man," Alasdair Penhallow remarked.

She was thrown for a moment by the change of subject. Then, cautiously: "Yes, he can be very hard indeed. But he's also a canny chieftain. It's thanks to his diligence that our clan thrives in many ways."

"I've heard that too. Still, some women, under such circumstances, might be eager to make a new home elsewhere."

"Yes, some women might, I suppose."

"Especially if that home was a fine one."

"An added inducement for some, perhaps," she said coldly.

"Don't you want children, Miss Fiona Douglass?"

She considered prevaricating, but it really didn't seem worth the trouble. "Yes."

"Well, then?"

"I'll not marry only for that reason."

"Don't you think you ought to hurry, at your age?"

His voice was not unkind. It was even gentle. But still his words stung. "All the more reason to choose one of the others," she snapped. "As you've no doubt observed, they're considerably younger than I am."

"I have observed that, yes."

"And yet you sit here wasting your time with me."

"Wasting my time? Hardly. I find you very . . . entertaining."

Fiona could feel a hot, angry flush overtaking her face and throat, and she recalled Mother's breathless report from a few weeks ago:

Alasdair Penhallow has been scandalizing the Eight Clans for years with his disgraceful behavior. Not just on special occasions but every day! Consuming spirits to excess, presiding over debaucheries, and so on! A monster of irresponsibility!

"Yes," she said to him now, her voice full of pointed meaning, "I understand that you're very fond of . . . entertainment, laird."

Those brows drew together again. "And what might you mean by that, miss?"

"It would hardly be maidenly of me to say."

"You needn't spare me. I have no delicate sensibilities."

"Obviously." Fiona permitted herself a slight, a very slight sneer.

He leaned forward, frowning. "What in the devil's name are you insinuating?"

"I've heard some things about your . . . habits, laird, which would hardly inspire in a rational woman an ambition to become your wife."

"Are you criticizing me? You don't even know me."

"Nor do I want to. We've come full circle, haven't we?" Fiona smiled triumphantly, as if she had scored a well-deserved point. And indeed, she could almost feel the tension in those broad shoulders of his as he said, slowly:

"You give the distinct impression, miss, of being a shrew."

"I haven't the slightest interest in what you think of me."

"I pity the man who marries you."

"As long as we've established it won't be you, you may disburse your pity as freely as you like."

"Although now I begin to wonder why any man would want to."

"Now who's being blunt, laird?" It gave Fiona what did seem like slightly juvenile satisfaction to have shaken him from his posture of calm politeness, but he certainly deserved it, for his gibe about her age if nothing else. Deliberately, even a little ostentatiously, she settled herself into the corner of the sofa. Ugh. The pillow there was as stiff as a block of wood, and its elaborate beaded decorations pressed uncomfortably into her spine. All in all, a stupid pillow. It *looked* good, but *felt* bad. No doubt an acquisition of the Penhallow's sainted mother. Fiona jabbed her elbow into it, then looked measuringly at Alasdair Penhallow. Now that they'd cleared the air between them — in a manner of speaking — she couldn't resist satisfying her curiosity. "So *did* you ride your horse all throughout this castle?"

His frown deepened. "I beg your pardon?"

"It was just something I heard." Then Fiona remembered the other part of the story. That he'd done it stark naked. My, my. It was one thing to hear gossip when the person it was about was elsewhere; it was another thing entirely to think about that person without any clothes on when he was sitting right across from you. And even when that person wasn't your type and you didn't like him but he was still a tall, broad-shouldered, muscular man, who seemed to literally radiate provocative virility . . .

A hot red flush suffused not just Fiona's face, but her neck and chest, too. Resisting a powerful, even desperate urge to fan herself with her hand, guiltily she met his eyes, those brilliant amber eyes, and saw that he was looking at her with a hard quizzical gleam in them.

"You heard that I rode my horse here? Inside Castle Tadgh?"

Fiona cleared her throat a little. "Yes."

"Why?"

"On a dare."

"On a dare as a grown man?"

"Uh . . . yes."

"And you think I'd do it? Likely breaking the spirit of my horse by forcing it to do such a thing, and quite possibly risking its life for a prank?"

Well, when he put it that way . . . And clearly it would be a bad idea to mention the part about him not wearing any clothes. Fiona now felt more than a little foolish. Plus, that horrible red flush was still making her feel like someone had been poking at her with a lit candle. So she took refuge in prim hostility again.

"Since I don't know you, laird, it's not unreasonable to suppose you capable of anything."

Now he smiled at her in a way she didn't like one bit.

"I don't know you either, Miss Douglass, but to be listening to gossip? And you such a mature woman, too. I'd never have credited it."

"I notice you didn't deny it," she snapped, nettled despite herself.

"Since you seem to have an active imagination, I'll let you decide for yourself."

Oh, splendid. It was as if he was *making* her picture him stark naked on a horse. With a flash of temper Fiona got to her feet. "Well!" she said, with an affability that was utterly false. "This *has* been instructional, laird, hasn't it? Now, if you'll excuse my cousin and me . . . ? I'm sure those other *young* ladies are simply champing at their bits for their time with you. An apt metaphor, don't you agree, for are they not creatures to be bought and sold?"

"I will excuse you with pleasure," said Alasdair Penhallow, his smile a little grim, standing up as well.

She dipped a little curtsy and left the room with

long strides. That same feeling of mildly spiteful satisfaction remained even as she had to endure the breathless chatter of Cousin Isobel, who struggled to keep up with her along the various passageways to their rooms.

"Oh! That insufferable Duff MacDermott! I simply observed what a handsome couple you and Alasdair Penhallow make, and he had the *gall* to — I *wish* you would slow down, Fiona dear! Why must you *lope* so? It's not at all proper, I do assure you! — What was I saying? Oh, yes, that dreadful man, and his beard! I could barely keep my eyes from it the entire time. Why, he scratched at it in the most vulgar way!"

A sidelong glance revealed to Fiona that Cousin Isobel was herself digging her fingers into her armpits, but nobly she refrained from comment.

"This castle is massive, is it not? Oh, my dear, what a thing to be mistress of it! Are you *quite* sure we ought to go left here? Yes? Well, thank goodness you remember where they placed us! Isn't that a *magnificent* hanging? How ancient it looks, yet so well-preserved! But I haven't yet told you what that MacDermott said! *He* commented that you and the laird seemed a most ill-suited couple, with such very different temperaments! The *cheek* of that man!"

Fiona caught at Cousin Isobel's arm and steered her away from going into someone else's room. "He's right, you know."

Her cousin fairly quivered with outrage. "Nonsense! Such matters can't be deduced so quickly! Although with dear Logan and yourself, of course — but that's neither here nor there! *Do* slow down, Fiona dear! Else I fear a palpitation may come on, which would never do, as we've so much planned for tomorrow! Have you heard? An excursion to the Keep o' the Mòr, an old monastery. Isn't that delightful?"

"I adore crumbling ruins," answered Fiona sarcastically, "as every female must. If we're lucky, there will be a hermit, or possibly even a ghost or two."

"Oh, no, do you think so? A ghost, really? Surely not, in this day and age! But a hermit would be *most* interesting! I've always longed to see one. What on earth do they eat, do you suppose? And how do they protect their clothing from the damp? It seems terribly unhealthy. But what was I saying? Oh! Yes! Of *course* Laird Penhallow will choose you, for you are infinitely superior to those other girls."

"Well, I'm certainly taller than them. Here's your door, Cousin. Good night." Fiona practically bundled Isobel into her room, and swiftly went on to her own, sorry she had neglected to bring her knitting from home, and that she had finished the two books she'd brought along with her. It was going to be a long night. But then, they all were.

Later, much later that evening, Alasdair lay with his head resting on interlaced fingers and his elbows akimbo. He was a big man, but even so his own self took up but little space within the great laird's bed. Four massive oaken posts, carved long ago, upheld a canopy and looped hangings of rich cream-colored linen, upon which had been skillfully embroidered figures of falcons, hawks, eagles, does and stags, foxes and wildcats. At this canopy Alasdair gazed unseeingly, for he was thinking about the four women.

About Wynda of the extraordinary bosom, so generously displayed, he could only wonder what exactly was the jewel on her pendant necklace, it having disappeared like a climber descending between two close-set boulders. He supposed she had talked to him in the drawing-room, but for better or for worse he retained nothing, as he had primarily exerted himself not to stare at her deeply fascinating *balconniere*.

Little Mairi had told him, in considerable detail, about her dog: where he slept (on his very own pillow, right next to hers), what he ate, when he evacuated his bowels, his fear of squirrels, his hatred of baths, his love for a nice marrow-bone.

Green eyes sparkling, Janet was full of enthusiasm for the morrow's outing. "An ancient monastery!" she'd cried, clapping her hands. "What fun! I simply adore old ruins, the more ramshackle the better! Oh, I do hope there are ghosts. Or a hermit at the very least!"

He had been obliged to inform her that the keep was entirely free of hermits, and as for ghosts, he had yet to encounter one there.

Janet had been only temporarily daunted, and smilingly said: "Still, it sounds wonderfully romantic! So Gothic! How I look forward to exploring every inch of it! Now! I want to hear all about you, laird!"

Now *that* was the right sort of lass, positive and friendly, excited about visiting a local landmark, a good conversationalist, *and* all soft and plump and round, like a ripe hothouse peach.

As opposed to the prickly, sharp-tongued, aloof Miss Fiona Douglass. Her eyes, when they spoke, had been suddenly, strikingly blue against the drabber blue of her gown — and practically crackling with fiery intelligence.

She was not uninteresting.

But God's blood, she'd be a handful for a man.

Some *other* man. Not *him*.

He liked his private life to be easy, predictable, as smooth as silk. And nothing about Fiona Douglass suggested smooth, easy predictability.

Besides, she'd made it clear she didn't want him, either.

He wondered again why she was still unmarried. Was there, perhaps, a swain anxiously waiting for her back in Wick Bay?

Oh well, it wasn't his problem.

So now there was one lass crossed off his list.

Still, there was no point in saying anything to her about it. No use in sending her home early, under a cloud of humiliation.

He thought again about Janet, and Mairi, and Wynda. Good God — Wynda. He spent a few moments imagining himself spending the rest of his life, the rest of his nights, with his face buried between those prodigious, those delicious, yielding breasts.

His last thought, before sleep claimed him, was of Fiona Douglass, and the recollection that her breasts weren't prodigious at all.

Chapter 4

Riding on Gealag, who confidently ascended the steep, rocky path leading up to the massive crest on which lay the Keep o' the Mòr, Fiona took in deep breaths of the cool, bracing air as she gazed at the magnificent views all around her: gently rolling green hills, a lush meadow in which heather bloomed a vivid purple-pink, the immense mountain called Ben Macdui, and, past Castle Tadgh, a stunning blue loch, long and deep, whose placid surface reflected, mirror-like, the drifting clouds above.

Then she turned her eyes to the drawn-out caval-cade of which she was a part. Inevitably, it seemed, she looked, first and again, at Alasdair Penhallow. Wearing a tartan kilt and a close-fitting black jacket, he led the group riding his big handsome bay, with pretty Janet Reid alongside him perched on a horse she had chosen from the Penhallow stables. To Fiona's experienced eye it did not seem that Janet had full control over her spirited mount, but there was no doubt that Alasdair Penhallow could very quickly assist her should she re-quire it. Seldom had Fiona seen a more capable horse-man, even among her own North Highlanders who were justly renowned for their equestrian skills.

Wynda and Mairi, as did the other women, traveled up the winding path in carts drawn by sturdy donkeys, with servants sitting on a high bench at the front guiding them. Wynda seemed bored, and Mairi, wrapped in an amethyst velvet cloak whose hood she had drawn about her golden head (creating a fetching halo-like effect), clutched her little dog to her and stared fearfully at the precipitous drop that loomed to one side, a scrubby sloping expanse littered with rocks large and small, as if carelessly tossed in a giant's game of chance.

At length their party came around a bend in the path, and gathered on the broad, level crest which housed the old monastery. Despite her sardonic reply to Cousin Isobel last night, Fiona was, in fact, impressed by the Keep o' the Mòr — by its sheer size, the looming immensity of its crenellated towers, its brooding splendor. The countless gray, rough-hewn bricks were very faded now, many of its windows only gaping holes, yet still it was impossible not to be struck by a powerful sense of its former dignity, solemn and grand.

Wynda Ramsay yawned.

"How charming!" cried Janet Reid, and flung herself off her horse with such gusto that Alasdair Penhallow just barely had time to catch her, and help set her feet, in scarlet morocco slippers, onto the ground.

Two dimples peeped on alabaster cheeks as she smiled up at him. "Oh, thank you, laird! What are we going to see first?"

"The lower two levels only," he answered, "as the upper ones may not be safe."

"Is there a dungeon? I would love to see a dungeon! Chains, and pincers, and all manner of nasty things!" Janet gave a dramatic shudder which set her emerald ear-bobs flashing in the sun.

Fiona couldn't help it. She just couldn't. She said chattily: "Yes, for our ancient monks are renowned for their cruel practices toward the worshippers they'd so often throw into their dungeons, aren't they? And on the slightest of pretexts, too! A late arrival to services, a misspoken verse from a hymnal, and so on. I expect," she added to Alasdair Penhallow, "the Keep's dungeon has the customary walls that drip, bloodstains on the floor, bones scattered about, and rats?"

Mairi emitted a little shriek of horror and clutched at her father's hand, Janet gave Fiona a hard look of dislike, and Alasdair Penhallow laughed.

"Alas, there's no dungeon. I spent many a night as a lad camping up here with friends, and how we'd have rejoiced in such a thing! We had to satisfy ourselves with ghost stories, though, and the occasional brick falling down as we slept, scaring us out of our wits."

Janet moved to Alasdair Penhallow's side and slid her hand around his arm. "I'd be so frightened to do something like that! Unless I had someone to protect me, of course, and then I'd simply love it."

Goaded beyond endurance, Fiona said: "As long as a brick didn't fall on your head."

"Shall we move on?" Janet sidled closer to Alasdair Penhallow, pointedly ignoring Fiona's remark, and Fiona had just enough time to see the laughter fade from Alasdair's eyes and into them come a somber, faraway look, as if he'd just remembered something that caused him pain — and then that expression vanished, he smiled down at Janet, and they both turned away.

Everyone dutifully followed in the laird's wake and it took what little forbearance Fiona had left to remain silent when the subject of hermits came up and was animatedly discussed for a full half-hour; when Mairi (who felt a little dizzy looking down the twisting stone staircase) claimed Alasdair's arm and crept along with such hesitancy that it took *another* half-hour for the group to finally convene on the ground floor; when, as they went outside to a pleasant sunny spot where the servants had laid down blankets and set out all the inviting elements of a picnic, Wynda, predictably, exclaimed:

"Dining *on pleen air! Comment enshantee!* And so fashionable! One might even fancy oneself at the Regent's Park! That's in London, you know," she explained kindly.

"You are a veritable fount of information, Miss Ramsay." Janet Reid, her face alight with mischief, sank gracefully onto one of the blankets.

"*Merci,*" said Wynda, as one benevolently acknowledging a compliment from a pitiful ignoramus.

"Yes, a fount." Janet burst out laughing, and accepted from one of the servants a tall crystal flute of champagne.

Fiona sat by herself on a blanket at the furthest edge of the group, and proceeded to peacefully enjoy some very nice ham sandwiches as well as a generous serving of strawberries and two thick delicious slices of a fruit cake densely studded with almonds, currants, and raisins.

"My!" Janet Reid commented sweetly from afar. "You have quite the appetite, don't you, dear Miss Douglass? And yet you're so very slim! One might almost call you skeletal! I wonder, really, if you might not have a tapeworm."

"Very possibly," Fiona replied affably, and helped herself to a large wedge of buttery golden shortbread.

"I suppose," Janet went on, a little less sweetly, "you're sorry not to see haggis today, or the offal pot. Aren't those the traditional dishes you Highlanders love to eat?"

Fiona wavered within herself. *Mind your tongue,*

rise above. Her resolution held for exactly three seconds and then she said:

"Oh, dear me, no, Miss Reid. You mistake us for a clan that actually cooks its food. We normally eat our food raw. Why, we snatch the fish from Wick Bay with our bare hands, and eat it just like that, barefooted on the beach. Head, skin, guts, and tail. Still wiggling. Yes, it's a simpler life we lead in the wilds of the north." Reflectively she concluded, "I daresay that's where we get the tapeworms from. Eating live fish. Or perhaps it's the carrion. So hard to resist."

Hastily Cousin Isobel put in: "Now, Fiona dear —"

She was interrupted by Janet Reid as a servant, refilling her champagne glass, misjudged the speed at which he poured and the frothy liquid overflowed, dripping onto the hem of her soft woolen pelisse. "Fool! Get away from me at once!"

Apologizing profusely, he stepped back, and another servant quickly came forward with a cloth to dab at the hem.

"It was but an accident," said Alasdair Penhallow, pleasantly, and Janet smiled at him, saying with unshaken self-confidence:

"Oh, indeed, laird, but Mother says one has to be firm with the servants, or they'll try to take advantage. Drinking up the spirits and thieving from the larder, you know."

"On the other hand," interpolated Fiona, in that same reflective manner, "one may, it's said, catch more flies with honey than with vinegar. Or is that only your philosophy with the opposite sex, dear Miss Reid?"

Janet narrowed her green eyes, but before she could reply her mother said proudly, "My Janet is as clever as can be, laird! Once she caught a maid with a roll in her apron pocket and dismissed her on the spot — with *such* an authoritative air for one so young!"

Janet's father added, with a fond twinkle in his eye, "She's a brave one too, laird! Not the least bit afraid of bugs. Always squashing them, as bold as you please!"

"And so lively!" Mrs. Reid went on. "She insisted on making her debut at fifteen, and argued her case so convincingly, how could we refuse her?"

"Never saw such a girl who could hold her breath for so long without passing out," said Mr. Reid, smiling at Janet.

"Oh, Papa, do stop boasting! It's dreadfully embarrassing, and I simply loathe putting myself forward. The last thing I want is to make the other young ladies feel inadequate."

"No use hiding your light under a bushel, puss."

"It's very true," Isobel said judiciously, "but speaking of bugs, it seems only right to mention that they are all too often found living in bushels. Or would it be more accurate to say bushel *baskets?*"

"Well, if we're to talk of bugs," said Wynda Ramsay, "it's *outré* to squash them, in my opinion."

Fiona took another wedge of shortbread, and bit into it. She considered pointing out that certain types of spiders, for example, were actually very useful and ought not to be harmed, but why inject a note of dull common sense into this diverting conversation?

"And yet, Miss Ramsay," Janet said sweetly, "what would you do if someone dropped a bug down the front of your gown?"

Wynda looked amazed. "A lady would never permit such a thing. *Mon doo!* It would be very poor form."

"Then let us hope it never happens to you."

"Now, Janet, I know your playful nature," said her mother, laughing. "It's so delightful! But surely you wouldn't . . ."

"Oh, Mama, of course not," replied Janet at once,

demurely. *Too* demurely, and Wynda said, losing a little of her stateliness:

"At Miss Eglinstone's Finishing School for Young Ladies, one of my acquaintances attempted to apple-pie my bed, and was very sorry afterwards."

"And while we're on the subject of apples, I once bit into one and found a worm," Isobel said, with the air of one determined to steer the conversation into less controversial channels.

"Half a worm?" immediately inquired Duff Mac-Dermott.

She glared at him. "An *intact* worm."

"Lucky for the worm." He laughed.

Then, rather to Fiona's regret, Mairi said in a small, piteous voice:

"Laird, I'm getting cold. Please may we go?"

"You're cold?" Janet swung around. "But it's so delightfully warm up here in the sun, Miss MacIntyre!"

"Yes, but I'm delicate, you see, and very sensitive to the weather."

"What an affliction you must find it," Janet said, looking at Mairi as if she were a clump of thistledown about to blow away in the wind and scatter into a thousand little pieces of fluff. "I never feel the cold," she added casually, but rather spoiled the effect by turning her glance meaningfully on Alasdair Penhallow.

She might as well have declared, thought Fiona, something like: *Only a robust young lady will do for the wife of the great Penhallow!*

Alasdair stood up. "Of course, Miss MacIntyre, we'll leave at once," he said courteously, and extended his big hand to her to help her up, her small white one seeming to disappear within it.

Lithe as a spring doe, Janet Reid jumped to her feet, shaking out her skirts, and said dulcetly, "Laird, do send a servant to assist Miss Douglass to stand. She's not as young as she used to be, I fear."

"Dear, dear, how right you are, Miss Reid," responded Fiona, and allowed a servant to help her rise. She thanked him, and went on pensively, "I do hope I don't expire of old age on the way back to the castle. So *outré*."

"Yes," agreed Janet, with poison in the sweetness, "I hope so too."

As their group slowly made its way toward the horses and donkeys, Janet gaily darted about, joking with Duff MacDermott, flirting with Alasdair, hanging heavily on her father's arm. Then she danced off to a low stone retaining wall and jumped onto it. As they advanced, the wall rose steadily higher until Janet was nearly over their heads but easily she balanced upon it, arms held out wide, her skirts fluttering in the breeze and displaying (for those who were interested) quite a bit of her shapely legs in elegant silk stockings.

"Janet!" called Mrs. Reid, a little nervously. "Do come down, darling!"

"Yes," added her father, "go back, puss, to where the wall is lower."

"I don't believe in going back!" answered Janet, laughing. "I'll come down at once." And fearlessly she jumped, landing on her feet with the agility of a rope-dancer.

There were screams from some of the ladies and Duff MacDermott cheered, exclaiming: "Ach, the spirit of the lass! As bold as Scáthach herself!"

At this comparison of Janet Reid to the legendary warrior woman of Gaelic lore, Fiona said nothing, only looked on thoughtfully as a crowd gathered around Janet, praising, remonstrating, admiring, congratulating. Fiona went past them to where Alasdair

Penhallow supervised the grooms as they made ready the horses, the donkeys, and the carts. He himself was checking one horse's billets and girth, but straightened when she came close and quietly said:

"Laird."

Alasdair looked down into the slender face of Fiona Douglass. Her eyes, he noticed, were now gray and grave.

"Aye?" he said neutrally.

She paused. "How do I say this tactfully? I'm not certain that Miss Reid selected the ideal horse for her abilities, especially since she's now in a very — ah — high-spirited mood. Perhaps you might keep close to her on the ride back, as you did on the way here?"

He had had that very thought, but said, silkily, "And perhaps you might wish to ride on the other side of Miss Reid? Not only could you supervise her, you could continue to bait her as well."

To his surprise, in Fiona Douglass's expression there flickered what seemed to be genuine remorse. "Yes, it was very wrong of me. I shouldn't have done it. As for Janet, I don't suppose she can help herself, especially given how monstrously her parents indulge her. And she's so young."

"Here again we find ourselves discussing age. Why is that, I wonder?"

Her expression abruptly hardened. "That's a very good question, laird, and it reminds me. Why aren't *you* married? Being well on the way toward middle age, after all."

"As a wise and mature lady once said to me, Miss Douglass, it's none of your business."

"True. Though naturally I'm curious. By the way, do you suppose Janet really will drop a bug down Wynda's gown? If I were Wynda, I'd watch out."

Alasdair looked at Fiona Douglass, standing so

straight before him, so tall and slim, with that un-usual silvery-blonde hair in a fat, shining braid down her back. He was conscious of a feeling of annoyance, and in the back of his mind he took a moment to ponder exactly why he felt that way. Felt bothered. Especially since he'd already made up his mind that she was off his list. In weeks, or even days, she would be gone from Castle Tadgh. Gone forever, and good riddance, and life would resume its easy, enjoyable, predictable course. He answered:

"The way Janet's been looking at *you*, she may well drop a black-widow spider in your vicinity. And possibly apple-pie your bed, too."

Surprising him again, Fiona laughed. She said, "You could be right. I'll have to be on my guard."

By now, annoyance was positively rippling through him. "As much as I'd like to stand around here all day chatting with you, Miss Douglass, I should probably go back to checking on this girth."

"You're right again," she replied, unperturbed. "Don't forget the billet."

"I won't," he said coldly. "When I'm done with it, would you like me to inspect your rig?"

"No, laird, thank you. I prefer to do it myself." And off Fiona Douglass went toward her big white horse, who greeted her with a friendly nicker.

As the cavalcade wound its way down the steep path, Fiona, from her vantage toward the back of it, swept her glance over certain members of the party. Sitting tall and straight in his saddle, Alasdair Penhallow kept Janet Reid close to him, and she, in turn, seemed to amuse and delight him very much, for very frequently did his laugh ring out.

Mairi sat huddled in her velvet cloak, her little dog on her lap, her mother's arm snugly around her.

And there was Wynda, on her face once more a rather bovine look of ennui.

She looked again at Alasdair. She liked how he had, before the return journey began, gone over to talk a little with both Wynda and Mairi. Irritating he might be, but he *did* have good manners. Goodness, how red his hair looked in the bright sunlight!

She heard a faint little clucking noise, and realized it was Cousin Isobel, sitting alone in one of the pretty carts. With her graying curls flying loose from her coiffure, she was having a conversation — an argument? — with Duff MacDermott who rode alongside her, and he alternately chuckling and gesticulating frowningly. Isobel, in turn, looked rather like a plump little hen pecking at him.

A wry smile curved Fiona's mouth. Now *there* was a well-suited couple, each of them, evidently, equally itchy. All that was needed was for him to scratch her arms, and her to scratch his beard, and it would be a match made in heaven.

When her amusement at this silly notion faded away, Fiona's thoughts drifted on without direction.

Her visit to the stables, early in the morning, had been a fruitful one, for she'd been pleased to see that they were well-kept, well-staffed; the Douglass horses were well-tended. And the head groom, a grizzled, barrel-shaped fellow named Begbie, had stoutly promised to rid her carriage of fleas.

When it was time, Cousin Isobel could travel home in comfort.

Home.

Was she herself looking forward to being back there? To the massive old keep in Wick Bay, always turbulent with Father's shifting moods, ever filled with the shadows of her own disappointment?

She heard in her mind Alasdair Penhallow's voice:

Here again we find ourselves discussing age. Why is that, I wonder?

Was it possible that she was, in fact, rather jealous of Janet Reid? So young, so lovely — so attractively plump — and with so many years of promise, of potential, ahead of her?

Fiona rolled this unpleasant idea around in her mind.

Good heavens, had she somehow become a sour old maid?

She was only twenty-seven.

Or, stated another way, she was all of twenty-seven.

Were the best years of her life behind her?

You face in the wrong direction, lady, you stare at the moon, ever changing.

The solemn, eerie voice of little wall-eyed Sheila now insinuated itself into her head.

You look but you do not see. Turn about, lady, turn about.

Despite herself, Fiona shivered a little in the brisk breeze that swirled about her, playing with the hem of her gown, the white ruffles at her wrists.

Her slender — bony — wrists.

My! You have quite the appetite, don't you? And yet you're so very slim! One might almost call you skeletal!

She really shouldn't have teased Janet Reid like that. Father was right about her sharp, sharp tongue.

Janet, boldly jumping off that high stone wall, landing as gracefully as a bird.

Sheila's eerie voice, directed toward Janet:

You leap, but should not. You go, but you ought not.

Fiona's shiver turned into an involuntary shudder, and she turned her eyes again toward the head of the cavalcade, to where Alasdair Penhallow rode next to Janet Reid, whose emerald ear-bobs glittered so brightly in the sun that it almost hurt to look at her.

There was a tour of the castle one afternoon; then, on a warm halcyon morning, a walk through the gardens, which were exquisite, followed by another picnic, this one by the river. Those who cared to could fish, and nearby, from a gracious old oak tree hung a wide wooden swing, on which Mairi joyfully allowed herself to be swung back and forth until suddenly she got nauseous, and had to lie down with her head in her mother's lap.

On the next day, they all visited an impressive waterfall.

The day after that, the men went shooting while the ladies hung back and watched; later, there was an archery competition on one of the wide lawns, and here the men were to watch while the ladies drew their bows.

Fiona looked over at Janet who, wearing a charming gown of snow-white lawn, was inspecting a cluster of arrows laid out on a table. Here, she thought, might be an opportunity to improve relations between them. She joined Janet and said in a pleasant tone:

"Which do you prefer, Miss Reid, those blue ones or the white ones?"

Janet turned on her a sparkling look of challenge. "Why? So you can have the ones *you* like better?"

Rise above, Fiona reminded herself. "Some people favor broader fletches. I was wondering what you've found most effective."

"It's hardly information I'd like to share, Miss Douglass."

Fiona tried another, more neutral tack. "You're from the Lowlands, I believe? I've heard archery is very popular there."

"Well, and what of it?"

"You've played the sport for a long time?"

"Oh, yes. But you, of course, have the advantage over me in that regard, Miss Douglass."

With an effort, Fiona kept her voice pleasant. "Inevitably, I fear. Have you lived in the Lowlands all your life?"

"Yes, but I'm looking forward to a change in the very near future."

Rise above. "Have you brothers and sisters back home, Miss Reid?"

"No, and aren't I lucky? How tedious it must be."

"I've always felt lucky to have sisters."

"Well, and there we go — differing yet again." Janet smiled, showing all her teeth in a grin that struck Fiona as rather feral. "It's been lovely having this time with you, dear Miss Douglass. But if you'll excuse me? I'd like to concentrate on choosing my arrows. I intend to win, you see. Win everything, if you know what I mean."

"Miss Reid, it's only a silly competition. And I'm not your rival."

"Well, you're mine." And Janet deliberately turned her back to Fiona.

That was that, then. Fiona was very fond of archery, but withdrew from the event and sat on the sidelines to watch, a goblet of cool lemonade in her hand. Looking on the bright side, she'd at least made the attempt. Also, nobody had dropped a bug down her gown.

So far.

Teas, nuncheons, dinners; long, festive evenings in the Great Drawing-room during which the company was treated to performances on the pianoforte by Wynda, whose playing was mediocre despite years of lessons, and also by Janet, who demanded her turn despite very little training, and whose playing was even worse (although glowingly acclaimed by her parents). Mairi sang in her high, sweet, true little voice, and sometimes Alasdair Penhallow joined her, his own deep voice harmonizing very pleasantly.

After one such duet, Alasdair thanked Mairi MacIntyre, smiling, and looked around the room. He'd already spent a half-hour conversing — if one could call it that — with Wynda Ramsay, whose mangled French made it sometimes difficult to follow her, and then another half-hour with Janet Reid, who was bubbling over with excitement about tomorrow evening's ball, and so it would have been less than civil of him to *not* go and talk with Fiona Douglass. Besides, they'd barely spoken a word since his curt rebuff at the Keep o' the Mòr.

Looking very self-contained, even rather aloof, she was sitting in an armchair near a window, her head bent over some sewing. She was wearing a white muslin gown, its hem and sleeves embroidered in gold thread, and with the dark green window-hangings behind her creating a vivid contrast, and her pale hair illuminated by flickering candlelight, she reminded him a little of a figure in a painting, perhaps something soft and infinitely subtle by Vermeer.

She looked up as he approached.

"May I join you, Miss Douglass?" he asked, a little warily.

"If you like, laird," she said politely, and went on sewing.

He sat down, crossed one leg over the other, and watched her needle flashing in and out of a length of soft crimson flannel. Well, now what? What could they talk about? He'd be circumspect, this time, and avoid any mention of age and marriage. There was always the weather. Christ's blood, not that, he'd already discussed it *ad nauseum* with a dozen people tonight. What else? Miss Ramsay had, as far as he could tell, been talking about London, unaware of the fact that he'd never been there and would never, ever set foot anywhere in the whole of England, as he despised everything Sassenach. So London as a conversational topic was decidedly out. Miss Reid, for her part, had gone on and on about dancing. He enjoyed dancing, but to listen to someone soliloquizing about steps, and slippers, and all the dancing-masters she'd had, because they'd had to let go one after another — because they all fell hopelessly in love with her —

Alasdair shifted restlessly in his chair. It occurred to him that this extended house party was starting to get on his nerves. He'd initially welcomed having a leisurely thirty-five days, but now they were, frankly, starting to drag. Maybe he should make his decision sooner, rather than later. Wouldn't it have been nice to have had more than four — no, three — viable candidates?

His mind leaped back to fifteen years ago, to the girl for whom he would have cheerfully moved heaven and earth.

To Mòrag.

But she was dead and gone . . .

With an iron inflexibility Alasdair brought himself back to the present moment. To the here and now, to reality, to the Tome's decree, and to his own desire to *remain* in the here and now, alive.

Fiona Douglass said, "That was a charming rendition of 'Annie Laurie.'"

She'd given him some purchase, and he seized upon it. "Thank you. Do you like to sing?"

"Not really."

"Do you play an instrument?"

"No. My mother tried to interest me, but I'm not very musical, I'm afraid."

"Nor interested in cards, either? You've not been joining in."

"No. Quite the dull stick, aren't I?"

He groped for something else to say. "Dancing?"

"No."

This was not encouraging. "What *do* you like to do for fun?"

"I like to ride. And read. And work in my garden. I enjoy sewing and knitting, too."

"Anything else?"

"Well, I do like food."

"And?"

"Isn't that enough?"

"I like to ride, and to read, too, Miss Douglass. And I'm fond of a good meal also. But it wouldn't be enough for me."

Fiona shrugged, as if indifferent. "To each his own."

He leaned forward. "Do I detect, perhaps, a hint of criticism in your voice?"

At last she looked up from her sewing, brows lifted. "Why on earth would I criticize you, laird? We're parting ways soon enough, after all."

She was so cool, so composed. So incredibly annoying. He said, edgily, "I could choose you."

She laughed. "Against my will? Dear me. What a delightful marriage that would be."

He couldn't stop himself, and replied, with mockery playing in his tone, "After nearly a week together, you haven't changed your mind about me?"

"No."

To his surprise, the cynical humor faded from her expression and she looked at him very thoughtfully.

"But I've seen how other women respond to you. As if — oh, I don't know, as if you're the sun, ever shining, and they're flowers seeking your warmth."

"Very poetic."

"A garden metaphor. It seemed to fit."

"Yes, but comparing women to flowers? A wee bit stale."

"True. I suppose it's the colorful gowns that made me think of it. The point is that women like you. And you obviously like them."

"There's nothing wrong with that."

"I didn't say there was. There's no need to be defensive."

"I'm not," he said, defensively.

"We've wandered off track. I've also observed how you wear your authority absolutely, but lightly. That you have a nice way with servants. That your clan obeys you without reserve. That you have great material wealth, and you live in a marvelous home in a breathtakingly beautiful part of the world. And yet . . ."

"And yet what?" he asked, more sharply than he intended. *And yet.* Together they were two of the most irritating — defiant — troubling words in the world. God's blood, but Miss Fiona Douglass got under his skin in a way he didn't care for one iota. "Should I prepare myself for a catalogue of my faults? Or a further recitation of all the scurrilous gossip you've heard about me?"

Fiona blinked, as if she'd abruptly been jerked from a dream, and focused on his face, on the fiery gem-like brilliance of his eyes. She'd gone and let her tongue run away with her. Again. She'd just been about to say *And yet there's something missing in you.*

Quickly she looked back down at her sewing. At the soft flannel bed-gown she was making for Nairna in her forthcoming confinement. For the baby she had conceived with Logan Munro.

Fiona almost laughed out loud. And with a certain bitterness. She was a fine one to talk about something missing.

"And yet nothing, laird," she said, and to her then came rushing a confusing torrent of thoughts and emotions: a strong desire to change the subject, a painful feeling of vulnerability, a sudden strange wish to see that hard look in his eyes soften. She went on, a little shakily and almost at random:

"Speaking of gardens, what do you —"

But here was Janet Reid, young and lovely in her emeralds and silk. "Oh, laird, won't you show us that card trick again? We all want so much to see it!"

And she swept him away.

Fiona kept her eyes on her sewing, glancing up only once, when she heard the now-familiar sound of Alasdair Penhallow laughing. Apparently he'd made the jack of spades appear and disappear seemingly at his will. Sitting on the arm of his uncle Duff's chair, his white teeth displayed in an engaging smile, Alasdair held the deck in one long-fingered hand as he swept a mock-complacent half-bow while the others applauded.

"Again!" cried Janet Reid playfully. "I'll learn your ruse, laird, I swear I will!"

"Never, Miss Reid," he answered, just as playfully. "I must keep some of my secrets intact."

"To be sure, to be sure!" chimed in Duff Mac-Dermott, chuckling, lifting his brandy glass in salute. "Come hell or high water, a man's life is his own!" He saw Isobel frowning at him and added facetiously, "Begging your pardon, ma'am, at my rough language!" Then he finished his brandy at a gulp and managed with only partial success to suppress a burp.

It was at this precise moment that Fiona realized she was getting tired of this absurd event at Castle Tadgh. Being around Alasdair Penhallow was getting increasingly less pleasant, for somehow, he seemed to make her question things about herself — her life — in an unsettling way.

Well, so *what* if she was a dull stick?

It was nobody's business but hers.

Fiona looked back down again at the crimson flannel she'd selected with such care — its color would set off to great advantage Nairna's white complexion and dark hair — and felt her heart twist within her. Grimly she went back to her sewing, and was glad, glad, when the evening was over and she could escape to her luxurious bedchamber, shutting the door firmly behind her. But some ten minutes later, as she sat at the dressing-table, brushing out her hair with long strokes of the brush, there was an agitated tap on the door.

"Yes?" Fiona said reluctantly, already knowing who it was.

"My dear, may I come in?"

"Certainly, Cousin."

Isobel opened the door and hurried inside, very nearly quivering with outrage, and plunked herself in the little chair next to the dressing-table. "You'll never guess what that awful man told me!"

"Which awful man?"

"Why, Mr. MacDermott, of course!"

"Ah." Fiona didn't stop brushing. "Let me guess. He loves you and wants to marry you," she said flippantly.

"My *dear!* What in heaven's name are you saying? If I didn't know better, I would think you've been imbibing! No, Mr. MacDermott — who decidedly *had* been drinking! Did you see how many brandies he consumed? — told me that the local gentlemen are placing bets among themselves as to whom the laird will choose!"

"Oh, who cares? Some men do that sort of thing all the time. I remember one night Father went outside with his cronies, put down a pan of oatmeal, and they bet each other as to how long it would be before a raccoon would come along and eat it."

"Really?" inquired Cousin Isobel, diverted. "Who won?"

"Nobody. One of the dogs got out and ate it."

"Well, that simply proves my point about betting! At any rate, Mr. MacDermott says that Janet Reid — and by the way, I'm nearly *positive* she cheated during the archery competition! — is the frontrunner, and that you and Wynda Ramsay are tied for *last*. It's outrageous, and so I told that man, but he only laughed. I vow I had to *stop* myself from tweaking that beard of his!" Isobel's eyes now shone with tears. "Fiona, dear, I'm so sorry we ever came here! I practically forced the girl who brings my chocolate in the mornings to tell me all about Alasdair Penhallow, and the things she *said*! I absolutely cannot repeat them to you. But the drinking, and the wenching! I've never been more horrified in my life. Why, for his birthday celebration last month — no. I *cannot* repeat it. But the drinking, and the wenching! I know this sounds dreadful, but I'm *glad* you're last! I wish we could leave *tomorrow!*"

Fiona's hand halted, and, not for the first time, she puzzled over Cousin Isobel's lightning-fast thought process — if it really could be considered a thought process at all. Were little Sheila standing by, she would in all probability say, *You are a leaf in the wind, madam, blown hither and yon, without rudder or sail*. Then Fiona went back to brushing her hair, with long, deliberate strokes. "If it's a comfort to you, Cousin, I couldn't care less where I'm situated in the rankings. But given that I'm faring so poorly, the odds are good you'll get your wish."

Isobel brightened. "That *is* a comfort to me, dear! Now! What are you going to wear to the ball tomorrow night?"

"Oh, good heavens, what a bother. You know I

don't dance. I'd much rather stay here and have a bath and read a book."

"But all the local gentry are to come, and there's to be a full orchestra — and I heard they may play some *waltzes!* Oh, I'd love to try that. It's been so long since I've danced . . ."

"You have my permission," said Fiona, bored, and stood up. "Now, may I escort you to the door? I'm to bed, for —" She smiled a little, but very ironically. "For I need my beauty sleep, you know."

This had instant appeal to Cousin Isobel, who at once departed in a hurried bustle, only pausing on the threshold to adjure Fiona, most earnestly, to sleep on her back, by far the best preservative of the female complexion. When Fiona did get into her bed, she blew out her candle and promptly turned onto her side. And stared, without expression, without hope, into the darkness.

The ball was a huge success, and Mairi MacIntyre was indubitably the belle of it, looking so much like a fairy princess in her shimmering white gown that Janet Reid was catapulted into a barely contained fury. From her seat among the matrons and dowagers, Fiona observed with mild interest as Janet threw herself into every dance with a coquettish energy bordering on abandon, and also she noticed that while Alasdair Penhallow danced every dance — although not with her, for she adamantly refused all offers including his — he also was several times in deep discussion with little clusters of the local gentlemen, their voices low and their faces serious.

It was a new glimpse of the great Penhallow: no smile, no laugh, no light riposte or lively flirtation.

What, Fiona wondered, was going on?

Her curiosity was heightened when, the next morning, she went to the stables to have Gealag made ready for a ride and was informed by Begbie with gruff politeness that the laird had forbidden such activities for all his guests.

Not long after that, at breakfast, Duff MacDermott told everyone to remain inside.

"Oh, but why?" said Janet, scowling. "We were to hunt today, and I was *so* looking forward to it!"

"Laird's orders."

"Where *is* the laird? And if these are his orders, he ought to be telling us himself!"

Looking goaded, Duff said, "There've been some problems from the Dalwhinnie clan. They're notorious horse-thieves — and worse — and in the last day or two have gotten too close to home for the laird's comfort."

"What do you mean by 'worse'?" cried Mairi, her face as white as snow.

Janet laughed scornfully. "How stupid it all is! I'm not afraid in the least! *I* think it's terribly exciting!"

"No, it's dreadful!" worriedly put in the father of Wynda Ramsay. "What is being done?"

"The laird and a goodly number of his men are patrolling as I speak, and he's set other men to guard the castle and the stables. But as a precaution, he asks that everyone obey him in this matter."

There were nervous murmurs among the guests, and many went immediately to their own quarters, as if to barricade themselves from harm. An ominous quiet seemed to descend upon the castle, and the air itself to vibrate with unease. Fiona saw Cousin Isobel, anxious and fluttering, to her bedchamber, then went to her own rooms where she changed out of her light morning-gown into a heavier day-dress, fastening underneath it a large pair of heavy cotton pockets.

Hardly fashionable, but very practical, especially at a time like this.

Fiona pulled on her tall sturdy boots, braided her hair, and removed from one of her trunks a flat leather case. In it were her pistols. Carefully she checked them, loaded them, slid them into her pockets. Finally she wrapped a large, warm tartan shawl about her shoulders, and made her way downstairs. When she came to a side hallway that led outdoors and to the stables, she encountered Duff MacDermott emerging from stairs that, she assumed, led to the cellars, for in each hand he carried a tall bottle of some spirit or another.

"Here now, lass!" he sputtered. "What're you about? Can't leave the castle! Laird's orders, don't you know!"

"Stand aside, old man," answered Fiona coldly. "If you believe I'm going to allow the Douglass horses to be harmed, you're even stupider than I thought."

"There are guards, and grooms!"

"Yes. But they're *my* horses, and I take care of my own."

Duff was plainly so astonished — and also, perhaps, already half-drunk — that he made only a feeble resistance as Fiona strode past him.

She met with stouter opposition when she reached the stables, but brushed it aside with such cool implacability that reluctantly, the men allowed her to go inside. She checked on the Douglass's carriage horses. Satisfied, she found a stool and placed it just outside Gealag's stall. Softly she spoke to Gealag, who with a troubled whinny had stuck his great white head over the gate; she stroked his velvety ears and forehead, gave him some chunks of sugar, and at length he calmed, relaxed. His head drooped and he seemed almost to lapse into an easy slumber.

Fiona sat on the stool, pulled her shawl tightly

around her to ward off the morning chill, and waited. Aside from low-voiced exchanges among the men from time to time, all was quiet. The long hours ticked by, and still Fiona sat, upright, listening.

Then, as the cheerful yellow sunlight of afternoon reached its peak, she heard in the distance faint, hoarse shouts and the muted *crack* of muskets firing. She slid her hands into her pockets and groped for the reassuring feel of cool metal.

The men muttered; moved about, shuffled their feet as if longing to be out and into the fray.

"Stay at your posts, lads," one of the guards commanded. "The laird said we must stay."

"Aye," Fiona heard them say, "Aye," and was impressed by their instant obedience.

Suddenly, startling her, there was a commotion from within, protests from the men, and Fiona caught the high-pitched sound of a woman — a girl — laughing.

Oh, Lord in heaven, no, she thought angrily, standing up.

Floating to her from across the vast stables came Janet Reid's voice, gay and vibrant.

"*Move,* you dolts! I saw them from my window! I'm going to show the laird that I'm *just* like Scáthach!"

The sound of rapid hoofbeats. A triumphant peal of laughter.

"Marston, get your horse, quickly, man, and you, Waldroup, get my own!" barked that same guard, "the rest of you stay here," and for a few seconds, Fiona was so furious at Janet she considered the simple expedient of doing nothing. But she remembered her own words to Alasdair Penhallow — *I don't suppose she can help herself, especially given how monstrously her parents indulge her . . . And she's so young* — and thought of her little sisters, and in a flash she had pulled open the stall door, thrown a bridle over Gealag's head, was on that broad white back, astride it, and riding after the foolish, the terribly foolish Janet Reid.

Fiona burst into bright sunlight, and saw ahead of her Janet on a raw young piebald too strong for her. Nor was Janet a capable enough rider to be on him without a saddle. The piebald bolted, veering toward a cluster of men in ragged tartans, their faces painted blue and all of them wielding muskets and swords. Janet screamed, a high, desperate sound that carried all too clearly over the shouting, and to her right came an answering shout from — quickly Fiona glanced to the side as she bent low over the racing Gealag — Alasdair Penhallow, riding fast on his bay toward Janet, a large group of his men right behind him.

Fiona saw him say something over his shoulder to the men, and several of them immediately separated, making straight toward the blue-faced men, and he continued toward Janet, whose screaming seemed to go on and on, as frantically she pulled on the pie-bald's reins. Behind Fiona came hoofbeats from the stable, but not quickly enough; she herself gained on Janet, got closer, but when she was about fifty feet away, watched helplessly as the piebald, plainly resenting the desperate rider sawing clumsily on its reins, twisted its mighty head and reared up on its hind legs, sending Janet tumbling to the ground, where she lay very still.

Within seconds, Alasdair Penhallow was there, had leaped from his horse, knelt down by that unmoving form. There was a whoop from behind him and a *crack,* and Alasdair abruptly pitched forward. One of the Dalwhinnies, some thirty paces away, grinned and dropped his musket, then reached for the other one strapped across his chest. He cocked it. Aimed it at Alasdair. Wanting to be sure the laird was dead.

But he hadn't reckoned on Fiona, who had swiftly brought Gealag to a halt, slid to the ground. Pulled out from her pocket one of her pistols, and without hesitation shot the blue-faced man in the heart. Looking surprised, he dropped the musket and crumpled to the ground. Fiona pulled out her other pistol and held it steady, keeping watch, waiting until Alasdair's men had killed — been killed — and captured any remaining Dalwhinnies, and it was all over.

It wasn't till much later, when Fiona was alone in her bedchamber, that she cried, covering her face with hands that still smelled of gunpowder and steel.

Cried without making a sound, and for a very long time.

Then, slowly, carefully, she washed her hands. Dried them, and her face, too.

And she went to find Janet's parents, to see if she could do anything to help them.

Chapter 5

Dr. Colquhoun had come and gone, telling Alasdair he must remain in bed for several days longer, for though the wound in his shoulder was healing well enough, infection remained a danger, movement could set him to bleeding again, and the fever still flared from time to time.

"You've lost enough blood as it is, laird," the doctor had sternly said, "and if you don't eat more of that good bone broth, I'll come and feed you myself."

With his sound arm Alasdair now waved away the bowl his manservant Grahame was proffering. "What day is it?"

"It's Wednesday, laird," answered Grahame.

"No. How many days is it since I was injured?"

"It's been a week, laird. Laird, may I not give you just a wee bit of broth?"

"No." Alasdair did the sum in his head. He was nowhere near the deadline of thirty-five days. Still, he'd had the news from Grahame, and there was no point in putting off the inevitable. "Send for Miss Douglass and her chaperone."

"Aye, laird."

While he waited, Alasdair hitched himself up on

his pillows, ignoring the stab of pain this induced, and ran a hand along his jaw, bristly with beard. He looked at Cuilean, who lay in a large shaggy ball near his feet.

"Well, sir?" he said, in a rough voice which imperfectly concealed his affection. "No gestures of condolence from you?"

Cuilean only thumped his tail agreeably, not lifting his head from the bedcovers.

Alasdair smiled faintly. But his smile faded as the minutes passed and it felt as if the waiting was interminable. Where in the devil's name *was* she? Was she defying his order — defying *him* — already? This, he thought morosely, was a bad omen, a bad start to things.

A wave of heat swept over him and he shoved the blankets down to his waist. To his left was a pitcher of cool barley-water but he didn't dare reach for it; his shoulder was still throbbing ominously, as if warning him. He ground his teeth, felt himself sweat, and irritably wiped at his face.

At last there was a tap on the door.

"Enter," he said curtly.

The door opened and Grahame came in, stepping aside to admit Fiona Douglass and her plump middle-aged companion. He then placed a chair by the fire and conducted Dame Isobel to it, while Fiona came toward him, very pale and grave, wearing a high-necked gown of brown figured muslin, her hair in a simple knot at the nape of her neck.

To Alasdair's annoyed surprise, Cuilean jumped from the bed and went to greet her, tail wagging. So big a dog was he that he nearly reached her hip. Without fear she held out a slim hand, and he very affably licked it.

Traitor, thought Alasdair, and snapped, "Come!"

They both looked over at him.

"Which of us do you mean?" said Fiona coolly.

"Both of you, damn it!"

Without the slightest air of guilt, Cuilean bounded back to the bed and leaped up on it. Fiona remained where she was. Dispassionately she gazed at him, her gray eyes flicking from his face to his bare chest, and to the silver pitcher on the table. Then she advanced, until she was some two feet from his bedside. She poured some barley-water into a glass and held it out to him.

Without moving he said, unpleasantly, "What took you so long?"

"I was in the kitchen garden, gathering herbs."

"What for?"

"To make a salve. Your cook scalded her arm yesterday, and I thought it might help."

"That's the business of Dr. Colquhoun."

"I was the one who sent for him. He agrees that a lavender salve can be very soothing."

"And what were you doing in the kitchen, may I ask?"

"Asking your cook about some recipes."

"I hardly expect my guests to be wandering into the kitchen."

She only shrugged, and ungraciously Alasdair took the glass from her. Already he was losing control over his life, and he hadn't even yet told her what was on his mind! He gulped down the barley-water — not for the world would he have admitted how refreshing it was — and handed back the glass. "Grahame! Bring a chair for Miss Douglass."

Grahame hastened to obey, then just as promptly retreated.

"Sit down," Alasdair said to her.

"I'm not your dog."

He curled his lip. "Please."

"As you will." Without haste she complied. She sat very straight, and folded her hands in her lap.

Frowning, restlessly he plucked at his blankets. He supposed it was highly improper for her to be seeing him like this, but as the view of his exposed torso didn't seem to be sending her into a spate of missish blushes (or a raging torrent of lust), evidently it didn't really matter.

"I understand," he finally said, "that Janet Reid is dead."

For a moment, just a moment, he would have sworn that Fiona's eyes filled with tears. But steadily she answered:

"Yes. Her parents have left, and taken her body with them."

"I blame myself," he said harshly.

"It wasn't your fault."

Anger, hot as the fever, surged through him, and he spoke even more harshly. "She's dead, don't you understand that? Or are you stupid?"

From across the room came an indignant twitter and Dame Isobel said, as if directing her remark to the leaping fire, "Well! A fine way to treat the person who's saved your life!"

Fiona paid no attention to her companion and replied to him with that same steadiness, "I'm not stupid. It's a tragedy, laird. How could it not be? And oh, such a sad, sad one. But I don't see how you could have prevented it. No rational person would have felt the need to lock people in their rooms. Janet's parents were berating themselves for not having kept a better watch on her." Fiona looked down, though whether or not she actually saw her hands, clasped loosely in her lap, was unclear. And then she looked up and directly at him again. "In the end, Janet brought it on herself, the poor reckless girl. Nor should you forget how her actions resulted in a dreadful injury to yourself — and I saw two of your men killed as a result. That is a tragedy also."

He stared at her. Noticed again how pale her face was. Saw, now, the dark circles underneath her eyes. "You speak like a chieftain's daughter," he said slowly.

"Which is what I am."

"My men told me how cleanly you made your shot. Your father taught you?"

"Yes."

"Why?"

"He did so when I was twelve, and began riding alone, all across our lands."

"He allowed you that freedom?"

"He knew I'd do it no matter what."

"Why?"

She shrugged again.

There was a silence, and finally, as if the words were dragged from him, Alasdair said: "Thank you."

"There's no need for that. I'd have done it for anyone. The Dalwhinnies should not have sought to harm you, or steal what is yours."

God above, she was cold, cold. He pulled his blankets up, hating the wound that rendered him so weak. Still he pressed on. "Wynda Ramsay is gone?"

"Yes, she left after Janet Reid was killed. She took all her mother's money and jewelry, and one of their horses, and fled in the middle of the night."

"To her home?"

"Apparently not. If I had to guess," Fiona added thoughtfully, "I'd say she went to England. I heard her say more than once that Scotland is so coarse and barbaric, so offensive to those of more refined sensibilities. The events of last week finally convinced her, I daresay. I wouldn't have expected such enterprising behavior from her, but people can surprise one sometimes."

"Yes, life here is very coarse and barbaric," he echoed sardonically, glancing around his elegant bedchamber.

"As compared to London," Fiona explained, in a carefully neutral tone. "*Où les rues sont pavées d'or, sur lequel les gens à la mode foulent.*"

Where the streets are paved with gold, upon which the fashionable people tread.

He snorted. "You'll not catch me among all those damned Sassenachs."

"I believe Wynda finally realized that. Are you sending anyone after her, for her violation of clan law?"

"No. Her parents may if they so choose."

"I think they desire nothing more than to be allowed to quietly return home."

"So be it. And Mairi MacIntyre lies ill in her bed, close to death?"

Fiona smiled slightly. "The reports exaggerate. According to your good Dr. Colquhoun, she is in the midst of an extended fit of hysterics."

"From which she will recover?"

Alasdair watched as Fiona's smile disappeared. "I expect she'll make a remarkable recovery as soon as she learns she too can go home."

"You suggest that her illness is a ruse?"

Fiona was silent, then reluctantly answered: "No. It's my opinion she truly believes she's at death's door. She is very fragile. In another week or two I think she may well somehow persuade herself to die."

"And the remedy is to tell her she's not to be my wife?"

"That is, of course, up to you, laird."

"I've no interest in murdering someone by marriage."

"A commendable attitude."

"Don't patronize me, Miss Douglass." He loathed this feeling of helplessness, of being supine in his bed when she sat so straight, so upright, in her seat. He gave a loud, lengthy, irritable sigh. "It seems there's only you left."

Her lips thinned. "Unfortunately, yes."

"You'll obey the decree?"

"I must, for I don't care to die. My father could very well see to that."

"He'd do that?"

"Quite possibly."

Alasdair looked hard at her. She puzzled him. Confounded him. Other lasses would be weeping, raging, at having such a parent. Other lasses would be crying with joy at their good fortune in having their hand secured by the laird of Castle Tadgh.

But not Fiona Douglass.

She sat very still, her eyes gone a wintry slate-blue.

"I too intend to live," he said slowly. "In that, at least, we are of one mind. You wish for a brilliant wedding, I suppose, as all women seem to do?"

"No. Nor would such a thing be appropriate given the recent deaths here. A small, private ceremony will suffice."

"At your home?"

"Here."

"With your family present?"

A shadow crossed her face — was it sorrow, or pain? — and stonily she said:

"No. My cousin will bear witness."

"Fiona, dear, this must not be!" protested Dame Isobel, who, obviously, had been eavesdropping for all she was worth. "Your family! All your sisters and their husbands! And let us not forget your trousseau! Naturally I am most *deeply* sensible of the honor you do me, but — oh, dear, I really haven't anything to wear! What would your mother say? I vow my head is all in a whirl!"

"Be quiet, Cousin, if you please. You must write to my father for his consent, laird, and by express if you like. A formality only, of course, and I'll write too, and ask for my things to be sent here. You may set the date at your convenience."

Alasdair felt an odd sort of sympathy for Dame Isobel. He himself was baffled by Fiona's brusque, businesslike response. It made him feel like —

Like what?

He thought it over.

It made him feel like she'd gotten the upper hand. That things were moving beyond his control. That he wasn't . . . safe.

It wasn't a feeling he enjoyed.

So he said, silkily, but with a barb in his voice:

"Since our union is clearly so repugnant to you, Miss Douglass, perhaps you ought to wait and see if I survive my wound? Sepsis might set in, you know, and carry me off."

"I doubt it. You are clearly very strong, and Dr. Colquhoun takes good care of you." She paused, drew a breath, for a moment looked uncertain. "I don't know if I have a dowry to bring to you."

Alasdair tried to shrug and immediately regretted it. His shoulder pulsed with a searing pain, and he was all at once exhausted to his very bones, and sweating again. "I couldn't care less," he responded testily. "I have plenty of money. Stop bothering me with petty details."

She rose, and to his surprise placed a cool hand on his forehead. "Your fever is rising," she said matter-of-factly. She poured him out another glass of barley-water, which he refused with a gesture that even *he* knew was churlish. "Grahame," she said over her shoulder, "help the laird slide down on his pillows — gently! — and cover him warmly. You must rest," she told him, "and I'll bid you good day, now that everything is settled. Come, Cousin."

And even before Fiona Douglass had left the room, Alasdair, hot, uncomfortable, in pain, was plunged into the welcome abyss of deep, dreamless sleep.

How many guests attending? Ask Lister. Their names?
Write to Father. Mother also
What to wear for ceremony?
Breakfast afterwards — see Lister, Cook
Clothes, etc., to be transferred to new bedchamber; who will do that?
Gealag — more oats in diet. Tell Begbie
Isobel??
Stop thinking about Logan Munro
More candles for chapel
One of Mairi's trunks left behind, have it sent to her
Is there a dame-school for children here?
STOP THINKING ABOUT LOGAN MUNRO

Ten days after her momentous conversation with Alasdair Penhallow, Fiona stood again in the same bedchamber, only now — why, only now she was his wife. She stood with her back to the closed door, and slowly she looked around the enormous room. A fire had been lit, the covers on the massive four-poster bed carefully, invitingly, turned down, a large candelabra was set on a table near the door and sent out a warm yellow glow of illumination. Giving that bed a wide berth, she went with measured step to the wide bank of windows which overlooked the courtyard below; all were covered with warm, heavy draperies and she pushed one aside to glance out through the window.

A full moon, fat and yellow, shone high in the dark sky. Around it, as if a brilliant setting to a jewel, countless bright stars flickered and twinkled, mysterious, remote.

Fiona let go of the drape and went into the passageway just to her left, which led to her dressing-room. She put her hand on its doorknob, then looked at the four other doors in the dim, high-ceilinged corridor. One led to the laird's dressing-room, she knew, and two others provided storage for furs and winter wraps and so on.

The fourth door was locked. Earlier today, when her things had been brought here, she had tried to open it. She'd asked the maidservant about it, but received only a shake of the head.

"I don't know what the room contains, mistress," Edme had replied. "The laird must have the key. Where would you like me to put your brushes?"

Fiona now turned the knob and went into her dressing-room. It was a luxurious suite unto itself, including two large armoires, a full-length cheval mirror, a satinwood dressing-table with all sorts of cunning little drawers, and an even nicer bathtub than the one she'd been enjoying in her previous bedchamber.

She went to the mirror and gazed at her reflection within it. She liked the long-sleeved pale green gown she had chosen, with its white slip and demitrain of soft gossamer satin. (And if she looked like a giant green twig in it, so be it.) Father and Mother had sent a beautiful diamond necklace, with pretty pearl and diamond ear-bobs, a gift that had, for a brief and dangerous moment, brought with it a powerful rush of homesickness.

And — on the fourth finger of her left hand was now a gleaming gold ring, exquisite in its simplicity. As he had placed it there, Alasdair Penhallow had said, in a firm, unhesitating voice:

With this ring I thee wed, with my body I thee worship, and with all my worldly goods I thee endow: in the name of the Father, and of the Son, and of the Holy Ghost.

His hand on hers had been warm, but it had not lingered, and from behind them in the castle's chapel Cousin Isobel had sobbed, whether sentimentally or sadly Fiona did not care to know. The other guests — Duff MacDermott, of course, along with the neighborhood gentry and as many of the local folk who could squeeze themselves into the chapel — had been, properly, silent.

Afterwards there was the customary breakfast. Determined to rise above the palpable awkwardness of this odd, this decidedly odd marriage, Fiona had exerted herself to be a pleasant hostess, while Alasdair, sitting at the head of the high table, impressive in his crisp white shirt and tartan kilt, his left arm in its linen sling (Dr. Colquhoun had sternly and publicly ordered him to continue using it, or he would not answer for the consequences), had done the same in his role as host, and together they had, she thought, managed to carry it off reasonably well. After the breakfast, after the guests had left, Duff MacDermott had drawn him off to the billiards room, both of them laughing, and Fiona had not seen her husband since.

Her husband.

Her face in the mirror looked back at her, and all Fiona could see was a ghostly pale complexion, with dark, bruised-looking smudges underneath the eyes.

This was not how, nine years ago, she'd thought her life would turn out. Tears suddenly rose into her eyes, and she fought them back, although for an awful, panicky moment she wanted nothing more than to wrench that gold ring from her finger and throw it out the window. She could almost hear the tiny distant *ping* it would make. Maybe it would roll into a sewer-hole and disappear forever. Maybe she would go to the window right now —

Instead, with slow, deliberate movements, she put away her necklace and ear-bobs. Undressed, and put on a plain white cambric nightgown. Unpinned her hair, brushed it out, braided it. Isobel had wanted to help her, had even (blushing a vivid scarlet, stammering, almost gasping in embarrassment) tried to lay before her the facts of what the night would bring.

"I've seen the animals all my life," Fiona had interrupted, with a kind of icy bravado, and dismissed Isobel and Edme, too.

Now that the evening was well advanced, and she was all alone in the laird's great bedchamber, she no longer felt quite so courageous. Still, Isobel had managed to offer what sounded like a useful piece of advice.

All you have to do, Fiona dear, is — well, it sounds terribly crude, but — a wife's duty is to lie there, and endure what happens. That's really all there is to it. Not that I myself — but my own dear mother did tell me before — although what happened — but that's neither here nor there! Keep your eyes closed, if that helps.

Fiona left her dressing-room and went into the bedchamber. She blew out the candles and slid into the unfamiliar bed, on the side furthest from the door, closest to the windows. She lay on her back. Waited and waited, thinking of nothing. It seemed like hours — it may actually have been hours — when, at last, the door opened, and Alasdair Penhallow came inside.

He took ten steps, fifteen, twenty, until he stood at the foot of the bed, looking very tall in the flickering light of the fire, his hair gleaming darkly, the deep red looking nearly black to her. She could see that in one hand he held a small pouch. A gift for her? How thoughtful. Good things, they said, come in small packages.

"Are you awake?" he asked.

"Yes."

"Excuse me for a moment."

He went away to his dressing-room, and when Fiona heard his steps returning, she lost all interest in the gift and shut her eyes. She lay perfectly still, her fingers laced across her breast, feeling her heart beating steadily, steadily, within its cage of bones and sinew.

Alasdair got into the bed.

There was a silence.

It was a heavy, expectant silence that somehow just seemed *loud*.

Behind the darkness of her eyelids Fiona thought of a baby, sweet-smelling, with soft pudgy cheeks, a delicious gummy smile, to hold and to care for. To love. Yes. Yes.

"Well," he said, "let's to it."

"Fine."

"My curst arm won't support me. You'll have to ride me."

"Ride you? What does *that* mean? You're not a horse."

"Come over here and I'll show you."

"No. Tell me what you mean."

He sighed. "I stay like this, on my back, and you go astride me."

"I still don't understand you."

"You sit on my cock, damn it! Is that clear enough?"

"Yes, thank you," she said coldly.

"Now that you understand, come here. We may as well get it over with."

"No."

"Are you worried you'll crush me? You're tall but you're a featherweight."

"I'm not worried I'll crush you. I simply won't do it that way."

"Why not, for God's sake?"

"I'm not one of your loose women. In case you hadn't noticed."

"I am all too aware of it," he answered in an annoyed tone. "All this tedious talking, for one thing."

"I'm sorry if I'm boring you," Fiona said, more coldly still.

"I didn't marry you so we could lie around prattling to each other."

"Well, if it comes to that, you're not very interesting either. When you're prepared to do your husbandly duty properly, let me know."

With heavy sarcasm he shot back: "I didn't realize there were rules about the positions."

Here, Fiona acknowledged, she had stepped onto thin ice. The best defense being a strong offense, she took refuge in primness and promptly said, "For gently born ladies, there ought to be."

"You refuse, then?"

"Yes."

"Flouting your wifely obligation on the very first night?"

"Are you going to beat me, as my father so often

vowed to do to my mother?" she snapped, then instantly regretted such a personal revelation.

There was another silence.

Fiona opened her eyes and very quietly turned her head on the pillow, to find that he had turned *his* head to look at her in the warm dimness of the bed.

"I don't believe in that," he said, in a low voice. And as if he was sorry for his own admission he added gruffly, "Besides, I couldn't do a very good job of it with a shoulder that's yet to fully heal."

"The luck is with me then."

He laughed shortly. "Luck. Yes."

How strange it was, Fiona thought suddenly, having a conversation — tedious or not — in bed with someone who was essentially a stranger to her. Was this how things were going to be between them? *With this body I thee worship.* Ha. She steeled herself against an unwelcome torrent of sorrow, fixed her mind on other things.

Isobel. Tell her tomorrow. Wick Bay
Why is there no housekeeper? Ask Lister
Linens. Where are they kept?
Children here inoculated? Ask Dr. Colquhoun
Cook re meal planning
Stillroom needs a thorough cleaning — assign
*   a maid*
When is wash day? Baking day? Brewing day?
Find head gardener (name?) — flowers for my
*   morning-room*
Go riding. Tell Begbie: no groom

Alasdair said something, interrupting her train of thought.

"I beg your pardon?"

"Duff," he said gloomily, "was right."

"That you really should have taken Mairi to wife?" she retorted at once. "That way he wouldn't have lost his bet. How much did he lose, by the way?"

"You knew about that?"

"Yes."

He paused. She could see him frowning. Stiffly he said: "I only found out about it today. I'm sorry. Had I known I would have forbidden such disrespectful behavior."

"It doesn't matter."

"It matters to me."

She absorbed this, then asked, "What was he right about?"

"Oh, that tonight would be difficult. He gave me a sporran filled with pig's blood just in case."

A lingering feeling of sadness now gave way to fury so strong that Fiona could willingly have leaped out of bed, sought out Duff MacDermott wherever he had lain his scrofulous self, and strangled him with his own beard. And she didn't even know exactly what bad thing she'd like to do to Alasdair Penhallow. Instead she said, icily, "What a charming wedding gift."

"It seems, however, he may have spared us both the shame of gossip tomorrow, so that the maidservants don't see unsullied sheets."

"Oh, and you're confident he filled a pouch with pig's blood in perfect secrecy?"

Alasdair was silent.

Fiona gave a mocking laugh. "Go ahead, laird, spill the blood anywhere you like. Ruin some perfectly good bed linens. And what will happen when finally we do consummate our union?"

She could almost feel, from the five or six feet that separated them, his own surging anger. "May God in His heaven intervene, madam," he growled, very slow, very deep, "and preserve me from your damned infernal logic!" With his uninjured arm he grabbed one of the pillows and flung it across the room, where it landed with a soft *plop* on the floor.

Fiona pondered his invocation of both heavenly and demoniac forces, considering whether it was worth another mocking jab at his inconsistency, and in the end decided it wasn't. She also thought about getting out of bed to retrieve the pillow, as she longed to do, but didn't care to expose her person (even in her demure high-necked nightgown) to his scrutiny. At least not at this exact moment. What, she wondered, was *he* wearing? A frisson of shivery alarm overtook her, and sternly she repressed it. Things — it — the act, whatever one wished to euphemistically call the conjugal duty — *was* (were) going to happen. Maybe Alasdair would tonight, in his wrath, find a way to overcome the limitations of his still-healing arm, and summon her over. She'd just have to grit her teeth and lie there like a wax dummy. It couldn't last for more than a few minutes, anyway, could it? And what about that loathsome pouch of blood? *He'd* better dispose of it, or else she'd take it and dump it down the back of Duff MacDermott's shirt.

At dinner.

In front of everyone.

And laugh, laugh, laugh.

While she was thinking about all this, Fiona gradually, very gradually, became aware that beside her, Alasdair's breathing had gentled into a soft, steady cadence.

His chest rose and fell, rose and fell.

His eyes were closed.

He was, in fact, asleep.

No doubt he was exhausted from the many hours of roistering with his boon companion Duff.

Fiona looked balefully at his peaceful face in the dim flickering illumination of the fire. His nose, she suddenly noticed, although a well-formed organ, had a slight bump on the bridge, as if, at one time, he had broken it.

It was strange, she now thought, abruptly distracted from her thoughts of vengeance, how sometimes a small imperfection could render an object more pleasing.

Not, she reminded herself, that she cared two hoots for his profile, attractive or otherwise.

She rolled onto her side, her back to him. She didn't expect sleep to come, but over the years she had become quite expert at waiting, patiently, submissively, for the night to crawl along. If she was fortunate, she might drift into a doze toward dawn.

The luck is with me then, she had said earlier. Oh, for a few hours' blessed slumber, and she would count herself, despite everything, lucky indeed.

Alasdair woke to the muddled consciousness that although he was in his own big, comfortable bed, something was different.

Oh yes, *that*.

Yesterday he'd gotten married.

Cautiously he opened his eyes, saw that it would soon be morning, saw that somehow, during the night, he had gotten himself closer to Fiona. Not close enough so that he could reach out and touch any part of her. But closer.

She lay facing him on her side, resting her cheek on the palm of one hand, her thick silvery braid draped across her shoulder. Her lips were slightly parted as she slept, and it struck him that they were —

That they weren't unattractive.

Really, they were almost kissable.

He hadn't noticed that before.

How surprising.

And in the wake of this realization, he felt an odd sort of guilt, as if by studying her face while she slept he was doing something wrong. Illicit.

It was time, then, to go.

With nearly superhuman quietness, Alasdair got out of bed, dressed (putting his arm back in the damned sling), picked up the sporran Uncle Duff had given him, and stepped outside into the hallway, softly closing the door behind him.

Curled up there was Cuilean, who immediately leaped up, stretched, dipped an elegant play-bow; and, tail wagging, he sniffed curiously at the sporran in his master's hand. Alasdair slid it into the pocket of his buckskins, rested his hand for a moment on that shaggy head, and by means of an obscure passageway he made his way outside into the bracing chill of early morning. Unobserved, Cuilean frisking at his side, Alasdair strode into the woods that lay far beyond the beautifully maintained gardens, his boots alternately sinking into damp earth and crunching on twigs and crisp fallen leaves. Here in the light of day, he didn't know whether to feel he'd had a fortunate reprieve on his wedding night, or whether he had made a complete and utter mull of it.

Had he behaved badly, ordering her around in bed like that?

Of course, she hadn't exactly been friendly herself, but still . . .

Perhaps he could have shown a little more finesse.

The truth was, he did have a lot to drink with Duff and some of the others who'd wandered into the billiards room, and so by the time he'd arrived at his bedchamber, he'd not been at his best.

And really, she ought to have been softer, more welcoming, more obedient.

Hadn't she?

Or *had* he been at fault?

Damn it all to hell, he thought grumpily, his brain was a mad jumble today, looping round and round in this unproductive way. He was glad when, arriving far into the woods, he could stop, could use a stout stick to dig a deep hole. In it he buried the sporran. Most earnestly did he hope that symbolically he was also burying useless thoughts and questions.

He required sons. He had a wife now. They needed to create offspring. Things didn't need to be any more complicated than that.

Alasdair tamped the dirt firmly beneath his boot.

Threw the stick aside.

Watched Cuilean dash after it.

Contemplated the day's agenda.

Back to the castle. Breakfast. A long ride. See some of his tenant farmers, visit some pastures, inspect some crops. Meet with his steward Lister. Perhaps a hearty nuncheon in the village — he'd take Duff along. Also, a new crate of books had recently arrived and been placed in the library at home; he could look through them, choose one to read right away (probably that one about sheep breeding he'd been waiting for). And so the day would nicely pass. Filled with a comfortable sense of routine, Alasdair began walking briskly back.

Chapter 6

There was a tentative knock on the door, and Cousin Isobel sidled into the morning-room which Fiona had appropriated for her own use. Repressing an impatient sigh, she glanced up from the sheaves of papers she'd been poring over.

"Yes, Cousin?"

"Good morning! How are you, Fiona dear?" Isobel came up to the desk at which Fiona sat, on her plump face an expression of concerned anxiety which Fiona found almost unbearably irritating. "I mean — that is — how are you *really*? You do look troubled! Are you — oh dear, are you in pain? That is —"

"I'm fine! I look troubled because I've been studying these household receipts. Someone has apparently been spending a shocking amount of money on French champagne."

Cousin Isobel bridled. "I'm sure we can guess who *that* is! I don't even need to say the name — *just* the initials! D.M.! Do you know what he had the temerity to say to me yesterday? Why, he — mercy me, look at all those china figurines! Why are they all pushed to one side? And who has pulled all the curtains down?"

"I have. They're too heavy for this room. Besides, I like the view, and sunlight."

"Oh! And the figurines? How delightful they are! I'm very fond of those pastoral scenes. So picturesque."

Fiona shrugged. "If I want to be surrounded by shepherdesses and goose girls, I'll go outside and find some to talk to. Besides, I can't stand their vacant painted-on eyes — they look so stupid I want to break them in two. Ugh. After I'm done here, servants will take them away, to a different saloon, and move my desk closer to the window."

"How busy you are, and so terribly brave," said Isobel, with a sympathetic titter that had Fiona clenching her teeth, "and despite the dreadful circumstances! How I wish we could leave! Of course, we'd have to somehow go back in time, before your marriage! How *complicated* life is! What was I saying before? Oh! The figurines! If I may be so bold, Fiona dear — since you don't want them here — they do remind me of — perhaps I might be permitted to dust them, when they've found their new home? They are so very, very delicate! I wouldn't trust even the best housemaid to be careful with them!"

"There's no need for that, Cousin. Now that the wedding is over, I no longer require a chaperone. It's time for you to go home."

Although Fiona had, for many days, been looking forward to Isobel's departure with enormous pleasure, she took care just now to keep her tone mild. Yet she was unprepared for the way her cousin's soft round visage seemed to crumple like that of a child who'd just been harshly scolded.

"*Home?* Oh, Fiona dear! I — I haven't any home! I had to sell my house in Edinburgh, you know, for though that delightful Mr. Watson — so handsome, so charming! — assured me his investments would yield an *enormous* return, he took my cheque and I never saw him again. I was never so deceived in all my life! I — I am afraid I am quite penniless now." Isobel sat abruptly, and wept into the lacy scrap of handkerchief she tugged from her little reticule.

"Yes, Mother had mentioned something about your house." Fiona fiddled with a dry quill, running her fingers along the feathers. "I meant you would go home to Wick Bay, and bear Mother company. I know she'd be glad to have you."

Isobel lifted a red, wet face. "Oh! Your mother is the dearest, kindest person in the world, and I love her most sincerely, but — oh, my dear Fiona, I am — well, I'm ashamed to confess that I'm rather afraid of your father! I — I do try my best to conceal it, but when he is in a bad mood, which he so often is, my very bones seem to *melt* with terror. Not that he would *hurt* me — at least I do not think so — but he is so tall! And so fierce! The knife he always carries at his belt, positively murderous! And the way he frowns at one! *Please* allow me to stay here with you! I'll do anything you like, and endeavor diligently to not be an added expense! In fact, you may move me to a smaller room at once. Anything will do! I'm sure I don't need a fireplace, or a window!"

Now here, Fiona realized, was a difficulty. If she did what she wanted, and sent Isobel back to Wick Bay, she would feel like a monster. Her heart already felt like a lifeless stone within her. She didn't need *more* weight hanging upon it. Oh well, she told herself, the castle was enormous. Isobel could potter around from dawn till dusk, dusting figurines, and (with luck) keeping out of Fiona's way.

"Very well," she said, trying to keep the grudging reluctance out of her voice, and hoping she wouldn't regret her change of mind. "You may stay, Cousin."

The sudden radiance on Isobel's face brought no answering smile from her; she added, as pleasantly as she could, "If you'll excuse me? I have so much to do this morning."

Isobel jumped to her feet, cramming her sopping little handkerchief back into her reticule. "Of course! Oh, thank you, Fiona dear! I will make myself very useful to you — I promise!"

As Fiona once again turned her attention to the household accounts, she had no idea, no prescient little prickle, that one day, Cousin Isobel's words would come back to haunt her.

It was late in the afternoon when Alasdair and Duff returned from the village, where they had enjoyed a hearty repast at the Gilded Osprey. They strolled into the Great Hall, and came upon a veritable army of servants busily rearranging the long tables within it. His steward Lister, whom he had left not three hours ago happily totting up columns of numbers in his small office off the Hall, now stood supervising.

"What's going on here?" he asked.

Lister turned to him at once. "Mistress's orders, laird," he explained in his quiet, calm way.

"Orders for what? To throw my household into chaos?"

"The mistress felt the tables had been poorly placed, laird, causing great inconvenience to the serving folk as well as slowing the delivery of hot dishes to the high table."

Alasdair scanned the Hall. It was immediately apparent that the tables had not, in fact, previously been arranged in the best configuration, but even as he tried to stop himself the fatal words came out:

"This is how it's always been done."

"Women!" commented Uncle Duff, and that single word was like spark to tinder. Alasdair felt his temper rising sharply and he demanded of Lister:

"Where is the mistress?"

"In her morning-room, laird. The room that was —" Lister hesitated, as if wondering if there were a better way to say it. But, of course, there wasn't. "It was your mother's, laird. The Green Saloon."

"I see." Scowling, Alasdair at once proceeded there, walking with long strides along the spacious corridor that led toward the back of the castle. It was exactly as he'd feared. His officious new wife was already changing things, and without so much as a by-your-leave. He stalked into the Green Saloon, and stopped abruptly three or four paces past the threshold.

His mother's precious figurines — gone. The heavy damask drapes — gone. Half the furniture — gone. The desk moved from its usual spot and now set perpendicular to the tall windows overlooking the gardens. And sitting at the desk, several neat stacks of papers arrayed upon it as well as a large vase filled with pink and white dahlias, was his wife, herself neat as wax in a simple day-dress of palest blue and a delicate cashmere shawl draped over her shoulders.

He said:

"Just what do you think you're doing, madam?"

Her eyes were also blue today, blue and pensive as she looked up at him.

"Your head gardener — Monty — says the bee-hives aren't doing well. He showed me a loose brood pattern, which is a problem, and also some sunken cappings. I was wondering what could be done about that."

Caught off-guard, Alasdair replied without think-ing, "He never said a word to me."

"Well, I had to winkle it out of him. He's not very talkative, is he? But I've never seen someone with such a way with flowers."

"That's for certain. Did you have to fight him for those dahlias? He's notorious for that — as if the flowers belong only to him."

"Oh no," Fiona answered. "He just gave them to me. Perhaps because it was a relief to talk about the bees. But I'm not sure he'll ever let me have some roses."

Alasdair laughed, but then he remembered why he'd come in here. She was a presumptuous, high-handed, *managing* female who — to very appropriately employ a botanical analogy — needed to be nipped in the bud. He scowled again. "You've completely altered this room." Warming to his task, he added (completely forgetting that he had always despised those prissy china figures), "And had items removed."

"Yes, there was too much furniture in here," she replied, with what struck him as unseemly breeziness. "And I had the figurines placed in that chamber upstairs — what is it called? All pink and frills? The Little Drawing-room? There's the perfect cabinet to display them to best advantage. In fact, my cousin Isobel is probably there right now, fussing over them — if you'd care to see their disposition?"

"No," he said, scowling even more fiercely. And before he was in danger of admitting that he could easily go the rest of his life without setting eyes on the damned things, he said, unpleasantly, "What gives you the right to come in this room and muck it up?"

Those cool blue eyes were flashing now. "As you have endowed me with all your worldly goods, the domestic matters are mine to manage as I see fit. It is my right as your wife."

"When you behave in the night as my wife, madam, then during the day you can move every cursed piece of furniture in the entire castle if it pleases you!" Even as he spoke these acrid words, some part of him wondered if she would cry, or perhaps angrily fling the vase of flowers at him. Wouldn't it be nice if she would simply yield, like a proper woman would?

Instead, to his fury, she settled her shawl so that it draped more evenly about her shoulders, doing it with a deliberateness that seemed almost to insult him.

"Feel free to inform me, laird, as to when you decide to behave in the night as a husband should."

He stared at her, tempted, very tempted, to smash the vase himself, and while he was at it, rip all her tidy stacks of paper in two. If he were to be dragged to the rack and stretched out twice his natural length he would not have told her that he'd today been to see Dr. Colquhoun to discreetly find out just when he might discard the sling. It was for *her* sake he had endured Colquhoun's raised eyebrow and instantly repressed half-smile. And now she had the brazen gall to instruct him as to his own business?

"I am master here!" he roared, and, turning on his boot-heel, left her morning-room — no, damn it to hell, the Green Saloon! — without another word. He gathered up Uncle Duff, whom he found in the library, glancing through a racing journal and placidly puffing on his pipe, and practically dragged him to the stables. It wasn't until they were on their horses, and riding away, that Alasdair realized he hadn't even mentioned to Fiona the aggravating rearrangement of the tables in the Great Hall.

Not only did he blame her for that, he blamed her for his own forgetting.

Damn it, damn it *all*. He realized he was grinding his teeth, and consciously relaxed his jaw.

He couldn't wait to get to his cousin Hewie's house, off past the heather meadow, where he could eat and drink and make merry and, for a little while, forget that he'd been forced into marriage with the most exasperating woman in Scotland.

Alasdair did not return for the evening meal, nor was his uncle Duff anywhere to be found, so it was only Fiona and Cousin Isobel at the high table. Fiona ate with her usual robust appetite, listening with only half an ear as Isobel rattled on.

"Oh my dear, I feel so *conspicuous!* The day after your wedding, and here we are, all alone! I'm sure that everyone is staring at us! That is, I mean, at *you!* I heard that the laird positively *thundered* at you this afternoon! How terrible it must have been! Why, oh why, did we ever come to this dreadful place? Oh yes, thank you," she said to the servant proffering an aromatic dish of juicy roasted beef, "just a very small serving. No, no sauce — I couldn't possibly — oh, wait! On second thought, just a dab. Thank you. Might you bring me another roll? Upon my word, how different the Hall looks, my dear Fiona! Better, in fact, although I had not thought any improvements were needed. Did you have fresh tablecloths put down?"

Fiona, accepting some of the beef, contemplated telling the truth, but didn't think she could stand any further conversation about the rearranging of furniture. She merely nodded, and continued to eat her excellent dinner. She knew that she was, in fact, being speculatively eyed by everyone in the Hall — and honestly, who could fault them? — but without disrespect, so there wasn't anything to be done about it. On the one hand, she could go on, pleasantly and indefinitely, without having to be in the same room with Alasdair; on the other hand, however, there was no question that his absence was rude. Insulting. What happened to all those good manners he'd previously been displaying during the delightful Let's Get Married Or Die competition? Wasn't she good enough to warrant a modicum of civility, now that she was — more or less — his wife?

Wasn't she good enough . . .

Yes, it was a question that had been haunting her for some years now.

Fiona kept herself busy for the rest of the evening by sewing, reading, and taking a long hot bath, but by the time she had made herself ready for bed, and was under the covers once more, his defection rankled to the point that she felt like a plucked harp spring, vibrating angrily.

Naturally sleep did not come, and the hour was well advanced by the time Alasdair finally came into the room. He stopped, as he had the night before, at the foot of the bed.

"Are you awake?"

"Yes," she replied coldly.

"Now there's wifely devotion for you! Did you miss me, madam?"

Coldly, coldly, she said: "Oh, yes, laird, I missed you greatly, especially at dinner, and most especially your scintillating conversation."

He only laughed, and went away for a while. When he returned, Fiona had forgotten to close her eyes this time, and was taken aback to see that he was completely naked. Goodness, but he had a lot of muscles, and quite a bit of hair on his chest, and also lower down —

And on his long legs —

Which were also very muscular, and —

This is what he would have looked like riding that horse around the castle.

Imagination, Fiona realized, wasn't always better than seeing the real thing. Especially when the real thing — the real person — was magnificent.

Oh, by the hammer of mighty Camulos, she was *staring*.

Quickly, then, she looked up at the canopy over her head, knowing that she was blushing a fiery crimson and deeply grateful that the room was dim. But, of course, he said as he climbed into bed:

"Had your fill? Or I could pull down the covers if you like."

Fiona wanted to do different things.

Part of her wanted to explode with anger, like fireworks in a dark sky, and fizzle away into humiliated nothingness.

Another part of her wanted to hurl herself across the space between them so that she could clap a hand across his lips and make him stop talking.

Yet another part of her wanted something else . . .

It was all very confusing. As if suddenly she had splintered into different Fionas. One was the Fiona who was cool and imperturbable, steady and reliable. One was a furious Fiona, roiling, boiling, with hostility. And another was a Fiona who — oh my, oh my — wanted to be soft and yielding and vulnerable, whose body suddenly seemed to have a mind of its own here in this large sumptuous bed where more could happen than sleeping.

It was this third Fiona which made her very, very nervous.

So she said to him, bitingly, "You smell of alcohol."

"Yes, I'm probably a little drunk."

"Why? Did you need to be drunk in order to bring yourself to do the deed with me?"

Oh, her unguarded tongue! Another painfully re-velatory remark she wished she could take back. She hadn't thought herself a particularly prideful person before becoming ensnared by the great Penhallow, but she was fast coming to learn that, apparently, she was.

How lowering.

Nor did it help when he laughed again.

"You're safe, madam, as I've been forbidden from, uh, using my arm for another week. Unless you've changed your opinion as to positions? Has the sight of my unclothed self incited in you a new resolve?"

"Hardly."

"A shame."

She only sniffed. And recoiled when he asked, ca-sually:

"Do you always wear nightgowns with necks up to your chin?"

Involuntarily she drew the covers higher. "Yes."

"It's not surprising, really. You've no fat on you, so I expect you get cold easily."

"I can't help being thin. It's how God made me."

"There's no need to sound so wrathy."

"I detest personal remarks," Fiona said, feeling that she had gained the safety of the high road, then promptly lost her footing when she added, "*I* would never criticize you, laird, for — as an example — that red hair of yours."

To her chagrin he only said, pensively, "Some people seem to find it attractive."

"I can't imagine why."

"What color hair do you prefer?"

This was dangerous, dangerous. She couldn't help but think of someone else, another man, another time, a caressing voice and enveloping arms; and fire, sweet fire overtaking her. With a kind of desperation she blurted out, "Where did you go tonight?"

"Why, madam, you *did* miss me. I'm touched."

"Never mind! It's of no interest to me, I'm sure."

Alasdair turned onto his side (his good side) and looked over at her. He could see the ruffles of her absurd nightgown framing her chin like the white petals of a flower. A Fiona flower, he thought suddenly, ridiculously enjoying the consonance of the two Fs. *A frilly Fiona flower. A frilly fine fearless Fiona flower. A frilly fine fearless familiar fetching forthright formidable fragrant Fiona flower . . .*

But then there came to him — penetrating the cheerful fog produced by the aged whisky Hewie had poured with such liberality — that earlier, that uneasy sense of his own behavior.

He had, in fact, left his bride of less than forty-eight hours to preside over the Great Hall, alone. He'd spent several delightful hours with Hewie and his company, which included Hewie's recently widowed sister-in-law, Nora, who seemed to rise above her affliction with remarkable resilience, giggling, flirting, pulling him to his feet to dance Strip the Willow when someone began sawing on a fiddle, even, at one point, plumping herself square onto his lap. How sorry she was, she'd confided with lips pressed close to his ear, that she had been ineligible to compete for the privilege of winning his hand in matrimony, for she would have tried so hard — and here her hand had boldly groped down past his waist — so very hard, but then again, people lost their spouses every day, didn't they, and who knew what the future might hold?

At the time, he'd been too distracted by the whisky, by that sweetly pandering hand, to take in the full meaning of Nora's words. But now they returned, almost like a blow to his brain, and mild uneasiness jolted toward something else. No matter what he felt about his recalcitrant wife, such things ought not to be said, ought not to be listened to, and he should have dumped bonny, winsome Nora off his lap onto the cold stone floor.

But he hadn't.

He had sat there, awash in the golden paralytic haze of whisky and mindless lust, held fast by a wet little tongue that had toyed with the rim of his ear and a sweet little voice saying evil words.

But now shame — like a bucket of icy water dumped upon him — had broken the spell, and he lay in his own bed, warm and snug, and abruptly, utterly sober.

He tried to tell himself that he *could* have wed little Mairi MacIntyre, she of the golden hair, the tiny waist, the tinkling laugh, the delicate fairy maiden who seemed to float rather than walk and who looked up worshipfully into one's eyes as though one deserved it.

He tried to tell himself that Fiona had brashly put herself forward. Had practically *made* him marry her.

But he was having a difficult time convincing himself of that.

Shame, and uneasiness, and a new feeling of uncertainty all got in the way.

Yet —

He summoned the memory of Uncle Duff saying blithely, *What is a wife but a brood mare? You'll pick one of the lasses, get her with child as many times as it takes to produce a son or two, and that's the sum of it.*

Now *that* was the smartest tack to take.

And luckily, tomorrow was another day.

And he had somewhere to go.

And if his wife had to eat alone for a while, no one would think twice of it again.

"Well," he now said out loud, as pleasantly as humanly possible, "good night, madam," he said to her, and firmly shut his eyes.

"Good night, laird," answered Fiona, with heavy

irony in her tone, and turned away from him. Memories, she thought to herself, were dangerously alluring, not unlike the apple in the old German fairy tale — that poisoned apple offered by the evil queen to her credulous stepdaughter: red, delicious-looking, tempting, and fatal.

It was still dark when Alasdair shook his uncle out of a sound sleep.

"*What?*" gasped Duff. "God's toenails, what's happening? Who died?"

"Nobody," Alasdair said. "Come on. We're going to Crieff."

"What? Now? Bloody hell, lad, do you know what I was dreaming about when you rudely rousted me? I was rescuing an endangered maiden from a dragon —"

"Wonderful." Rapidly Alasdair picked up Duff's clothes, which still lay in an untidy heap on the floor, and flung them onto his bed. "Let's go."

Grumbling, Duff sat up. "Light a candle for me. Why are we going to Crieff?"

"Cattle meet."

"So?"

"So I want to go look at some cattle."

"Three days after you're married?"

"Aye. You're putting your shirt on backward."

"Ach, so I am." Duff laughed. "And you're running away."

Alasdair frowned. "Nonsense."

"I'm not judging you, lad. A man must do what a man must do. Besides, we've had some good times in Crieff before, haven't we?"

"Aye. Hurry up."

"Not just running away, but *sneaking* away, eh?"

"Shut up. Here are your boots."

Ten minutes later, they came down the last steps of the staircase into the still-dim Great Hall, heading for the side hallway which would take them outdoors and to the stables. Alasdair turned sharply left around the carved newel post, just as someone was quietly coming around it, and they collided.

"Sorry —" they both began, stepping back, and then stared at each other.

"Oh!" exclaimed Fiona, just as Alasdair said, as pain from his arm winged through him, "What the *hell* —" He gathered himself. There was absolutely no reason for him to feel guilty. He went on, "What are you doing, madam?"

She glared up at him. "I might ask the same of you."

"I," he said loftily, "live here."

"As do I, thanks to you."

"And isn't it splendid. Were you *following* me?"

"Of course not! I was hungry, so I went down to the kitchen for something to eat. Where are *you* going?"

Duff chuckled. "So much for sneaking away."

"Sneaking away?" she echoed. She crossed her arms over her chest. Over her non-prodigious breasts. And added, in a rather snappish way, "Had enough of me already, laird?"

"Not that it's any of your business," he answered, "but my uncle and I are going to Crieff."

"Why? Are there going to be some Roman-style bacchanals?"

"Let's hope," said Duff, and Alasdair overrode him.

"There's a cattle meet, if you must know."

"I see. And were you planning to inform me of your departure, or was I just going to find out on my own?"

"You're not my keeper, madam." No, there was

no reason in the world for him to feel guilty. None at all. None, none, none. "I was going to have one of the grooms tell Lister, and Lister would, of course, tell you."

"Thereby, of course, keeping my dignity intact. How thoughtful of you, laird."

"Oh, by the body of Christ, madam, go back to bed," he said, also in a rather snappish way.

"Don't tell me what to do."

"Fine! Do whatever you like. I couldn't care less."

"Thank you for that! Go have fun in Crieff. Since *fun* is what you're all about, isn't it?"

"I'm going to look at *cattle*, damn it!" he shouted.

"And now you're shouting at me. Excellent. I think I've had just about enough. Go, then! Stay as long as you want. The longer the better, as far as I'm concerned." And Fiona stalked past him and then Duff, and went rapidly up the stairs, at a pace clearly intended to convey a strong desire to absent herself from him as soon as possible.

When she was gone from sight, Duff chuckled again. "Well," he said, "that went well."

"Shut up, Uncle," growled Alasdair, and continued on his way to the stables.

Fiona did, after all, go back to bed where, to her surprise, she managed to doze off for an hour or so. When she woke, it took her a few moments to realize where she was. And *who* she was; her right hand as if of its own accord went to her left hand, to feel the solidity of the gold ring upon it.

Fiona looked over at the empty space next to her.

It just so happened that she enjoyed going to cattle meets.

But did anyone ask her if she wanted to go, too?

No, nobody had.

Not that she'd want to spend more time with *him*. And his awful uncle. Off, the two of them, to roister about Crieff.

She'd do just fine without him. She'd do *better* without him.

And what, exactly, would she be doing?

Fiona remembered Duff's remark about the laird's late mother, that evening in the Great Drawing-room:

She did so much here in the castle, during her day, there'll be little for the laird's new wife to do, beyond producing offspring, of course.

Of course, there wasn't much she could do about offspring. And wouldn't it be delightful to lie around all day, eating chocolates and reading novels? Or buying new dishes, when there were already several very attractive sets lying around, not even used?

God in heaven.

Fiona got up, dressed, and went to the sunny breakfast-room. There she had a very nice bowl of porridge with cream and sugar and two cups of tea while she went over her list for the day. Then, briskly, she began addressing the items before her.

It was wash day, and she spent a couple of hours overseeing the laundresses at their work. She walked through the kitchen garden with Monty, and after that they moved on to look, worriedly, at some of the beehives. She went for a ride on Gealag. She began the inventory of household linens, a daunting enterprise given the sheer quantity of them. She wrote letters to her mother and to her sisters. She went up to the attics, vast and cavernous, curious as to what they contained, and was stunned by how crowded they were with furniture (bedsteads, bureaus, sofas, tables and chairs of all description, tall mirrors, desks, and so on), piles of clothing and bedding seemingly beyond numbering, along with a staggering array of wooden boxes, crates, and trunks. As she went downstairs she bypassed the nursery (too soon, too soon), and found herself in the long gallery whose walls were filled with portraits.

She paced slowly along, studying them. Before her was plainly evidence of a long and noble heritage dating back hundreds of years. Here was a little girl from James the Fourth's time, dressed like a small adult in her quaint gable hood and heavy, mulberry-colored brocade gown with its wide fur-trimmed sleeves. Here was a medieval prince (with dark red hair!), very arrogant in his fine silk-trimmed tunic and cross-gartered leggings that displayed sturdy, muscular calves and thighs. Here was a beautiful middle-aged woman of the previous century in her lavishly pleated *robe à la française;* her face was white with powder, her lips deep red, and on her right cheek had been placed a tiny fashionable patch.

Fiona came to a large painting with a more modern look, and paused. Two boys, one about five, the other a few years older. The smaller one with red hair and brilliant amber eyes, the taller one blond, with eyes of dark brown, and very handsome. They were in a sunlit glen, with thickly clustered woods in the background, and a shimmering blue loch in the far distance — surely, Fiona thought, the same one which lay beyond the castle. The two boys stood side by side, not touching, and each with a dog at his feet. The little red-haired one was looking at his wolfhound puppy, and on his countenance the painter had captured a charming expression suggestive of fun and mischief. The taller blond boy stared directly at the viewer, giving a distinct impression of proud authority, and paying no attention to the handsome sable and white Collie which sat gazing adoringly up at him.

The red-haired boy had to be a young Alasdair. But who was the older boy? They shared some physical similarities in the shape of their heads, the lines of their jaws, even to the curve of dark eyebrows.

It had to be his brother. Or perhaps a cousin?

As she stood there, puzzled, Fiona realized just how little she knew about her new husband.

Oh well, what did it matter.

He didn't like her, and she didn't like him.

Still, it could have been worse. She could've married Niall Birk. Ugh. And spent her life making sure he wasn't creeping up behind her to shove her down the stairs. Or she might have been wed to the extremely stupid Walraig Tevis, or the spindly knife-wielding Ross Stratton who, now that she thought of it, reminded her in a very nasty way of a rat.

Instead, she had married Alasdair Penhallow, who wasn't stupid, who didn't remind her of a rat, and who, she was sure, wasn't going to shove her down the stairs.

They just didn't like each other, that's all.

She wished these prudent reflections would make her feel more cheerful, but there was no use in wringing one's hands and bemoaning the state of things. She hated when people did that. Besides, to complain about her lot would be like feeling sorry for yourself when you'd been given a perfectly practical and serviceable pair of stockings for your birthday — and pining in a very immature way for, say, the moon. Luckily, there was always so much to do. Right now, for example, there was still time before dinner to ask Lister about the leak in a big copper tub one of the laundresses had mentioned, and to send a message to Dr. Colquhoun, asking him to check on a footman with a sprained ankle. If she hurried, she could go to the library and find a new book to read for later.

Fiona turned away, and as she did she noticed that on the walls in this section of the gallery, there were very faint discolorations, nearly invisible to the casual eye of a passerby. She paused again.

It seemed that the portraits had been rearranged.

Yes, for now that she noticed it, the paintings here weren't as densely set together as in other areas of the gallery.

How curious.

Then she went on and elsewhere, her mind filling up with other, more pressing things.

After dinner, she and Isobel went to the Great Drawing-room. There, Isobel produced an intimidatingly large puzzle and Fiona, shrugging, helped her sort through the pieces and make a start on the perimeter. Having found the four corner pieces, Isobel announced both her satisfaction and her fatigue, and proceeded to doze in a chair next to the fire. Fiona sewed up a jagged rent in one of the chapel's altar cloths — knowing that now that she was wed, working on baby garments for her sisters would evoke an irritating array of inquisitive reactions — and then turned to her new book, a collection of Walter Scott's poetry. She was reading "Marmion," and had just gotten to the lines *Oh! What a tangled web we weave / When first we practise to deceive*, when she gradually became aware of that odd creeping feeling of being stared at.

She looked up from her book. Sure enough, little Sheila stood next to her chair — within three feet of it, in fact — and Fiona had to suppress a gasp. How on earth had the child gotten so close without her noticing it?

One of those peculiar pale blue eyes was fixed on

herself, the other seemed to be resting thoughtfully on Isobel.

"She dreams of the past and what could have been."

Fiona reached for the girl's hand. "You're a shrewd little lass. What brings you here, hinny?"

"I came here, lady, because . . ." Sheila trailed off, looking down at their clasped hands. "Fences," she murmured, sounding troubled, "high fences." Then she pulled her hand free and glanced around the elegant room. "How can you breathe in here, lady?"

Before Fiona could reply, someone said sharply, "Sheila! You ought not to be there!" A very old woman, bent over her stick, came stumping toward them, on her deeply wrinkled face disapproval written large.

Sheila suddenly became simply a little girl who had been apprehended in an act of naughtiness, and stuck a rather dirty finger in her mouth, around which she spoke cajolingly. "Oh, but Granny, the lady doesn't know that tomorrow is my birthday."

"So it is, but you'd no right to come disturb the mistress," scolded the old woman. "I do apologize, lady, I was at my devotions and the lass slipped away from me like a *kelpie*."

There certainly was something unusual about the little girl, but hopefully she didn't number shapeshifting among her talents. Fiona responded civilly: "There's no need to apologize, I assure you. And you are . . . ?"

The old woman dipped a creaky little curtsy. "I am Margery, lady."

Ancient might she be, but there was nothing vague or doddering about Dame Margery. A flash of inspiration came to Fiona and she asked, "Have you lived here all your life, madam?"

"Aye, lady, that I have."

"Can you tell me aught of the laird's family? There's his uncle here, of course, and *he* once mentioned that the laird's parents had passed away, but other than that I know nothing."

Dame Margery looked consideringly at Fiona. "That's so, lady, both of the laird's parents have gone on, and his older brother as well."

"How sad! Were these recent losses?"

"Nay, madam, there was a single event, and that some fifteen years ago."

Fiona stared. "A *single* event?"

"The loch," Sheila remarked, in the tone of one passing along some mildly interesting information, "is deep, and a monster lives in it. It ate them all up."

"Hush, child!" said the old lady severely.

"But it's true, Granny. The monster warned them not to come, but they did, and it swallowed them."

Cousin Isobel had woken, and now interposed in a quavery voice: "A *monster*? Oh, surely not! But still, one can't be *too* cautious, can one? Fiona, my dear, *pray* don't ever ride your horse anywhere near there! Your mother would never forgive me if you were to be swallowed up by a loch monster!"

"I've seen it," boasted Sheila.

"That you have not," the old lady said, "and it's long past time for your bed, child! Forgive us, lady, for our intrusion! Come!"

With dragging steps the little girl went to her grandmother, pausing only once to twist about and say, "Please, lady, can Cook make me something nice for my birthday? The laird's mother never did anything for the children of Tadgh. It was only and ever her *things* she cared about."

"To be sure I'll speak to Cook," promised Fiona, and watched, bemused, as Dame Margery pulled her wayward little charge from the drawing-room. Her

book was still open in her lap, but her mind was occupied in sorting through Sheila's words, as if trying
to separate wheat from chaff.

Of course there was no loch monster, but it did
sound all too true that a disaster had befallen Alasdair's family there. And what was that all about —
the laird's mother not doing anything for the castle's
children? How would Sheila even *know* that, or make
the claim, given that Alasdair's mother, Gormelia,
had been dead some fifteen years? And . . . was Sheila
referring to Gormelia's own children as well?

Into Fiona's head came an uncannily clear image
of the portrait she'd viewed earlier that day, that of
the two little boys, one with dark-red hair, the other
with bright yellow-blond hair. Surely he was Alasdair's older brother, lost to the loch along with their
mother and father?

She remembered, then, that excursion to the Keep
o' the Mòr, and Alasdair recalling cheerfully, *I spent
many a night as a lad camping up here with friends.*
She had seen how, unexpectedly, the laughter had
gone from his face, to be taken over by a look of
haunting sadness — and just as quickly been replaced
by a smile.

Now she wondered if Alasdair's brother had been
part of those enjoyable long-ago nights at the Keep,
and if the memory had caused him pain —

Her musings were interrupted by Isobel saying,
"Such an *odd* little creature! And those eyes! *So* unsettling! Still, her birthday — I could sew her a wee
stuffed doll, do you think she would like that? I have
just the right scrap of fabric for a little gown, and
some narrow lace for the hem."

"Yes, I think Sheila would love a doll, Cousin,
how kind of you," answered Fiona, a little absently,
but touched by Isobel's thoughtfulness.

"I'm so glad you agree! Oh, my dear, speaking of gowns, I had the strangest dream just now. I was sixteen, and I was wearing the white silk gown Papa allowed me to have for my debut, with the skirt draped *à la polonaise*, and the prettiest striped caraco in the world, with long sleeves and three rows of ruffles! It was the very one I wore when I met Captain Murdoch, you know."

"Captain Murdoch? Do I know him?"

"Oh! No, you wouldn't. I do *try* not to talk about him. It was just that silly dream of mine that reminded me."

The quavery note had returned to Isobel's voice, and Fiona looked at her curiously. Her cousin had long seemed to be an open book: someone whose rampant garrulousness could never conceal anything. And yet here was — as it were — a new paragraph revealed.

Not a happy one, clearly.

Fiona hesitated. She didn't wish to pry. But then Isobel said suddenly:

"Dreams *are* so odd, aren't they? In my dream I had the merest glimpse of Captain Murdoch, and then he was gone. Just like in real life. It was only for a while — for such a *little* while — that we were betrothed."

"Betrothed? But only temporarily?"

"Yes. On the very eve of the wedding, Father discovered that Captain Murdoch had — well, he had a great many debts, which none of us knew about." Isobel smoothed out her skirts with punctilious care, and Fiona watched as a single tear rolled slowly down her cousin's soft white cheek. "I told Father it didn't bother me, that thanks to a legacy from an aunt I had *more* than enough money for the both of us! But he told Jimmie — that is, Captain Murdoch — that although he would permit the marriage, he refused to settle the debts. He held all my money in trust, for I was not yet of age. And — the next morning Jimmie was gone. I never saw him again, nor heard from him."

Fiona drew a deep breath, and said with a new softness: "I didn't know, Cousin. I'm very sorry. Surely you — you had other offers?"

Isobel smiled faintly. "Oh yes, but somehow — I don't know how it was, but somehow I could never like anyone quite as well as I liked my Jimmie. And so time passed, and my parents died, and I stayed on in our house. Of course I kept myself busy, but — well, how happy I was when you came to visit me, my dear! And you only eighteen! How much fun we had, didn't we? And then there was Logan! So charming! That is — until he — oh dear —"

"Goodness!" Fiona interrupted with a brisk, bright, inauthentic affability. Softness fled, leaving in its wake a sudden raw feeling of desolation; into her heart had crept again that secret stony feeling. "Only look at the time! How late it is!" Quickly she stood. "I'm to bed, Cousin. If you'll excuse me? I hope you sleep well. Good night."

Without waiting for a reply, Fiona left the Great Drawing-room. Her steps were graceful and dignified, she told herself, not ignominious scuttling. No, she wasn't running away. Not like *some* people did . . .

It wasn't long before she was in bed, hopelessly wide awake.

Her thoughts turned to Isobel. Poor Isobel. How strange: never had she thought she'd feel for her the slightest pang of sympathy. Maybe she wouldn't have, if Isobel had cried without abandon, as she had yesterday, but there was something about that one tear, slowly making its lonely way down that white, lightly powdered cheek.

She'd been so used to viewing Isobel as a nuisance. Almost an enemy.

This small, soft, vulnerable person — without a home, without money, without prospects — her *enemy*?

Was it possible she had been carrying her old grudge beyond what was reasonable, what was fair?

Was it possible that she had, over the years, become so hard, so cynical?

These were troubling ideas.

She had long prided herself on her good judgment.

A different perception of Isobel somehow altered her perception of herself. She wasn't quite sure how she felt about that.

Fiona's thoughts, inevitably it seemed, now turned to her husband.

There was still so much she didn't know about Alasdair, but she *had* learned that his parents, his brother had died. How dreadful for him and how sad. She could only imagine what that might feel like, especially the loss of a sibling — but she didn't *want* to, for dearly did she love her sisters, had adored and protected them all her life. Nonetheless, it was an unexpected glimpse of Alasdair. He would have been twenty years old at the time. Would he have looked very different then? Fiona wondered. At thirty-five, there wasn't a trace of gray in his hair, and he moved with effortless vigor.

Really, the only thing she could think of were those lightly grooved lines that bracketed his mouth, but they didn't suggest diminishment, but rather authority . . . laughter . . . sensuality.

In fact, they were the sort of lines over which one might want to run one's finger, tracing them, teasingly.

If one were an idiot, Fiona told herself caustically.

If one were that soft, yielding, vulnerable, *foolish* Fiona.

She snatched at the covers and bundled herself tightly within them. Stubbornly she closed her eyes, made her breathing regular, relaxed her tense limbs.

A log collapsed within the fireplace.

A gust of wind rattled the panes of the windows.

Somewhere, a dog barked.

It occurred to her, then, just how big the bed was. It was ridiculous, it was bizarre, but after only two nights of being married, after two nights of coldness and bristling hostility between them, she — well — she actually missed having him there with her.

Not *if* one were an idiot, she told herself.

She *was* an idiot.

Chapter 7

"Slow down, lad, slow down," pitifully groaned Uncle Duff, "your footfalls are making my head pound."

Alasdair adjusted his pace and with a listing Duff at his side went up the broad stone steps at the entrance to Castle Tadgh. The week in Crieff had been very productive — during the days, at least. The nights had been devoted to other pursuits. And now his uncle was paying the price. Glancing at his haggard face (even that immense beard looked wan), Alasdair was conscious of a twinge of impatience. He shook it off, though, and stepped warily into the Great Hall, wondering what bad things might have happened in his absence. And where was Cuilean, who usually bounded out to greet him?

Mellow early-afternoon sunlight illuminated the long tables which lay in the tidy geometrical lines of their new formation. Was it his imagination, or did the suits of armor flanking the great fireplace seem shinier? And were the colors of the enormous fifteenth-century tapestry hung on the wall behind the laird and lady's chairs looking a little more vivid?

Over by one of the tables was Lister, a reassuring sight at least. He was talking with a middle-aged woman in an immaculately clean gown and ruffled cap, whom Alasdair didn't know. They turned as he came forward, and advanced to meet him.

"Laird," said Lister, "may I introduce to you our new housekeeper, Mrs. Allen of Aberfeldy. She is," he added with his air of scrupulous correctness, "a cousin of mine."

Mrs. Allen dipped a respectful curtsy, and Alasdair nodded. Of course she was a cousin, everyone in Scotland had a cornucopia of cousins, but — "I hadn't realized," he said carefully, "that we required the services of a housekeeper."

"The mistress asked me, laird, if I might know of any suitable candidates, and at once I thought of Eliza Jane, whose elderly master had recently died."

"Yes, I see," answered Alasdair, and he really *did* see. The officious hand of his wife, yet again! "Where is the mistress?" he inquired grimly.

"When last I saw her, laird," said Mrs. Allen, her expression now a little anxious, "she was in her morning-room."

His mood rapidly souring, he couldn't keep himself from saying: "Do you mean the Green Saloon?"

Mrs. Allen looked nervously to Lister, who answered for her. "Yes, laird. It's what the mistress calls it, so we've fallen into the habit of it."

A querulous moan issued from a nearby table. "Ale," demanded Uncle Duff weakly, slumping low in a chair. "Hair of the dog! And some cold meat — scones also. Hot! With jam."

"Right away, sir," said Mrs. Allen, and hurried toward the archway that led to the kitchens.

Alasdair registered a flicker of irritation at Duff's peremptory order — would it kill him to say "Please" or "Thank you"? — but said nothing, only turned and went on to Fiona's morning-room — to the Green Saloon, damn it. He came to the threshold and stopped short.

On a long chintz-covered sofa lay his wife, on her side, fast asleep, with a big tartan shawl draped over her slender form. And curled up at her feet, in a familiar shaggy ball, was Cuilean, who opened his intelligent dark eyes and thumped his tail, but gently, as if not wanting to disturb his human companion.

Feeling an absurd sense of betrayal, Alasdair frowned at Cuilean, and then at Fiona. No wonder she was sleeping. She was exhausted from interfering where she ought not. He came into the room, exasperated to notice himself lightening his tread, but before he'd taken more than two or three steps Fiona started awake and abruptly sat up, blue eyes wide.

It was then that Cuilean jumped off the sofa and frisked toward him, tail wagging wildly.

"Oh!" Fiona said, reaching up to smooth hair tousled by sleep. "It's you! Must you creep up on me like that?"

"Must you make off with my dog?"

She frowned back at him. "He's been following me around since you went away."

That, he realized, was unanswerable, so he chose another angle of attack. "What the devil do you mean by hiring a housekeeper?"

"Are you going to sit down? You quite tower over one. It's very unpleasant."

Reluctantly he did sit, in an attractively upholstered high-backed chair, somewhat mollified when Cuilean soulfully laid his big head on his knee. But he stuck to his guns, albeit with a slightly different tack.

"I don't recognize this chair. Don't tell me you've been buying new furniture the moment my back was turned."

"It's from the attics. I didn't care for all those Rococo chairs that were in here before."

"My mother," he said heavily, stubbornly, "thought them very handsome."

"It's stupid to quarrel about taste. I prefer furnishings that are less ornate." Fiona pulled away the tartan shawl that had remained tucked over her, revealing a simple day-dress made in a singularly beautiful shade of lavender that even in his peppery temper Alasdair had to acknowledge as strikingly flattering to his wife's pale complexion, dark-lashed blue eyes, silvery-blonde hair, even her slim figure. Why, she almost looked —

She almost looked —

He blinked.

For a moment there, he had thought her lovely.

Attractive.

Desirable.

Don't be daft, man, he told himself harshly.

Such sentimental thoughts were a trap, the chain around the ankle that jerked and tightened and dragged you down into the depths.

Cuilean lifted his head and fixed those intelligent eyes on him, ears pricked as if questioningly, and Alasdair said shortly to Fiona:

"Is that a new gown, madam?"

"No."

There was a silence, during which Alasdair fought within himself. Why was he being so churlish? He ought to tell her how bonny a dress it was. But it felt like he would be giving away something he wanted — needed — to hang onto.

Finally he said, all too aware of how awkward he sounded, "I thought you'd been having new dresses made."

Two bright spots of color burned on her cheeks. "Why would you care?"

"I don't. But what's this about hiring a new house-keeper?" Oh, God in heaven, he was only digging himself deeper. Was this really *him* talking? Needling her about domestic concerns? If he'd taken ten seconds to think about it, it was completely obvious they needed a housekeeper; no doubt Lister and Cook had been bearing the burden for too long. Why hadn't he noticed it before? He *should* be thanking her for being astute enough to not only observe the problem, but to have dealt with it so swiftly.

But he just couldn't force out the words.

He was, in truth, behaving like a complete and total ass.

What was happening to him?

Where was the blithe, light-hearted, easygoing Alasdair?

She was sitting very straight on the sofa, eyes sparkling with anger, and had just opened her mouth to speak when he said coldly, "Never mind!"

It was the best he could do.

"Very well. While we're on the subject of house-hold matters, laird, are you aware that in one of the cellars there are a hundred and fourteen cases of Veuve Clicquot?"

Alasdair felt his mouth dropping open. "What?"

"Yes, I went down there in search of some drying racks and there they were. It took me half an hour to count them all. Oh, and after questioning Lister, I've also learned that the staff hasn't had their wages raised in five years."

"But I —" He stopped. "But I told my uncle to — I distinctly remember — it was, in fact, five years ago —"

She said nothing.

Slowly he rose to his feet. It felt like his familiar world was crumbling all around him, and that noth-ing would ever be the same again. If, in fact, he were prone to hyperbole, he might even have said that the sky was falling. But he did not give voice to such fancies. Instead, he gave a small, formal bow and said, "If you'll excuse me, madam?"

"By all means," she answered coolly. "I have a great deal to do this afternoon."

Cuilean trotting happily at his side, Alasdair went in search of Duff, and found him in the Great Hall spreading a lavish dollop of strawberry jam on a tattie scone, which very generously he held out to Alasdair. Which Alasdair curtly refused.

The conversation that followed was difficult — for him. Duff cheerfully admitted his mistake, acknowledged he had forgotten to speak to Lister about the wages (for it was, he reminded Alasdair, the morning following their exceptionally convivial Lammas Day celebrations), and also confessed to purchasing all that pricey champagne. One never knew, he added helpfully, what with the tumultuous state of European relations, when the supply would be cut off.

Alasdair held onto his temper with an effort, then went off to find Lister, to whom he gave an order for wages to be immediately increased (and back wages tacked on), and after that he sought out the housekeeper Mrs. Allen and reassured her as to her welcome.

All in all, it was a less than delightful afternoon, and nor was dinner any better. Nobody talked much, although Dame Isobel kept clucking under her breath about *aging roués* and *hoarding French champagne* and *feckless profligates,* looking so much in her red gown like an angry little hen, wanting to peck out Duff's eyes, that for once Alasdair felt himself to be entirely in charity with her. His uncle, however, oblivious to atmosphere, ate and drank with undiminished cheer.

And what was on his own mind, speaking of things

more or less delightful? Progeny. Dynastic imperatives. Responsibility for his clan. All the while sitting next to a wife who was as warm as a block of ice, and about as cordial. He'd never done the deed under such circumstances and he hoped he was — so to speak — up for it. As soon as good manners allowed, Alasdair was up and away, and off to the stables where he surprised Begbie and the grooms by wanting to discuss new tack for the horses, at great length and in considerable detail, long into the evening.

"**A**re you awake, madam?"

"Yes," Fiona said with her eyes closed. When she had heard the door to the bedchamber opening, she'd quickly shut her eyes. She wasn't going to take any chances. She wasn't going to be confronted by the sight of his naked self (tall, lithe, muscular) strolling with unsettling self-assurance from his dressing-room toward the bed. Especially since the very first thing she had noticed, earlier that day when Alasdair had surprised her in her morning-room, was that his sling was gone.

Tonight was it, then.

She took a deep breath.

Felt, heard him getting into bed. The shifting of the mattress, the rustle of bedclothes.

Here he was.

A tall, lithe, muscular, and (very likely) naked man.

Her husband.

Her life's partner, supposedly, now and forevermore.

She remembered Isobel's advice.

All you have to do, Fiona dear, is to lie there, and endure what happens.

She waited.

After what felt like a year of strained silence, very cautiously she opened her eyes and turned her head on the pillow. Alasdair was looking at her and it took all her will to not slam her eyes shut again.

He moved a little, and she felt in her body a kind of instinctive tremor. And then he spoke.

"Are you well, madam?"

His voice was quiet, careful, civil.

"Yes," Fiona said, just as carefully. It seemed only decent to add: "And yourself, laird?"

"Aye."

Another year passed.

"Thank you," he said.

"You're welcome." Time dragged by. Oceans rose and fell, forests grew and withered. Fiona cleared her throat. "So how was the cattle meet in Crieff?"

"It was excellent."

"Indeed?"

"Yes, the Watsons were there, describing how they're — but I don't want to bore you."

"I've heard about the Watsons. Were they speaking of the Buchan humlie?"

"Yes, they're cross-breeding it with the Angus doddie."

"Oh yes, at home we've been thinking of doing that too. Did you hear anything about the Shorthorn strain?"

"It was the talk of the meet. In fact, I bought a bull from a factor sent up by the Colling brothers. A Sassenach, but he seemed to know his business."

"Was the bull sired by Young Jock, by any chance?"

"Aye. This one in particular had a very broad chest, and its knees looked very sturdy."

"Ah, that *is* excellent. When does it arrive?"

"Next month." Alasdair paused. Then: "Would you . . ."

"Yes?"

"Would you like to see it?"

"What?"

"Would you like to see the bull when it arrives?"

"Oh. Yes. I would."

"I'll let you know, and we can ride out together."

"Thank you, laird."

"You're welcome, madam."

They stared at each other, and Fiona wondered if her expression was as surprised-looking as was Alasdair's. Suddenly, abruptly, she wished she had banked the fire so that even its current dim glow was gone.

"Well —" he said. Now he was a little awkward, but polite, careful, businesslike, impersonal. A new transaction was about to happen. Needed to happen; there was nothing to discuss, or argue about. She answered in a calm, steady voice:

"Yes."

"Speaking of, uh, breeding —"

"Yes."

"I thought perhaps we ought to —"

"Yes."

"You are amenable?"

"Yes," she repeated.

Underneath the warm, cozy covers, he slid a few feet closer, and closer still. "You're certain, madam?"

"Yes."

"I gather you have an understanding of what will happen."

Fiona stared up at the canopy. "Yes."

"I'll do my best not to hurt you."

"Thank you." For a crazy moment she wanted to laugh. Suddenly they were being polite with each other, and at this juncture! But when he came even closer, all desire to laugh vanished. The bedcovers had slipped down and she could see how densely muscled his shoulders were. How *large* he was, and why did his body seem to give off so much heat?

"I wonder if you might, uh —"

"Yes?"

"If you would lift your nightgown up? Just to your waist."

He said it as he would ask someone to pass the salt cellar.

"Certainly." Still staring at the canopy overhead (though she could not, to save her life, have articulated what those embroidered figures were), Fiona hitched up her nightgown, bunching it around her middle. "It's done," she said.

"Thank you."

Still underneath the covers, Alasdair slid closer — closer — and she could smell the clean scent of him, soap, damp hair, a hint of the stables, ever so faintly pungent. It was a good smell, attractive in her nostrils. Then he was on top of her, and with a pulse of intense awareness she received his warm, heavy weight and just as quickly closed her eyes, plunging into the safety of self-imposed blindness. But she could not ignore the long length of him, hard muscles, the electrifying brush of wiry masculine hair against her bare legs. His knees gently nudging her own apart, her will allowing it, allowing her thighs to part to him.

He moved, gently rocked himself against her, and she could feel his hardening shaft. Far, far past the part of her brain where every vivid new sensation was felt, registered, noted before cataloging another one, she was thankful that he was able to bring himself to this necessary state.

"Are you all right?" His voice, low and deep, polite, so very close to her ear.

"Of course."

"You're certain?"

"Yes."

"Well then."

She kept her eyes closed, let herself be soft, not taut. She could tell that he braced his arms on either side of her, and she wondered what she should do, if anything, with her own arms held close to her sides. Then his shaft was there, at the very center of her. For a moment her breath stopped. Then his hand was there too, briefly, and back again, wet with his own saliva.

"Ah —" he murmured, as gently he moved, entered into her; paused.

"You needn't stop," Fiona said.

"All right." Alasdair moved again, in short, careful strokes, was in her, within her, there was a brief and momentary discomfort, sharp and then gone, like a thought one had and forgot. Gradually his strokes lengthened, filling her up with him. Fiona was a little surprised, somewhere, at how gracefully her body gave way to his hard largeness, how gracefully he moved above her, but in her blindness still she wanted to turn her mind elsewhere: and into it flashed an image of the soft wee doll Isobel had made for little Sheila, Sheila's preternaturally wise little voice saying *Turn about, lady, turn about,* and then to Fiona came a rush of anguished memory: big, tall Logan Munro, an empty parlor, his arms around her, his tongue in her mouth like a hot, wet, insinuating hint of his intentions as he drew her trembling hand down his chest, lower, lower still . . .

What if it were Logan above her, upon her, now?

Logan with his deep dark eyes, all agleam, Logan with the bold black hair she loved to toy with, Logan who would say, caressingly, *My beautiful one, when we are wed . . .*

Between her legs, deeply within her, was hot, hard

maleness, rhythmic, and Fiona, yielding without hesitation, allowed memories, fantasies, to flood her mind and body, like a flower blooming with artificial speed and violence. *My beautiful one . . . my beautiful Fiona. Here. Touch me here.* Her hand, timid, against the fall of his trousers, before retreating. Logan's clever fingers at the back of her gown. Never had she let him undo the buttons, or lift up her skirts, but oh, with a sweet ache at the core of her, she had wanted him to.

Wanted him.

A hard chest brushed against her breasts, as if snapping her awake, and she opened her eyes to the shock of his face so intimately close to hers.

Alasdair's face, and no other's.

Red hair, not black. Those amber eyes were shielded, dark lashes upon his cheeks, upon his countenance was a look of — she puzzled over it. A kind of grave, remote concentration. He reminded her of a statue from Greek antiquity, regal, aloof, untouchable.

But magnificent.

He, Alasdair, was magnificent.

Suddenly she was too frightened — frightened of *herself* — to keep looking at him, and tried again to put her mind elsewhere, but it was impossible now. Alasdair's breath had quickened, he moved his body more quickly. Then: his peak, a shudder, he let out his breath on a guttural sigh. Stopped. She felt the warm wetness of his seed as gently he withdrew.

It was over.

They had done their duty.

He lay next to her, and she listened as his breath evened, softened. She pulled the covers up a little higher. Wondered what she should do about the wetness between her legs. She decided to get up later, when he was deeply asleep.

Finally he said, "Thank you." As he would acknowledge someone who had, in fact, passed the salt cellar.

Fiona was conscious of a welcome flicker of irritation. She'd die before she would say, "Thank *you*" in return. Or, even worse, "You're welcome." Instead she made a soft, vague, neutral sort of noise. It seemed to suffice, for he responded politely:

"Are you all right?"

"Yes."

"Is there anything I can do for you?"

"No."

"You're sure?"

"Yes," she answered calmly.

"Well then, good night." And he shifted over to his side of the bed, rolled away with his broad muscled back to her.

"Good night," she said, her tone just as civil as his. She lay listening to the sound of his breathing. It was but a few moments, she could tell, until he had fallen asleep. A kind of bitter jealousy flared, then subsided into her customary resignation.

She spent a few minutes eyeing the canopy above her. Now she was able to identify the figures. Stags, does, wildcats, foxes, hawks, eagles. It was remarkable embroidery work. Perhaps she'd do some embroidering herself. Not tomorrow, no, for she and Mrs. Allen, who now was helping her, still had many hours of linen inventory ahead. And it was baking day; she wasn't sure if the starter yeast was as vibrant as she would like. Also, she wanted to . . . Her mind stuttered somehow, and she realized that not tomorrow, but right now, she wanted to know what Alasdair had been thinking above her with his eyes closed.

Had he been picturing some other woman? A lovely, rounded woman, all voluptuous and responsive, shameless and loud? The sort of trollop who'd agree to ride her man like a stallion?

A hot blush came over her, guilt manifesting itself in the blood that rushed to her face, and she was glad, glad, that Alasdair had turned his back to her. Hadn't she been thinking of Logan, dreamily and treacherously, as she lay beneath her husband, as limp as a little doll?

So what? There's no harm in it, a part of her cried out defensively, and she pressed cool hands to hot cheeks. It occurred to Fiona that Alasdair hadn't kissed her, hadn't even tried to kiss her.

Did she want him to?

Memory, insistent, undeniable, snaked its way into her head.

The empty parlor at Cousin Isobel's, Isobel conspicuously gone out into the garden. Logan and herself on a sofa, Logan pressing her down upon it. His mouth on hers, soft, wet, his tongue fully within her, probing with such boldness, licking at her teeth, that she felt an excited kind of panic (half-wondering if she would suffocate), felt her knees start to shake as a hot giddy fire seemed to roar through her whole body. Logan laughing softly, obviously aware of her response to him, pulling her bashful hand to where he could display his desire, showing her how to stroke him through the fabric of his trousers. *My beautiful one, when we are wed . . .*

Now, here, in the warm coziness of her bed at Castle Tadgh, Fiona abruptly felt chilled. She pulled the covers up to her neck.

Baking day. Yeast? Also, new pans needed?
Linen inventory. One hour at least. Check: moths?
Lister's father — dentures — where is closest dentist (reputable!)
Rumor re bedbugs in servants' quarters: find out for sure

*Sewing scissors need sharpening. Who does
    that here?*
*Shaw's retrievers. Ask Cook to give them meat
    scraps. Cuilean also?*
*Talk to Monty about beehives — could
    foraging ants or toads be the problem?
    Show him section in Maxwell's Practical
    Bee-Master*
Dallis birthday next week. Send note
*Cow-house. How much milk, cream? Any
    village families who need some extra?*
Go for ride on Gealag. LONG RIDE

Yes indeed, she was going to be busy.
Thank God.

The next morning Alasdair found himself whistling
a little as he rode out to take a look at the hay fields.
Relief — he was feeling relief. Things had gone all
right last night. It had all been accomplished with a
minimum of fuss and botheration. Fiona hadn't been
missish, their exchanges had been amiable enough.
The pattern had therefore been easily established. They
could go on about their business from now on, knowing what to expect during these interludes.

As he rode in the bright sun of late summer, Alasdair observed with pleasure the crisp amber of the
hay all around him. The harvest was going to be a
good one this year.

Her legs, he suddenly remembered (for no apparent
reason), were long, slender, white and soft-skinned,
and strong, too. In his determination to get it over
with, he hadn't really paused to notice that.

It was an interesting combination, that soft femi-
ninity and supple strength.

Of course, during the days Fiona was active and energetic — that would explain it. He'd caught glimpses of her, up and down the staircase, walking with her brisk step here and there, in and out of the castle, and he knew she rode almost every day.

Last night, though, she had been calm, quiet, remote. What, he now wondered, would it feel like to have those long, strong legs wrapped around him?

An intriguing thought.

But . . .

In its wake came uncertainty.

A certain sense of risk. Of disruption.

And so he dismissed it.

He had carefully shaped his life these past years, to a form and a flow which suited him admirably. To this form, to this pattern, he would adhere. *Continue* to adhere.

Relief came again in a welcome wave, and he whistled "Bonnie Leslie" from start to finish, three times straight.

While Alasdair was riding, Fiona was in the breakfast-room, eating with enjoyment a freshly baked scone and reading her letters. There was one from Mother, with her flowing, looping writing, which wasted a great deal of space on the page, but was cheerful and affectionate. It had rained on Sunday, wrote Mother, but her charming new kid ankle-boots in the most delicate shade of aquamarine had, most fortunately, not been damaged on the way to and from church. Osla Tod had recovered beautifully from her tooth-pulling; the whitewashing in the Great Hall had gone smoothly (aside from Father twice losing his temper and subjecting the workers to a furious tirade). Oh, and there was interesting

news from Henrietta Penhallow in England, Mother
added. *Her grandson, Gabriel, is engaged to a Miss
Livia Stuart from Wiltshire. Wherever that is. English geography is so dreadfully confusing, isn't it?
Do you suppose Miss Stuart is related to our own
poor lamented Queen Mary? I can't image Henrietta
settling for anything less than an exceedingly highborn addition to her family.*

Also in Fiona's pile was a letter from Nairna,
joyful with reports of her advancing pregnancy, so
long desired, a very miracle; the wisewoman Tavia
Craig in constant attendance, and oh so kind! There
was a letter from Rossalyn, too, happily settling into
married life with Jamie MacComhainn.

Fiona put down the letter, and sipped her tea. How
nice to hear that everyone — including the workers,
she assumed, now the whitewashing was complete —
was doing so well.

As for herself, she was doing well also. Of course.
Last night had gone very well. Now that she knew
what to expect, why, she wouldn't have to think about
it at all anymore.

While Fiona was reading her letters, Isobel was trotting up the stairs to the Little Drawing-room, holding a soft sheepskin shammy Mrs. Allen had kindly
found for her. It was perfect for dusting those exquisite figurines she so admired. Her handkerchiefs
— made from inexpensive bleached cotton she'd purchased in Edinburgh and hemmed herself — simply
weren't good enough for such an important task.

When she entered the room, she cast an appreciative glance around. All pink and frilly it was, with
billowy lace curtains and lovely chairs and sofas up-

holstered in French toile. And as a centerpiece to it all, there was that enormous cabinet with its leaded glass windows and arched pediment. All told, it was a delightful chamber, and so cozy! It was a mystery as to why dear Fiona seemed to despise it.

Poor dear Fiona, trapped in a loveless marriage to that great hulking red-haired man! (Who had the misfortune of being the nephew of that detestable Duff!) It was dreadfully sad how things had turned out. And there was so little she could do to help her poor suffering cousin!

Isobel ran her shammy along the fluted edges of the cabinet's middle section, a narrow mahogany shelf gleaming with satinwood inlay. It was then she observed that beneath the shelf was a row of little doors, which could be opened by means of shiny oval knobs set with black onyx. How strange that she hadn't noticed them before.

Surely no one would mind if she just peeked inside?

Her heart pattering in excitement, Isobel sank to her knees and cautiously pulled on one of the knobs.

The door opened easily, almost as if it wished to reveal what lay inside.

But there was only a big, dusty book, bound in faded and cracked leather.

Normally Isobel didn't care for books. She had never been much of a reader. But the vanquishing of dirt struck an instant chord. It seemed to be, in a very small way, something she could do to be helpful. How gratifying.

Isobel pulled out the book — so big and heavy that it took much of her strength — from the dark recesses of the cabinet, and ran her shammy across its binding. Gracious, it even had cobwebs clinging to it. She brushed them away, and read the words now more clearly visible in gilt — or was it actual gold leaf?

Laws of the Eight Clans of Kilally.

She stared at it. "Laws" did not sound the least bit interesting. And yet —

And yet a kind of irrepressible curiosity flickered within her.

Isobel looked over her shoulder, as if she was about to do something that was forbidden and needed to make sure she was alone (which, thankfully, she was), then reached down, and slowly opened the great hoary Tome.

While Isobel was opening up the Tome, Duff Mac-Dermott stood before the round mirror that hung on a wall in his dressing-room. He turned his face this way and that, inspecting it. Not bad for a middle-aged fellow, if he did say so himself. A few wrinkles, a few gray hairs, but a truly magnificent beard, the epitome of masculine vigor. To be sure, he'd gained a few pounds over the years, but that only gave him added stature. Really, he didn't know what Dame Isobel had been muttering about last night. Himself an aging roué? A feckless profligate?

She obviously didn't know a dashing *bon vivant* when she sat right opposite him at dinner. The poor aging spinster-lady. Why, she was probably so over-whelmed by his masculine charm that she could only sputter and cluck around him! He'd be sure to behave more kindly toward her in future. They were of an age, he reckoned, but she was so fragile, so delicate, when compared to his own robust state. Perhaps he might offer a strong arm when escorting her up some stairs, or pick up her handkerchief when she dropped it. That sort of thing. *Chivalry,* he thought contentedly as he smoothed his mustache, *was not dead, at least not while Duff MacDermott was around.*

Humming under his breath, Duff now shrugged himself into one of his nicest jackets. Earlier, he'd run into his nephew, been greeted cheerfully. Not only that, Alasdair willingly agreed to meet him at the Gilded Osprey for a nuncheon. Things were coming along just as they should. A long, hearty meal, a bottle or two of port, extended flirtations with the serving girls. Yes, it was going to be a good day.

While Duff was putting on his jacket, little Sheila and her grandmother Margery stood before a table in their cottage, which lay just at the edge of the heather meadow. Sheila was rinsing potatoes in a bowl of water, and passing them to Margery, who patted them dry and peeled them.

Sheila sang little snatches of an old tune as she worked, and Dame Margery shot a measuring glance her way. The child's pale blue eyes showed none of the opaque, absent look they got sometimes, but the old lady did observe upon her narrow face a faint look of mischief, and upon the hem of her dress a trail of clinging cobweb.

"You were up early today, sweeting," she said to her grandchild, accepting a damp potato and enfolding it in her cloth. "Where did you go?"

"I had something to do at the castle, Granny, that's all."

"What might that be?"

"Oh," answered Sheila vaguely, "nothing, really. Granny, didn't Dame Isobel make me the prettiest doll in the world? Oh, Granny, your hands are bothering you, won't you let me peel the tatties?"

Margery's look sharpened. "You've not been to the castle to stir up trouble?"

"Never, Granny, never!" swore Sheila, with such fervor that the old lady relented, and said:

"Aye then, you may peel, for my fingers do pain me this morning. You're a good lass."

Proudly Sheila took up the little knife. "I try to be, Granny. Though it's not always easy."

The old lady rested a gnarled hand on her granddaughter's head. "You're more right than you know, sweeting. Now! I'll wash the tatties, and we'll have a lovely pottage for our dinner tonight."

Chapter 8

As Alasdair confidently expected, the days ticked along smoothly, like a well-oiled clockwork, and a week swiftly passed. The usual rounds of work and play; and the nights alone with his wife had indeed fallen into a predictable pattern. He wandered in, greeted her, they had quick, uneventful congress, and he went to sleep.

On the eighth night, he came into their bedchamber very late.

"Are you awake, madam?"

The question had become a ritual, only now she said:

"Yes. But it's my woman's time."

"Oh."

"And I wish," she added waspishly, "you would stop calling me 'madam' in that pompous way."

"I wasn't aware," he said, offended, getting into bed, "that I was being pompous."

"Well, you were."

There was a silence. Alasdair settled himself comfortably. He had heard that during this monthly interval, women could be rather touchy. So, cautiously, he asked, "What shall I call you then?"

"Isn't it obvious? My name is Fiona."

"Very well — Fiona."

She only gave a sniff. Huffily, he turned on his side with his back to her, and closed his eyes. Adjusted the bedcovers. Shifted his pillows around. After a while he said, over his shoulder and with a little growl in his voice:

"I can hear you being awake."

"I'm just lying here. Minding my own business, I might add."

"It's practically the middle of the night. Why aren't you asleep?"

"What do *you* care?"

"Oh, for God's sake, Fiona. Please just tell me."

There was another silence. Finally, she answered, reluctantly, as if unwilling to share anything personal:

"I have insomnia."

He remembered finding her in her morning-room, napping. He recalled the dark circles under her eyes. Now he wondered how many hours she had spent in this bed, awake in the darkness, while he had serenely slept, oblivious.

He rolled onto his back. Turned his head and looked at her. The fire in the hearth provided just enough light for him to see that she, too, lay on her back, her eyes fixed — as they often seemed to be — on the canopy above their heads.

He cleared his throat a little. "Why do you have insomnia?"

"I developed it as a child."

"Why?"

"Oh, I don't know," she said grudgingly. "I suppose when I realized my father was often unkind to my mother."

"Was he — unkind to you?"

"He was . . . is . . . volatile. Was he unkind? Well, he would sometimes threaten to beat us. So I began to lie awake at night, in case he did come into the room I shared with my sisters, in one of his rages."

"Were you afraid?" He turned onto his side, facing her.

"Not really. I lay awake thinking about what I would do if he came in."

"What you'd do?"

"Yes. I kept a fire iron next to me in bed."

"Would you have used it on him?"

"I told myself I would. I couldn't protect Mother, but I could at least try to protect my sisters."

"That was brave of you."

He saw her shoulders, covered by her prim white nightgown, lifting in a shrug. "I don't know about that. He never hit us, never came into our room. Perhaps I overreacted. But the end result was insomnia."

"Surely there are remedies. Maybe Dr. Colquhoun could help."

"I doubt it. I've tried everything. Chamomile, hops, lady slipper, lavender, valerian. Hot baths, cold baths. Warm milk. Wool socks. More exercise, less exercise. Oils on my feet, oils on my forehead. Nothing has worked."

How far apart in the bed they were, he thought. The space between them seemed vast; her face was a little ghostly in the dimness. He tried to think what it would feel like to be unable to sleep, night after night, year after year. Naturally he at once felt a tremendous desire to sleepily yawn. He repressed it. Out loud he said, sincerely, "I'm sorry."

"It's not your problem."

Did he imagine it, or was there, beneath her level, dispassionate tone, a note of melancholy?

He said, on an impulse:

"Just so you know. I *didn't* ride my horse through the castle."

She didn't respond for a few moments. Then: "I

believe you. I've seen how you're too good to your horses to do something like that."

"Thank you." He added, still impulsively, "May I ask you something? It's something I've been curious about."

He saw her quickly turn to him, as if alarmed. As if there was something she didn't want him to know. "Curious about what?" she asked.

"About how you learned to speak French so well."

"Ah." She sounded rather thankful. "There was a French family who came to Wick Bay, very poor and in distress. I spent a lot of time with them, and eventually I picked up their language. And what about you? You understood me at that dinner with Wynda? *Avez-vous un tuteur, ou vous avez été envoyé loin à l'école?*"

"The tutors came later. School came first, when my brother and I were sent to one in Glasgow, where after six years there they finally kicked us both out."

"Kicked you out? Why?"

"Well, we didn't ride horses through the buildings, but we did accept other dares." He laughed. "We were, in fact, the terrors of the school."

"What did you do?"

"What *didn't* we do. The pranks, the fights, the defiance. We *did* manage to sneak some learning in, but we hated it there. We just wanted to be home."

"Were your parents angry?"

"Our father didn't care, but our mother — my God, she was furious. She wanted to send us to Eton, but Gavin and I vowed we'd run away on a pirate ship before we'd ever set one toe in England. She knew us well enough to believe we really would do it, so we stayed home, evaded the poor tutors she brought in, and more or less ran wild after that. She gave up on us, as long as we didn't interfere with her endless renovations."

Fiona was quiet, as if absorbing this, and Alasdair was already sorry he'd said so much. He hated looking backward, hated thinking about the time before —

She said, very quietly, "I hope you don't think I was listening to gossip, but Dame Margery did tell me about . . . what happened on the loch . . ."

With an effort he made his voice light. "Don't worry about it. What about you? Did you and your sisters ever go to school?"

Again, a silence, as if she were registering his rebuff, and deciding how she wanted to react.

Then:

"No, we didn't. We had a governess for a few years, a very earnest and capable lady, but eventually Father's ambivalence about the value of female education overcame him, and he let Miss Dwight go. She found a more congenial situation in Dumfries, and Father let me buy as many books as I wanted, so it all worked out fairly well, especially since my mother was so intimidated by Miss Dwight that she completely went out of her way to avoid her." Suddenly Fiona laughed, with what sounded like genuine amusement. "Once I found her underneath the stairs. Just sitting there. Poor Mother!"

Alasdair smiled. And he said, still in that interested, impulsive spirit: "May I ask another question?"

With laughter still in her voice, she said, "Yes."

"What's your favorite dish?"

"Cook's *boeuf à la Bourguignonne*."

"Favorite color?"

"Periwinkle."

"Writer you most admire?"

"Shakespeare."

"Season?"

"Spring."

"Dogs or cats?"

"Dogs. Of course."

"Can you swim?"

"Yes. But don't tell anyone."

He laughed. "Why not?"

"Why not?" she repeated. "That's a good question. I suppose it's felt like a secret for all these years. Back home I used to swim sometimes in the bay, when no one was around. Even though Father told us not to."

"A renegade! Weren't you cold?"

"I almost froze to death. But it was worth it."

He very nearly said, *Gavin and I used to swim in the loch,* but caught himself just in time. And his brain, very agile and quick, served up something else he had wondered about, thanks to her mention of the bay, and home. Was there, back there, a swain who had lost her to her precipitous marriage?

So he instead said:

"Why were you still unmarried at twenty-seven?"

"Still harping on that, laird?" In an instant the mirth was gone. "Worried that there's something wrong with me? Some defect I ought to have disclosed? After all, you've never seen the upper part of my body, have you? I could have three breasts, or bloody sores there, or worse. I suppose you can't bear to look —"

"Fiona, I only —"

"Or perhaps I am — as you so discreetly hinted that evening in the Great Drawing-room — past my best childbearing years. Maybe it's hopeless, and all these delightful romps together have been a waste of time."

Her words were blistering and sharp. If they'd been fencers in a duel, she'd be flying at him, without a *fleuret* on the tip, lunging to kill. And in this kind of situation, you either retreated, or you parried, just as aggressively.

"Yes, delightful," he said, with a snarl in his voice.

"Didn't you listen to the marriage vows we made? Our task is that of procreation."

"Task. It's very obvious it's a task."

"And just how would you be able to make such a judgment, madam?"

"Are you accusing me of being unchaste?" she snapped. "Surely you were aware of the state of things when you first had me? Or was your mind elsewhere?"

Oh God, oh God, he'd backed himself into a corner. How had things gotten so ugly so quickly? And yet, even in the heat of the fight, a little, awful part of him was rejoicing. *Safe, safe, safe.*

"This," he said coldly (and yet comfortably), "is a highly indelicate conversation."

"Indelicate?" She gave a sardonic laugh. "I had no idea your sensibilities were so refined, laird. Do forgive me."

"And I, madam, had no idea you were capable of such coarseness." Now he was simply being an ass. He knew it. But he couldn't seem to stop himself.

"Well, we've learned quite a lot about each other tonight, haven't we?" she said icily.

"I'm afraid so."

"Very enlightening."

"And exhausting." He yawned, loudly and ostentatiously. "Good night then."

He could hear her scornful huff as she flounced onto her side, with her back to him. "Yes. Good night."

Alasdair closed his eyes. It was almost as if the angry, ugly words they'd exchanged were still hanging in the air, taking up space in the darkness of the room. He waited, waited, for them to subside. And as he waited, it came to him then — that despite the mechanical nature of their coupling, he'd been assuming she found him attractive, as women generally did. He'd brushed aside her reply to his provocative question in the Great Drawing-room, when he'd said:

You do not find my person comely?

Not particularly, she had coolly answered.

He let this startling possibility sink in.

Yes, he'd been assuming that she wanted him, while he was the one dispensing his — ah — favors at his own convenience. That *he* had the upper hand, *he* was in control.

Maybe, maybe, he was wrong.

Then came another unwelcome thought, like an angel (or devil?) perched on his shoulder:

Well, lad, you haven't exactly done much to excite her passion, have you?

He countered, *She's not my type.*

What's wrong with her?

Too thin, too pale, too blonde.

The angel (or devil) seemed to say, slyly: *Have you really looked at her, lad?*

Alasdair almost groaned out loud. Here he was, having a dialogue with himself. What the hell was wrong with him?

The sly little voice made itself known again.

Have you, lad? Or have you locked yourself in?

Shut up, he tried to tell the voice. *I've worked everything out to my satisfaction. Don't you go —*

Rocking the boat? said the voice, a little cruelly.

I'm done with you, Voice.

But you're not done with Mòrag, are you?

Shut up. Go away.

Never.

Alasdair shifted in the bed, raked a hand through his hair.

Which reminded him. What was so wrong with red hair, by the way?

Not a damn thing.

He had nice, thick hair which he kept clean and well-barbered.

He opened his eyes, turned his head to glare at her back.

Look at her? Locked in?

Damned stupid voice.

And he closed his eyes again, waiting — a little guiltily — for sleep to claim him. His last waking thought was the belated realization that with the advent of her woman's time, a hope for conception had been dashed.

Well, he'd certainly been the compassionate husband, hadn't he.

Later, much later that night, Alasdair dreamed he made passionate love to his wife, who sat astride him, her curious silvery hair released at last from its braid. It covered her like a living mantle of silk. And in this dream, her pale, slender body actually glowed, as if she were on fire. It was his touch that ignited her.

A deep coldness lay between the laird and his lady, and little Sheila was overheard saying casually to her playmates a few days later:

"There are ghosts in the castle."

"We *wish*," one of the other children answered, just as casually, tossing out a little piece of crockery for a marker, and they all went on with their lively, occasionally contentious game of hop-scotch.

And a few days later after that, on a beautiful morning that held in it the tiniest hint of autumn, Fiona stood in the warm, clean kitchen conferring with Mrs.

Allen, the housekeeper, and with Cook. All around her was well-ordered bustle; on a low stool near the hearth sat Sheila, playing with her doll. Isobel had made a white lace wrapper and a wee nightcap for the doll to wear, and Sheila was carefully tying the tiny ribbons, one after another. On her lap was also a big lemony biscuit, sweet with sugar and dotted with caraway seeds.

One of these delicious biscuits Fiona had just sampled and approved. Now she was looking over Mrs. Allen's menu suggestions for the week's dinners. "Yes, Monday and Tuesday look fine, thank you. Cook, have you the ingredients for the vermicelli soup on Tuesday?"

"To be sure we do."

"Excellent. But one of the entrees for Wednesday — I do not think the laird cares for beef tongue roast, and nor do I overmuch, so perhaps you might reserve that for staff. A roasted sirloin instead for the high table?"

"Aye, mistress, and we'll enjoy the tongue, thank you."

"Good. And a salad of potatoes and peas, if the peas are fresh?"

"Indeed they are."

"Then I think we're done." Fiona smiled. "Now, do you need more salve for your arm?"

Cook rolled up her sleeve to display the inside of her forearm, where the skin was pink and healthy. "Nay, I thank you, mistress. Only see how well the burn has healed!"

"It has, and I'm so pleased," said Fiona warmly. "Thank you, Mrs. Allen, you may go. Cook, if you could have a nuncheon brought to my morning-room in an hour or so, I'll take it in there, and —"

She broke off as she realized that Sheila was tugging at her skirt. Goodness, how that child crept up on one! But she smiled down at her and said, "Yes, hinny?"

"Lady, lady, have you a magic salve for my granny's hands? They're paining her greatly."

Fiona looked inquiringly at Cook, who nodded and said, "It's the rheumatism which plagues poor Dame Margery, mistress."

"I'll bring some salve for your granny," Fiona promised, "and herbs for a tea. It will help, although it's not magic, hinny."

"When, lady, when?"

"I'll come tomorrow, if you'll tell me where you live."

"You must go past the village to the heather meadow. We live on the very edge of it, just where the forest begins. *I* think there are boogeymen within it, but Granny says I'm wrong."

"There's no such thing as boogeymen, child!" interpolated Cook reprovingly, and Fiona only said:

"Tell your granny I will come in the afternoon."

Sheila nodded, and picked up her biscuit which had fallen to the floor. With casual nonchalance she began to eat it, and Fiona smiled again and went off to the stillroom, where she began assembling the herbs she needed. As she worked her mind wandered, thinking for the hundredth time about the other night in which she and Alasdair had quarreled so fiercely.

She'd been feeling very low, for there was no babe within her womb, no little one to dream of, look forward to. Why couldn't he have said, *What if tonight I held you? Simply held you?*

Why couldn't *she* have said, *Please will you hold me?*

Because they couldn't. Obviously.

But oh, she *had* wanted to be held, *had* wanted a

little comfort. It might have been nice to be clasped in those strong arms, to feel her body brought close to his, to lay her head on that broad chest and listen, just listen, to his heartbeat. Who knew, maybe — what a wild, wild hope — maybe it would even have lulled her into sleep.

That wasn't how it had gone, however. Oh well. The truth was, you couldn't have everything in life. You didn't want to be like that foolish farmer in the cautionary tale by Aesop — greedily killing the goose that laid the golden egg. Wasn't that the key to, well, if not happiness, at least not being miserable? Accepting things the way they were?

That's what people said, at any rate.

And so here it was, another day.

Time, as the saying goes, was marching on.

Whether you liked it or not.

Fiona reached for a fragrant sprig of lavender, and focused again on her work. Despite everything, she was looking forward to riding out to the heather meadow. Exceptionally lovely it was, surrounded by dense woodlands of pine, juniper, yew, and with the majestic Grampian mountains in the distance, rising up to meet the wide blue sky. Beautiful, calm, and peaceful.

She could, she thought wryly, aware of a faint, but unmistakably lonely ache within the far reaches of her heart, certainly use the peace of mind.

On the very next day, in the fullness of a glorious afternoon dappled with the light and shadow of drifting clouds, Alasdair, riding with his bailiff Shaw to visit some of the tenant farmers who lived on the remote northern border of the Penhallow lands, saw that one whole length of fence, a cattle enclosure, had been hacked away. Inquiries among the farmers elicited the information that it had just happened last night, and that half a dozen cattle had been stolen — a heavy toll.

"I'll send some men to help you rebuild, and to stand watch during the next several nights," Alasdair told them. "And we'll try to find your cattle."

"Think you it's the Dalwhinnies again, laird?" asked Shaw, as they rode swiftly back toward the castle.

"It's hard to believe they'd be that bold, after what happened so recently. You heard that old Dalziel Sutherlainn died last month?" At Shaw's nod, he went on, "A hard man to mourn — a twisty mind, an improvident leader, rash and selfish. His son Crannog is now the chieftain."

"Know you him, laird?"

"Nay, we've not met, but I wonder how far the apple can fall from its tree. I want twenty men out there at least, and word sent out to all the farmers to be on their guard."

And at exactly the same time when Alasdair turned his horse back toward the castle, Fiona was giving Dame Margery a pot of salve and a cloth bag of herbs, and glancing around her cottage. It was small and simply furnished, but clean and comfortable. "Where is Sheila?" she asked. "I've brought some lemon biscuits as well."

"Thank you, mistress," said the old lady smilingly, "most kind of you! Sheila went off to gather some kindling for our fire. Though I thought she'd have returned by now. She'll be sorry to have missed you, for she wished to show you her slate, with her letters drawn upon it."

"I'll walk out to meet her if I can," answered Fiona, and said her farewells. Holding Gealag's reins, she led him along a winding track into the shadowy woods that lay behind Margery's cottage. Boogey-men lived here, little Sheila had said. Fiona remembered how, when she was small, her garrulous nurse had terrified herself and her sisters with bloodcurdling tales of trolls, wraiths, demons, and, worst of all, the Sack Man, a phantomlike figure said to descend upon wandering children, scoop them up in his foul sack, and carry them off in order to eat them. How incensed Father had been when he'd discovered this. He'd sent the nurse away, back to her family, and secretly Mother had confided to Fiona how grateful she was, for the stories had been petrifying her, too.

Fiona smiled faintly.

Then she heard men's voices, low and rough, and paused, her smile yielding to an abrupt tense alertness. It was hearing Sheila's voice that compelled her to pace cautiously forward, to the lip of a clearing, where she saw some ten or twelve men, plainly not of the Penhallow clan, for their clothing was ragged and unkempt. Their horses, tethered, were thin, but the half-dozen cattle were fat and robust; and in this dark clearing stood Sheila, gazing up at the men whose postures indicated both fierce hostility and more than a little fear.

They were all armed, with muskets and daggers, and Fiona briefly but intensely regretted not bringing her pistols. Then again, why would she? She'd merely ridden out to visit one of their own. Besides, she'd have been badly outnumbered anyway. These men were cattle thieves, and she was deeply afraid that the belligerence they were displaying toward Sheila — looking more than usually otherworldly with her pale, wandering eyes, very blank just now, and her seemingly unlikely attitude of calm imperturbability — would erupt into swift violence.

"You're empty, empty," said Sheila, matter-of-factly. "Hollow, hollow."

One of the men, bearded and balding, hissed: "Kill her, laird, and be done with it! We must be away!"

The man just addressed slowly lifted his dagger, and took a step forward. "Aye, I'll do it, just as you say!" He was very tall, cadaverously thin, and reekingly filthy, with a rough sort of mantle flung over his shoulders, made of shabby animal pelts loosely stitched together.

"Stop!" Fiona came three, four, five paces into the clearing. She could feel her heart thumping hard in her breast, but made her voice loud and imperative. The men all swung around to face her, weapons raised, and the leader jabbed his dagger menacingly.

"Who are you?" he cried out.

"It's our lady," answered Sheila calmly. "Good day, lady, you came as you said you would."

"The Penhallow's wife!" hissed the bald man. "Leave the little witch, laird, and let's take *her*, and that horse of hers! A fine ransom the Penhallow will pay for her safe return!"

"Aye, that's for sure," agreed the leader. "But — how do we do that?"

"Bind her wrists," the bald man replied, "and have her put on your horse. And you ride that horse of hers! Do it!" he barked at the other men, who moved quickly to obey.

Fiona submitted to the indignity of having her hands tied together and being tossed up onto an old sway-backed mare, but when the leader approached Gealag, he found that short of killing the beautiful white horse he'd not mount him, for Gealag threw out his sharp front hooves with vicious intent.

"I'll lead him, the brute," said the bald man, moving toward Gealag, "and whip him if he balks."

From atop the mare on which she perched astride, displaying far too much of her stockinged legs, Fiona said, with steel in her voice, "Harm him, and I'll make you wish you were dead."

"Ha!" retorted the bald man, snatching at Gealag's reins, "as if you could, trussed up like a chicken as you are."

"She'd shoot you in the heart, empty man," remarked Sheila, then staggered as he stalked past her, cuffing her across her head, hissing, "Quiet, you witch!"

The leader swung up behind Fiona, holding her about the waist with an unnerving tentativeness, and kicked his heels into the mare's flanks. "Let's go!" he cried, and the ragtag cavalcade began making its way deeper into the forest. Fiona, nearly gagging from the smell of the man behind her, turned her head to stare at Sheila, first to make sure she wasn't harmed, and second to try — foolish though it seemed — to communicate an urgent thought.

Go tell the laird, hinny!

Sheila only stared back at her, a grubby finger stuck into her mouth, her face utterly blank, and Fiona felt her heart sink.

Alasdair was very busy when he got back to the castle, organizing his men, sending out messages, looking over all the horses. The last thing on his mind was dinner, but as the hour arrived, he knew he and the men would be awake all the night and would benefit from having had a meal, so with them he quickly made his way to the Great Hall, only to find that his wife wasn't there. How odd. Perhaps she was caught up in one task or another, or napping somewhere. He dispatched both a servant boy and her maidservant Edme to go find her.

Naturally it had begun to rain, so not only was Fiona tired, hungry, sore from the lack of a saddle, and unhappy, she was soaked to the bone and shivering in the cold. She had whiled away the long hours of this weary journey by eavesdropping, and had learned that the skeletal, bad-smelling leader, behind her, was named Crannog Sutherlainn, and that he'd only recently become the clan's chieftain. She learned that the balding, bearded man, Faing, was Crannog's uncle. As she listened to them openly rejoicing about not only stealing several fine, fat cattle but also looking forward to receiving an enormous ransom from Alasdair Penhallow, she refrained from pointing out that her absence at Castle Tadgh *would* be noticed (sooner rather than later, if Sheila bestirred herself), someone would come after her, and because cattle couldn't travel particularly fast, the plodding pace of their escape was, frankly, a bit of a problem. For them.

The moon was high in the sky by the time, after a great deal of complaining among the men, their party stopped and made camp for the night in a small clearing filled with concealing underbrush. Fiona was relieved to be lifted down from the poor nag who'd been made to carry two people, and also to see that Gealag — although clearly nervous — was all right. She was pushed down into a wet patch of leaves to sit and given some malodorous venison jerky to eat, with her hands still bound together. Even in the darkness she could see the green patches of mold upon it, and so she turned to Crannog Sutherlainn who was beside her, and held out the jerky. "Here."

"You don't want it?" His long, thin face was suspicious.

"No. It's nasty."

"It's the best we've got," he said defensively, accepting it, and as he immediately began gnawing upon it, Fiona looked around the group of men who surrounded her, all of them, she now observed, as thin as their horses and eating their single pieces of jerky with undisguised avidity. Nothing else was produced to eat. She was pondering this, when Faing spoke to her.

"Wouldn't mind having a bit of you," he said with a smile that revealed several distinctly unappealing teeth, "before we let you go. You're a rare beauty, lass. The Penhallow's a lucky man."

Fiona took a moment to wonder if a compliment coming from such a one could in any way be viewed as flattering, especially since she knew for a fact he couldn't possibly be drunk and so it wasn't just alcohol talking.

"I wouldn't recommend it," she responded coolly. "Violating me would only make my husband quite a bit angrier than he's already certain to be." *My husband*. Was this the first time she'd said those two words out loud?

"She's right, Uncle," interpolated Crannog Sutherlainn, sounding more than a little anxious. "Come to think of it, maybe we ought to be pushing along right now."

The men began loudly grumbling, and Faing replied, "No. We're fatigued," and Crannog promptly subsided, his eyes darting worriedly about. They came to rest on Fiona. "You're cold?" he asked, softly, as if hoping the others wouldn't hear him.

"Yes."

He took off his shabby fur mantle, and laid it around her shoulders. Its smell was awful, and as it was already wet it provided little real warmth, but Fiona couldn't help but be touched by Crannog's gesture. She saw, as he bent near her, that he couldn't be more than twenty years old.

He's only a boy! she thought. Aloud she said quietly, "Thank you."

He nodded, and without his mantle she could see just how painfully thin he was; his shoulders were knobby and his Adam's apple huge in the scrawny column of his throat. Here was someone considerably thinner than herself, but she doubted very much that he was anywhere near as well fed.

Empty, empty, hollow, hollow, little Sheila had said.

The castle and the stables and the gardens had been thoroughly searched and his wife, apparently, was missing. Alasdair stood in the Great Hall, frowning. Annoying and perplexing Fiona might be, but she wasn't flighty, or one to play pranks. He was wondering uneasily if there was a connection between the Sutherlainns and Fiona's mysterious disappearance, when Cook approached him, and said, twisting her hands in her apron:

"Laird, it's come to me, 'twas yesterday that the mistress mentioned she was to ride out today to Dame Margery with some herbs."

The words were barely out of her mouth before Alasdair was gone from the Hall, off to the stables where he had a half-dozen men saddle their horses along with his own. Twenty minutes later, he stood just inside Dame Margery's cottage, having woken her and little Sheila from their beds.

The old lady was baffled, alarmed, and turned to Sheila, who, barefoot and in her nightgown, stood sleepily rubbing her eyes.

"What know you of this?" she said urgently to her granddaughter. "You told me you saw the mistress in the woods, but nothing else."

"You saw the mistress, lass?" put in Alasdair quickly. "When?"

"Oh, this afternoon, laird, I was looking for kindling for Granny."

"What happened then?"

"The men took her away with them."

The little girl was calm, vague, so casual in her speech that Alasdair had to keep himself from what felt like literally exploding. He'd been exasperated many times prior in his life, but he now knew, with soul-shaking certainty, that this moment was the absolute topper.

Sharply, from between clenched teeth, he said, "What men?" just as old Dame Margery exclaimed in horror:

"You never said a word of this!"

"Oh, Granny, when I saw those lemon biscuits I forgot all about it. Aren't they so good? I wish we could have them every day."

Patience, he told himself sternly. *You mustn't frighten the child.* "What men did you see, little Sheila?"

She looked up at him (at least one eye did, the other seemed to be directed at a stoneware crock in which, he suspected, biscuits were stored). "I didn't know them, laird, but one of them called me a witch, which is a terrible lie. They had some of our cattle, and they also stole our lady and her horse."

"Can you tell me which way they went, lass?"

She nodded. "Oh yes, laird, they're following the northwest trail, but they're not going very fast, and if you ride hard you'll find them in about an hour and a half. But be careful, because the rain has made the trail very slippery. Although the rain will stop soon."

Now the lass was all about sharing useful information. Hours had passed since Fiona had been taken — long, treacherous hours in which anything might happen. That they were going northwest confirmed his suspicion that it was the Sutherlainn clan they were dealing with, led by a man of whom Alasdair knew nothing: a lack of information which made him very, very uncomfortable.

As he and his men began riding as rapidly as they dared along a trail which was, as Sheila predicted, dangerously slippery, Alasdair thought of Fiona, alone, vulnerable, unprotected, and he felt the cold hand of fear take hold of his heart. If the Sutherlainns so much as hurt one hair of her head, he told himself grimly, he would wreak such vengeance upon them that the entire clan would wish it had never seen the light of day.

Chapter 9

All the other men had fallen asleep in their dirty blankets, but next to Fiona, Crannog Sutherlainn remained awake, his own filthy blanket draped around him and his thin face drawn, gloomy, as he stared ahead, lost in his own thoughts.

"Laird," said Fiona quietly. He started, and whipped his head toward her.

"What?" he whispered back.

"Stealing my husband's cattle wasn't a wise idea."

She watched various expressions flit across his countenance: defensiveness, fear, anguish, then resignation. Finally, he nodded, and hung his head.

"I know. 'Twas my uncle's insistence. I didn't want to offend the mighty Penhallow. But he said it was the only way."

"Your people are hungry?"

He gave a sigh which seemed to emanate from the depths of his being. "Lady, they are starving."

"Why? What happened?"

"My father —" Crannog paused as if painfully, swiping his hand across the dank hair plastered to his forehead. "These past three years my father wouldn't let the farmers tend their fields, he forced them to

make war upon the Balfours — the Hearns and the
Pòls as well."

"Who?"

"They're small clans along the Firth of Lorne. They
had insulted him, he thought. His mind was unhinged
those last years," Crannog went on, "he feared and
reviled everyone, the whole world seemingly."

"Including you?" Fiona said, very low.

He nodded again. "I — I *hated* him! We all did!
I was *glad* when he died. But the damage was done.
We'd so little food! I've given the farmers back their
fields, but how can we survive until the crops grow?
Uncle Faing said the Penhallow wouldn't miss a few
cattle, when our need is so great." Crannog Sutherlainn sighed again. "I told him I'd rather go to the
laird directly, and ask for his help, but he said that
begging is worse than death. He said I'm a coward,
and womanly in my fear."

"He's a fool. Your instincts were the right ones."

He lifted his head. "Think you so, lady?"

"I know so. My husband is a good man and a
generous chieftain." With wonderment, Fiona heard
herself saying these words, saying these words with
sincerity.

For a moment, hope flared in the dark-ringed eyes
of Crannog Sutherlainn, but just as quickly faded. "It's
too late now."

"It's not too late. If — *when* — when my husband's
people come for me, make sure your men lay down
their arms."

"I — I am not sure they will listen to me."

"You must *make* them do so! Otherwise there will
be bloodshed, and things are certain to go very bad
for all of us."

"But how do I do that, lady?" He looked so young,
so anxious, that Fiona couldn't even find it within

her to continue resenting all the misery of this very
bad day.

"It is their duty, their sacred duty, laird, and their
honor is at stake. And *your* duty is to do what is
right."

"I'm not ready for this," he said softly, looking so
unhappy that had her wrists not been tied together
with a length of horribly scratchy rope she might have
put an arm around the poor lad. "I am afraid, lady."

"It's all right to be afraid," she whispered back.
"You can be afraid, and still lead your people."

He was silent.

Fiona hoped that what she'd said was making sense
to him, because from across the clearing she had seen
Gealag move restlessly, lift his great head as if listening, and it seemed possible, just possible, that the
Penhallow men were quietly approaching. Very much
did she hope so, but at the same time she now felt
more fear than she yet had — if Crannog Sutherlainn
did not rise to the occasion, there could indeed be
bloodshed. Her stomach tightened into a knot. Not
just blood, but death, possibly her own or among the
Penhallow men. Or poor young Crannog's. She didn't
wish *anyone* to die, even that dreadful, stupid Faing.

She strained to listen, tensed her body to spring
up, away, among the trees if she could manage it.

Yes.

There it was.

A faint sound of boots on sodden leaves, a twig
giving way, then another.

She opened her mouth to warn Crannog, but all
at once, like ghosts materializing, into the clearing
strode — why, there was Alasdair. He had come for
her. He *had* come. And he was flanked by half a dozen
of his men, muskets drawn. He himself held extended
a long silver-plated pistol, looking so fierce that Fiona
almost didn't recognize him, for in him now was

nothing but a cold and deadly intent. No laughter, no
playfulness, no fun. His eyes came to her, searchingly,
then passed around the scene before him. Even as he
did so, Fiona's captors stirred, roused, grabbed guns
and knives, jumped up. Crannog leaped to his feet
also, but unarmed. "Weapons down," he ordered his
men, but only a few obeyed.

"We must fight, you dolt!" exclaimed Faing, and
gladly would Fiona have kicked him, hard (if she
weren't afraid she would startle him into shooting
someone). Instead she nudged Crannog with her shoulder, as pointedly as she dared. He didn't glance down
at her, but she saw him pull himself up straighter.

"Weapons down!" he repeated, shakily, but loudly.
"As your laird, I command you! 'Tis your — your
sacred duty to obey me!"

At this, all his men did slowly drop their muskets
and knives onto the ground, all except for Faing,
who remained belligerently holding his musket, now
pointing it directly at Alasdair who, in turn, very
steady, aimed his pistol at Faing.

And then Alasdair lowered it.

Fiona wanted to scream out her fear.

In the air itself, like a poisonous mist, seemed to
thrum the very real possibility that Faing, now the
lone defiant one, desperate, his pride and authority
challenged, would do something rash. Her gaze flashing to the Penhallow men, Fiona saw at once that they
were very nearly on the brink of all shooting Faing,
slaughtering him, in the impetuous hope of killing
him before he could do the same to their leader. Only
their absolute obedience held them back, but in the
meantime Fiona could see Faing, perspiring copiously,
tightening his grip on his musket. Her icy terror froze
her in place, and she looked with her own desperation
at Alasdair.

He stood there very cool and calm, completely

steady and in control, the sheer force of his own personality seeming to Fiona the only thing keeping this awful situation in check. Horrifying her by not even acknowledging Faing, he flicked his gaze to Crannog and said, with a civility that in other circumstances she would have found amusing:

"Laird Sutherlainn, I believe?"

Crannog dipped his head awkwardly. "Aye. You are Laird Penhallow?"

"Aye. Your men follow your orders save for one. What is your clan's punishment for such behavior?"

"Dishonor, banishment, death, should I so desire it," slowly answered the younger man.

"You wouldn't dare!" growled Faing. "You stripling! You callow beardless wonder! You —"

"Be — be quiet, Uncle," interrupted Crannog, very pale. To Fiona it seemed as if he was somehow drawing strength from Alasdair's powerful presence. "You are not laird," Crannog went on. "I am. Put down your musket, or you'll face my judgment."

Looking comically astonished, Faing slowly laid his musket on the ground.

Relieved, relieved beyond measure, Fiona felt like applauding. Which reminded her. She nudged Crannog again, and quickly he bent down to help her to her feet. She was stiff, cramped; she staggered a little, and then to her pleased surprise Alasdair was there, his arm around her, supporting her, and gratefully she leaned against him, his solid warmth, as together they made their way across the clearing, where they were flanked by the Penhallow men.

"Are you hurt, Fiona?" he said quietly.

"Nay, laird."

"I'm thankful to hear it." With swift efficiency he pulled a knife from his boot and cut through the rope that bound her wrists. She rubbed at them, thinking ruefully that she was going to bear the marks for some days to come. Much better to enjoy the marvelous feeling of Alasdair's strong arm around her again, and to lean into him. It was only now that she fully realized just how tired, how cold, how hungry she was. She shivered and burrowed a little closer, and with pleasure flickering through her felt his arm tighten. Goodness, but he had a lot of muscles. How very nice they felt.

"What now, laird?" said Crannog. "I — I deeply regret the theft of your cattle. 'Twas wrong. But I take full responsibility. Your punishment should be directed only at me, not my men." His voice trembled a little, but he squarely faced Alasdair with such desperate courage that suddenly Fiona wanted to cry. Instead she tugged at Alasdair's jacket and whispered:

"Laird, have you any food?"

He smiled a little (giving her just enough opportunity to admire those lines bracketing that very attractive mouth of his). "You're hungry, lass, of course. Aye, we've enough for an army. Begbie insisted on filling up our saddlebags before we left. Can you wait just a little?"

"No, laird, it's for them. Only *see* them, Alasdair."

He did look. Then, in a quiet voice, to one of his men: "Marston, the food Begbie had you stow — you and Waldroup place it before Laird Sutherlainn."

They moved quickly to comply. Dried beef, oatcakes, apples, neatly wrapped hunks of cheese, small brown loaves of bread. Crannog stared at Alasdair with wide eyes.

"For us, laird?" he asked tremulously. "After the harm we've done to you?"

"It is yours," responded Alasdair, as one chieftain to another, and Crannog nodded to his men, who — his uncle Faing among them — fell ravenously upon the food. With newfound dignity Crannog took for himself an apple and some dried beef, and ate more temperately, although his hands were, very obviously, shaking from hunger and, perhaps, with relief.

To Marston Alasdair now said, "Bring me one of the flasks, please, opened."

Marston reached into a saddlebag and brought to Alasdair a small silver flask, which he then placed in Fiona's hand. "Drink, lass," he ordered softly.

"What is it?" she asked, looking up at him.

"Brandy. 'Twill warm you till I can get you home."

"I don't —" she began, but broke off when, gently, he put his hand on hers, brought it and the flask to her lips, and tipped her hand just enough to allow some of the brandy to flow. Pungent and slightly sweet, with a tang of old wood, it burned a little in her mouth and down her throat, and then, as she accepted more at his urging, and then a little more after that, a welcome warmth seeped languorously through her limbs, bringing with it also a calm, hazy relaxation, very pleasant after those many long hours of tension.

"Better?"

She smiled. "Better."

"Good." To Crannog he said: "Are all your people in a similar state?"

"Aye, laird," replied the younger man, a healthier color in his emaciated face, and briefly explained just how his clan had fallen into such desperate straits.

Alasdair listened, nodded, then said: "We will leave you now. I'll not give you the cattle, for they belong to my farmers. But tomorrow I'll send several wagons with food. Write to me with a list of the supplies you need. Dispatch your bailiff here if you like, to confer with mine. We'll ensure your survival through autumn and winter, and assist you in the spring as you need us, so that your clan may thrive again." He held out his hand, which Crannog, tears in his eyes, came forward to clasp.

"I thank you, laird," he said. "And you as well, gracious lady."

Fiona smiled at him, and Alasdair replied, "Farewell. You've made a good beginning as chieftain."

Much later, Fiona would only fuzzily recall being placed before Alasdair on his big bay horse. "I can ride on my own," she protested, vaguely surprised to hear the words running together a little.

"And likely fall off," said Alasdair, his breath warm at her ear. "You wouldn't want to do that to Gealag, would you?"

"No," she answered, allowing him to wrap a clean dry blanket around her, allowing his arm to come firmly about her middle, and watching as Crannog's shabby mantle was given back to him.

Goodbye, smelly thing, she thought. *Hello, lovely strong chest*. Out loud, she said:

"Laird."

"Aye, Fiona?"

"I'm worried."

"There's nothing to worry about anymore. You're safe."

"I know that."

"Well then?"

"I'm worried that I smell like that nasty bundle of furs. Or worse."

He laughed. "If it's a comfort to you, I've been riding all day and I doubt that I smell much better."

"It *is* a comfort to me," she replied, quite seriously, leaning back against him, and it occurred to her then that she was, perhaps, more than a little drunk. She listened contentedly as Alasdair gave orders to his men, and watched as their party broke up into different groups: one man sent ahead to the castle, riding fast; another to accompany Alasdair and herself and to lead Gealag; the others to bring the cattle back at their slower pace.

He clicked his tongue and his horse began to move.

"We've a few hours' ride," he said. "Will you be all right?"

"Yes." Fiona could feel her body relax, almost as if it were melting against the solid muscled hardness of Alasdair's, both of them perfectly in tune with the steady rhythmic movement of his big bay. Suddenly, something funny floated up in her mind and she laughed. Actually, she giggled. Which was very uncharacteristic of her. But what a cheerful sound it made.

"What is it, Fiona?"

"Oh, Alasdair, I'm angry at you," she answered, smiling, a little loopily, at his arm draped firmly around her. "Don't you remember that terrible fight we had the other night? I've been angry at you ever since. So angry. Not," she added punctiliously, "that I wanted Faing to harm you."

"That's nice to know. Are you still angry at me, lass?"

She thought about it. "I *should* be. My *head* says I am. But I don't feel it, really."

"That's nice, too. How *do* you feel?"

She thought some more. "I feel . . . happy. Happy that everyone's all right."

"Happy is good."

"Yes. Were you worried about me, before?"

He brought his arm yet more snugly around her. "Aye," he said, and she heard in his deep voice the unmistakable ring of truth.

She smiled again, and he went on:

"I was so worried, lass, that it was impossible to stay angry. You were very brave and stalwart, you know."

"So were you. When you lowered your pistol!"

She felt him shrug, casually. "I had the uncle's measure," he said. "That type tends to shoot first and ask questions later."

"He said he wanted to have a bit of me," remarked Fiona.

"What? Did that bastard so much as touch you? I swear to God I'll go after him right now, and —"

Fiona interrupted him with another slightly loopy giggle. "No, he didn't, Alasdair. Dear me, how fierce you sound. He also said I was a rare beauty."

His arm, which had tightened at her mention of Faing, loosened a little. But — thank goodness — not too much. "I wouldn't have credited him with that much perceptiveness."

"My head feels all swimmy," Fiona said, "but I *think* I just heard a compliment."

She wasn't sure, but he might have dropped the lightest of kisses onto her hair.

"Aye," he answered, "you did."

"How nice." Fiona sighed, feeling very warm and comfortable, which was funny, what with her wet gown and soggy boots, and being filthy and exhausted, but there it was. She drifted into a kind of waking dream, in which everything was easy, in which everything was possible. It was even possible, in fact, to rest her head on Alasdair's shoulder, on his strong, lovely, muscled shoulder, and to slide her hand along that firm, heavy arm around her waist.

And so when finally they stopped at the wide stone steps of Castle Tadgh, Fiona was, almost, sorry.

Even more was she surprised to see so many people there to greet and receive them despite the outrageously late hour, their voices warmly hailing the safe return of their lady, congratulating Alasdair and his men, inquiring as to their respective well-being, and did they wish for anything to eat or drink?

Fiona was helped down by someone, but before she could take a step forward, Alasdair had dismounted and lifted her into his arms, as easily as he would cradle a babe, and bore her up the steps. Once inside, in the Great Hall, she saw that there was Mrs. Allen alongside them, smiling, and to her Alasdair said: "Is the mistress's bath prepared? And a tray ready for her? Thank you, Mrs. Allen. We'll go up directly."

"I can walk," said Fiona, although secretly she was glad when Alasdair only said firmly:

"I'll carry you."

"Thank you, Alasdair."

"You're welcome, lass."

As they went up the staircase she said, "Alasdair."

"Yes, Fiona?"

"I don't think I've ever been this tired before."

"It's understandable, under the circumstances."

"I suppose so. I feel rather fuzzy." Fiona felt her head lolling back against him. After a few minutes she said thoughtfully, "This is very luxurious, being carried. One feels a little like Cleopatra, although of course without the carpet. Gracious, I've never looked at ceilings quite this way before. Did you say my bath will be ready?"

"Aye."

"Oh, good. Are you sure I'm not too heavy for you?"

"I'm sure."

"You're very strong. Oh, Alasdair, look, there's something painted on the ceiling in this gallery. I never noticed it before. What is it?"

"It's a bad reproduction of some of the frescoes from the Sistine Chapel. See? There's the Creation . . . Noah and the Flood . . . the Twelve Prophetic Figures . . ."

"Oh my. They *are* bad."

"An enthusiasm of my great-grandfather, apparently. He brought in an artist from Italy, who swore he was a direct descendant of Michelangelo himself."

"I doubt it."

Alasdair laughed. "So do I. My mother always meant to have them painted over, but never got around to it."

"Look, there's God dividing water from Heaven. And He has red hair, just like yours! These must never be painted over." And Fiona laughed, too.

All too soon, they were at and into their bedchamber, and she was given into the competent hands of her maid Edme, even as two other maidservants came in, one with a covered tray that smelled delicious, the other with an armful of fresh toweling, and Mrs. Allen was there, to check on things, and at the same time as Fiona was thanking Alasdair again, an exuberant Cuilean bounded into the room, excited to see everyone, and Alasdair said something to Fiona which she didn't catch and was also ordering Cuilean to calm down, and then another maidservant came in and the next thing she knew she was being bundled off to her dressing-room, stripped of her soggy clothes, and put into a warm bath which felt *wonderful*.

Next she was helped into her nightgown, hustled into bed, propped up with pillows, and the tray, uncovered, placed in front of her. On it was a bowl of rich beef broth, a plate of warm bannocks, all soft and buttery, and a large roasted chicken drumstick. She ate it all, every crumb, every drop of broth. And then, sated, surrendered her tray to Edme, who betook herself to her own bed, and Fiona was alone in the great bedchamber.

She leaned back against her pillows, yawning, but vowed to stay awake until Alasdair came. Within her was a new little glow, unnamable, fragile, yet it

seemed to somehow warm her whole self. She hardly
knew what she wanted to say to Alasdair; she only
knew that she wanted to see him.

Maybe, just maybe, she'd even keep her eyes open
when he came out of his dressing-room. She'd just
spent several hours snugged up against that magnificent body of his, and had gained a new appreciation
for it. In fact, it now occurred to her, she wouldn't
mind getting close to Alasdair again.

Quite a bit closer.

A fiery blush heated up her face, her neck, even
her chest, and her hands went to the high soft ruffles
around her throat, as if finding them confining, as
if wanting to do away with them. Fiona hesitated,
then shoved back the covers and hurried into her
dressing-room. Quickly she went to the armoire
in which her night things were kept, and fishing
through a drawer she pulled out a different nightgown, of silk rather than cambric; she swept off the
one she had on, and swapped it for the other, then
nervously eyed herself in the full-length cheval glass.

Did she look ridiculous with the daringly low
neckline, without those concealing ruffles? And heavens, silk seemed to accentuate one's form, rather than
to conceal it as did the more demure cambric. How
soft it felt against one's bare skin . . .

Fiona hesitated again, as if checking within herself.

Yes, that tender little glow was still there, warm
and brave.

That decided her. She put the cambric nightgown
away. Meticulously cleaned her teeth, smoothed her
hair in its long thick braid. Hurried back to bed,
plumped up her pillows, lay flat, sat up, then finally
settled for something in between. She tucked the bedcovers around her. And waited for Alasdair.

And waited.

And waited.

But he didn't come.

The little glow flickered. Waned. And, finally, it died out. Toward morning she drifted into a light, restless doze, aware, as she shifted in and out of wakefulness, that she was sad. Painfully sad. And even a little ashamed. When finally she gave up on sleep and pushed herself out of bed, the first thing she did was to rip off the silk nightgown and shove it back into its drawer.

The next thing she did — of course — was to look for a quill and a piece of paper.

Items for Sutherlainns
Stop thinking about Alasdair
Gealag — check hooves. Stones, mud from
    last night?
My boots. Ruined? Or salvageable? Ask Edme
Write to Father; has he tried those warm oat
    & burdock poultices for the sheep?
Salve — wrists
Ask Cook: boeuf à la Bourguignonne soon?
    With bannocks
Kitchen garden. Blackberries. Preserves.
    Plums?
Any new remedies for insomnia? Research
STOP THINKING ABOUT ALASDAIR

It had been a long night. Alasdair sat at the breakfast-table, tired, but satisfied. He'd come straight from the stables, ravenous, and now was no longer hungry, in itself a pleasant state of affairs, but his cheerful mood was due only in part to that. He felt good — sanguine. The situation with the Sutherlainns had been successfully resolved; most importantly, Fiona was safe.

Thank God, she was safe.

And they seemed to have moved past the cold, icy cold tension of the past few days.

Thank God for that, too.

And today was a new day.

Today, perhaps, they could have peace between them.

Sweet, calm, easy peace.

That wasn't so much to ask, was it?

"Black pudding! Excellent!"

It was Duff, ambling into the breakfast-room in a distinctly bleary way, and Alasdair searched his memory: had Duff been among those who'd gathered last night to welcome his safe return home with his mysteriously absent wife?

Not that he could recall.

He frowned a little, watching as Duff sat down, called imperiously for ale, filled his plate with black pudding, baked beans, grilled tomatoes, fried mushrooms, buttery toast; he himself waved away the ale a servant proffered, but accepted a second cup of coffee, and nodded his thanks as the servant removed his plate.

"No ale?" inquired Duff, with such concern that Alasdair felt a sharp prickle of — well, there it was again, annoyance. There was no law that said one *had* to have ale every day, even if, perhaps, it had long been a convivial custom shared with one's uncle. He answered:

"No."

"Really? Are you all right, lad?"

"Aye."

"If you say so." Duff stared at him, looking perplexed, then finally took a long ostentatious draught of his own ale, as if somehow proving a point, and went on with his meal.

Alasdair's annoyance intensified.

Finally, when Duff reached for his fifth piece of toast, Alasdair said, with deliberate casualness:

"You may remember that my wife went missing yesterday."

"Did she? Oh — ah — yes, now that you bring it up, lad, I *do* recall somebody mentioning it. Big castle, this. Off somewhere mending something, I suppose? Never saw such a lass for sewing. Always with a needle in her hand! Hmmm — wonder if she'd fix this shirt of mine? Look at this rip — d'you see it? How it got there I've no idea. Might've been Hewie jabbing at me with a billiard stick — only in fun, of course. I *think* it was only in fun. Though he may not have liked it when I kicked him in the seat of his pants. For a lark, you know! Did you try some of that whisky he brought over last night? Only one bottle, but superb! Jameson, 1782! Let's buy some, lad, what do you say?"

"I wasn't in the billiards room last night."

"Oh, weren't you? Could've sworn it was you making that bank shot that put away four balls in a row. Superb!"

"No, I was riding into the Dunstan woods in search of my wife."

"Why? Ran away, did she?"

"No, she was kidnapped."

"Kidnapped? Really?" Duff lifted his tankard to wave it in the direction of a servant. "God's blood, the trouble these women make! Ah! To the brim! That's the dandy."

It occurred to Alasdair, then, to think suddenly of Crannog Sutherlainn's uncle Faing, a man whose guidance of his young nephew was questionable at best.

He'd been twenty years old — just about Crannog's age, he reckoned — when Duff had come to live at Castle Tadgh. He'd been young, in trouble, desolate with grief. Vulnerable.

Alasdair looked across the table at Duff and with that same deliberate air of relaxation made himself lean back in his chair. It was, he thought, lucky for Duff that he didn't have a billiard stick in his hand, for he might have been tempted to jab it at him. And not in fun. He said:

"Would you like to know if I found my wife?"

Duff gave a start. "What did you say, lad? I was wondering if we might want to go to Pitlochry for the races. There's a filly to be running there I've had my eye on for many a week. We ought to go today, though, if we wish to find good lodgings."

"No. I've plenty to do here."

And he did. For one thing, he wanted to confer with his bailiff Shaw about sending the promised supplies to the Sutherlainns, and with Fiona as well, about what they could include in the way of linens, clothing, and household supplies.

From his place at the head of the table, Alasdair glanced over at the foot where the lady of the house would sit. It was empty at the moment, but he realized with a sense of surprise — pleased surprise — how good it felt to know that here in his home was his wife Fiona, and that he could rely absolutely on her capabilities. It was not something he'd known in his fifteen years as chieftain, ruling alone. He really had done just fine on his own. But now he had a helpmeet — a partner.

It felt . . . different.

It felt . . . better.

Because it was better for the clan, of course.

Thoughtfully Alasdair ran a hand across his beard-stubbed cheek, jaw, chin, his thoughts shifting in an entirely different direction. Surely, surely, Fiona did not find him repulsive? Unattractive? Surely it had not been only fatigue — and brandy — that made her relax

into his embrace as last night they rode together . . . ?
Lord, but he needed a bath, a shave, clean clothes —

Then he heard her voice in the corridor, speaking
to a servant, and he glanced toward the doorway with
an alacrity that a few days ago, that *yesterday,* would
have been unimaginable to him.

She came into the breakfast-room, wearing a
simple and elegant gown of the palest, softest green,
a white fringed shawl around her shoulders, and her
hair, thick, lustrous, in a loose knot at the nape of her
neck. Why had he failed to notice, before, just how
striking she was?

How bonny.

How unique.

And then he also saw the dark circles of fatigue
underneath those long-lashed eyes of cool gray. Her
slender face was pale. Had she not slept? he asked
himself. How could she not, after such a long and
difficult day? It seemed impossible. He had left their
bedchamber confident that on this of all nights, she
would sleep.

He wished, powerfully, that somehow he could
be of service to her. As it was, he could only stand,
smile, say pleasantly:

"Good morning, Fiona."

His heart seemed to sink a little when she replied,
courteously but without warmth, "Good morning."

A servant pulled out her chair and she sat; in
answer to his query she said, "Chocolate today,
please." He poured it out for her and she thanked
him, then curled her fingers around her cup as if to
warm cold hands.

Having sat again, Alasdair gazed down the length
of the table at her. It was not a particularly long table,
perhaps some fifteen feet of gleaming oak and meant
for cozy *en famille* gatherings, but there did seem to

be quite an immense distance looming between them. He felt oddly tongue-tied. And it did not feel right, somehow, to begin their conversation on the subject of organizing household goods.

So, instead: "How are you?"

She took a sip of her chocolate, then met his gaze with her own. "I'm fine, thank you. And you?"

His heart sank a bit lower. "I'm fine."

"Good." She asked the servant for oatmeal, cream, currants, sugar, then, dauntingly aloof and self-possessed, she applied herself to eating, without hurry, and Alasdair couldn't come up with anything else to say. He would, he thought darkly, stop his mouth with his own napkin if he started to make a lame and platitudinous remark about the weather. Morosely he accepted another cup of coffee. Fiona was halfway through her bowl when suddenly Duff chuckled.

"There's your wife right there, lad."

"Yes," answered Alasdair coldly. "I can see that for myself, Uncle."

"Well then! All's well that ends well. I don't hold with lasses running off into the woods, and most especially at night. Disruptive, and not the *thing*," he said, addressing this last sentence to Fiona with an air of avuncular sternness.

She gave him a look over her spoon that might otherwise have smote a more sensitive individual. "I'll remember that the next time I'm carried off by bandits."

It was possible that Duff would have said more on the topic of proper behavior, but just then Isobel hurried into the breakfast-room and he jumped to his feet, nipping in ahead of the servant to draw out her chair with a grandiloquent gesture. "Do be seated, Miss Isobel," he said, then leaned down to pick up the reticule she had dropped in her evident astonishment. Even from where Alasdair sat he could hear the bones in Duff's back creaking at his unusual speed of movement and sure enough, when Duff straightened, he winced, then groaned under his breath as stiffly he resumed his seat. Still, he managed to smile at Isobel, then said, with ponderous gallantry:

"Where were you, madam? We've missed you."

"Oh! Am I late? How dreadful of me!" Isobel exclaimed, and although ordinarily Alasdair found little about his wife's cousin of interest, he was mildly surprised to now see her face turn an exceedingly bright red.

"I was — I was reading, you see," she explained to Duff, rather breathlessly, "and I'm afraid I lost track of time. Oh! Black pudding! One of my favorites! Yes, please, I'd love some — thank you!" Busily she unfolded her napkin, rearranged her silverware, added sugar to her tea, filled her plate.

If he didn't know better, Alasdair might even have said that Dame Isobel was looking rather guilty. What on earth for, he wondered, still with only faint interest. As far as he knew they had no salacious books lying around the place. And even if they did, it was difficult to imagine short, plump, fussy, chattery Dame Isobel poring over them.

Still, one never knew about people.

It occurred to Alasdair that he hadn't seen her among the crowd welcoming them home, either. Not that he cared one way or the other for himself, but he'd have thought she'd be concerned as to the welfare of her cousin.

So he said to her, "I trust you passed a pleasant night, madam?"

She turned round, anxious eyes to him. "I *wish* I could say yes, laird, but what with my terrible worry for Fiona, and my fear that the castle would be under attack at any moment, I'm sorry to confess to you I did not! I locked my door, and even took the precaution of wedging a chair underneath the doorknob."

He frowned a little. "Someone told you the castle might be attacked?"

"Oh, no, laird, it was my own assumption. It's such a different life here from the one I'm used to in Edinburgh, you see. Why, I hardly dare to venture out of doors these days! One might be murdered by blue-faced men, or abducted without warning, to suffer a fate worse than death! One never *really* feels safe!"

"Nonsense!" heartily interposed Duff. "You're safer here than on the muck-filled streets of Edinburgh, where ruthless cutpurses roam about and ruffians break into people's houses at all hours of the day and night!"

"Oh! Do you think so?" responded Isobel, timidly. "That is, I am sure you are right, sir, but in *my* neighborhood — so quiet, so genteel! — that is to say, my *old* neighborhood, for I no longer — well! I'm sure that's not a tale worth telling — so grateful as I am to dear Fiona for — It's just that one feels so *nervous* here."

"That's but womanly foolishness," Duff told her, with such genial condescension that Alasdair could only wonder why Isobel didn't swat angrily at him with her little beaded reticule. "You'd not catch *me* in a city!" went on Duff, warming to his topic. "Foul, crowded, degenerate places, filled with sloth and vice! Dankness and darkness! Here in the countryside, the air is pure! Clean! Fresh! Nature everywhere, humans and beasts in divine harmony! Where men protect their women, and cherish them, and keep them from harm! Just the way it should be!"

"Speaking of beasts, you have an enormous rent in

your shirt," commented Fiona dispassionately. "Were the wolves after you?"

"Wolves?" echoed Isobel, knocking her napkin off her lap in a convulsive gesture. "Here *inside* the castle?"

If Fiona had laughed, Alasdair might have also, but when he looked down the length of the table at her, he saw that her expression was cool and remote. Why would that be? Last night they'd parted so amicably. Puzzled, Alasdair only half-listened as Duff spent several minutes reassuring Dame Isobel as to the complete absence of wolves roaming the hallways of the castle or lurking behind a cabinet, deviously waiting for the unwary to come along and be promptly ripped to shreds.

"Although," Duff concluded, "there *was* that time a buzzard somehow got into the Great Hall, do you remember that, Alasdair my lad? Devilish hard to capture it. I had to cast that old fishing net just so —" He shot his arm upwards to demonstrate and there was an audible sound of ripping fabric.

"And now," said Fiona, "the rent is even bigger."

If it weren't for the hair everywhere on his face, Duff might, perhaps, have been seen to be flushing self-consciously.

"Sir," Isobel said timidly, "if you like, I could sew that up for you."

"Would you, madam?" He looked hopefully at her.

"Oh yes, to be sure! I do love to be helpful! I wonder if I have the right color thread? Yet no matter what color I choose I'm afraid the repair will still be visible — unless I'm very, very careful with my stitches, and I —"

Isobel proceeded in this animated vein for some time, and Fiona, with what felt like superhuman patience, refrained from interrupting and, instead, ate another bowl of oatmeal and had some more chocolate. When finally her cousin subsided, Fiona pushed away her bowl and said in a businesslike tone:

"Laird, will those wagons you mentioned have room for bed linens and clothing? I expect the Sutherlainns will need such things, and badly too. I've already spoken with Lister and Mrs. Allen, and we've been to the attics as well, to see what's been stored there. We've plenty to spare — if this is agreeable to you?"

Alasdair was looking at her from his seat at the head of the polished oak table. He was looking at her as if she was a mystery he was unable to fathom, but she'd volunteer to sew up every rip and tear in Duff's large wardrobe of scruffy clothing before she would offer any clues. How *could* Alasdair have gone off like that last night?

"Aye, madam," he replied, "it's agreeable to me," although in his expression was nothing that suggested laughter, pleasure, or anything at all agreeable.

Which, thought Fiona, served him right. Dreadful, cruel, hard-hearted man.

Chapter 10

Later that day, after an excellent dinner featuring the roasted sirloin and salad of fresh peas and potatoes she'd planned with Cook a few days earlier, Fiona rose to her feet, as did Isobel.

"If you'll excuse us?" she said to Alasdair and Duff.

Alasdair also stood up. "You're going to the Great Drawing-room?"

"Yes." Her tone was just as chilly as it had been all day. "As we always do. In the evening. After dinner."

His tone was a trifle grim as he said, "May I join you?"

Fiona didn't know who was more shocked, herself or Duff, who sputtered:

"What? I thought we'd go to the village, or to Hewie's, or — or —"

"You are certainly free to, Uncle." Alasdair turned to Fiona. "Madam?"

"You may do whatever you like, laird."

He bowed, slightly. "I await your convenience, then."

"Well!" exclaimed Isobel. "Isn't this nice? Of course we're only going to sew, and no doubt Fiona

will read, and we may, perhaps, work on our puzzle
— it's *very* complicated, with hundreds of pieces, so
tiny, you know, and so finely cut! An historical map
of Glasgow — very educational! Fiona is exceptionally clever at it, laird, I assure you! Why, she found all
the pieces for Bogton House in one sitting!"

"I'm not surprised to hear of Fiona's cleverness,"
Alasdair answered, albeit rather grimly still, and
Fiona haughtily wrapped her fine woolen shawl more
tightly around her, as if encasing herself in impenetrable armor.

Together they left the Great Hall, Isobel fluttering
and animated, herself and Alasdair silent, with Duff
trailing behind them, brushing crumbs from his shirt-
front and also — ugh — picking out a few stray peas
from his beard. Servants had preceded them to the
drawing-room, and so several candelabra had been
lit, as well as a fire in the hearth; the green velvet
window-hangings had been closed against the chill of
the evening.

Fiona sat on the same sofa, near the cozily crackling
fire, where she'd had her first extended conversation
with Alasdair. She and Isobel had just that day arrived
at Castle Tadgh; there had been that long, formal ban-
quet during which those other three women had tried
very hard to catch the interest of Alasdair Penhallow.
She, on the other hand, had composed in her head a
letter to Mother. And little Sheila had come up to her,
and said:

You look but you do not see.

It seemed like a lifetime ago.

She hadn't dreamed she would become Alasdair's
wife. It was the last thing in the world she wished for.

And yet here she was.

Now, her back very straight, Fiona reached automatically for her sewing but only held it on her lap,
and let her gaze wander round the room.

Isobel had gone to the large marquetry table on which lay the Glasgow puzzle, and was instantly absorbed in it. Duff, disgruntled, was stretched out on a sofa on the other side of the room, his feet, in scuffed evening shoes, resting on the sofa's arm, providing anyone who cared to look an excellent view of his laddered stockings with spectacular runs in them.

And Alasdair had seated himself opposite her, just as he had that very first time. She had not, then, found him the least bit appealing. But even a person who was furious and ashamed and all frozen inside would have to admit that he was very distinguished in his tartan kilt, patterned in dark greens and reds, and close-fitted black jacket.

He crossed one long leg over the other, thus also providing anyone who cared to look an excellent view of nicely shaped calves in checkered hose and garters. Also a pair of sturdy knees and even a bit of his thighs, muscled and attractively hairy.

Fiona repressed a sudden stupid gladness that she had on one of her prettiest gowns this evening, a robe of carnation-pink crêpe worn over a white silk slip, along with the lovely diamond necklace that had been a wedding gift from her parents. Hastily she dropped her eyes to her sewing and picked up her needle.

After a while, Alasdair said:

"We got a great deal accomplished today."

She didn't glance up. "Yes."

"The wagons for the Sutherlainns will leave tomorrow at first light."

"Excellent."

"Thank you for all your help."

"I was glad to do it."

"Were you glad? You gave the impression of wanting to murder someone."

"I was glad," she clarified icily, "to help the Sutherlainns."

"Oh, and murder me?"

"Maybe," she answered, because she couldn't help herself, and looked him right in the eye. He still had that baffled expression on his face.

"Why?" he asked, simply.

And the words just came out. "Because," she hissed, "you left me last night, and didn't come back."

"But —"

"But what?"

"I told you where I was going. That I was going to wait for the men who had followed behind with the cattle, see to their well-being. That it was important to me to greet them personally."

"What?"

"Didn't you hear me tell you that before I left our bedchamber?"

Fiona thought back to last night, to the confusion, the servants coming and going, and Cuilean romping around, and her own dazed exhaustion, and . . .

And Alasdair, in a warm and pleasant voice, saying something which she hadn't quite caught . . .

"Oh," she said, feeling rather like a balloon abruptly deflating. "Did you, laird?"

"Aye. And I told you I probably wouldn't see you again until morning."

"Oh."

"I was sure you understood me. You nodded and smiled at me."

"Oh. Well. I didn't understand you. There was too much going on. But," she added scrupulously, "it wasn't your fault, laird."

"Ah."

"It was good of you to wait for your men," she also added.

"They had a hard slog of it."

"Was everyone all right?"

"Aye."

"And the cattle?"

"Unhappy. But all right."

"Oh, that's good." Suddenly Fiona realized that she was feeling like a balloon that was *filling* with air. She was, in fact, a light and happy balloon, floating up into skies of blue. So she said, "I'm sorry for the misunderstanding."

"Is *that* why you've been so —"

"Murderous? Yes. I'm sorry, laird."

"It's fine. But yesterday you called me by my first name."

"That is so . . . Alasdair."

He smiled at her, and tentatively, she smiled back. Really, his face was quite pleasing when he smiled. It emphasized the strong line of his jaw, the firm beveled shape of his chin. She didn't like it when men had weak chins.

Logan Munro has a weak chin, whispered a sly little voice in her head.

He did? Fiona tried to summon an image of Logan, but it seemed impossible here in an illuminated room, with her eyes open.

Wide open and looking at her husband Alasdair.

You look but you do not see.

"What are you working on?"

Fiona blinked, flustered, as if she had been caught out, caught between two worlds, one of which she had no business to be in. "I beg your pardon?"

"Your sewing. What is it?"

"An altar cloth." She told herself to be here, now, and put her focus analytically onto Alasdair's face. But a cool cataloging of his features — two eyes, two ears, one nose — fell away in a giddy rush of impressions, almost as if she was encountering him for the very first time. His broad shoulders, the sturdy column of his neck; the strong planes of his face, those remarkable amber eyes. The dark red of his hair, contrasting vividly with the black fabric of his jacket. Actually, now that she gave it her consideration, it wasn't a dreadful color at all, that hair of his. It was thick, alive with color, with a charming tendency to spike upwards a little above his forehead. How unusual it was for someone with red hair to have dark eyebrows and eyelashes — how striking. He still smiled at her, highlighting those intriguing lines on either side of his mouth. They were sensual, inviting —

"What is the embroidery upon it?"

"What? Oh. A Nativity scene," she answered, almost at random.

"Very nice." That subject seeming to be fairly well exhausted, he fell silent, and shifted a little in his seat. She couldn't help but notice as he did so the hem of his kilt moved up a little higher, revealing a more expansive length of muscled thigh.

Don't stare, don't stare, she told herself, and hastily picked up her needle again. She had once more splintered into a Fiona abrim with intense and contrary emotions, and it made her both excited and afraid. And awkward, gawky, jittery; her heart was beating a little more quickly than usual, she could almost feel her blood rushing faster through her veins. She remembered again how yesterday, in that horrible confrontation with Faing Sutherlainn, Alasdair had seemed to dominate, not with a weapon or through any kind of violence, but by his very presence, the sheer strength of his will. She had felt it in her bones, with an almost physical reaction juddering through her.

Now, with Alasdair sitting opposite her, she again responded to the pull of his being, as if his body called out to her body, and her mind — her busy, sensible, clever mind — had nothing to do with it. She was sharply aware of the smooth, silken fabric against her breasts, encasing her arms, surrounding her legs as if confining her, overheating her; very much did she all at once want to pull off her shoes, her stockings . . . her gown, her chemise. Everything.

Her hands, Fiona saw suddenly, were shaking, and so she put aside her sewing, reached blindly for the book that lay on the little table at her elbow.

"What are you reading?" asked Alasdair.

Fiona seized upon the title as a way of cleaving through the wild confusion that had taken hold of her. "*Modern Methods of Crop Rotation.* I found it in the library."

He looked at her. Curiously. Smilingly. Then, as if willing to follow her lead: "I got that a few months ago, and liked it. Have you gotten to the section about alternating oats with turnips or potatoes, then planting barley, hay, and pasture?"

She was on solid ground again. Thank goodness. "Yes, it was very interesting. I found the diagrams very helpful. Did you see the one about planting at a diagonal, allowing for better distribution of the manure?"

"I did. It seems a very good idea. What do you think about the suggestion to maintain pasture for three years? With one season of oats after that, and then back to pasture?"

"It might depend on how the winters have been, and the general condition of the sheep and cattle."

"Aye. And I don't like to depend too much on turnips and hay for their feed. I always like to have several clover fields in cultivation."

"Although too much clover can weaken their digestion, don't you find? I remember once when a flock of Father's sheep got into a clover field, they got so bloated that we had to treat them with a sour milk and oatmeal mash for a week, which was a great deal of work for everybody."

They continued in this vein, easily and enjoyably, until the tea-tray was brought in. Fiona realized that all her self-consciousness had dissipated, her confusion, her crazy desire to strip off all her clothing as well. She was back to being steady, practical Fiona.

Which was good.

Wasn't it?

"Brandy!" said Duff, ambling over. "About time."

"Tea," said Fiona, nodding her thanks to the servant who had placed the tray on the low table between herself and Alasdair. "Sandwiches and biscuits and macaroons. No brandy."

"A frivolous Sassenach custom," growled Duff, sitting next to Alasdair and giving all the appearance of a long-suffering figure from Biblical times. So might hoary Moses have frowned, gesturing sternly to the stone tablet's Eleventh Commandment: THOU SHALT NOT SERVE TEA IN THE EVENINGS.

Fiona only shrugged, and passed Alasdair a cup of tea, the way he liked it, with a little cream and no sugar. Isobel came then, and she gave her a cup also. Then, for herself, tea with cream and sugar. Ten minutes later, it was clear that the food was fast disappearing, and Duff said in an offhand manner:

"I'd take a cup of tea, lass, if there's any left."

It would have been churlish to grin in a triumphant fashion, and so Fiona only said, politely, "To be sure there is, Uncle. How do you like it?"

"However it is least objectionable."

She laughed, and handed him a cup with plenty of cream and sugar. "May I give you a plate?"

"Aye," he replied, and when he received from her a pretty china plate heaped high with delicacies, he added, gruffly, as if trying to remember a word in another language, "Thankee."

"You're welcome, Uncle." Fiona leaned back against the sofa, feeling very mellow. There really was something unifying about good food. Thoughtfully she picked up a macaroon from her plate and bit into it. Sweet, soft, chewy: so delicious she had to keep herself from saying *Mmmmmmm* in a rather lascivious way. Was it sinful to relish a macaroon with such sensual pleasure? As if of their own volition her eyes strayed to Alasdair. Who sat perfectly at his ease, studying her. Smiling.

A memory flashed through Fiona, back again to their first conversation here. She had thought of a great cat, toying with a mouse. She of course had been the mouse, who had not wanted to be played with. Or eaten.

A shudder rippled along her spine. Not of fear exactly, but something else.

Maybe now she wanted to play.

Just maybe.

And so, when, a little while later, Alasdair stood and stretched and casually announced, "I'm for bed," she hesitated, heart hammering within her. Then, with extreme care, she put her plate back onto the table, noticing that her hands were shaking again.

She stood up also.

"I'll come with you," she said, just as casually.

And together, they left the room.

Fiona was self-conscious again, afraid, more afraid than excited now. She sat before her satinwood dressing-table, eyeing her pale, slender face in the mirror. In a horribly cowardly way, she had changed

into a plain white cambric nightgown, with (yes) a
high ruffled neckline. Had taken down her hair and
quickly braided it. Nervously she plucked at the fabric
over her bosom. Why did she have so little substance
there? She ran her palms over the flesh of her torso,
and even through the nightgown the outline of her
ribs was apparent, she was sure of it. There was no
getting around it. She was scrawny. No wonder Alasdair could only bring himself to look at her legs.

Although *they* were skinny too.

Well, there was nothing for it, Fiona thought
gloomily, but to go lie down in the bed, and wait for
him to ask her to lift up her nightgown. As usual.

She sniffed.

Stared at herself.

And then two large, fat tears rolled down her
cheeks.

And then a sob escaped her.

And then there was a knock on her dressing-room
door.

Fiona jumped, as might a prisoner summoned to
the chopping block. "Yes?"

"You've been a long while. Is everything all right?"

No. She said, "Yes."

There was a pause. "Are you sure?"

No. She said, "Yes."

Another pause. "May I come in?"

No, she wanted to say. She wanted him to go
back into his own dressing-room, so that she could
flee unseen to the bed and crawl in. Hide. But she
summoned a shred of courage, mixed together with
a large dollop of misery, swiped at her face with her
sleeve (oh, how prim were those ruffles around her
wrists), and answered curtly:

"If you wish."

The door swung open, and in came Alasdair.

Fiona did not turn around, but caught bits and pieces of him in her small mirror. Evidently he had on a dark blue dressing-gown, belted around his waist. She supposed she should have been grateful that he hadn't waltzed in stark naked, but it was a thought without emotion. She laced her fingers together in her lap and locked her eyes upon them. There were ten, there were ten; she tried to focus her mind by actually counting them —

Alasdair stopped behind her. "Have you been crying?"

"No."

In his silence was a certain skepticism; just as in some mysterious way, the weight of his gaze was a physical sensation upon her, though she hardly knew if she liked it or not. When lightly he ran his hand along the length of her braid, the muscles in her shoulders tightened and she had to force herself to stay still. Stay quiet. Not break away in panic.

"May I?" he said, and in her blind confusion she gave a quick nod.

Then his fingers were gently pulling apart the thick bunches of hair that she'd woven together and hastily tied at the bottom with a ribbon. They moved through her hair without hurry, with a slow, caressing touch.

"Give me your brush," he said.

"No," she answered, in an ungracious, grumbling way.

"Please."

"No."

"Please, Fiona."

"Oh, all right," she snapped, and thrust her brush over her shoulder, still without turning around.

"Thank you."

Slowly, gently, patiently, he brushed her hair, from the crown of her head down to her waist, with long, easy, rhythmic strokes, as if he had all the time in the world, as if there was nothing better he had to do. As if he would never stop. As if there was no future, no past — only this moment, this very private, quiet moment between the two of them.

Gradually, very gradually, Fiona relaxed. Her shoulders lost their tense hunch. She gave herself up to the steady rhythmic movement of the brush. She breathed in. Breathed out. Easily. Her eyes drifted shut. She wasn't sleepy, but had somehow slipped into a realm of pure and mindless sensation.

"Beautiful."

Alasdair's voice, softly, from behind her.

"Your hair is like silk, lass."

"My only beauty, so it's been said," she murmured.

"That's nonsense."

He leaned past her to place the brush back onto her dressing-table, and Fiona's eyes flew open. Alert again, she watched, repressed a little gasp, as with effortless strength he turned her pretty chair — with her in it — so that she was sitting perpendicular to her dressing-table.

"What are you doing?" she asked nervously.

"This." He bent down, and lightly touched his lips to hers.

Shocked, dazed, even frightened by this unexpectedly intimate contact between them, Fiona didn't respond. Her mind was skittering wildly, even as her heart thumped hard within her. Which Fiona *was* she right now? Oh God, which one?

He pulled away a little, and gravely said:

"Do you not want me to?"

She shrugged, hanging onto her composure for

dear life. "You can," she said, a little raggedly. "If you want to."

"I do," he answered with that same gravity. He kissed her again, gently, just to the side of her mouth, and then at the tender pulse-point underneath her chin, and then her cambric-covered shoulder.

Fiona did not resist, but remained very still.

And then —

He sank to his knees before her, and although she was glad to observe that the dark blue sash of his dressing-gown remained firmly belted, the lapels did gap open and she could see quite a bit of his chest, its hard planes, the springy dark hair, so very, very masculine. *With my body I thee worship.* One of their vows. It was *allowed* to touch that tempting hardness, but fear held her back. Fear paralyzed her. And then Alasdair reached for her interlaced fingers, took them in his big, warm hands, and turned her palms upward. Although her salve had helped, her wrists were still red, chafed, from the rope that yesterday had bound them.

Alasdair touched his lips to each wrist in turn, gently and deliberately, and Fiona jerked as if an electric current ran through her. His lips were soft and firm all at once, and such was the tenderness of his gesture that she almost felt as if he kissed her body, her self, her soul, entirely and in a way that sparked within her a wild, all-consuming hunger.

"You are courageous, Fiona," he said, looking into her eyes which she knew were wide, wide open.

"No," she whispered. "I'm afraid."

"Right now?"

"Yes."

"I won't harm you."

"I know you won't. But I'm still afraid."

"Why?"

"This is — different — from before."

"Aye. Different."

"Why?"

"Our nights together," he said, "you didn't enjoy them, did you?"

She hesitated. Then decided, now, to tell the truth. "No."

"Of course you didn't. I was not as I should have been. Would you like to try again?"

"Can we?"

"If you wish it, Fiona. The choice is yours."

"I — I *think* I do." Her mind seemed to drift and glide, like a bird dipping over the water, and then something shifted inside her and she said, "I would like to try. Yes."

"I'd like that also." He smiled a little. "I'd like to think the marital duty can be more than what we've known so far."

"When you call it 'the marital duty,' it's hard to believe."

"Point taken. What shall I call it then?"

"Call it what it is."

"I think sex can be more than what you and I have known so far."

"That's better."

"Good. Are you still afraid, lass?"

"A little. Yes. Or a lot. I'm not sure."

"You need not fear. All will be well." He kissed each palm, first one, then the other, his gaze steadily meeting hers, and then there was a sort of pause, almost, she thought dreamily, like that odd shivery stillness before lightning strikes. She waited for him to bring her roughly against him, to press his lips hard on hers, perhaps, to blatantly push his tongue full and heavy into her mouth, to take one of her hands and press it against his shaft.

Just as Logan had.

But Alasdair did nothing of the sort.

Instead he leaned back a little. He curled his hands around her bare ankles, slid them in a caressing stroke — back and forth, back and forth — across the sensitive tops of her feet; slowly, oh so slowly, underneath her nightgown, his hands slid up her calves, to the back of her knees where the skin was yet more sensitive, where his fingers lightly, confidently lingered, as if relishing the feel of her. How warm it made her feel, how languorous and excited all at once, but when, she wondered, would this slow delicious interlude end and his own needs take over? Instead, he only said:

"Do you like this?"

She thought about it. "Yes," she answered cautiously. But had to add, "Do you?"

"Very much. Why wouldn't I?"

There were so many reasons, but she picked the most obvious one and blurted it out. "Well, for one, my legs are like sticks."

"No. They're soft and strong. Powerful. Beautiful." He slid his hands higher, around her thighs, and in the very core of her Fiona felt a giddy flutter of pleasure. Oh, it felt good. *He* felt good.

He said, "Any other concerns?"

"Yes." She was a little breathless now. "Isn't this boring for you?"

He laughed. Not mockingly, but softly, kindly. "No." Then he grasped her hips with that same gentle, deliberate touch, and tugged her forward on her seat, slowly pushing up her voluminous nightgown as if he was unwrapping the nicest, most wonderful gift in the world, exposing all the length of her legs, bunching the fabric up around her waist — but not as before, there was nothing brisk or businesslike about Alasdair now. He drew his fingers up along the soft inside of her thighs and Fiona quivered.

He had used the word *beautiful* twice. And about

her. And he *seemed* sincere. She wanted to believe that he found her beautiful, wanted to trust his words and the messages conveyed by his caresses.

But trust did not come easily for her. Life — and by this she meant Logan Munro, of course — had taught her that a man could say something, but then do something which contradicted his soft, beguiling words.

Yet . . .

Here before her, on his knees, as a man might genuflect before some higher being, was Alasdair, his hands, like a sorcerer's, conjuring from out of her cool composure a carnal fire that made the saliva pool in her mouth and her breath come heavily between parted lips.

"Open for me," he said quietly.

"What — what are you going to do?"

"I'll show you. If you don't like it, I'll stop."

"Do you promise?"

"Yes."

Fear warred with curiosity.

After several moments ticked by, each and every one an eternity, curiosity won.

Or maybe she was more courageous than she knew.

Carefully, Fiona brought her legs apart. She had only a few moments in which to feel dreadfully vulnerable, exposed, nervous, before Alasdair slid his hands around her hips, brought his mouth to the white, soft skin of her thigh, and —

He licked it, in a long, warm, wet stroke of his tongue.

Did it in a way that seemed to her he *liked* it.

Fiona made a choked sound deep in her throat. Reached down and gripped his forearms, hard.

"Should I stop?" he asked. His face was calm, serene, but there was a kind of eager intentness in his expression also, as if she had interrupted him from doing something he very much wanted to do.

"N-no."

"All right."

Starting from the inside of her knee, all the way to the juncture where her leg ended and the soft intricate folds of tender flesh began, his warm tongue traced a path, slowly, lazily, without any hurry at all, then went — there. *Oh my God,* Fiona thought, *oh my God,* as he licked at her very center, found concealed like a sweet pearl amidst the soft skin, soft hair, an exquisitely sensitive nubbin of flesh, and with an appetite, an assurance, that she thought might stop her hard-beating heart, with wet, sure strokes of his tongue he made pleasure begin, and build, and heighten, like a grace note that went on and on, as an angel might sing, once and forever.

She hadn't known.

Hadn't known her body, her spirit, was capable of this.

This joy made incarnate, flowing from the sweet primal core of her, out and down her legs, up through her torso, blazing along her arms, her neck, and for all she knew creating an ecstatic halo around her head. Joy and bliss and pure sensation.

Vaguely Fiona realized that from her throat issued soft noises, somewhere between a hum and a gasp. They were moans, really, but quiet ones, because she had to hold back a little, had to hang onto her restraint, her dignity.

Didn't she?

Did self-control have a place in all this, when she now was having a hard time figuring out where she ended, and where Alasdair began? When he knelt before her, was without haste worshipping her with his clever, kind, knowing tongue, his hands still holding her as if he would never let her go?

Her eyes closed, her head tipped back, and it seemed to Fiona that she was in danger — danger of the best and wildest kind — of flying off a high cliff, soaring without shackles into the ether.

She didn't know why she stopped him.

All at once she wanted, *needed*, with a curious ferocity, to be yet closer to him, face to face. So — panting, sweating — she pulled away, sat up a little straighter, sharply aware that much of her was draped, imprisoned, in her prim white nightgown even as the rest of her body was free.

Deliciously free.

Alasdair sat back on his heels. Studied her face. Lifted his dark brows. "Everything all right?"

"Yes."

"Did you like that?"

"Yes."

"Would you like me to keep doing it?"

"No."

"All right." He said this with easy casualness. He didn't get up, or yawn, or frown, or look impatient, or grab at her hand to make it do something for him. No, he sat on the soft, dove-gray carpet of her dressing-room like someone who had all the time in the world. For her.

Fiona wanted to laugh out loud, to clap her hands with glee. But that would have been childish. She didn't feel like a child right now. She felt quite adult. More to the point, she felt very, very womanly. And, she realized, she felt —

Beautiful.

Strong.

Powerful.

Much like, she imagined, a butterfly, transformed, emerging from its cocoon.

So when Alasdair said, casually, "What would you like to do now?" she answered:

"I'll show you."

And rapidly she undid the long row of little white buttons at the neck of her nightgown, which she then ripped up and over her head, tossing it aside without a second glance. And she slid off her dainty velvet chair onto his lap, grabbed his face between her two hands, and said, "Kiss me again."

Chapter 11

A week ago Alasdair had had a vivid dream in which he was making love to Fiona, who sat astride him with her shining hair freed from its braid. In his dream, her pale slim body had glowed as if on fire, set alight by the touch of his hands upon her.

Now, here in her dressing-room of all places, as he received her upon him, felt her hands upon his face, saw the glow in long-lashed eyes gone blue, he wondered for a stunned moment if he was, in fact, dreaming. She *seemed* real, there was something very reassuring about the weight of her, the rapid rise and fall of her chest, the scent of her lemony soap and her rose perfume and her sweat mingling in a rather intoxicating way, but still —

It was easy to imagine that despite their prosaic surroundings, he, they, had been transported to some kind of mystical paradise.

Here they were, here was Fiona, naked as the day she'd been born. With her hair streaming about her like a shimmering silvery-blonde cloak, here was his Eve, he was her Adam, and he had just tasted of the Fruit of Knowledge: the sweet musky taste of her still lingered, but he hadn't had enough and he wanted nothing more than — why, he wanted more of her.

As he had come to her closed dressing-room door, he'd been confident that their marital relations — sex — could be improved, but never in a million years would he have guessed *this* would happen. That the nice little flame he'd expected had instead exploded into a roaring conflagration of desire: a bonfire of absolute, devouring, splendid lust that took them both, remaking them anew. Had he really once thought her too thin, unappealing? Christ, but he'd been blind. She was magnificent. And with that same ravenous longing he wanted to run his hands along the long slim line of her torso, devour her beautifully rounded little breasts, and more, so much more, but she had said firmly to him:

Kiss me again.

Who was he to disobey?

Especially with that pretty mouth, the color of pink spring roses, so temptingly close, revealing between parted lips a glimpse of white straight teeth. Maybe she wanted to devour him too. Alasdair knew a strong impulse to ravage her mouth with his own, but instead, acting on a kind of deep instinct, he remained still, meeting her eyes with his own, and didn't even pull her against him.

"You," he said, quietly, calmly, affably, "kiss me."

He could feel her react. The indrawn breath, her fingers tightening against his face.

"Do you want me to?" she asked.

"My God, yes."

She seemed to be satisfied then. She smiled slightly. Leaned closer, and closer still, until there was only the merest hairsbreadth between their mouths. A kiss without a kiss. How could such a thing be so erotic? But it was: he was hard now, ragingly hard, she had to know it and feel it, his shaft beneath his robe pressed insistently between her legs as she sat with wonderful abandon on him, the silken barrier between them damp with the wetness of her desire, her readiness. *Hurry, hurry,* clamored his body, but with a supreme effort of will, guided by instinct, he did not hurry. Instead, he waited. His breath came faster and his own lips parted; expectancy surged through him like a storm.

But he waited.

She did not kiss him, though their mouths were so close and he could feel the warmth of her breath like a siren's song. No, she slid her fingers down along the column of his throat, to the muscles of his shoulders, slid caressingly around his biceps, and then up again, to travel across his chest, lingering, dipping into the hollows of his collarbone and trailing down his chest.

He couldn't prevent himself from groaning a little.

"You're torturing me, lass."

"Am I?" She didn't sound at all sorry. She sounded rather pleased. And she shifted herself upon his lap a little, in a very purposeful, very cruel way.

He groaned again.

"You," he said, "are not a nice person."

"No," she agreed, in a pleased voice. "I'm really not, am I?"

But she did touch her lips to his, just a little, a whisper-light touch, and Alasdair broke out in a sweat.

"More?" she asked.

"Aye."

"Very well." She tilted her head, kissed his upper lip, *licked* it. Pleasure shot through him, keen and exquisite.

"Again?" she asked.

"Aye."

She licked his lip again, boldly now, then brought

her lips more fully upon his, and when she gave a long, soft, satisfied sort of sigh, he judged the time was right, and he deepened the kiss, touched his tongue to hers, explored her, tasted her, but with a slow approach, without haste, sensitive to her response, and savoring — relishing — *experiencing* every second of it. Yielding, returning, she was all wetness and heat here, too; Alasdair groaned again, a raw, rough sound which seemed to give her considerable enjoyment, for she gave a little purring noise, broke the kiss, and pressed herself against him, whispering against his ear, "You *do* like this, don't you?"

"You know I do."

"Good." She bit his earlobe, just sharply enough to make him twitch with surprise and excitement.

"No, you're not a nice person at all," growled Alasdair, and took his revenge at once by wrapping his hands around her shoulders, creating a distance between them, and taking one pink, hard tip of her sweet little breast into his mouth, suckling at her and enjoying very much the spasmodic way *she* twitched. Two could play at that game, after all. After a while he went to her other breast, glorying in the way she clutched at him, murmured feverishly, "Oh, Alasdair, oh my God . . ."

He could have gone on like this forever, yet did not object when her hands found the silk sash at his waist, fumbled at it. Her face was flushed, her expression one of intense urgency.

In a lazy, leisurely way he leaned back from her, bracing his hands behind him, amazed at his own self-control. It seemed possible that he'd never been quite so racked with lust, but here he was, not even assisting her one tiny bit to speed things along.

"Your hands are trembling," he remarked.

"Help me, you awful man," she hissed.

He smiled. "If you insist." He lay back onto the soft carpet, Fiona shifting to straddle his thighs. He undid the knot she had created in his sash, but did not open the robe, only folded his crossed arms behind his head. "There."

Fiona sat back a little, breathing deeply, and said, politely, "Thank you."

"You're welcome," he replied, just as courteously, then commented, "You've stopped trembling."

"For now."

There was a pause. Alasdair wondered what was going to happen next. He hoped his body wouldn't disintegrate into a million little pieces of unfulfilled desire. He gazed up at Fiona, slim and strong and naked and with her magnificent hair all about her.

"You look like Belisama, lass." The mystical goddess of light and fire.

"That's a lovely thing to say."

"I mean it. You're beautiful."

"When you say it like that, I almost believe you."

"Believe it."

"I'll try. Alasdair."

"Yes, Fiona?"

"I wish our wedding night had been like this."

"So do I. I'm sorry I was such an ass."

She smiled a little, and he admired again the lovely curves of her rose-pink lips, although he did wish they weren't so far away from his own mouth.

"Better late than never," she said.

"True."

"Will it always be like this?"

"Like how?"

"Magical."

"No."

Her dark brows went up. "No?"

"It will be better," he told her.

"That seems impossible."

"Trust me."

"I will."

"Fiona," he said.

"Yes?"

"There's a very real chance I'll die unless I have you very soon."

"We wouldn't want that to happen."

"I'm glad you feel that way."

Still she didn't move. "Alasdair."

"Yes?"

"Do you remember what you asked me to do on our wedding night?"

"Aye, to my shame. Must you remind me again of my boorishness?"

"I only brought it up because — well, I want to do it."

He really *was* dreaming, Alasdair thought, in a kind of wonderful agony. "Fine."

"Is it all right for a wife to do that?"

"Yes."

"And you would like it too?"

"Yes." He lay at his ease — or with as much appearance of it as a man could in his situation, with a blatantly erect shaft, poorly concealed by a panel of silk, and his naked wife only inches from it — and waited for her to make the next move, for still that deep instinct of his told him to do so. He wondered if she would slide open the panels of his robe with a certain tentativeness, but instead she whipped them aside. And then, in a heartbeat, she was upon him, he was within her, they were joined completely and it was, in fact, magical.

Fiona could not have said how long it was after they had made love, after they had both reached their peaks, first her, then Alasdair, that she lay next to him on the carpet in her dressing-room, still rather breathless. She *had* cried out, had lifted her voice in joyful abandon, and oh, how wonderful it felt to do that.

Now her head rested comfortably on the perfect hollow between the base of his neck and his collar-bone. One of her legs was draped across his; one of her arms lay across his broad chest. Her hair was everywhere. Tomorrow it would take her a long time to smooth out the snarls and tangles. But why consider tomorrow when the present moment was so delightful?

She said to Alasdair:

"Thank you."

One big hand had been stroking her arm, but it stopped. "Don't be daft, lass."

"Why am I daft?"

"If anyone's to be doing the thanking, it should be me."

"Really? Why?"

"Do you need to ask?"

Fiona smiled. His pleasure had been as exciting, as satisfying, as her own. She reached out and ran a teasing finger along those sensual lines near his mouth, then down the firm hardness of his chin. Now *that* was a chin for you. Manly, handsome, neither too protuberant nor receding.

Goodness, she hadn't thought of Logan Munro at all. Before, in those brief mechanical interludes with Alasdair, she'd allowed seductive memories to dance across her mind. But tonight, Alasdair had filled her senses, richly, completely. Filled *her*. Nothing that had ever happened between herself and Logan — the stolen kisses, the secretive caresses — could compare with making love with Alasdair.

A little voice, solemn, oracular:

You stare at the moon, ever changing. Turn about, lady, turn about.

Fiona suddenly remembered that evening in the Great Drawing-room some weeks back, when, unguardedly, she'd compared Alasdair to the sun.

Another memory superimposed itself, one she hadn't thought of in a long time. A few weeks before she had left home on that fateful journey to Edinburgh at eighteen, to visit Cousin Isobel, an eclipse had come upon Wick Bay. She'd been riding with Father to visit one of their tenant farmers, whose sow had just given birth to an astonishing nineteen piglets, when the sky had begun turning to a deeper blue before fading into gray and continuing to darken, and day had somehow, bizarrely, become night. She had been shocked, and afraid, but Father had said, "It's the moon passing across the sun. 'Twill soon pass away. There will be all kinds of tumult and gibbering among the poor folk, and they'll talk of nothing but the devil casting his own shadow. Ignore it." He had been right, and before long the afternoon had brightened again.

Then she had gone to Edinburgh and met Logan, with his jet-black eyes, gleaming black hair, who had said he loved her but changed so completely. It was not difficult, as she lay here replete, entwined, to think of Logan — the memory of Logan — as the moon, ever-changing and inconstant; and Alasdair, here, now, real and solid, her future, as the sun.

Alasdair, filling her with warmth and pleasure.

Maybe filling her with a baby, too.

Fiona closed her eyes. Her breathing had softened to an easy cadence. Images formed, as if fully fleshed in her mind: herself all rounded and pregnant, a chubby red-haired baby, all smiles and dimples, Alasdair holding the baby in his arms; *another* baby, with silvery-blond hair and a determined little face . . .

"Alasdair," she said, keeping her eyes closed.

"Yes, lass?" He was stroking her arm again.

"I'm feeling very sleepy."

"That is gladsome news."

"I'm not sure I want to sleep on the carpet."

"No, lass, I quite agree. Wait a moment. Don't move." He extricated himself from her embrace, and with easy strength he picked her up in his arms, lifted her, and carried her to their bed. He laid her down, gently as a feather; she gave a contented sigh, still with her eyes shut, and said, "Thank you."

"You're welcome." The mattress shifted as Alasdair got in next to her. Not all the way across the length of the bed, either. He lay on his side, with a big, splendidly heavy arm across her midsection, just below her breasts. "Good night, lass."

"Good night, Alasdair."

There was a short, comfortable silence.

"Alasdair?"

"Aye, Fiona?"

"I'm too happy to sleep."

"Oh?"

Fiona opened her eyes and turned onto her side, facing him. How strange it felt to not have on a nightgown. But how . . . convenient. She slid closer to him, until their naked bodies were touching — skin to skin, her smooth breasts against his muscled chest, her hips pressed up against his — and felt his pleasingly immediate response. She smiled in the warm dimness of their bedchamber. "I know what we could do instead."

"Do you?" His deep voice was lazy, amused.

Fiona curled a leg over his hip, and snugged herself even closer. "Do you want to?"

"You *are* daft," he said, and kissed her, and she kissed him right back, and they began again.

Later, later, when their breathing had slowed and their sweat had dried, Alasdair lay watching as Fiona, this time, did fall asleep, on her back, one hand flung out toward him, on her face an expression of pure tranquility.

Ah, good for you, lass, he thought.

Carefully, so as not to disturb her, he brought the blankets a little higher, to cover her bare, smooth-skinned shoulders, then settled back against his pillows. He'd have thought he would have preceded her in sleep. Especially since he hadn't slept at all last night.

Still, he could certainly lie here for a little while, and enjoy this marvelous feeling of satiation. And happiness, yes?

Yes?

Wasn't he happy?

He *should* be.

The sex had been more than satisfactory.

Alasdair rolled onto his side, away from Fiona.

He should be happy, for now, for sure, there would be peacefulness between them.

And peace was such a nice, safe feeling.

It was all he wanted.

All he needed.

And on that thought, his body relaxed. His eyelids grew heavy. And at last, he slept too.

He was having an argument with Gavin. Or, rather, he was trying to have an argument with Gavin, who, taller, older, only looked down his finely chiseled nose at him and smiled in that aloof, condescending manner he deployed when he was trying to prompt Alasdair to explosive outbursts of fury.

It usually worked.

They were standing on the shore of Loch Sgàthan, deep, blue, beautiful, with Castle Tadgh clearly visible in the distance. Here in this loch they had swum, fished, sailed for all their lives. *Don't do it, you daft fool!* he was saying to Gavin, only he noticed that he was shouting, for the wind abruptly rose, and the blue waters of the loch had turned a troubling dark green, no longer smooth and glassy but choppy and angry-looking.

But I want to, calmly replied Gavin. *When have you ever stopped me from doing what I wanted to do, little brother?*

Never, damn you, Alasdair said, waiting for the mood to shift, for the affection — which for all their lives had knitted them together — to return, as it always did, even after their ugliest fights.

I'm ready, someone cried, *I want to be the first one on the boat.*

And there was Mòrag, her black curls whipping crazily in the wind, looking not at him, but up at Gavin.

And Gavin smiled at her, took her hand, just as Alasdair heard a loud *crack* that could have been thunder, or, equally possible, his heart breaking. He prayed it was thunder, for pride was clearly all he had left.

I'm ready too, Gavin told Mòrag, and then as Alasdair reached desperately for them both, to try and stop them by physically restraining them, a crowd of people had suddenly appeared between them, blocking his way. Friends of Gavin: the large party he had invited from Glasgow, charming young men, bonny young ladies, their pleasant chaperones. And Father and Mother, too:

Mother, saying proudly, *Gavin is such a fine sailor, isn't it a handsome boat we've given him for his birthday?*

Father nodding, nodding, nodding.

Don't do it, he shouted, *don't go,* but his words were lost in the howl of the wind, and even as he glanced in despair at the loch, a dark, menacing shape, enormous and sinister, swam up near the surface, and only Alasdair saw it.

The crowd of people in front of him had gone oddly transparent, and he could see through them as he would an ordinary pane of glass. He could see Gavin backing away from him, smiling, Mòrag clinging to his arm.

Gavin, saying, *We're going whether you like it or not, little brother. Stay on the shore if you wish. We'll miss you; won't you change your mind?*

Goodbye, goodbye, everyone said gaily, Father and Mother too.

Mòrag, laughing, her black curls suddenly a morass of deadly snakes, alive and writhing and furious, as if entirely separate beings from Mòrag and transmitting their black anger to Alasdair, who shouted, *You're daft, all of you, you shouldn't go, it's unsafe, can't you see that?*

Nobody listened, nobody heard him, and furiously Alasdair tried to turn and walk away from them, but he had looked at the snakes and been instantly turned to stone. He was forced, then, to watch as the boat, already full of passengers and in the middle of the loch, went slowly down. Forced to hear the screams, the pitiful cries for help. It seemed to take years for the beautiful new boat to sink within the ugly green depths of the loch.

The last one to go under was his brother Gavin,

his golden-blond hair like a shining helmet in the gloom.

Gavin didn't scream or cry like the others. No, he stood there very calm, smiling at Alasdair triumphantly, as if even in death he'd gotten yet again the very last laugh.

Gavin! he shouted. *I'm sorry I turned away from you! So sorry!*

Too late, little brother. You should have come with us, you know. We're having so much fun.

No. No —

You should have come with us.

No! You were wrong to insist!

I'm never wrong, little brother.

You're daft!

What's the matter?

I'm sorry —

Wake up.

What? I can't hear you, Gavin!

Alasdair, wake up. Wake up!

Mother, Father, Gavin, Mòrag, all of you — you can have her with my blessing, Gavin, if only you'd come back —

Wake up, Alasdair!

A hand was upon him, shaking his shoulder, and Alasdair was swept away, jerked from his dream, opening his eyes to find himself in his bed, sweating, and in his blind disorientation he had no idea who was touching him: with a rough noise he shoved the hand away, wrenched himself across the bed. "Stop," he said hoarsely, "don't touch me."

There was only silence.

Alasdair was waiting for his heart to slow its racing. Waiting for his eyes to adjust to the dimness.

He saw Fiona, sitting up, the covers clutched to her breasts and her hair a mad nimbus all around her, looking, he thought dazedly, not unlike a seraph who had come from the heavens into the human realm.

"I'm sorry," he said, his voice still a little rough. "A nightmare, nothing more."

"You called out," she said softly. "For your parents. For Gavin, and for Mòrag. Was she someone whom you lost, too?"

A wave of anger, of pain and desolation, crashed over Alasdair and he had to fiercely fight back the urge to snarl at Fiona or to simply get up and go away somewhere, anywhere, to avoid having to answer questions he didn't wish to hear, let alone answer. Instead, he brought himself closer to her, through sheer will made his voice just as soft.

"It was nothing, lass," he said, "only a dream," and before she could say anything else he coaxed her down with persuasive hands, to lie against him, and to let him kiss her and touch her, gently, slowly, until she was breathless, eager, carried off with desire. And then he, too, was subsumed, all thoughts of the past gone, as if they were only flotsam taken back by a remorseless sea.

After, Fiona slept again, and Alasdair did too, for a little while. But sentience came again, far too soon, and for a long while he reflected in the darkness on the irony of Fiona sleeping and himself wide awake. Somehow they seemed to have traded places. He'd have laughed out loud — although perhaps not entirely with amusement — except that he didn't want to disturb her.

Finally, in that uncertain hour between waning night and early sunrise, very quietly he rose, dressed, slipped out of their bedchamber, leaving behind a sleeping Fiona. There in the hallway was Cuilean, tail wagging, and together they went downstairs and outside, where they walked to the river. Alasdair watched the sun begin its slow climb into a blue cloudless sky, and Cuilean enjoyed himself nosing along the riverbank and chasing squirrels up into the trees. Ordinarily Alasdair would have enjoyed just such an early-morning walk too, but today . . .

Today was different.

And not in a good way.

So he was glad — inappropriately glad — when he returned to the castle and was greeted in the Great Hall by his bailiff Shaw, his boots and trousers spattered with mud, his rough hat gripped in his hands, and anxious to let him know that during last night's thunderstorm, lightning had struck a great oak tree. "It toppled, laird," Shaw said, "and it's completely flattened old Norval Smith's threshing barn."

In his dream, Alasdair recalled, he had heard the storm. It had been real. *Not* his heart cracking in two.

Well, that was a relief.

"Was anyone injured?" he quickly asked.

"Thank God, no, laird. But the Smiths were badly spooked, and their animals, too. Their horses broke away from their stables, and a whole flock of sheep is scattered. And you know how frail Norval is."

"To be sure. Let's go there at once." To Lister, standing near, Alasdair said, "Tell the mistress where I've gone, would you?"

"Of course, laird. Will you be wishing for breakfast before you go?"

"No, I thank you." With that, he was off and away to the stables, aware, with some shame, that his concern for the Smith family was tainted by his gratitude at having an excuse to go.

If he was running away, just a little, there was nobody who could possibly have suspected it.

To Fiona came the slow realization that she was being gently delivered from the depths of slumber into a new day. Goodness gracious, she was actually waking up, rather than stirring blearily from out of a restless doze. How novel, how incredibly, wonderfully, amazingly, miraculously novel.

She sighed happily and stretched, filled with an unusually powerful sense of well-being. She was rested. And naked. *And* her body felt . . . well-loved. Quickly, now, she opened her eyes, looking for Alasdair.

But he was gone.

A disappointment, especially after last night.

Don't be impatient, you'll be seeing him again soon enough.

However, when Fiona had bathed and dressed, and made her way downstairs, Lister informed her that the laird was already gone out. A further disappointment, but hardly a tragedy. She had, after all, slept uncharacteristically late. Cheerfully Fiona thanked him and went on to the breakfast-room.

The disposition of a widow's bedstead, should she remarry and die, without new issue, before her current spouse does.

The age at which a young man might become a soldier.

The proper investigatory procedure for anyone suspected of being a witch.

The protocol for May Day celebrations (with specific additional instructions during a leap year).

The invalidation of a wedding ceremony performed when the presiding minister is observed to be in an obvious state of intoxication.

The punishment for arson.

The formalities of becoming a guardian of orphaned children.

The sale of personal possessions acquired in a state of summer madness.

The resolution of violent disputes among elderly siblings.

The proclamation that any calf born an albino automatically belongs to the chieftain or his designated successor.

Isobel sat back on her knees, her brain whirling. The Tome was simply *stuffed* with rules, procedures, and ordinances, as well as the occasional retraction or clarification, as in the archaic material about witches, demons, and spells. She felt a delightful shudder ripple up her spine. How confusing it all was, yet so endlessly fascinating. And she was only up to page 418.

She glanced at the elaborate ormolu clock set on the fireplace mantel and gasped. The breakfast hour had already commenced, and she was going to be late again. She didn't want that. Mealtimes had become so pleasant; she'd had such nice conversations with Duff lately. It had been a long, long time since a gentleman had taken such an interest in her, and she in him. He was so intelligent, and so handsome. At first, it had been difficult to notice these attributes, but it was as if her perception had somehow, mysteriously, begun to sharpen.

Quickly Isobel closed the Tome and put it back into the cabinet, pleased to notice that it was getting easier and easier to move it.

Sheila lifted her head from the sampler on which she was laboriously sewing a simple floral border. "Granny," she said suddenly, "are you always right?"

Old Dame Margery glanced at her over the shift she was mending. "Nay, child, only the Lord above is always right. Why do you ask?"

"Oh," replied Sheila vaguely, "I was just wondering. Granny, Granny, your hands are better, aren't they? The lady's magic salve worked, didn't it? And Granny, only see! I've finished one side entirely, isn't it pretty?"

"Very pretty, child, very pretty indeed." Margery smiled at her grandchild, and watched as that strange, opaque look passed from her eyes and she turned them once more to her sampler.

"Do it, man!" Duff said, with a certain urgency, to Grahame, Alasdair's manservant whom he'd summoned to his own rooms.

"All of it, sir?" asked Grahame, sounding more than a little astonished.

"Aye. Now! Before I lose my courage."

"Very well, sir." Grahame took his shears, drew a deep breath, and clipped off Duff's long beard. *Snip snip snip.* And it was done. Slowly Duff turned to look at himself in his mirror. After a minute inspection, he said:

"Shows off my jaw. Excellent. Now for a shave. And while you're at it, you may as well trim my hair."

"And eyebrows, sir?"

"Why not?" replied Duff, recklessly. "If a man's got a good face, there's no point hiding it."

"Very well, sir," Grahame repeated, and obediently set to his work.

Fiona sat at her desk, looking not at her notes and lists and letters, but out the window. It was a golden September day, breezy and mild, with perfect weather for the harvesting that had already begun. The sky was vast and so beautiful a blue it almost made her heart ache to see it.

Movement, somber color, caught her eye, and she saw Monty the gardener stumping past in his dark jacket and somehow managing to carry as if it were weightless the longest ladder she had ever seen. Curiosity, and the temptation of a golden morning, decided her.

In a flash Fiona was up and on her way outside.

Chapter 12

Alasdair had talked with the Smiths, seen for himself the damage to their barn, made arrangements for help. Now he sat astride his horse, aware that within him were competing desires.

A part of him wanted to hurry back to the castle, find Fiona and sweep her up to their bedchamber. Lose himself within her. And make her cry out, again and again, with pleasure, as she had done last night.

Yet another part resisted — stubbornly, very stubbornly.

It was this hard, seemingly intractable part of him that won out, and so he dismissed Shaw and rode, alone, to the shore of Loch Sgàthan, the site of that epic disaster fifteen years ago, today as smooth and as placid as if it had never — would never — roil up in a storm and swallow a handsome new boat and all its occupants.

He dismounted, flung the reins of his bay over its neck, allowed him to wander, knowing a single whistle would bring him back. He walked slowly to the rocky stretch of shore which met up with gently lapping water, that liminal space between solid earth and infinitely yielding water. He picked up a stone, expertly sent it skipping along the blue surface, and smiled a little, remembering Gavin's annoyance when here was something his little brother could do better.

Alasdair's smile faded as he thought back to the day Mòrag Cray, and all the others, had arrived from Glasgow. She came alone, without parents, the boon companion of one of the other young ladies, and no sooner had he caught sight of her than he'd fallen madly in love.

So too had Gavin.

They'd liked the same girl before, had competed to win the affections of this young woman or that young woman, but it had always, before, been in fun; had never tested the bond between them.

It was different with Mòrag.

For one thing, she was heart-stoppingly beautiful. And even though you could tell that she knew it, you couldn't bring yourself to hold it against her, for she was, simply, dazzling, with her luscious round figure, her wild black curls, those black eyes that always seemed to gleam as if with a secret you wanted to know.

Easily, effortlessly, she charmed all the young men who had come to Gavin's house-party — captivating them with her playful, teasing ways, swinging hot one moment and cold the next, flirting with you at breakfast and ignoring you at dinner, then casting warmly provocative glances at you just when you thought you'd give in to despair. She danced, she rode, she played cards to win and threw them down if she didn't, but in the next moment was laughing again and ready to find something else fun to do.

For a while Mòrag toyed with them all, and finally he himself — impetuous, bewildered, lovesick young fool — had one evening gathered all his courage and invited her for a stroll in the gardens.

There, underneath a golden harvest moon, alone with her for the very first time, he had told her he loved her, asked her to marry him. Had actually gone down on his knees.

And Mòrag laughed.

Don't be silly, she said. *Get up, before someone sees you like this.*

But don't you even like me? he had stammered, clambering to his feet.

Oh, I like you well enough, my boy, she'd replied with a shockingly brutal honesty, *but you aren't the heir to Castle Tadgh and all its holdings, are you?*

It was as if she had whipped out a little, sharp knife from her dainty slipper and stabbed him with it. His chest — his heart — literally hurt him.

My God, he had slowly said, *I ought to tell Gavin what you really are.*

She'd laughed again. *Do you think he'll believe you?*

He didn't know what to say to that.

Then Mòrag had whisked herself away and back inside, and he'd been left alone, his boy's pride cut to the quick, and wondering what he should do. Things were already strained between Gavin and himself, and if Gavin really cared for her, who was he to stand in his way?

He didn't know.

And so he did nothing.

His last glimpse of Mòrag had been of her standing on the boat's beautifully varnished deck, her arm slid possessively through Gavin's, her black hair, blown free from its demure chignon, blowing wildly in the rising breeze.

Gavin had organized the sailing expedition. He'd laughed at the wind, the clouds massing overhead, the ruffled waters of the loch. And everyone laughed along with him — except for himself. He'd tried to dissuade Gavin from taking out his boat and been kindly patted on his shoulder and dismissed. He'd appealed to their parents: Mother had told him not to be so nervous, and his father had urged him to come along so that he could learn from Gavin's skill in handling his new boat. In a rage, he'd flung himself away and over to his cousin Hewie's, and persuaded him to join him in several hard rounds of boxing until his equilibrium had returned and the image of Mòrag's lovely face had begun to fade from his mind. He'd ignored the wind and the rain, assuming, of course, that they were all back at the castle, safe and sound, and quite possibly primed to make fun of him for his silly caution.

It wasn't till very late at night, when the storm had finally waned, that some of his father's men had found him at Hewie's and told him the news.

They were all dead.

And he was now the laird of Castle Tadgh and all its holdings.

He had fallen again to his knees, only this time he was howling.

If only he had tried harder to dissuade them —

He could have somehow *made* them stay on land — Couldn't he?

Short of knocking them all senseless, what else could he have done?

He didn't know that, either.

Afterwards, later, when the mourners had come, he had met Mòrag's dazed parents, who came creeping into the Great Hall like mice, timid and overwhelmed, he a faded, stooping clergyman, she a graying slip of a woman in a cloak that had been repaired many times over. He'd understood at once Mòrag's determination to have Gavin, to reinvent herself as a nobleman's wife, a lady of superior social standing, wealthy, privileged, every whim obeyed. There was no way of knowing, then or now, if she'd truly cared for Gavin.

Not that it mattered, Alasdair thought, sending another stone skipping lightly along the water. They had gone, and left him alone. But Duff had come, and together they had — why, they had seized the day.

When he was twenty-three, he'd carried on a delightful flirtation with Lady Rodina Breck that had come to nothing. The year after that, he'd fancied himself in love with his distant cousin Kenna Salmond, but after a while his interest there had also dwindled away, into a tepid sort of friendship. His other *amours* had been strictly conducted with women who understood that a wedding ring was not in the offing. Marriage, then, had been the last thing on his mind.

Alasdair remembered, suddenly, Fiona turning the tables on him at the Keep o' the Mòr by saying sardonically, *Why aren't you married?*

He also remembered her saying to him, a few days after that, while sitting together in the Great Drawing-room:

I've observed how you wear your authority absolutely, but lightly. That you have a nice way with servants. That your clan obeys you without reserve. That you have great material wealth, and you live in a marvelous home in a breathtakingly beautiful part of the world. And yet . . .

She had broken off, on her face a sudden, unguarded look of sorrow, and soon after Janet Reid had playfully interrupted them.

Poor Janet — who, now that he thought about it, reminded him more than a little of Mòrag. But somehow he couldn't remember either of their faces particularly well anymore. How strange.

Now he found himself wondering what Fiona had been going to say to him that evening. He had, seemingly, everything in the world, and yet . . .

And yet there's something wrong with you.
And yet you're missing something.
And yet you've never married.
And yet you've never found love.

Alasdair now sank down onto his heels, his gaze fixed on the smooth, shimmering surface of the loch. Prior to his thirty-fifth birthday, his life had been for years very much like that: smooth and placid. Easy. He knew the rumors that had been circulating about him all these years, wildly exaggerated rumors of his dissolute way of life, and for these he cared not a whit. He was a good laird, dedicated to the welfare of his clan; what did it matter how he privately conducted himself?

Did he need an excuse for how he'd lived his life?

And yet . . .

Loss had shaped him, there was no doubt about it.

Maybe he'd become a limited sort of man.

In China, so he had heard, there was an enormous wall, stretching for thousands of miles, creating a high impenetrable boundary around its perimeter.

Maybe he was like that, too.

But there wasn't any point in beating one's chest and bemoaning the state of things. He hated when people did that. Besides, to complain about his lot would be like feeling sorry for yourself when you'd been given a perfectly practical and serviceable pair of socks for your birthday — and pining in a very silly way for, say, the moon. He was married now, and determined to fulfill his responsibilities.

And he liked Fiona, he respected her — wasn't that good enough?

It was going to have to be.

You couldn't, as the saying went, wring blood from a stone.

As if to prove his own point, he picked up one more stone and squeezed it in his fist, hard.

No blood, of course.

He was safe inside his wall.

His old familiar wall.

Alasdair sent the rock skipping across the shining blue water, watched it sink, then rose to his feet. He whistled for his horse, which came at once; without hurry he rode back to the castle where, when he stepped into the Great Hall, he overheard one of the maidservants saying to another, with a distinct note of awe in her voice:

"The mistress is up in a *tree?*"

"What?" Alasdair said. "Where?"

They turned quickly, each dipping a little curtsy, and the other maidservant said, "Out in the back, laird, so I heard, among the very treetops!"

Naturally he had to go.

As soon as he was outside he saw the tree with an enormously long ladder propped up against it, and there was Monty, too, with a gnarled hand upon one of the rails — all too casually it seemed to Alasdair. And there, high above, on the uppermost rung, was Fiona, peering with interest at something concealed among the branches.

She too gave the appearance of great casualness, and Alasdair could not suppress a vision of her falling, falling, lying crumpled and broken at his very feet. He had feared for her life as a captive among the Sutherlainns, but at least it had not been her fault she'd been thrust into danger. Nobody had forced her to climb this damned ladder!

He was afraid for her. And he didn't want to be afraid for her. To care about someone so much his heart was in his throat. From head to toe his body was alert to the possibility she might be harmed . . . Oh, God in heaven, here he went again. He glared down at Monty and said in a low, fierce growl:

"What the devil is my wife doing?"

"Goldfinch nest," said the laconic Monty. "Rare."

"And you let her go up there?"

He shrugged. "She wanted to see it."

"It never occurred to you that it might be dangerous?"

"Very sure-footed, the mistress is."

It was then that Fiona turned her head and smiled down at him, and Alasdair, with the ease of long habit, steeled himself to stay guarded, even as he smiled warmly back. He wasn't, he told himself firmly, being duplicitous. He hadn't done anything, or said anything, to deceive Fiona.

He'd simply acknowledged his boundaries.

That's all.

An understanding achieved within the private depths of a man's being: how small a thing, impossible to see or touch or quantify, how invisible to all the world. Yet a single silent act can change everything, altering the flow of events, influencing behavior, shaping outcomes. A butterfly in Africa, so it has been said, can — by flapping its wings in a certain way — trigger a hurricane thousands of miles away.

Thus did Alasdair shut a door.

At precisely the same moment that Fiona would, as it were, open a window.

High above, Fiona felt her heart bloom. It would have taken supernatural abilities for anyone to see that in the warmth of Alasdair's smile, the flash of his white teeth, the glow in his extraordinary eyes, that something was a little lacking, something was held back. Fiona only saw her handsome husband, only thought of last night's bliss, and felt a rush of fiery anticipation that made her grip a little harder at the ladder's railing.

Good God, was it possible — she caught her breath in wonderment — that she was falling in love? That such a gift was being given, when she'd thought it denied to her forevermore?

Yes.

Happiness seemed to roar through her, like a cataclysm released.

Yes.

Oh, but life was good! She gave a last quick glance to the little clutch of faintly speckled eggs all clustered together in their cozy nest. The promise of something rare and special; the hope of new life. Perhaps for her, too, and even now within her . . .

Could it be that her dreams were coming true at last?

"Goldfinches, laird!" she called joyfully. "We'll have goldfinches this autumn!"

"Naturally I am delighted to hear the news, madam," he responded smilingly, "but won't you come down? I want to talk to you."

Her brow furrowed. "Is everything all right with the Smiths?"

"Aye, to be sure."

"Oh, good," and Fiona began to descend, moving swiftly and safely to the ground. Not for her the dangerous tumble, the precipitous fall. And there he was, big and solid, strong and handsome, to have and to hold, forever. He took her hand, lifted it to his lips, and Fiona felt her knees go rather rubbery. "Oh, Alasdair," she murmured; she couldn't help it. And she didn't care if she sounded a little breathless, because she was.

"Madam," he said, and in his deep voice was a caress, and wasn't it lovely that he didn't let go of her hand after he had kissed it.

It was only Monty clearing his throat that seemed to break the spell. "I need the ladder elsewhere," he said dourly. "Could be we've worms in the apple grove."

"Oh no," replied Fiona, but absently, and Monty shot her a darkling look before reaching for the ladder. He *had* been planning to let her have some brilliant red and orange helichrysums, but now he changed his mind and grumpily trudged off by himself to see about those worms.

Alone in the garden, Fiona looked up at Alasdair. "What did you wish to talk about?"

"I'll tell you later," he said, softly, "tonight."

He wanted her. He *still* wanted her. She knew it; could feel it. And she wanted him, too: an answering desire, delicious and sensual, sparked fiercely, flew along her limbs, pooled in the secret juncture between her legs, and Fiona took a step closer to him. How wonderful it was to be married. How marvelous to — yes, to be in love. Why, she almost felt like a giddy girl again, as if the world was made over again, just for her.

"I look forward to that, Alasdair."

"As do I." He released her hand, only to offer his arm. "Would you care to stroll through the gardens?"

"I'd like nothing better."

They began to pace, in a deliciously leisurely way, along the graveled path. They talked about the harvest, and the annual clan celebration that was to come later in the month. They talked about horses, they talked about Fiona's plans to expand the kitchen garden, and they agreed to host a dinner party next week. Their conversation flowed as if with the sweep of a river, lightly and easily, and Fiona was happy, happy, even if, strangely, at one point her feet seemed to tangle clumsily underneath her, nearly tripping her, and unfortunately Alasdair had just the moment before turned away to look at something, and for a few uncomfortable moments she felt just like she had as a girl long ago, awkward and ungainly.

At dinner they were greeted by the extraordinary sight of Duff's newly shaven face. The upper part was tanned, and the lower part was dead white, giving the impression that he was somehow sporting the features of two entirely different people. Also, his unruly gray and white locks had been severely cut, and were — Alasdair squinted in disbelief — smoothed flat with pomade. And if that weren't enough, Duff was wearing formal evening clothes that had obviously been in storage for some time, the scent of mothballs adding a pungent top note to the sickly-sweet fragrance emanating from his hair.

The change, to say the least, was extraordinary, and Alasdair struggled to tamp down a juvenile desire to burst into raucous laughter. But it was more than that, he realized uncomfortably. He was surprised to notice that he actually resented what Duff had done. What the hell was the matter with Duff?

And what was the matter with *him*?

He looked away from Duff's strangely bare face, and accepted from a servant a delicately poached chicken breast. He turned his attention to that. For years their mother had said to him and Gavin, *If you can't say anything polite to each other, don't say anything at all,* which of course only egged them on the moment her back was turned.

No: he wasn't going to think about Gavin.

Or about walls or fences.

He was going to focus on the delicious meal set in front of him.

It wasn't until the third course arrived — a grilled

salmon and sweet mashed carrots piped into decorative swirls — that finally Duff said, in a loud aggrieved voice:

"Are you all *blind*, for the love of Christ?"

Alasdair glanced at him. "Your new look, Uncle?"

"Aye, damn it!"

"It's, ah, very noticeable."

"Noticeable? Is that all you can say, lad?"

"Give me a minute. I'm trying to think of a different adjective." Alasdair signaled for another glass of wine, hoping that his tone was light and playful, and not, as he feared, a trifle mean-spirited. Surely it was beneath him to begrudge what Duff had done.

Wasn't it?

Silence fell once again, heavy with Duff's displeasure. It was only broken when Isobel said, timidly, "I think you look very distinguished, sir."

"At last! *Le mot juste!* Thank you, madam!"

"And I think," said Fiona, "you look years younger, Uncle."

Mollified, Duff ran a hand across his chin. "Well, that's two compliments, at least."

Stubbornly, Alasdair only took a sip of his wine, and refused to meet his uncle's gimlet eye.

When dinner ended, Duff ostentatiously escorted Isobel to the Great Drawing-room and sat near her as she opened up her work basket.

"And what is that you're sewing, Miss Isobel?"

"Oh, it's — well, it's only a stuffed doll," replied Isobel, flustered and fluttery. "I made one for little Sheila, for her birthday, you see," and continued in her meandering way about the upcoming birthday of Lister's niece, and how she had asked Isobel so *very* nicely for a doll of her own, and how she had, after an intensive search, managed to find a piece of fabric that very nearly matched the little girl's own dress.

At first listening only to keep his back turned to his unappreciative nephew, Duff nodded perfunctorily, but as Isobel went on, found his interest in the project was piqued, and even made a few helpful suggestions which Isobel immediately championed with enthusiasm.

"Of *course*, my dear sir! How right you are! Yellow yarn for the hair! It will match dear little Erica's locks to a *nicety!* Only look — I've just the thing!" Isobel pulled an untidy ball of yarn from her work basket to show Duff, and promptly dropped it.

Duff picked it up and handed it to her with a courtly gesture that made his shoulder twinge a little, but he tried hard not to show it and was rewarded by the sight of Isobel, blushing a youthful pink, as she accepted it with a murmured word of thanks.

Alasdair, restless, oddly uneasy, opened his book, closed his book, opened it again, and just as quickly closed it. Finally he stood before Fiona.

"Madam," he said, "I find I don't care to wait for the tea-tray. If you'll excuse me?"

She was looking up at him, and in her eyes was a newly kindled light. "Would you like some company, laird?"

"Aye," he answered. "Aye, I would."

And so they left the drawing-room together, and made their way to their bedchamber, and there found pleasure, release, oblivion in each other's arms. And so the pattern was set, day after day, for twelve of them in total.

Fiona knew it was twelve, because she'd been counting them.

Her days of joy.

But on the thirteenth day, there came to her a certain sense that something wasn't quite right, though she couldn't exactly put her finger on it.

Something not quite right between herself and Alasdair.

It may have been her sensitive nature, or the fact that she was reflexively observant; who knows? He was warm, he was affectionate, he was passionate. Yet it was as if — oh, she hardly knew how to describe it. Like being on a boat, pulling away, watching someone you cared for inexorably, irretrievably, recede into the distance?

That night, after tossing about for several hours, she drifted into shallow sleep, and dreamed that she was hungry, so hungry. Starving. After fighting through a deep dark thicket, filled with bristling brambles that pricked and stung, she stumbled across a chunk of bread, stale and moldy-looking, and as reluctantly she reached for it, into her mind popped the old adage *Half a loaf is better than none.*

And in her dream Fiona kicked the bread away, shouting angrily, *It's not, it's not better, it's not nearly enough!*

And a few hours later, having eaten an extremely large and satisfying breakfast, she went to her morning-room to jot down some notes for the dinner party's menu, sketch out some additions to her kitchen garden, examine a sheaf of papers she'd found stuffed inside a vase in one of the storage closets. They were, she realized in surprise, thirty years old — tradesmen's bills for tasseled, green velvet window-hangings, expensive chairs and sofas, costly decorative tables with fine mother-of-pearl inlay, as well as invoices for artwork, both paintings and sculptures. Why, these were all items in the Great Drawing-room. And now Fiona felt her eyes go wide in astonishment. The sum was astronomical. Had all those people been paid? She'd need to talk to Lister —

A maidservant came in then, with the mail, and

Fiona pushed aside the old bills to eagerly receive them. Another letter from Nairna, joyful, reporting with insouciance that she'd gotten so big so early, and had been experiencing some pain — only the ligaments stretching, said Tavia Craig, to be expected as there was a good chance she was carrying twins; and so she'd been put to bed, and how kind everyone was, she was surely the most petted, most pampered person in the world!

Twins, thought Fiona, how splendid for Nairna! It wasn't surprising she had to be in bed — Fiona had heard this was quite common in such situations. Which reminded her: there was a tenant farmer's wife who'd already had one set of twins and now was hugely pregnant again, and fatalistically expecting another set. *I'll visit her tomorrow*, Fiona thought, *and wasn't there a problem with some strange fungus in their shed? Did the vinegar treatment I sent over for her husband to try on the walls solve it?* Something else to follow up on, too.

Fiona turned to Dallis's letter; she had written, in comical resignation, that her rambunctious toddler insisted on trying on all the baby clothes both old and new, and then added an indignant diatribe against people who *would* pat her stomach and talk to it as if she herself wasn't there.

Fiona smiled, then looked down at her own flat stomach. Perhaps . . . perhaps . . .

She reached for a fresh piece of paper and picked up her quill.

Maisie
Elspet
Rose
Ùna
Annag
Bonni

And then:

Ethan
Archibald
Carson
Tàmhas
Domnall
James

Weren't they all beautiful names for babies? She looked out into the garden, dappled all green and gold in the vivid early-autumn sun, and wished she could stop thinking about her silly dream of nasty bread and her own violent rejection of it.

The day wound itself along, busy, challenging, interesting, filled with minor disasters and small triumphs, and she managed to suppress her odd uneasiness until they'd all gathered once again in the Great Drawing-room. She had her sewing — and Alasdair was laughing at something Duff had said — and Isobel was working happily on her puzzle —

And Fiona said, "Laird, I found some old bills."

He turned to her, smiling, and she wondered why, precisely, she didn't feel like returning his smile.

"Did you, lass?"

"Yes, all for things here in this room, hundreds of pounds' worth. Lister couldn't find any records of their being paid, so I suppose I'll need to contact the merchants and artists right away."

"I'll take care of it. You needn't bother."

"Oh, I don't mind. I'd be glad to handle it."

"Nay, I'll do it."

"I insist, Alasdair. Surely you have better things to do."

"These events occurred long before your arrival. I'd prefer to look into it myself."

Fiona couldn't stop herself. Pointedly she looked over at the green velvet window-hangings. "Three hundred and eighty pounds for the fabric alone," she said with a sniff. "And nineteen pounds for the tassels. Dear me."

At that, Duff turned around. "Are you talking about those green curtains? God in heaven, the way my brother-in-law Stuart's eyes bugged out when he heard how much they cost! I laughed so hard I nearly gave myself an apoplexy! He looked *exactly* like a toad! Your mother's renovations, lad, began in this room, but you wouldn't remember that, of course — you were only a wee bairn, but *I'll* never forget it, for Stuart came to stay with me for nearly a year. Maybe more. The noise, the dust, all those extra people in the castle were unbearable, he said." Duff shook his head, but nostalgically now. "It was like old bachelor times for Stuart and me both. The fun we had! And Gormelia could rip up the castle to her heart's content."

Alasdair said nothing, and Isobel put in, diffidently, "She certainly had good taste."

"So everybody said," Duff agreed. "Gormelia was famous among the Eight Clans for her deft ways with furniture and paintings and carpet! Buying, and buying again! Stuart used to say that the only reason she married him was for the opportunity to redo the castle." He chuckled. "Well, she certainly took on a job for herself. Fifty bedchambers at least, and I don't know how many drawing-rooms there are. But Gormelia did, you can be sure. Never knew anyone so obsessed with furnishings! Heaven help you if you moved a cushion to a different spot on a sofa." Thoughtfully he added, "Not exactly the warmest person in the world, I must say. I always thought she liked *things* better than people. One day I said it to

her face, and she booted me out on the spot and told
me to stay away. Bit of an overreaction, I thought, but
in any event I never came back until the funerals."

Fiona looked at Alasdair. On his face was a
wooden expression, which as she watched shifted
into a pleasant one as he returned her gaze and said
lightly, "Are we having macaroons this evening with
the tea-tray, my dear? I hope so."

Her impulse was to reply in kind, politely, but
instead she said, taking an instant dislike to being
addressed as *my dear* in that somehow impersonal
tone, and still not sure why she felt so stubborn about
the whole business: "Gracious, to think of spending
almost four hundred pounds on window-hangings!
I've never heard of such a thing."

He only shrugged, and Fiona went on, doggedly,
"Maybe this is why I've never really liked this room."

Still he was silent.

Fiona felt her back stiffening.

And before she could prevent it, she found herself
paraphrasing Sheila — *little Sheila!* — and saying
snippily, "I suppose your mother was too busy stuff-
ing the attics with perfectly good furniture to do
anything for the children of Tadgh. Including you
and your brother, I daresay," she added fiercely.

Alasdair did not reply, and Duff said, "Alasdair
and Gavin did all right, lass. They had each other,
you know."

"That may be so, Uncle, but I still feel like ripping
down those curtains. I can tell they're going to bother
me more every day. Alasdair, can I put them somewhere else? In the attics? Assuming, of course, I can
find any space in there."

His eyes had the cool brilliant gleam of citrine. "I
appreciate your soliciting my opinion," he said lightly,
"but I couldn't care less what you do with them."

The words were pleasant, yet Fiona felt as if she'd been shoved into the icy waters of Wick Bay. She stared at him. What on earth was going on here? She wasn't insulting him, wasn't harming him! Was it because she had been criticizing a long-dead mother-in-law whom she had never met? Not, perhaps, very high-minded of her, but what sort of person cared more for *furniture* than for her children?

"Fine!" she snapped. "I'll have them taken away first thing in the morning."

Alasdair shrugged, and opened up his book.

"You really don't care where they go?" She could hear the shrillness in her voice and hated it, but didn't seem able to subdue it.

"I really don't."

"Fine! I'll have them dumped in the loch then." No sooner had the hasty words come out of her mouth than she wished them unsaid. God, the loch! Why had she said that? The place where his family had perished! A scarlet flush of shame blazed on her face, her neck, her chest, and for a moment Fiona longed to be a victim of spontaneous combustion and disappear into a little, smoldering pile of ashes — especially when she saw how Alasdair's expression was now one of remote, polite, utter blankness. He gazed back at her as he might look at an odd sort of bug that had landed on his shoe.

Was this the man to whom in the nights she'd given herself, body and soul? Who had brought her to the heights of unimaginable pleasure? And to whom she had, equally, given pleasure?

Hadn't she?

She *thought* she had.

It was as if their connection was painfully fragile, ephemeral, like an exquisite flower — whose time was bound to be brief — fading in front of her eyes.

Really, now that she thought about it, not unlike
the dream of Logan which also had turned to mist
and disappeared.

Fiona blinked. She remembered something else
from that night when they had first made love, *really*
made love. Alasdair, calling out in his own dream, as
if desperately trying to summon those lost in the loch.
And after, she now realized, distracting her from
talking about it. And so now, with a hard, desperate
edge — half wanting to clutch at him, half wanting
to hurt him — she said abruptly, "Who is Mòrag?"

Alasdair's jaw tightened, but coolly he said, without looking up from his book, "Only ancient history,
my dear."

"Stop calling me that!" she snapped, and with a
violence that surprised her, flung her sewing to the
floor, scattering pins everywhere. "And answer me!"

"We may be married, but that doesn't mean I'm
obliged to dredge up meaningless anecdotes from my
past, simply for the purpose of satisfying your curiosity."

Fiona reeled back, as if from an actual blow, her
body vibrating with rage and frustration. "You —
you're — you're *nothing* to me," she said, nearly chok-
ing in her urgent desire to hurt him, to wound him for
pushing her away. "I'm so sorry I married you!"

She heard Isobel gasp and glanced over to see both
her and Duff looking shocked. With *his* eyes bugged
out like that, *he* looked like a toad too, Fiona thought
meanly. In fact, they both did. She turned her furious
glance to Alasdair, who, with a slow deliberateness
that seemed only to mock her, closed his book, set
it aside, stood up, and said, with that same remote,
light, frighteningly courteous voice:

"Nothing. I see. I'm afraid, though, that you're
stuck with me. My apologies for being such a bad

bargain." He bowed slightly. "A most elucidating evening. And now I bid you good night."

He turned toward the door, and Fiona shrieked, "How *dare* you walk away from me! Don't you *dare* leave this room!"

But he did leave the room, and without pausing, without a backward glance.

And with a vicious gesture she swept her work-box off the sofa, creating an even bigger mess of needles, scissors, thimbles, pins, a wild ugly jumble of thread.

In the heavy silence that seemed to blanket the room like a looming black raincloud, Fiona found herself shaking from head to toe. Good Lord, had that really been her, shrieking like a harpy, flinging things around? What had happened to calm, rational, reserved Fiona? Gone, she thought bitterly, gone like petals dropping from a dead flower. She turned her eyes to Duff, and watched in acrid amusement as he seemed to shrink back a little.

"Do *you* know who Mòrag is?"

"Was," he replied, but cautiously, as if fearful she'd start throwing things at him, too. "She was on the boat that went down that day. They said she was young and beautiful. But that's all I know."

"Of course she was young and beautiful," said Fiona, in a hard, bitter voice. "And I'm neither. I'm jealous of a dead woman."

"Oh, Fiona *dear*," Isobel said uneasily.

The minutes ticked by, with agonizing slowness, some ten or fifteen of them, Fiona guessed, and then a servant, William, came in with the tea-tray. Well, here was one small comfort, she thought, he'd come too late for the fireworks. And speaking of fireworks, it occurred to her that it felt as if her entire *life* had spontaneously combusted, and all she had left was a pile of black ashes.

Nothing seemed to matter anymore.

Carefully William set the tray on the low table before her. Of *course* there were macaroons. Delicious macaroons. She knew that if she tried to eat one, it would stick in her throat like sawdust.

"Thank you, William," she said.

"You're welcome, mistress," he answered, then crouched down and reached for the jumble of threads.

"No. I'll do that."

"Mistress?" He was puzzled.

"I'll do it. Thank you, William. You may go."

"Very well, mistress." He stood, left the room, still looking puzzled.

Isobel approached, moving as one would toward a formerly friendly dog who had just sunk its teeth into someone's ankle. "Fiona dear, please let me help you."

"No. I made the mess, and I'll clean it up. Have a macaroon." And Fiona laughed without humor. She slid from the sofa to kneel on the soft floral-patterned carpet, where with an awful punctiliousness she began picking at the spools of thread.

Twisting her hands together, Isobel stood uncertainly. She looked from Fiona to Duff, whose expression was as taken aback as her own. "I'm — I'm not hungry," Isobel said softly, apologetically. "Can't I at least pick up *something?*"

"No."

In Fiona's voice was nothing but steel, and Isobel's eyes began to fill with tears.

"I think I'll — I think I'll go to bed then, Cousin. If you'll excuse me?"

"By all means." Fiona did not look up.

Duff hastily rose to his feet. "I think I'll do the same," he said. At the doorway he paused, with a discombobulated Isobel at his side, and added awkwardly: "Well — good night, lass."

"And to you," Fiona responded mechanically, not lifting her eyes from the seemingly impossible snarl of colorful thread. And she too added something, only with terrible irony.

"Sweet dreams."

Chapter 13

Fiona could not have said how long it took for her to pick up everything from the carpet as well as from the polished wood floor beyond — how many minutes (hours?) it took to neatly separate the spools of thread. Her legs hurt from kneeling, and behind her eyes there developed a painful ache from the strain of peering so minutely in the flickering light of the candles. Somewhere in the back of her mind, she realized she didn't have to restore the thread to its usual tidy state. So what if she missed a pin or two? She *knew* it wasn't of any real consequence. But still she persisted, her fingers moving without conscious volition as the great violent storm of rage and frustration within her slowly receded, leaving her awash in a dreadful all-encompassing state of —

Fear.

A cold, nasty, desperate sort of fear.

What if Alasdair hated her now?

After their inauspicious beginning, things had been going so well between them. *Better* than well.

Yes, swimmingly, said a cruel little voice inside her brain, forcing her to think of the loch, a sinking boat, the loss of life and hope.

Her eyes caught a tiny glimmer underneath a large wing chair and grimly she inched toward it, still on her knees. Yes, another pin. God, God, had there been *millions* inside her work basket? She picked it up and knew a brief temptation to stab herself with it as she realized she had gradually crept all the way across the drawing-room to the green velvet curtains — curtains she now hated with a vehemence she knew wasn't rational. But still. Was she really going to have them taken away tomorrow?

She had no answer.

The thought of tomorrow only made her feel anxious, weak, alone.

Quick, make a list, she told herself hastily. Order out of chaos. Her old standby. It had never failed her. Do this, then this, and after that, do this.

For years, making lists and keeping busy had allowed her to move on reasonably well from her . . . disappointment. It had saved her from falling into despair. Hers had not been a perfect life, of course, but it had been a useful one, a productive one. How many items had she crossed off her lists? Hundreds. Thousands. There was something to be said for that.

Making lists had proved to be an excellent coping method.

But it failed her tonight.

Like a magician whose tricks failed to materialize, her mind felt undone; she couldn't think of a single comforting task that called out to her.

Tomorrow was only blank slate, frightening in its abject emptiness.

A creeping panic came upon Fiona now, and even though she wasn't actually cold, she shuddered as if with a chill. Her chest felt tight, and it was hard to draw a complete breath. Quickly she stood, her eyes searching the room for — what?

For help.

For Alasdair.

She had enough presence of mind to drop the miscreant pin into her work basket, but that was all. Then she was hurrying to her bedchamber. *Their* bedchamber. She wanted to run, but it was only *not* running that kept her from giving way to true hysteria, especially since traversing the labyrinth of stairs and passageways in the dead of night was bad enough. She half-expected doors to fly open and monsters to leap out at her, or to feel an icy hand grabbing at her skirts from behind. *Oh, the Sack Man, the Sack Man,* her old nurse would say with gloomy relish, *he'll put you in his nasty sack and there's nothing you can do to stop him. He'll eat you alive, and laugh at your screams . . .*

Fiona's heart pounded hard, frantically, as if trying to escape the confines of her chest. *There's no such thing as a Sack Man,* she told herself, *I am safe, I am real, slow down, just put one foot in front of the other, BREATHE —*

Nonetheless it still seemed like years, agonizing years, before she finally found herself in the long high corridor of the laird's great suite. There was faithful Cuilean, who promptly rose to greet her, tail wagging, then subsided into a large furry ball at her soft command.

She put her hand on the doorknob, reassuring in its solidity. Turned the knob. Slipped into their bedchamber. Oh, God, what if he wasn't even there?

He was, he was. The candles were extinguished — or had burned down — but the heavy draperies had been left open to admit wan, spectral moonlight, and she could make out his big long form in the bed.

Fiona waited for her heart to slow its rapid beat, but it seemed she might have to wait forever for it to do that: a frantic need had her in its grip and her heart, her body, knew it. She *had* to span the divide between them, she *had* to turn back the clock and restore what they'd had, only a day before. She took five, six paces into the room. And in a strange reversal, into the dimness she said:

"Are you awake?"

There was a pause.

"Aye," he answered, without inflection. Even so, that one word was enough. In an instant she was at the bed — and ripping back the covers — and *on* the bed, on *him*. He was on his back and with unhesitating boldness she straddled him, groin to groin, her elegant, delicate gown of celestial blue crêpe puddling in disarray around her thighs.

Was it genuine desire that was driving her? Or something else (pure desperation, for example) that made her behave like an animal leaping upon its prey? Not for the world would Fiona pause to try and figure it out. It was time for *action,* not words, or so she told herself, and so she grabbed Alasdair's wrists, shoved them up and back on either side of his head as if restraining unwilling arms; leaned down and pressed her breasts onto his bare hard chest, and urgently found his mouth with her own. She kissed him roughly, wildly, all moistness and heat and sinuous urgency.

For a few moments — possibly the longest, most terrible interlude in her whole entire life — his only response was absolute stillness. Cold, cold despair threatened to rise up within her and defiantly Fiona tightened her fingers around Alasdair's wrists and ground her hips against his.

Then:

His tongue met her own, demandingly; his shaft, now rapidly hardening beneath her. From Fiona's throat rose a guttural noise of satisfaction and with a provocative twist of her head she withdrew from their kiss, only to slide her tongue, wet, knowing, along the underside of his jaw, to the hard column of his throat to where the skin was tender. And without warning, but with provocative deliberation, she bit him — just hard enough to leave her mark upon him.

Alasdair jerked, and softly she laughed. Laughed when with ridiculous ease he broke her hold upon his wrists, brought his hands to her shoulders, pushed her upright and slid his hands down to play upon her breasts, still hidden within the soft silken bodice of her gown.

But her laughter was silenced as Alasdair's clever fingers, his strong body beneath hers, evoked unspoken answer from her own body, and Fiona heard herself begin to pant, felt a molten energy begin to ignite within her. Lust. Glorious all-consuming lust. She lifted her hands to cover his, pressed fiercely upon them as if to urge him on. *He* laughed then, pulled down upon the fabric of her bodice, and when it resisted, with a casual purposefulness he simply tore it apart, baring her breasts to him.

Fiona registered first the sound of the crêpe ripping and gasped, a giddy half-shocked excitement rippling through her; next she felt the sudden sensation of cool air upon her exposed chest, and then Alasdair was sitting up, arms wrapped around her, his mouth suckling at her so insistently, so hungrily and hotly, that she began pulling at her skirts, wrenching them up and out of the way, until she found his hardness, until she was upon him, until she joined them together, and they were one, together, moving in the most primal dance of all, and all at once she knew.

He was the center of everything.

He was *home* to her, everything that was familiar and real and solid.

And wonderful.

And true.

The past had been swept away; she had opened up her heart again, she had changed. And change had made her free.

The words tumbled out of her in a breathless rush.

"Oh, Alasdair, oh, Alasdair, I'm so sorry for what I said, please forgive me," and then the naked vulnerable truth, "I love you, I love you so much, I —"

He didn't stop, but kissed her, his mouth slanted hard on hers as they moved together, and she thought she might go mad with pleasure, but even as she kissed him back she felt the cool machinery of her mind stir to life. She tried to push aside the unwelcome intrusion, to drift away on the powerful tide of passion, but her brain wouldn't be denied. It pointed out, in a horrible, dry, rational way:

You told him you loved him. Then what happened?

Be quiet, you. Go away. This feels too good. We're back where we were last night, everything is all right again. Oh God, this feels so good.

The inexorable rejoinder came back. *You told him you loved him. And what did he say?*

It's stupid to say such a thing and expect to hear it repeated back to you.

Is it? coolly observed her brain. *My, how easily you're satisfied.*

Shut up, shut up! Fiona hoped she didn't blurt those words out loud, but by then it was too late. It was as if a beautiful symphony had been waylaid by another song being played at the same time, jangly and discordant and distracting.

"Stop," she said to Alasdair.

He did stop, almost as if he too was aware of the discordance. Fiona made herself pull away from him, and sat, as stiff and straight as a poker, among the rumpled bedclothes. She was just as rumpled, she knew, with her ripped gown and tumbled skirts, and no doubt her hair was a ghastly mess, but to this she was indifferent. Her only remedial act was to pull together the two pieces of her bodice, creating a mockery of modesty. She watched as Alasdair leaned his back against the intricately carved headboard, carelessly pulled up a blanket to his waist. His broad chest was damp with sweat and he smelled so good —

Fiona set aside this tempting fact. Instead she folded her hands in her lap, just as if they were sitting fully clothed in a warm well-lit drawing-room. And she said, in a level tone:

"You don't love me, do you?"

She saw that tempting chest rise and fall as he took a deep breath. "Fiona," he said, "lass, let's not do this."

"There, I suppose, is your answer."

He reached out to cover her hands with his own big warm one. "I like you," he said, with unmistakable sincerity. "I like you, lass. And I admire you, I respect you. It's more than a lot of married people can claim to share."

"True."

"Isn't that enough for you?"

"No."

"You mean that?"

"Yes."

"Well," he said, "that's a problem, for it's all I have to give to you."

Fiona pushed his hand away. "It's not enough."

"You knew this was to be a marriage not of our choosing." His voice was a little cooler, a little harder. "Your expectations — they ask too much of me. You've no right to be changing the terms as we go along."

Here again the words tumbled out of her. "Life is *about* change, don't you see that? It's because of *you,* you wonderful maddening man, that I've finally learned it! *You* taught me how to love, truly love, and I don't want to give that up!"

He stared at her. And finally he replied: "Can't we agree to meet in the middle? Each bringing to the table what we have?"

"Oh, Alasdair, don't you understand?" It was a plea, raw and vulnerable. "It's not enough for me — not enough after all these years! I'm afraid I'll dwindle away, until my existence is nothing more than — than a pathetic half-life. I'll be a machine that gets things done — that's all. I'll be a ghost." Two great fat tears spilled from her eyes and angrily she swiped them away. "I won't live that way anymore! I want a real, full life! Can't you understand? Don't you want that?"

"I have a real life that I enjoy," he answered, coldly now. "And here's what I think, for what it's worth. I think you're being greedy."

Greedy.

The word sounded so harsh. Like a reproach, a slap in the face. A confirmation, once again, that she simply wasn't good enough. Would never be good enough. In that instant Fiona wanted to crumple. Wanted to bury herself under the covers, hide her head as well. But then her pride reasserted itself. She lifted her chin:

"You are, of course, entitled to your opinion."

"I thank you," Alasdair said, in his tone a certain irony, and he saw Fiona sit up even straighter, if that were possible. Coldness, irony, detachment — all excellent defenses for a man who felt he'd been sent reeling with his back against a wall. Christ in His heaven, he thought with more than a prickle of resentment, but he hadn't wanted to have this conversation at all. What was the point of all this yapping? What could possibly be gained from it?

Why, he asked himself, couldn't she simply leave well enough alone?

There she was, some three feet away from him, her silvery-blonde hair shimmering in the pale faint glow of the moonlight, her eyes huge and blazing in her slender face, her body lithe and taut, to it clinging a subtle intoxicating scent of wild roses. She was tousled, disheveled, magnificent. Even now, with hostility practically crackling out loud between them, he wanted her.

But when she spoke again, there was nothing in her manner which suggested that any sort of rapprochement was possible. She was as dry and analytical as a lawyer. "You say you have only *liking* to give me? But not love?"

"That is so."

"It's a lie. It's not that you *can't* love me. It's that you *won't*. There's a world of difference, Alasdair."

She knew. She knew. Her words were like a brilliantly aimed sucker punch to his solar plexus, hard and painful, but he willed himself not to show it. "You think yourself very shrewd."

"But I'm right, aren't I?"

No matter what he said next, he was doomed. If he told the truth, that she *was* right. If he denied it — he *would* be lying. He was many things, but not a liar. Which meant he had nowhere to turn, nowhere to run. Savagely he ran a hand through his hair. And to think that lately he'd felt so confident, so buttressed by his certainty it was all going to be easy. It was all going to be fine. *Smooth sailing.* He'd laugh at himself if it wasn't so bitter a humor that now took hold of him. Oh yes, very smooth sailing. His wife was staring at him as if she'd like nothing better than to throttle him. Or worse.

"Answer me," she hissed.

All at once Alasdair wished there was a cattle meet somewhere he could sneak off to in the middle of the night. But weariness swept over him then, weighty and hard, implacable, as if pinioning him to the bed. This, he thought, is what Sisyphus felt like, after being made to push a boulder up a steep hill all day long. It almost seemed like a boulder was on top of *him*. Would this excruciating, pointless exchange never end? "Oh, for God's sake, Fiona, have done," he said heavily. "I've had enough."

He heard her sharply indrawn breath. Then she said, "I've had enough also."

"Good. Let's go to sleep. And if you like —" He exerted himself; he wanted to be generous. He wanted to at least offer her something; said, "If you like, we can talk more tomorrow."

"No. No more talking. Enough."

"It's up to you."

"Is it? How nice."

Alasdair didn't know what to say to that, so he only replied, "Good night then." He slid back down, feeling with intense relief the pleasant sensation of his head resting against his pillows. But he realized she hadn't moved. "Lie down, Fiona, under the blankets. You must be cold."

She was still staring at him. "Yes. I *am* cold."

"Come under the bedcovers, then."

"It's apparently escaped your notice that I'm still wearing my evening-gown."

"Does it matter?" He could hear how he was almost slurring his words with drowsy fatigue. His eyelids were impossibly heavy. Sleep, like an irresistible sorceress, beckoned.

Did it matter? For the life of her, Fiona didn't know how to answer him. Why not crawl underneath the warm bedclothes, still in her gown and jewelry and blue silk slippers? What possible difference would it make?

She thought about it.

Somehow — it came to her in slow realization — somehow it would seem like giving in.

Involuntarily she shuddered. She really *was* cold. Her fingers were starting to feel numb. Alasdair, she saw, was already deeply asleep; his set, shuttered expression had given way to an unguarded relaxation.

Well, there's added insult to injury, Fiona told herself with a kind of wry desolation. He had slammed a door in her face and then promptly fell asleep, while she sat ramrod-straight, exhausted yet wide awake, feeling utterly alone.

Blearily, hopelessly, she got off the bed and eased from it one of the heavy blankets, then took one of her pillows and went quietly into the dark, high-ceilinged passageway off the bedchamber. She meant to go into her dressing-room, but somehow her steps led her to that mysterious locked door and she found herself standing in front of it with her hand on a doorknob that turned but did not yield.

An *actual* closed door, and not simply a metaphor for her life, Fiona thought with that same bleak amusement. She gave the doorknob a last futile twist and made her way into her dressing-room where she lit a single candle.

Without haste she folded the blanket into a makeshift bed, changed into her heaviest nightgown, took off her jewelry, brushed and braided her hair, cleaned her teeth. She did all this methodically, like an automaton. And finally she blew out the candle, lay down, and snugged the blanket around her.

Ha, I've made my bed and now I must lie in it, she thought, staring into the obliterating darkness. She couldn't even make out the shapes of the armoires, the

dressing-table, anything. She did catch a whiff of the
rose perfume she had, earlier in the evening, dabbed
with joyful anticipation behind her ears. That seemed
a lifetime ago. She had been reasonably happy then.

And now?

Now she was — nothing. Empty. With nothing to
say, nothing to talk about.

The long minutes ticked past, one after the other,
just as slowly as they had in the Great Drawing-room.

Eventually, she supposed, they would all add up
into an hour. And then another hour. Morning would,
whenever it was ready, come.

A deep sigh escaped her.

She turned onto her side.

She wished that rose scent would go away.

Oh, she was weary, so weary. But not the least bit
sleepy. Her mind churned uselessly, on and on. Was
she right? Was she wrong? Was she greedy and de-
manding? Was she foolish to have allowed herself to
fall in love with Alasdair Penhallow? And could these
things even be controlled? Her love for Alasdair was
like — oh, God, it was like a wild riot in her heart.
Unstoppable, as exuberant as wildflowers in the
spring. Nothing you could do would ever keep them
from blooming in dazzling profusion, as far as the eye
could see.

Suddenly her brain served up a new idea: *I could
try to make him love me.*

And just as quickly it was rejected. What, manipu-
late Alasdair, lie to him, be someone she wasn't? And
what sort of sorry love would *that* be?

No, he had made it clear what his limits were. And
you couldn't lose what you never had.

People were — what they were. She couldn't help
but feel more than a little foolish for issuing her passionate speech to him about change.

Take *her,* for example.

She thought back to the second night of her marriage, when Alasdair had come strolling toward the bed, naked, jolting her into awareness of his intense and alluring masculinity. *Had your fill?* he had said in his deep and equally alluring voice, mocking her, unsettling her. At that moment she had somehow splintered into different Fionas: the cool, efficient, everyday Fiona; a cracklingly angry Fiona; and, surprising her, a Fiona so alive with desire she practically caught on fire with it.

Here in the silence of her dark, dark dressing-room she could almost feel herself reverting to that first, fundamental, reliable Fiona. It was like putting on an old pelisse that you'd had for years. It wasn't in the best condition, perhaps, and was tight-fitting in certain areas (because you'd outgrown it?). But it was familiar. And with familiarity came a certain comfort. A certain sense of safety, cocooned in which she could acknowledge that a great love was, clearly, to be denied to her. Well, that was life, wasn't it? And after all, she had a lot to be thankful for.

As if by magic, a sheet of paper presented itself to her mind's eye.

Good health
Meaningful work
A beautiful house to live in
A library filled with books
Delicious meals
Wonderful rides with Gealag
A husband who doesn't berate or beat me

This imaginary sheet of paper, only partially filled with her neat, efficient writing, seemed so vivid that Fiona felt she could almost reach out in the darkness to touch it.

And there, you see? she told herself. *You're back to making lists again. How splendid. Congratulations.*

If there was a rather sardonic quality to this little interior commentary, well, she could live with that.

And immediately, with a sort of horrible fluency, she turned her mind to the tasks that awaited her tomorrow — no, today, actually, given how late in the night it was. Hand over those old bills to Alasdair (there was no point in hanging on to those, that was plain). Talk to Cook about the dinner party. Visit the heavily pregnant farmer's wife. Take the lovely, elegant, damaged, celestial-blue evening-gown, cut it into small pieces, and stow them away in her scrap-bag. Oh, and it was brewing day; she must see how the fermentation was coming along. Write letters to her sisters, and to Mother —

Suddenly Fiona knew a sharp, painful stab of homesickness. For soft, sweet Mother. For her old bedchamber, in the high turret room with a view that seemed to go on forever. For Wick Bay. For Mother's cheerfully messy solarium, the horribly draughty drawing-room, even the interminable parade of mutton dishes. Even — yes — even for Father.

She'd be there right now, if . . .

If Alasdair had married one of the other women.

Bold, vivacious Janet Reid. She would have been a spirited mate for Alasdair. Perhaps, in time, she'd have matured. Mellowed. Possibly she would have been kinder to the servants.

And the dainty, ethereal Mairi MacIntyre? Not a terribly useful sort of girl, but oh so lovely to look at. Some men liked a wife high on a pedestal, as an ornament to admire from afar.

As for the bovine Wynda Ramsay and her obsession with the English *ton* and her execrable French — well, at least she had a tremendous bosom, which is more than *she* could say about herself.

Oh, that wretched clan decree! If not for that, she'd never have met Alasdair. Married him. Would never have fallen in love with him. She'd still be home in Wick Bay, no doubt, and wouldn't that have been better?

Fiona wrestled herself onto her other side, bunching the blanket firmly around her. She tried to tell herself it was true.

When Alasdair entered the breakfast-room that morning, he did so a little warily, not knowing quite what to expect. How would it be between himself and Fiona? Hostile, difficult, peppered with barbed comments, thinly veiled insults? Would there be a loaded question, perhaps, about how well he had slept?

There she was in her place at the foot of the table, wearing a charming long-sleeved day-dress of softest periwinkle, her hair smoothly coiled into a low knot at the nape of her neck. She was her usual elegant self, slim, upright, neat as a pin and pretty as a picture.

She looked up from her teacup as he entered. Pleasantly she said, "Good morning, laird," and Alasdair was aware of a rush of relief.

"Good morning," he answered, and nodded at Duff and Isobel, who were, he noticed, eyeing him with trepidation before glancing with the same nervousness at Fiona. Yes, there *had* been quite a scene last night in the drawing-room, and no doubt they were expecting something of a similar nature.

But Fiona had obviously set the tone, and Alasdair gratefully took his own seat at the head of the table. Today was, after all, a new day. Perhaps they *could* talk things through. He saw that next to his plate and silverware was a dark red brocaded document folder.

He looked at Fiona.

"The old invoices," she said calmly, "for your review." And that was that. A servant offered her more tea, and with that same pleasant manner she accepted.

"Thank you," Alasdair answered, pushing aside the brocade folder with a sharp repugnance he didn't, at the moment, care to analyze.

"You're welcome."

Silence then filled the breakfast-room, which was illuminated by a particularly beautiful and piercing September sunlight, warm and golden. It wasn't until halfway through the meal that Alasdair became aware of that silence. Usually Isobel would be chattering about this or that. Duff might be mentioning his plans for the day, and urging Alasdair to join him. Fiona would at least be saying *something*.

It was then he realized that Duff and Isobel kept glancing between him and Fiona. And that Fiona, usually so hearty in her appetite, had barely touched her food. That underneath her eyes were the heavy dark circles of one who had not slept much the night before, if at all. But to this she had not referred, and had only sipped calmly at her tea.

"Madam," said Alasdair, "is your breakfast not to your liking?"

She turned her eyes — cool gray today — to him. "I find I'm not very hungry this morning, laird."

"Ah." He paused. "Are you unwell?"

"By no means."

"I'm glad to hear it."

"Thank you for inquiring."

"Of course."

It was all very civil. Her tone was still pleasant. So what exactly was bothering him? It was like having a pebble in your shoe. Such a small thing, yet impossible to ignore. Doggedly he continued:

"My bailiff Shaw says that the bull sent by the
Colling brothers has arrived. I know we talked about
riding out together to see it. Would you like to do
that?"

"How kind of you to ask. But I'm afraid I've so
many things to do today. Perhaps another time." Fiona
rose to her feet, smoothed out her gown. "In fact, I
really ought to get started. If you'll excuse me?"

Briskly she left the breakfast-room. Baffled, strug-
gling within himself, Alasdair stood and caught up
with her in the long high-ceilinged passageway. Servants bustled to and fro, but he *had* to speak.

"Madam," he said, "Fiona —"

She turned, her eyebrows lifted inquiringly.

He came close to her, and saw with a certain gladness that she didn't step away. In a low voice he said,
"Would you like to talk?"

And lightly she answered, "About what, laird?"

"About last night."

"No."

"No?"

"You were honest with me," she said, lightly, pleasantly. "I appreciate that. We understand each other
now. And when I agreed with you about no more talking, I meant it."

"Yes," he said, "but . . ."

She waited. His eyes searched her face. His brain
searched for words. Abruptly there flashed into his
memory an experience from long ago, when at a dare
from Hewie — both of them reckless fifteen-year-olds
— he had agreed to climb a sheer rockface on Ben
Macdui. Initially he'd done well, and had easily ascended to a point some fifty feet above the ground.
And then his fingers could no longer find purchase
above him. It had been a sickening sensation. He
could go no further.

That's what it felt like right now.

Fiona wasn't cold, wasn't furious. Those luminous eyes weren't blazing with passionate emotion. Yet it was as if he could gain no purchase on her; she was in some fundamental way inaccessible.

"Well," she said at last, "if that's all, laird?"

"Yes — no." He groped for her hand, held it gently. She did not resist, but there was about her the slightly distracted air of a busy person who was mentally already somewhere else.

"How sweet," Fiona said, and with equal gentleness withdrew her hand. "I do hope you have a nice day."

And she turned and walked away from him.

Although he had long finished his breakfast, Duff lingered at the table while Isobel poked at a strawberry tart, picking away at the buttery crust until a pile of golden crumbs had accumulated on her plate and the sweet red interior lay exposed but uneaten. Her white brow was wrinkled and her lips pursed distractedly, her eyes downcast. She wore this morning a high-necked gown of soft violet, trimmed at the neckline and sleeves with a modest fall of white ruffled lace, and it came to Duff, as he observed her, that she rather resembled a pansy.

He liked pansies.

One of his favorite flowers, now he came to think on it.

He said, unconsciously echoing Alasdair, "Is your tart not to your liking, madam?"

She started. "Oh! Only look what I've done. How wasteful of me! I'm sure it's delicious, sir, but —"

"Call me Duff, won't you?"

"Oh! Ought I? I should hate to appear forward."

He observed with pleasure the pretty blush on her plump cheeks. "Not a bit of it," he declared. "And might I have the privilege of calling you by *your* Christian name? I've always thought 'Isobel' to be a lovely name. That's what I called a terrier bitch I had when I was just a lad. What a hunter! She must've killed a hundred badgers if she killed a one." Nostalgically Duff added, "Had bright eyes like little shiny buttons, just like yours."

"How sweet of you . . . Duff," answered Isobel, fluttering a little at the compliment, and he felt in the region between his stomach and his shoulders an unfamiliar, but agreeable sensation. In his lungs? What else was in there? Kidneys, liver? Yes, and also one's heart. He smiled and said:

"Now then! What's had you so preoccupied that you've torn that pastry to bits?"

At once Isobel looked worried again. "I was just thinking about what happened last night in the Great Drawing-room. Such a *fierce* quarrel! And it was so *tense* just now between dear Fiona and the laird. Underneath, if you know what I mean? It's dreadful! I can't help but be upset."

"Yes, well . . . But . . . Oughtn't to dwell on . . . I mean —" Fumblingly Duff struggled to think of something consoling to say. It didn't come easy; he hadn't been in the habit of paying much attention to the feelings of others. But there was something about Isobel that made him want to try. And then, in a stunning bolt of inspiration, it came to him. "Did you notice how — well — snappish Fiona was last night? They say that in a certain — ah — delicate state, ladies can be peevish — and consider how she didn't eat her breakfast this morning. Maybe she's . . . you know . . ."

Isobel's eyes were round. "Goodness! Why, yes! Of course, it would be early days yet, but still . . . It certainly would explain . . . How *terribly* clever of you to think of it!"

"It's nothing, really," he said modestly. God's eye-teeth, but it was nice to bask in some womanly admiration, and from a lady, too, none of your silly little tavern wenches either. To be sure, Isobel's face *did* have some lines upon it, but so did his, truth be told, and conferred upon them both, he thought, a fine sort of shared dignity. He was especially glad, now, that he'd lopped off that unruly beard of his, and that today he'd put on one of his better shirts.

Which reminded him. He called to one of the servants: "There's a basket of mine out in the hall — bring it in."

When the servant returned bearing the basket, he said, "Place it by Dame Isobel." And added, as if the words came to him a little rustily, "Thank you."

"You're welcome, sir," said the servant, and Duff realized that it didn't feel so bad to acknowledge when people did you a service, either.

Isobel was staring in bewilderment at the brilliantly colored heap of garments before her. Bright yellow. Loud green. Vibrant chartreuse. Blazing red. "Your — your waistcoats, Duff? Shall I mend them for you, as I did your shirt?"

"No — no, you misunderstand me," he answered quickly. "I'm discarding them. They are, perhaps, a trifle too — er — vivid for one of my age. What may have suited me most excellently in the past might not be quite so — ah — *comme il faut*. I thought — well, I thought they might find new life as wee dresses for the dolls you make."

"Oh, Duff, how *very* kind of you!" exclaimed Isobel, touched. "And the fabric will make the most *delightful* little gowns. Thank you so much!" She smiled at him, eyes shining with gratitude.

Duff opened his mouth to reply, but found himself at a loss for words. It had been a long time since a lady had looked at him in that way. Maybe never.

A servant broke the spell, by offering to take away his empty plate. "Oh — um — yes. I thank you," said Duff, and was filled with a surprising regret when Isobel rose to her feet, saying:

"Oh dear! We're keeping the servants from their work, I'm afraid." She ran a caressing hand over the smooth, bright material of a gaudy yellow waistcoat. "How lovely. Well! Thank you again! *So* considerate of you! Good day to you, Duff."

"And to you, Isobel. I trust I'll see you at nuncheon?"

"Yes," she said, a little breathlessly, her face pink, and thus they went their separate ways, Isobel with her basket to the Little Drawing-room, Duff to the library where he intended to pore over the latest racing journal but instead stood at the window, thoughtfully puffing on his pipe in a state of pleasant — very pleasant — abstraction.

Chapter 14

By late afternoon Fiona had accomplished all the tasks on her list, moving through them capably and efficiently, one after the other. So what if she felt like a machine? At least she might felicitate herself on disguising that fact reasonably well.

Or so she thought.

She was in the kitchen garden, clad in an old muslin gown, on her knees among the mint, fennel, basil, and dill. For quite some time now she had been trimming, watering, uprooting weeds, picking off snails. Cook, surprised and solicitous, had more than once sent servants out to help, but Fiona had waved them away. In particular, there were several prickly spear-thistle plants which had recently sprung up and she was determined to eradicate them. A large bushy heap had piled up in her basket when, abruptly, a shadow fell upon her. Quickly Fiona looked up.

But it was Monty.

No "but," she corrected herself.

It was Monty.

"Madam," he said in his gruff way, "that's enough for today."

Fiona looked up at him and with a grimy palm

wiped the sweat from her forehead. "I've more thistles to pull up. It won't take but an hour or so."

"Madam," he said, "your hands."

She glanced at them. Not only were they filthy, but they were scratched and bleeding in several places. "Oh," she said, feeling oddly embarrassed, as if she'd been caught out in some way. "It's nothing. Is there something you need?"

"I thought you might wish to look at the beehives with me."

"Not today. Thank you."

"Very well."

But he continued standing there, looking at her from underneath craggy eyebrows.

Finally she said: "What is it, Monty?"

"Only the bees, madam."

"Perhaps another time. Tomorrow, or the next day. Or next week."

"Aye, madam," he answered, stolidly, and left her. To her prickly spear thistles and her damaged hands.

So relentlessly did Fiona attack the thistles that by the time she'd bathed and changed for dinner, she was almost late. She smiled impartially at Alasdair, Isobel, Duff, and the servants ready to begin serving the meal. It wasn't so bad, she thought, as she lifted a spoonful of an exquisitely clear beef consommé. It wasn't so bad living on this plane of existence. Today, for example, had gone by fairly quickly. Why, the days and the months and the years would simply fly by. There was no excuse for the secret sadness that seemed to pervade every inch of her and make her feel as if the sheer weight of it would cause the floor to collapse beneath her. Thank goodness for one's pride.

A few spoonfuls of the consommé, she found, was enough. Her stomach felt full of the sadness. She managed a bite of the glazed ham, a nibble of the savory jelly, half of an asparagus toast. None of it tasted particularly good, either. After she had rejected the pork cutlets, a duck ragout, the cauliflower with a creamy *velouté* sauce, the apple loaf, and a lemon *soufflé*, she gradually became aware of the fact that she was being stared at by her tablemates.

She looked back at them. Duff and Isobel, she noticed without any particular interest, shared a smiling conspiratorial glance. Alasdair was somber.

"What ails you, Fiona?" he said gravely.

"Nothing, laird, I assure you."

"You do not eat. 'Tis troubling to me."

"You needn't concern yourself. I am well."

"Shall I ask for something else to be brought?"

"No. Thank you."

"Fiona —" Then he stopped. And he said, "What happened to your hands?"

"Nothing. A little work in the garden."

"But —"

He had that baffled look on his face again.

She didn't care. Wouldn't care. She was an automaton, good enough to be liked, but not worthy to be loved. Everything was fine. You couldn't lose what you never had. Time marched on. She smiled pleasantly, looked away, had a sip of wine.

And so the evening meal went by. As did the subsequent interval in the Great Drawing-room. Quietly, with every appearance of placidity, she mended another torn altar cloth, and neither flung it to the floor nor shoved her work-box off the sofa. For the most part she kept her eyes on her stitches, concentrating on making them uniformly tiny and even, one after the other. The tiniest, most even stitches ever sewn. As if she were competing in the world championship for Best Repair of an Altar Cloth (White

Linen of Excellent Quality, Origin Likely Dating to
Early 1800s, Several Rips in Fabric Due to Unknown
Causes, Possibly Aging and/or Neglect). She did not,
once, look at those green velvet curtains, not even
for a second. For all she cared now, they could stay
up forever, or until hell froze over, whichever came
first.

Isobel and Duff seemed to be finding a great deal
to say to each other, but she paid no attention to
them, and very little to Alasdair, either, who was up
and down, pacing restlessly around the room, until
finally Duff commented jovially:

"Lad, you're like a prisoner in a cell."

"Or perhaps an animal in a cage?" put in Isobel,
obviously meaning to frame things in a more positive
light.

"You ought to get some exercise tomorrow," Duff
added, in a kindly way. "Remember how, when I first
came here, you used to go out and chop wood until
the axe-head would fly off? I nearly lost an eye one
day." He laughed.

Alasdair did not laugh, or smile, and Duff's own
smile faded. With concern, he asked: "What's the
matter, lad?"

Alasdair finally came to a stop opposite the sofa
on which Fiona was sitting. She knew this but did not
lift her head from her sewing. After all, she was busy
competing for the Best Altar-Cloth Repair Award of
1811.

"I'm waiting for Fiona," said Alasdair. "It's time
for bed."

Once, and quite recently, too, Fiona mused, these
words would have thrilled her to her very soul. But
now they were just that — words. Conveying information but without evoking an answering response
within her. "I'm not quite finished, laird." How af-
fable and polite she sounded! How easy it was to

manufacture the tone, too. Dreadfully easy. "You needn't wait up for me."

He sat. "I'll wait," he replied grimly.

"As you wish." One stitch, another stitch, and another after that. She could feel him staring at her, but composedly she sewed on. The chatter between Isobel and Duff dried up, and altogether, she supposed, another rather awkward scene was being enacted here in the Great Drawing-room. Oh well. The tea-tray came and went (she had nothing), the moon rose or sank (she hardly cared); one stitch, another stitch, another after that. Then: "Well!" she said brightly. "It's done, and quite nicely too, if I do say so myself." She folded the cloth, put away her sewing things, rose, daintily patted back a yawn.

"Good night," she said pleasantly to Duff and Isobel, whose expressions reminded her a little of blanched almonds, poor dears, and then she turned to Alasdair. "I'm ready, laird."

He stood. Together, with an odd ceremoniousness, they left the drawing-room and without speaking made their way to their bedchamber. Alasdair ushered her inside, then shut the door behind them.

"Let's talk."

"Dear me, how *chatty* you've become," Fiona said lightly. "In a moment, then, laird," and she whisked herself off to her dressing-room. When at length she emerged, in one of her ruffled high-necked nightgowns, he was already in the bed. Oh, not for her to run over there and wrench away the covers in a wild rush of passion. No, sedately she went to her side of the bed and got in, plumped up her pillows, pulled the covers snugly around her armpits, fixed her eyes in the dimness on the canopy overhead. Just like old times. Could people die from sadness? she wondered. And just how much would it hurt?

She feared it would hurt very badly indeed.

"Fiona."

Alasdair's deep voice.

"Yes, laird?"

"Talk to me."

"Certainly. What would you like to talk about?"

"About us."

"Well, as to that, laird, you'll have to do all the talking. As I trust I've already made clear, I've nothing to contribute. I am, of course, happy to listen, as a good wife should."

There was a silence, empty and vast.

Fiona stared unblinkingly above her.

Alasdair slid closer to her in that immense bed.

"Fiona," he said.

"Yes?" she answered politely.

"I want you. I want to finish what last night we began."

In his voice she could hear the desperate urgency which she herself had experienced some twenty-four hours ago. She could feel the bewitching heat of his body. Could smell that fascinating scent which she'd come to associate with him alone, soap and clean damp hair and just a musky trace of the stables.

And she felt — nothing.

Nothing could penetrate the sadness which had apparently turned her into a living statue.

But neither did she resent his words. In all fairness, she had to admit, yesterday in this very bed she had tried to do the same thing.

"Fine," she told him. "Just a moment, and I'll lift up my nightgown for you."

"What?"

"As a dutiful wife, naturally I will accommodate you, laird."

"Oh my God," he said, revulsion in his tone, "stop it, Fiona. I'll have none of that."

"As you will. I'll wish you good night, then." And she turned on her side, presenting him with, should he care to peruse it, an excellent view of her back. A kind of shield which would conceal the fact that she was crying. Silently, without sobs or sniffles; simply a stream of tears falling, one after the other, as if they sprang from an infinite well.

It was on the following morning, when Fiona had stepped onto the front portico to check if the weather was sufficiently auspicious for wash day, that she saw Sheila sitting on one of the stone steps, loudly weeping. Quickly Fiona went to her, and placed a gentle hand on the little girl's bony shoulder.

"What's the matter, hinny?"

Sheila raised a wet, woebegone face. "Oh, lady, I was running to help catch a chicken that got loose, and I fell." She pulled up the dirty hem of her gown to show Fiona a pair of badly scraped kneecaps. "See?"

"I do see. Won't you let me clean those poor knees? I have some very nice salve for them, too."

"All right." Slowly Sheila stood, wincing, and suddenly a strange, opaque look came into her pale blue eyes. "Why must trouble come in threes? Why, lady?"

"I don't know, hinny. But I do know that Cook has made a lovely batch of gooseberry dumplings. Maybe you'd like one after we fix you up?" Fiona watched as the little girl's face cleared and she swiftly nodded. Hopefully there wouldn't be two more incidents to plague poor Sheila.

But, of course, Fiona could not have guessed that Sheila wasn't referring to herself but to the troubles of some other person entirely.

The days passed. Fiona went about her business, Alasdair went about his. The harvest this year was abundant and the weather benign; the threshing barn of old Norval Smith was promptly repaired, made even better than new; the bull sent by the Colling brothers was pronounced entirely satisfactory. The dinner party hosted by the laird and his lady was talked about for some time, so elegant, so enjoyable an affair it was. The very pregnant farmer's wife was successfully delivered of healthy twin girls. Everyone marveled over how nice the altar cloths were looking. Isobel's beautifully attired dolls were much clamored for by the little ones of the clan, and Duff took to fashioning sticks into delightful little fishing-rods that were equally sought after.

In fact, everything really was going remarkably well. Somehow, though, in some mysterious way, somehow the atmosphere at Castle Tadgh, which had been brightening, dimmed bit by bit. It wasn't palpable, it wasn't anything you could touch or quantify, but there it was. Yet nobody could have suspected that despite his usual smiling, easygoing exterior, the laird was greatly troubled. Or that behind her calm, pleasant façade their lady took refuge from her anguish in an inflexible pride.

No one could have had any way of knowing that the laird and lady lay far apart from each other in the night, so divided in their relations that they might as well have been in separate beds, separate rooms, separate countries.

Isobel, perhaps, had some inkling of this deep estrangement, and more than once, as doggedly she read on through the Tome, sad tears would drop onto the timeworn pages, and carefully, so carefully, would she dab at them with her cheap, lacy, ineffective handkerchiefs from Edinburgh.

A fortnight after Sheila had fallen and hurt herself while pursuing an escaped chicken, she sat in a corner of the Great Hall, playing dolls with Lister's niece Erica. Abruptly she froze, as if hearing a disturbing, far-off sound.

"That's one," she said mournfully, and hugged her doll close.

The next afternoon, having been implacably ordered by her grandmother to climb into the wooden tub set before the crackling fire in their cottage, Sheila briefly interrupted her stream of complaints to say, to Dame Margery's bewilderment:

"That's two." And then: "Oh, Granny, I *hate* taking baths, everybody knows that bathing makes your skin fall off. Do I *have* to wash my hair? Soap gives you freckles, Granny, and I've got too many of those already. Why do I have to be clean for the feast tomorrow? I'll just get dirty all over again. Oh, Granny, the water's not hot enough, and also my fingers are getting all wrinkly. If you make me stay in here any longer, they'll be that way forever."

While Sheila was taking her bath, Fiona realized that her woman's time was upon her again. She was not pregnant. And the way things were going between Alasdair and herself, she never would be. Alone in her dressing-room, she thought of the Bonni, or the James, or the Maisie, or the Archibald — such beautiful, beautiful baby names — who would never be, and of the loving family she had once hoped to create with Alasdair.

She was tired. There was a low cramping in her belly. She wanted to lie down, to sleep away the afternoon, forget about her cares for a little while . . .

But there was so much to do.

Cook had asked her to come taste the dishes she had already prepared. Mrs. Allen wanted to go over last-minute arrangements for the decorating of the Great Hall. Lister was waiting for her to review the list of wines he had selected. A man from the village, the leader of the musicians she'd engaged, was downstairs, needing her approval of the songs they were to play tomorrow.

And so on.

And so forth.

Fiona looked absently into her mirror. Gracious, she thought, but I've become the skeleton Janet Reid once taunted me about. How she'd laugh to see me now! And those circles under my eyes — I look like some kind of ghastly clown.

She shrugged at her reflection. She left her dressing-room. And she went back to work.

Alasdair walked slowly downstairs toward the Great Hall, alone. Feeling very much alone. He could hear the clatter and bustle from below, servants talking and laughing, musical instruments being tuned up, little snatches of this and that being played. It was all very cheerful, and it only served to highlight the desolation within him. He felt, he imagined, much as a man did who'd been clouted in the head by an oar — vigorously and repeatedly. Such a man would be dazed, befuddled; the world around him might even stop making sense to him.

What had gone wrong between himself and Fiona?

How had things gotten so bad?

If he could have, he'd have left the castle at sunup, and stayed away till late in the night. He was in no mood for a party. For a dirge, yes, or an exhumation. But he was the laird, and nothing short of illness, incapacitation, or actual death would keep him doing his duty, which was to preside over the evening's festivities.

He walked on, hoping that in his eyes wasn't the stunned, hopeless look of a man who'd been savagely beaten within an inch of his life.

It was, everybody agreed, the best clan celebration anyone could remember. The food, the drink, the music — all were simply splendid, and the Great Hall had never looked so convivial and inviting. It was a grand thing for the clan, everyone said, when the laird had married the lady. And just see them now, sitting up at the high table — he so tall and handsome, she so lovely and kind. Just like a king and queen. And so happy together! Oh yes, a grand thing for the clan. Here — have another ale, won't you?

Fiona sincerely hoped her face wouldn't crack in two from all the smiling she'd been doing. The muscles in her cheeks had begun to pain her. But it was as nothing compared to the hurt in her heart, so she supposed she could keep on looking pleasant and gracious for as long as the celebration went on. In a sense, she mused, it was all a play, and she was merely an actor performing her part. And sufficiently well, too. There would be no applause, no standing ovation, but it was nice, at least, to see everyone enjoying themselves.

Although not quite everyone, she suddenly realized, even as Duff, at her left, leaned toward her and said, "Lass, where's Isobel? Is she unwell?"

"I've no idea, Uncle. She sent no word. I'll ask for her maid —"

"Nay, lass, you're needed here, and why call her maid away from the fun? I'll go tap on her bedchamber door."

"You might also try the Little Drawing-room. That's where she often spends her mornings, I believe. And let me know if there's anything I can do."

"I will." Duff stood, and surprised Fiona by briefly placing a hand on her shoulder. "You're a good girl," he said, and went away, and Fiona sank again into her abstraction.

More food, more wine and ale, more music, more of everything. Time passed, and passed, and passed, and the cheerful noise levels in the Great Hall went up and up, obviating the need to try and make stilted conversation with Alasdair. He sat next to her at the high table, magnificent in a dark jacket and tartan kilt, his dark-red hair spiked upwards a little above his forehead in a way she loved with ridiculous fervor. She wanted to run her fingers, languorously, through his hair. Wanted to kiss him, for hours on end. There was no denying it: she ached for him, body and soul, but never again would she reveal it, never again risk being hurt that way once more. She would infinitely prefer to be torn apart by wolves. In fact, she'd go out into the woods and *look* for them if necessary. She smiled at a group of children, pretty flower garlands in their hair, who had joined hands and were spinning in a circle in time to the music.

She had, quite frankly, nearly forgotten about Isobel, and was therefore startled to see her come into the Great Hall looking as if she'd seen a ghost. Duff, his expression as grim as Fiona had ever seen it, had

one arm around the tottering Isobel, and in the other
he carried the Tome.

Oh, heavens, Fiona thought sardonically, I must
have inadvertently violated clan law by allowing mar-
inated asparagus and broad beans to be served at the
annual harvest celebration. I suppose they're here to
tell me this dish can only be served in *October*. Ten
lashes with the cat-o'-nine tails for me, no doubt.

When finally they reached the high table, Duff first
courteously helped Isobel to sit, pressed on her a glass
of wine; then he moved aside a large platter to make
room for the Tome, which with a strange precision he
set at an equal distance between Alasdair and Fiona.

"What's this all about?" asked Alasdair, frowning.

Moving with an exaggerated slowness that didn't
disguise the fact that his hands were trembling a little,
Duff opened the Tome to a place some three-quarters
of the way through, and pointed to a small paragraph
of text in the middle of the right-hand folio.

"I'm sorry," Duff said heavily. "So sorry. For both
of you."

Fiona watched as Alasdair read the text. She
watched as he read the paragraph over and over. She
watched the muscles in his jaw tighten.

Twenty lashes with the cat-o'-nine tails, she thought
flippantly.

Then Alasdair pushed the Tome closer to her.

"Read this," he said.

He stood up and scanned the Great Hall.

Afterward, everyone agreed that the laird hadn't
shouted or thundered; he had spoken in only a slightly
louder voice than usual, yet it was strange, they later
commented with awe, how effortlessly it had cut
through all the noise and merriment, like a knife slic-
ing through a thread.

"Where is Dame Margery?"

Something about the way he said it made the musicians put down their instruments, the children pause in their games. Servants stopped serving, ferrying dishes, whisking here and there.

"I am here, laird." Margery got to her feet, stood leaning on her gnarled stick.

"Come here, madam, if you please."

"Aye, laird."

Fiona barely noticed all this, for now *she* was reading the text on page 758 over and over again.

The ancient clan decree specifying that any chieftain of Castle Tadgh who, having entered into his thirty-fifth birthday still in an unmarried state, must, on pain of death, cause to be brought into the castle all eligible maidens of noble birth from among the Eight Clans of Killaly and from among them select a bride within a span of thirty-five days is hereby rendered null and void. Consequently the obligation among such maidens to comply with this decree or else suffer ignominious death by drowning is also declared obsolete. Be it known that should any chieftain and any maiden have unwittingly obeyed said decree, the union between them is legally invalid and they are to immediately retrogress to their previously unmarried state. Be it also known that no disgrace is to come upon them. The lady is to be granted her original virgin status. All offspring from this specious union are to have their parentage acknowledged but must formally be known as bastards henceforth.

Fiona felt a crazy desire to laugh. *At least I'm not going to be whipped for serving asparagus and broad beans*. But instead of giving way to an unseemly bray of laughter, she loosely laced her fingers together in her lap, sat up straighter than ever, and made herself breathe in a steady cadence. She dared not look at Alasdair, who had once again taken his seat but was very still.

A leaden silence descended as slowly Margery made her way among the crowds thronging the Great Hall. People stepped away from her as if from an Old Testament prophet, respectfully but also uneasily.

At long last the old lady reached the high table.

"How may I serve you, laird?"

"I assume, madam, you are not familiar with this passage in the Tome?"

In a careful, controlled voice, Alasdair read it out loud, and Dame Margery went white.

"Oh, laird, on my life I was not! Surely you must know I was not!"

"*Anyone* might have missed it," Isobel put in, anxious to be helpful. "It was in the middle of a *tremendously* dull section about logging rights and timber sales, which seems like an odd place for such an announcement, when you think about it. It's a wonder *I* came to notice it, for I'm not the least bit interested in lumber transactions."

Margery's stricken gaze didn't waver from Alasdair's face. "I believed I knew the Tome from start to finish, laird, every page, every word, every statute and decree. My arrogance is unforgivable." She bowed her head. "You must punish me as you see fit. Banishment would be a mercy, but if it's death, then so be it."

"Nonsense," responded Alasdair, in that same controlled manner. "You may return to your seat."

"I thank you for your lenience, laird. 'Tis more than I deserve. With your permission, I'd like to go home. I've no stomach now for the feast, or for the festivities."

"Of course you can go home. Need you an escort?"

"Nay, laird. In my spirit I am shattered, but my legs will carry me. For your benevolence I thank you yet again." As sorrowful as a mourner at a funeral, Dame Margery turned and, leaning on her stick, with plodding steps began walking away from the high table.

Alasdair saw before him a sea of stunned, troubled faces, saw the question in their eyes. He said, in a quiet yet carrying voice:

"Those who wish may stay. Those who want to leave may freely go."

At his words, the crowd quietly dispersed. Nobody actually ran screaming from the Hall, but there was no question, Fiona thought, that they were fleeing as they would from a disaster. A flood, say, or a fire. Possibly a plague of locusts. And it was remarkable how quickly the place emptied. How eerie it looked with the tables still laden, but with the vacated chairs set higgledy-piggledy all around them. Only Duff and Isobel remained, their faces pale and drawn.

"Christ, what an unholy mess," Alasdair said.

For a few seconds of wild confusion Fiona thought he was referring to the abandoned feast, and the monumental effort it would take to clean it all up, but when she looked at him she realized he was staring grimly at the Tome.

It was then that she finally understood. Not just in her brain but in every particle of her being.

She and Alasdair were no longer married.

Grief slammed through her, hard enough to make her grip her hands painfully together. These past weeks had been awful, worse than awful, yet never in a thousand years would she have dreamed their marriage would be severed in this way. So quickly, so cleanly. So decisively. But in the wake of that sad dark wave there came a sudden thought:

It's not too late.

What has been put asunder, can still be joined together.

Hope fluttered up.

Quickly Fiona half-turned in her chair, looked at Alasdair.

Even as Fiona turned, Alasdair did the same, within him an inarticulate longing.

Their eyes met.

And held.

A word, a whisper, the slightest smile, a hand extended, any sign of yielding could have brought them back from the brink. There was infinite opportunity in that locked gaze. There was a future.

But between them, separating them, was pride, like a high fence staked deeply into the ground. Fear. Anger. Stubbornness. Old hurts, new hurts.

How could hope stand a chance against it all?

And so the moment passed.

Their gazes fell away.

Accompanying Dame Margery home to their cottage, Sheila suddenly said, "That's three." A vague memory floated across her mind, how she had, weeks ago, gotten out of her bed, very early before anybody else was awake, and slipped off to the castle in the gloom of waning night. There she had gone into the Armament Room, an intimidating place under ordinary circumstances, filled as it was with old guns and sharp swords in large glass cases, alarming suits of armor, shields and nasty-looking spears set high on the walls. After Granny had told everyone in the Great Hall about how the laird must marry, and after the great fuss that had followed, somebody had put that big, dusty old book back in the Room, on its elaborate iron stand that looked just a little like an instrument of torture.

She had taken the book — oh, how heavy it was! — upstairs, as quick as any deer of the forest, and gone into that pink frilly room where a big mahogany cabinet stood. She had pulled open one of the little doors and slid the Tome inside.

Why, Sheila wondered now, had she done that? It had seemed so important at the time.

"Three what, sweeting?" Granny asked.

Sheila looked up at her grandmother. She'd already forgotten what she had said, and the memory of taking the Tome was swiftly fading. "Oh, nothing, Granny," she replied. "It was a strange feast, wasn't it? See? I *told* you I didn't need to take a bath. I'm still hungry, aren't you? What's for supper tonight, Granny? I hope it's something *good.*"

In the Great Hall, Fiona said to Alasdair, coolly, "That's that, then. I'll leave tomorrow."

He watched in numb disbelief as she slid the gold ring from the fourth finger of her left hand. It came off with an ease that somehow seemed a little obscene. Gently she placed it on the table between them.

Did she feel freed? From a burden so dreadful she couldn't wait to be gone? Had her feelings for him, then, dissolved so quickly? Or was there something monstrous — repellent — in him, some awful, fundamental aspect of his character that was driving her away?

Her face, calm, as remote as a medieval saint set in stone, was his answer. And he remembered that ugly exchange between them in the Great Drawing-room, when she had vehemently said, *You're nothing to me. I'm so sorry I married you.* And determined to hold himself aloof from her, he'd replied, *I'm afraid, though, that you're stuck with me.*

How wrong he had been.

How terribly wrong.

"But the baby!" blurted Duff, and Alasdair whipped around.

"*What?*"

"Fiona is — that is, Isobel and I assumed — the symptoms —" Duff stammered out, then faltered when he saw Fiona give a small shake of her head. "Ah, lass, I'm sorry."

"Look on the bright side, Uncle," she answered levelly. "No bastards to worry about."

My God, my God, Alasdair thought, but she's a cool one. Out loud he said:

"Are you certain, Fiona?"

"Oh yes, quite sure. Nature has told me so." She stood up. "If you'll excuse me? I've so much to do before I go. Laird, I trust you'll allow Begbie to assign some of his men as outriders on my journey to Wick Bay?"

"I will escort you myself."

"No. I'll go as I came, alone, a maiden —" Her lip curled ever so slightly. "— a maiden of clan Douglass."

He stood up also, and looked deep into those big, long-lashed gray eyes. "Fiona," he said, quietly, urgently, "there's no need to go in such haste."

"On the contrary, there's every need. I want to move forward with my life."

"You can do that here."

"You and I both know that's not true."

"Why is it not true?" he asked, feeling like a schoolchild who has failed, and spectacularly too, at a lesson that should have been learned some time ago.

"Because I'm greedy," she said evenly. "Because I'm greedy and I'm hungry. I'm ravenous. My God, I'm *starving*. But what I want you don't have to give me. It's not your fault. I don't blame you. It's just the way it is. And I don't want to fight against it anymore. That's why tomorrow I'm leaving here."

"But —" he said, "don't you — shouldn't we —" And abruptly he ground to a halt. Not knowing what else to do, he reached out his hand for hers, hoping that his touch might accomplish what his inarticulate words couldn't.

But she stepped back and away from him.

"No," she said. "It's not proper. That's all over now. Will you have Begbie assign some outriders for me?"

"As you will," he replied, numbly. "I'll speak to him myself."

"Thank you."

"And — and could he have readied a carriage for myself, please, laird."

They all looked at Isobel, in whose trembling voice was nonetheless a firm resolution.

"But —" said Duff, and stopped.

"My place," Isobel said, "is with Fiona." She too rose to her feet. "How can I help you, Fiona dear?"

"If I may, I'll share your bedchamber tonight, Cousin. And we'll need to get our things packed very quickly."

"Of course. Shall I — shall I send an express to your parents?"

"No. We'll surprise them," said Fiona with a small, sardonic smile.

"Very well." Distressfully Isobel pressed a hand to her forehead. "Oh dear, how dreadful this is! I can only *imagine* the reception we'll receive back in Wick Bay! Do you suppose your father will be *very* angry with us?"

"With me, do you mean? I couldn't care less. I'm too big to be left on the shores of the bay to die, after all, and if he sends me off to a hut on the marsh I'll have a very nice time there, away from his moods and his tempers. Well," Fiona added politely, "good day to you, gentlemen," and briskly she left the Great Hall, an agitated Isobel following behind, doing her best to keep up on her shorter legs.

Alone in the Hall, Alasdair looked at Duff, who had slumped, miserable, in his chair.

"I'm sorry, Uncle," he said at last, his voice low and rough.

"I'm sorry too, lad," answered Duff.

In a minute, Alasdair thought, he'd go off to the stables and find Begbie. Do everything that was needful to ensure a safe, comfortable journey for Fiona and Isobel.

He'd go in a minute.

Just until he could process the fact that his life had, in the blink of an eye, come crashing down around him, with an irrevocability that seemed to turn his insides to a solid block of ice.

Chapter 15

The next morning, under a bright blue sky filled with white, hurrying clouds, it seemed as if every able-bodied member of clan Penhallow had gathered in the courtyard to say farewell. Fiona couldn't help but be touched, and although it took everything she had to remain cool and calm amidst such a large crowd — *A chieftain's daughter doesn't cry in front of people,* she kept reminding herself — there was something to be said for a public goodbye to her former husband.

Duff had already, with exquisite care, handed a white and trembling Isobel into the carriage.

Now he came to Fiona. "Well, lass," he said, and paused, awkward. Then, as if language failed him, swiftly he hugged her, and stepped back, his gaze going to Isobel whose face was framed, as if in a portrait he would never forget, in the carriage window.

"Goodbye, Uncle," Fiona said. Uncle-that-was, actually, but why bring it up now? Behind her, held by his leading rein by Begbie, Gealag snorted, and she could hear the cheerful jingle of his harness as he tossed his great head, as if he were impatient to be off and on their way.

Then Alasdair was there, tall, grave, regal, his

dark-red hair glinting in the sun, his eyes pure amber and citrine. How odd it was, Fiona thought, that when she first met him, and for some time thereafter, she had not found him particularly attractive.

Now it occurred to her that she must have been blind.

You look but you do not see.

So she studied his face, allowed her gaze to sweep up and down the entire muscular length of him, memorizing every detail, for it would have to last her a long time. Forever: yes, a very long time indeed.

"*Mar sin leat,*" Alasdair said to her. "*Slàn leibh.*" *Goodbye. May you be well.*

"You also." She was glad her voice was so steady, for in reality she didn't feel very sturdy. No, her legs felt a little shaky and she could have sworn the ground beneath her feet was tilting ever so slightly.

"May I?" asked Alasdair, as Begbie brought Gealag forward.

"I — yes."

And for the last time Alasdair was intimately close to her, for the last time he was touching her, his big hands about her waist; with his immense strength he lifted her without apparent effort onto the saddle.

He stepped back.

"Thank you," Fiona said quietly, and just as quietly he said:

"You're welcome."

She gathered Gealag's reins in her gloved hands; gloved because today there was a distinct chill in the air. Summer was gone. Fiona looked at Alasdair for the very last time, looked down upon him where he stood in the courtyard, very still, very straight, his arms at his side. Into her mind came Juliet's anguished words to her Romeo when they parted for — as it would turn out for them also — for ever.

*Methinks I see thee now, thou art so low as one
dead in the bottom of a tomb. Either my eyesight
fails, or thou look'st pale.*

And trust me, love, in my eye so do you, answers
Romeo. *Dry sorrow drinks our blood.*

Fiona shuddered. She clicked her tongue to Gealag
and at once he broke into a playful trot. Together
they led the way out of the courtyard, followed by the
large handsome coach in which Isobel rode, and the
dozen armed men who would bring her safely home.

She did not look back.

When the cavalcade had disappeared from sight,
Alasdair went out beyond the kitchen garden and
chopped wood for Cook's fires, did it until blisters,
angry and painful, had sprung up on both hands,
until Duff came, until Duff came and with the soft
voice of one approaching a vicious and unpredictable
beast, finally managed to coax him away from the
towering pile of wood which might well last Cook
into, and through, a long, harsh winter.

Isobel managed to retain her composure until the
third day of their journey. She and Fiona had finished their evening meal, alone in a capacious private
parlor of the inn where they were to pass the night,
and they were sitting before a large comfortable fire
that helped chase away a threatening dampness. Rain
had swept down upon them late in the afternoon and
now they could hear it drumming hard upon the roof,
lashing furiously at the windows.

Isobel drew her shawl more closely about her and

looked anxiously at Fiona. "Are you *sure* you're not catching cold from riding in the rain?" she asked, for the third or fourth time. Maybe the fifth time.

"I'm sure," answered Fiona, staring as if transfixed into the leaping flames of the fire.

"I'm afraid you were utterly soaked — positively *dripping* by the time we got here. How brave you are! No word of complaint has passed your lips even *once*. Oh, my dear Fiona, I must say I don't care for this weather at all. I believe it's made me feel — well, I must confess I feel just a *trifle* low."

And with that Isobel burst into tears. She pulled from her reticule one of those absurd little handkerchiefs and, sobbing piteously, dabbed at her eyes.

Then and there Fiona vowed to make Isobel a large set of handkerchiefs, *big* absorbent handkerchiefs, lavishly embroidered and crafted from the finest linen money could buy. She stood, went to Isobel, gently patted her shoulder.

Isobel covered Fiona's hand with her own. She cried for a long while, and Fiona simply stood, patiently, until she was done. Saying nothing. But being there.

Then Isobel said, shakily:

"Thank you, Fiona dear," and took away her hand, to rub the back of it against her soft wet cheeks. "How silly of me to break down like that, when your troubles are so much greater than my own. Forgive me, please, won't you?"

"There's nothing to apologize for, Cousin, I assure you." Fiona went back to her seat before the fire.

Isobel drew in a deep breath. "Oh, Fiona, I seem only to bring you bad luck in love. I should never have permitted Logan Munro's advances — I see that now — and to *think* how *that* turned out for you. I *do* need to apologize! I should have done so *years* ago!

What a foolish, sentimental old maid I was — and *am!* And now, it's all my fault that your marriage is over. I am so *deeply* sorry!"

"You were not — are not — responsible for Logan's actions," Fiona said, slowly, her eyes once again fixed on the ever-shifting fire. "Or for mine. My God, how long ago that was. A lifetime ago." All at once the old resentment, the old stubborn grudge, which for so many years had been lodged in her heart like a thorn, finally fell away, and was gone.

Not that Fiona felt like hopping up and dancing a reel, but still.

It felt better. Was better.

She continued:

"It's not your fault, either, about discovering the other decree. It just — happened."

"That's how it seemed to me," replied Isobel, nodding vigorously. "There was something which seemed to *compel* me to read that boring old Tome! As if — as if I was somehow being pulled along! And when I saw how unhappy you'd become in your marriage, I just read more and more. As if by doing it, I would somehow be *helping* you!"

"Helping me . . ." Fiona murmured. A memory opened up. The morning after her wedding; she had agreed to allow Isobel to stay on with her at Castle Tadgh. A visibly relieved and grateful Isobel had declared, *I will make myself very useful to you — I promise!*

And so here she was, halfway back to Wick Bay. Isobel wasn't to blame, of course not. But there was no escaping the cold hard facts.

No husband, no baby.
No husband, no baby.
No husband, no husband . . .
It almost sounded like a child's refrain.

She could almost hear little Sheila's voice chanting it. Almost —

But instead she seemed to hear again Sheila saying dejectedly, *Why must trouble come in threes? Why, lady?*

It now occurred to Fiona, uneasily, that perhaps Sheila had not been tallying up her own misfortunes.

Maybe it had been an oblique reference to herself.

No baby. That was one.

No husband; love unrequited. That was two.

Or was that three, according to the vagaries of cosmic accounting?

If not, what then was the third?

Her mind revolved uselessly. A broken carriage wheel tomorrow, fleas in their beds, Father's fury when she arrived on his doorstep? News that Alasdair had, within hours of her departure, married someone else? Why did there have to be a third? Weren't things bad enough already?

"— and I do hope there will be ample room for both of us," Isobel was saying, "although I *cannot* think the marsh air salubrious. My petticoats will doubtless become mildewed, and it seems all too likely I'll succumb to an inflammation of the lung before the year is out. Which will at least make the hut less crowded," she concluded, in the tone of one looking hard for a silver lining and finding it decidedly meager.

Fiona blinked. "What hut do you mean, Cousin?"

"Why, the one to which your father will exile us."

"I was being sardonic. Mostly. And truly, Isobel, no blame could possibly be attached to you, even by Father."

"Well, I am preparing myself mentally, Fiona dear. I don't *wish* to live in a hut, but I will do it for your sake."

Recognizing this for the heroic sacrifice it was, Fiona was able to summon up a wan smile. "Thank you, Cousin," she answered, sincerely, and then both ladies were silent, absorbed in their own, less than sunny reflections.

Letters had come for Fiona; a small pile had accumulated in only the few days since she had gone.

"Shall I send them along to the mistress's — to Miss Fiona's home in Wick Bay, laird?" asked Lister.

"Yes," answered Alasdair shortly, but added hard upon: "No." Then: "Yes, of course, send them on."

"Very well, laird." Lister looked a little puzzled, but continued, gesturing to a different stack upon his desk, "These invitations, laird, how am I to reply to them?"

"Say yes. To all of them."

Another day of travel, another inn. Another night. After tossing and turning for several hours atop a mattress filled with — evidently — lumps of coal, Fiona finally fell asleep toward dawn. She dreamed of Alasdair. He was standing perfectly still on the deck of a boat, his arms at his side. The boat rocked wildly among the roiling waves of a storm-tossed loch. She watched him, helpless, from the distant shore. It was unclear whether he would survive, or sink. And then, underneath her feet, the ground abruptly gave way and she woke up, for several panicky seconds having no idea where she was and groping, futilely, in the empty space next to her for Alasdair.

It was at a glittering ball hosted by one of his neighbors that Alasdair realized that several of the young ladies in attendance — as well as their mothers — were eyeing him with hopeful speculation.

He was, after all, a single man again.

So he danced with all the young ladies. He smiled, he said all the right things, he laughed in all the right places. But he could not forget that he had never, not once, danced with Fiona.

In truth, Fiona hadn't a particularly clear sense of how she would be greeted upon her return to the Douglass keep, but nothing could have prepared her for what she found upon entering the Great Hall.

Her mother, clad in black; weeping.

Father, also in black, looking just a little bit stooped.

A coffin.

And —

Logan Munro, in black as well.

A terrible fear clutched at Fiona.

Why must trouble come in threes?

"What has happened?" she demanded, more loudly than she had intended. They all swung around in surprise.

"Fiona!" Mother gasped. "How did you *know?* How did you get here so quickly?" She hurried to Fiona, hugging her tightly.

Fiona hugged her back, but a little absently, her eyes — in them an urgent question — meeting Father's over Mother's shoulder.

"Nairna is dead," he said, his face a graven mask.

A blast of irrational anger now roared through Fiona as she pulled away from Mother and turned on Logan Munro, her hands clenched into fists. "I just had a letter from her," she said fiercely. "She was well. The wisewoman had put her to bed, that's all. She was *well*."

"The wisewoman was wrong," replied Logan, his voice heavy and somber. "She was a fool, an incompetent. There was no child. It was a tumor growing within her. It must have been just after Nairna wrote you that it all became clear." His voice shook. "By then she knew she was dying. And she asked that I bring her home."

"*You're* the fool!" snarled Fiona. "You're the incompetent one!"

"Fiona!" Mother exclaimed, horrified, but Logan Munro only shook his head.

"You don't need to tell me that I failed her, Fiona. I know it."

"Empty words from an empty man!" Fiona advanced toward him, hardly knowing in her rage what she intended, when Father intervened, catching her arm in a firm grip.

"Calm yourself, daughter. Munro is a guest in my house. I'll not have him dishonored by your vitriol."

Fiona looked up at Father with wild, blind eyes. He leaned close, and said with a softness she would never have expected:

"In all likelihood, there was nothing that anyone could have done. My own mother was taken the same way."

"Oh, Father, she was so happy —"

"I know."

And when Fiona couldn't think of anything else to do, wearily she leaned her head upon his shoulder, just for a few moments. And just for a few moments, Father — the hardest and most undemonstrative of men — put his arm around her, their shared grief bringing them together in a way that was completely new.

In a little while, Fiona was able to go to Mother and embrace her again, and Isobel, too.

She was able to make her way to the coffin and, with tears streaming down her face, say her farewells to Nairna. *Goodbye, my dearie. I'll love you always. I'll never forget you.*

She was able to say to Logan Munro, in a civil and reasonably steady voice, *I'm so sorry for your loss.*

And she was able to ask what needed to be done, what she could do to help, and to start on the herculean task of organizing a stunned and grieving household.

After, Fiona was never able to fully piece together the details of the days that followed: it was all a gray unreal blur, the clan gathering, her sisters Dallis and Rossalyn arriving with their husbands, the funeral, the sad interminable meals and the long sleepless nights.

More tears for Nairna.

A sudden hole in the fabric of the universe; a little, bright light winked out.

Solitary prayers in the chapel.

A quiet interval with Father, explaining her return, and its permanence, Father only nodding, saying nothing, accepting.

Mother collapsing, needing constant attendance and finding in Isobel an unexpected source of strength.

One day dissolved into another.

The mourners left.

Her sisters departed.

Mother slowly recovered.

But Logan Munro stayed on.

The fact of his presence barely pierced the shroud of misery in which Fiona was enveloped. He was simply *there*. At meals. In the evenings, in the cold

draughty saloon that served as their drawing-room.
She would come across him in a passageway, or see
him half-lounging on a sofa in the solarium, talking
with Mother and Isobel, or find him by the horse
paddocks, not riding, but leaning against a railing
and staring off into the distance.

Everywhere she turned, it seemed, there he was:
a handsome figure of a man, very tall, very broad-
shouldered, black-haired and black-eyed, dressed all
in black. An object of sympathy, a devoted husband
who had tragically lost his young wife. The soft-
hearted maidservants couldn't do enough for him,
and would endlessly watch him with tender, eager
eyes.

"**W**ell, that was . . . interesting," said Duff, as he
and Alasdair rode away from an afternoon event described by their hostess — well-known in the neighborhood for boasting that she had *twice* been to a
museum in Glasgow, and *four times* to a concert —
as a Lyrical Poetical Musical Entertainment. It was
remarkable, really, just how many of the local young
ladies were keen to display their musical abilities *and*
were fond of reciting the work of derivative, second-
rate poets specializing in lurid descriptions of hellish
landscapes, bad weather, love affairs gone wrong,
and very long death-scenes.

"Interesting? If you say so," Alasdair replied.

"Didn't realize harps have become so popular."

"Nor I."

"Not particularly fond of them, personally."

"Perhaps you should be, Uncle. As Lady Niocalsan
made a point of observing within my earshot, a *jeune
demoiselle* playing the harp is provided with an excel-

lent opportunity to display her figure to best advantage."

Duff laughed. "That," he said, "is inarguable."

They were riding along a wide trail flanked by trees whose leaves had passed their glory of red, orange, yellow; many had already fallen, littering the ground in a final display of brilliant but dimming color. In the far distance, the high craggy mountaintop of Ben Macdui was dusted with snow, and a chill, nippy and invigorating, was in the air.

"You've been quite sociable these days, lad," said Duff, mildly.

"Just keeping busy, Uncle."

"Aye. And you're very much a favorite among the *demoiselles*, I notice."

"You flatter me."

"You know I don't. And I couldn't help but notice this afternoon that you seemed rather taken with young Miss Hameldon."

"Did I?"

"Yes, but I also could see, at yesterday's grouse shoot, that Miss Rattray was constantly by your side."

"So?"

"So I'm wondering, lad, what's on your mind."

Alasdair looked over at his uncle. What could he say? *Fiona has been gone for seventeen days and sixteen nights, in our bedchamber I can still smell the faint pleasing scent of her rose perfume, and the castle has never been so desolate. Oh, and inside I seem to still be composed of a single block of ice, and also I wonder how, precisely, I'm going to get through this life. Other than that, my mind is as beatifically empty as that of an Eastern mystic.*

Aloud he said:

"I'm trying to move forward."

"Ah."

"The need for an heir and all that."

"I see."

"Weren't you the one telling me that a wife is nothing but a brood mare?"

Duff didn't respond at first. Their horses clopped along. Finally he replied, pensively, "I may have altered my beliefs about that."

"And here I thought you were the one thing I could count on not to change." Alasdair meant to sound wry, jocular, but somehow his voice was more serious than he wished.

"It's slowly been dawning on me, lad, that life is *about* change."

A memory of Fiona saying that very thing seared through Alasdair, painful and harsh. He said nothing, only listened as Duff continued:

"Never thought I'd shave off my beard. Or care what my stockings looked like. Never thought I'd begin to value courtesy over rudeness, kindness over selfishness. God's blood, I never thought I'd spend countless hours making fishing rods for the children, and enjoying every minute of it." He rubbed at his bare chin. "It's unsettling, to say the least — old habits die hard — but there you are."

In a kind of despair, hoping to turn the subject, Alasdair said lightly, "If we're to talk of being a favorite among the ladies, I notice you're causing a stir among a certain set yourself."

"What, among the old tabbies? Well, I can't help it. There's no getting around the fact that I'm a good-looking fellow."

Alasdair smiled. Success. A diversion.

But then Duff added somberly, "I'm trying to move on, too. I'll admit, though, that I'm not making much headway. I might flirt a little, but the truth is that my heart's not in it." He sighed. "I won't pry, lad. Not judging you, either. But if you want to talk — I'm here."

Alasdair met Duff's eyes, nodded his thanks. It was enough. It was all he could manage.

They had come to a place where the trail gave way to a vast rolling meadow in which the heather's violet bloom had quietly faded away. Alasdair pulled his horse to a halt. He looked around the meadow as if he had never seen it before.

"Where to now?" asked Duff.

"We've been invited to Hewie's. One of his mad dinner parties. You know — the usual."

"Wine, women, song."

"Aye."

"It's up to you, lad."

Alasdair thought about what the evening would, predictably, entail. The pattern of Hewie's parties had been long established. He could eat until he was ready to burst, get splendidly drunk, play billiards, dance reels. And, very likely, he could allow himself to be seduced by Hewie's widowed sister-in-law, the attractive — and aggressive — Nora.

Old habits die hard.

"I believe," he now answered Duff, "I'll pass."

"Then so shall I. Race you back home?"

Motion, speed, the chilly wind pressing hard on his face: a fast gallop in the gathering twilight. Yes. Alasdair nodded.

They both dug their heels into their mounts, and were off.

Reestablished at the Douglass keep, Fiona seemed to have been seamlessly absorbed back into her old routine, in a way that was deeply unnerving, as if her time

at Castle Tadgh had been collapsed into nothingness.
Nobody asked her about it, whether out of sensitivity,
respect, or lack of interest. It had been her hope that
as the long days passed, the image of Alasdair would
begin to fade from her mind and her heart, but it did
not. After a while, it occurred to Fiona that she now
had a better and more vivid understanding of that old
Greek myth about Eurydice, the girl who'd stepped
on a poisonous snake and been sent for all eternity to
live in the ghastly Underworld — a place of despon-
dence and woe from which ordinary mortals could
never escape.

It felt a little like she was living in a sort of underworld, too, invisible to everyone else but evident to
her, every minute, every hour.

She did her best to tamp down a restless longing to
be somewhere else.

Anywhere else, perhaps.

Alasdair stood in the Great Drawing-room, staring
at the window-hangings. Even though no one came in
here anymore — he and Duff now went to the library
in the evenings — apparently somebody had, at some
point, drawn open the heavy, tasseled lengths of dark
green velvet to admit the sun.

He remembered Fiona saying scornfully:

*Three hundred and eighty pounds for the fabric
alone. And nineteen pounds for the tassels.*

God's blood, but that was a lot of money.

There was a tap on the open door, and Alasdair
turned. In the doorway stood Mrs. Allen the housekeeper in her tidy spotless gown and ruffled cap.

"You sent for me, laird?"

"Aye. Come in." He gestured toward the curtains.

"Could you have those taken down, please, and cleaned?"

"Of course, laird."

"And afterwards — I want to give them away. To someone who'll find them useful. Any ideas?"

Mrs. Allen looked thoughtful. "You ordered more wagons to go to the Sutherlainns next week. The fabric is very thick, and will help keep a room warm. There must be a dozen or more lengths to divide up, laird."

"Do it, then."

"I'll see to it at once."

"Thank you, Mrs. Allen. By the way, what do you think of them?"

"Of the Sutherlainns, laird?"

"I was unclear. I mean those window-hangings. What's your frank opinion?"

Mrs. Allen hesitated.

"Your frank opinion, please."

"Well, laird, they're a wee bit much for the room, aren't they? And with all those tassels — I can't help but think them rather *busy*, if you know what I mean?"

He looked at them again. And nodded. "Aye," he said. "I do know what you mean."

Change was coming.

Change was coming, and it was good.

It was Fiona's seventy-second wedding. Seventy-third, she supposed, if she counted her own ephemeral one to Alasdair Penhallow.

But she wasn't going to.

So: her seventy-second wedding.

She sat once more in the very last pew of the church in Wick Bay, where, far to the front, her fourth cousin,

Boyd Iverach, was marrying *his* fourth cousin, Effie Bain. It was a small, local wedding, and the church was only half-full. Several rows ahead of her sat Father, Mother, Isobel, and Logan Munro. Next to Logan, pretty Helen MacNeillie (yet another cousin) had placed herself just a little too close for respectability, and Fiona, observing them from behind, noticed what a striking pair they made — he so tall and broad, and with his dark hair, Helen so plump and round, with curls of tawny gold.

She herself had come just a tiny bit late, having ridden out past the bogs to visit old Osla Tod, and had to quickly scramble into nicer clothing for the wedding. Now she looked down at the charming kid ankle-boots Mother had let her borrow. Aquamarine. So beautiful, that liminal shade between green and blue. Once in a while, the loch near Castle Tadgh had been that color, rendering it breathtakingly lovely.

The minister was going on and on in his sonorous voice about the duties and obligations of marriage, and surreptitiously Fiona loosened the silken cord of her reticule. She pulled from it a small pencil and a little piece of paper. As it happens, it was the very same piece on which, a few months back on that perfect summer's day, she had added to her list during Rossalyn's wedding.

Fiona turned over the paper.

It was blank.

Absolutely, totally blank.

Slowly, secretly, she began to write.

Things I like about myself:

Intelligent
Kind
Capable

Hardworking
Good sense of humor
Strong

Things I don't like about myself:

Stubborn
Too proud (?)
Insecure
A dull stick
Greedy

She thought for a while.

In the *Things I don't like* category, she crossed out *Greedy*.

She also crossed out *A dull stick*.

Then she looked up and to the front, where Boyd was kissing Effie, with a boisterous *smack* that resonated sweetly throughout the church.

She looked back down at her list.

Crossed out *Things I don't like about myself*, and wrote instead *Aspects to improve*.

Yes.

That was better.

She'd work hard to improve on her stubborn, insecure, overly proud aspects.

She gave a decisive little nod.

And finally, in the *Things I like* category, underneath *Strong*, she added:

Good enough.
I am good enough.
I am MORE than good enough.
I am worthy.
I am

She paused. What was the right word?

Then it came to her, and she wrote: *lovable*.

Capable of loving, and worthy of being loved.

Suddenly she noticed that the wedding was over. People were standing up, talking, laughing.

Fiona folded her paper, and put it and the pencil safely back into her reticule. With a firm step, she went to warmly congratulate Effie and Boyd.

Time marched on, relentlessly, inexorably, everywhere around the vast earth, yet for two particular people, in their separate parts of the world, long miles apart from each other, it had a distinctly peculiar quality. Was it going by quickly, or curiously slowly?

It must have been two months after she'd come back to Wick Bay, on a cool, cloudy morning, that Fiona stood at a workbench in the stillroom, using a stone pestle to grind the tough leaves of a house-leek into a pulp for a poultice. Isobel had a headache, and leeks were an excellent remedy. After she had delivered the poultice — Fiona glanced at the long list she'd set near the mortar — she'd go to the kitchen to talk with the cook, then stop by the stables, and after that sit with Mother for a while in the solarium, and do some sewing. Then —

"Hello."

Fiona paused. There was Logan, very nearly filling up the width of the doorframe with his massive shoulders. She looked up at him. "Hello." Then she went on mashing a particularly fibrous leaf.

"You've been avoiding me."

Fiona considered this. "No."

"No?"

"No. But it would be fair to say that I haven't been seeking you out."

"Are you still angry at me for Nairna's death?"

Fiona considered this also. "No."

"I'm glad."

There was a silence. Fiona finally mangled the leaf into a satisfying pulp. Logan leaned against the doorframe.

"A long time ago," he said softly, "we used to have conversations."

"True."

"Perhaps we could have one now?"

"What about?"

"Whatever you like."

Fiona looked up at him again. Goodness, but he was as handsome as ever. He really did have the most classically perfect nose she had ever seen — like the bold prow of a ship. And how had he managed to have just one lock of his black hair lying across his forehead in that dashing way? Had he done it on purpose, or was it one of those lucky accidents in life?

"Very well," she said. "I'll begin. Why are you still here, Logan?"

"I have a reason for staying."

"I see. Don't you have an estate to run at home? Fields, a house, servants, and so on?"

"I don't think you do see, in fact. And yes, I have an estate, but I also have a bailiff, who spares me the boredom of having to think about — or, worse, deal with — sheep and farmers and crops. And I have a mother and a sister to manage my house and my servants."

"What on earth do you do with yourself all day?"

"A gentleman can always find ways to keep himself occupied."

"If you say so."

"Trust me." He smiled, and there it was — the fetching little dimple in his left cheek.

She had always found that dimple incredibly charming. The very first time she'd met Logan, when she was eighteen, he had smiled at her — in just the way he was right now — and she had badly wanted to touch her tongue to that intriguing hollow. And immediately had turned as red as a strawberry, and made an inane, awkward remark about the weather, expecting him to turn on his heel and walk away in disgust at her maladroit manner.

But he hadn't. He had agreed that the weather *was* fine. And stayed. And she'd been lost.

"So," she now said, "what *is* your reason for staying on?"

"You."

"I beg your pardon?"

"You're the reason I'm still here."

"I don't understand."

"I want us to start over again."

Fiona pushed away the mortar and pestle. Already the house-leek pulp was losing its potency; she'd have to grind some more as soon as this absurd exchange was over. Because it *was* absurd.

Wasn't it?

"My, my," she said in an even tone. "Moving rather quickly, aren't you?"

He took a step toward her. "If life has taught me anything, Fiona, it's that anything can happen at any time. The past is gone. Right here, right now, is a second chance for us. We cared for each other once."

"Yes, but you jilted me for Nairna, as you'll recall."

He took another step closer.

"I liked you. I liked you very much." His voice, his eyes, everything about Logan was eager earnestness.

"But — I had debts, Fiona, large debts from foolish gambling while at university."

"And Nairna had a much bigger dowry."

"I'll not deny there was, in part, a mercenary incentive. I was desperate, in danger of losing my estate. I don't gamble anymore — at least not beyond my means. And I was a good husband to Nairna — you know I was."

"Yes. You made her very happy."

"So now let's look to the future, Fiona, you and I."

If he had touched her, she would have shoved past him and left the stillroom, poor Isobel's remedy be damned. But he simply stood there, so very tall, so very big. And whether he knew it or not, he was saying all the right things to a woman with a broken heart. The past is gone. Start over again. Second chances. The future.

Fiona said:

"Just so we're clear. Are you saying that you want to marry me?"

"Yes, my darling, that's exactly what I'm saying."

She let this sink in. Such marriages were far from uncommon among the pragmatic Douglass clan; no one would bat an eye. But more important, what would Nairna have said?

It was an easy question.

Fiona could almost hear her sweetest, kindest, most loving of sisters saying, *Of course! Marry him with my blessing. Take good care of him, won't you?*

"Well," Fiona said to Logan, "if you're looking to make money from marrying me, you'd better think again, because you never know with Father and his vagaries."

"It's not about money. I have a very competent bailiff and my income is ample for my needs."

"Have you spoken to Father?"

"No. You're no green girl."

"I need time to think about your proposal."

"Of course. Take as much time as you need. May I kiss you?"

"No."

"No?"

"No."

He smiled, those black eyes of his flashing. "You disappoint me, but I can be patient. Good day, my sweet."

"Where are you going?"

"Somewhere there's a fire. This keep is atrociously cold."

"Father's gone off to look at some fishing boats, if you're interested."

"I'm not."

"As you like. Good day."

His smile was caressing. "Till we meet again."

Then he was gone, and Fiona was alone again. She turned at once to the mortar and pestle. She threw out the old house-leek, and started on a new one.

Chapter 16

Alasdair whistled, and Cuilean came running, panting joyfully. They'd been to the river and back, and now, as they made their way through the gardens toward the castle, Alasdair saw the long ladder once more propped up against that tree, where once he had watched Fiona high above him. Monty was slowly descending, rung by rung, and when he reached the ground he said in laconic acknowledgement:

"Morning, laird."

Alasdair paused. Cuilean frisked round him, plainly wondering what next exciting adventure awaited them. Alasdair said, "So how are those eggs doing?" Never in his life would he have imagined he'd be asking after a nest of goldfinch eggs, but if Duff could shave off a beard he'd had for thirty-five years, anything, he supposed, was possible.

"Not eggs anymore. Hatched."

Alasdair hesitated.

Monty said, "Want to see them?"

"Actually, I do."

"Shall I hold the ladder steady, laird?"

"Monty, how long have you known me?"

"All your life, laird."

"Have you ever held a ladder for me?"

Monty reflected. "Nay, laird, though there *was* that time when you were stuck on the roof."

"You offended me grievously with your suggestion then also."

"You were nine, laird."

"I may have broken my collarbone jumping down, but my pride was intact."

Monty smiled, ever so slightly, which for him was the equivalent of a face-splitting grin. "You were ever a game lad."

"That's one way to put it. My mother used to say that I was an imp from hell. And that's when she was in a good mood." Alasdair went to the ladder and swiftly climbed it. There, high among the branches, was a cup-shaped nest, and in it were five little — what were they called? Not fledglings, for the tiny fragile creatures had no feathers to speak of. They were covered in a fluffy gray down that made them look at once rather comical and, he thought in wonderment, incredibly vulnerable. Their eyes were black and bead-like and utterly without guile. New life, new hope. He found himself wishing with a startling intensity that they'd survive, grow, fly.

A little flutter from a branch some three feet away caught his eye. An adult finch. A nervous parent. At once Alasdair went down the ladder. Cuilean greeted him with as much enthusiasm as if he'd just returned from a long sea voyage, and Alasdair reached down to affectionately rub that rough woolly head.

"Mayhap," said Monty, "we'll see goldfinches more often now."

Alasdair straightened. "What are the odds of that?"

"Time will tell."

He nodded, and was just about ready to move on when Monty added:

"Always felt —" He stopped, looked meditatively up into the tree. "A shame about that accident on the loch. Never had a chance to change, and grow, as a family. Hard for you, being on your own."

For Monty this was an epic speech, and Alasdair stared down at him, amazed.

"Aye," he answered slowly. "A shame. Thank you, Monty."

The older man dipped his head a little and cleared his throat. "Rosebushes need cutting back. If that's all, laird?"

"Aye." Alasdair watched him trudge off. Cuilean had gone to investigate an interesting smell underneath a hedge, but came instantly when Alasdair whistled, and followed obediently at his heel as he went into the castle and — to Cuilean's disappointment — not into the breakfast-room but up the stairs and eventually to the Portrait Gallery.

Alasdair slowed as he came to the painting of his ancestor Raulf Penhallow, the savage medieval warrior-prince said to have been the terror of half the island. Very fine he was here, in his handsome tunic and leggings. Very arrogant and proud. There'd never been a need to wonder, Alasdair thought, how he had come by his dark-red hair. Raulf was sporting a full head of it.

As a child he'd never spent much time looking up at old Raulf, for by some devious trickery the artist had managed to render his eyes in a way that seemed to follow you about, with an expression in them that suggested ill intent. One of the pleasures of adulthood was that he'd become tall enough to meet Raulf face to face, as it were, without a superstitious chill running down his spine.

Alasdair lingered there, his gaze resting thoughtfully on that haughty countenance. Not only was

Raulf renowned for his ferocity, he was also notori-
ously stubborn (which made all his sieges successful). But in the end, evidently, he was undone by his
insistence on eating oysters brought in from Cairnryan
— against the advice of his ministers, his astrologist,
his surgeon-barber, his wife *and* his mistress, and his
priest, for the distance was such to make consuming
them hazardous.

He was dead within the hour.

"You bloody old fool," Alasdair said out loud to
Raulf. "Hoist by your own petard."

He moved on.

At length he came to the portrait of himself and
Gavin. How they'd hated standing still for so long!
Also, he and Gavin had been in the middle of a long-
running feud as to who was better at spitting their
saliva the furthest, and the only way the harassed artist
could keep them from breaking out into fisticuffs was
to abandon his idea of posing them with their arms
around each other. But the entire time he and Gavin
had muttered crass scatological insults to each other.

Speaking of stubborn.

Suddenly Alasdair grinned.

Christ, maybe it all could have worked out all
right, no matter what would've happened with Mòrag
Cray.

Anything was possible.

His smile dimmed, and he reached out a hand to
one of those faint discolorations on the wall.

Then he walked on to the laird's bedchamber and
into his dressing-room. On a low shelf in his armoire
was a small box hewn from oak and fitted with orna-
mental brass along its curved lid. Inside the box was
a steel key, and Alasdair took the key, went into the
passageway, and stopped before the locked door.

Into his mind came little Sheila's voice, that odd

remark she'd made the day after his thirty-fifth birthday, right after Dame Margery had issued her stunning pronouncement.

A room with a door, a door with a lock, she had said in that dreamy way she had sometimes. *An egg that won't hatch, a bird that can't fly . . .*

There was no doubt about it, Sheila was an interesting child, with those pale blue eyes that could, apparently, see two things at once.

Alasdair unlocked the door.

Without windows, without candles to illuminate it, the room was dark, but Alasdair didn't need such things to know what was inside.

A dozen portraits of his family, set carefully against the walls.

Father, Mother, Gavin, and himself: painted from the time of his own infancy until shortly before their deaths.

After they were gone, he couldn't bear to look at these portraits. Somehow he couldn't bring himself to destroy them, and so had placed them in here. Not in the attics, where anyone might go and find them. Here, where they were concealed from prying eyes, and where they had been, undisturbed, for all these years.

Alasdair leaned against the doorframe, his eyes fixed on the dim shapes of the portraits. He felt it coming, the massive wave of grief, but he didn't brace himself against it or try to fight it, or ignore it, as he'd done before.

Instead he let it roll through him, an overpowering rush of sorrow so intense that for a brief moment or two he wondered if it would kill him.

But it didn't.

It rolled on and away.

Leaving him not empty, but filled with — why, it was love.

Love for Gavin, clever, mischievous, maddening, impulsive, merry, affectionate.

For Father, intelligent, kind, easygoing, maybe a little weak, but well-meaning and generous.

For Mother, brilliant and moody, a limited person, perhaps, whom he'd never fully understand, but she'd done the best she could, which is, in the end, all that anyone can do.

As for Mòrag Cray, what he felt wasn't love, or even the remnants of a boy's fiery infatuation, that was all in the past now, but he didn't feel the old longing anymore, the dreadful insidious pull of what might have been.

The wave would come again, he was sure of that, but next time, he thought, it would be a little less intense.

More bearable.

It was, he thought, possible, just possible, that he had begun to heal.

Alasdair took in a breath, and slowly let it out.

Then he left the door open, put away the key, and went downstairs to the steward's office, Cuilean trotting alongside him.

"Lister," he said.

"Aye, laird?" Lister, at his desk, looked up, promptly set aside his quill.

"You know the rooms off my bedchamber?"

"Of course."

"In one of those rooms are some portraits of my family."

"Indeed, laird?"

Alasdair smiled a little. "Haven't you been wondering, all these years, where they were?"

"It's not my business to wonder, laird," replied Lister piously.

"I'd like you to have the portraits put back in their place, in the gallery."

"To be sure, laird, I'll see to it."

"Good. Have you been able to pay those old invoices of my mother's?"

"Oh yes, it's all been taken care of."

"I'm glad. Thank you, Lister," said Alasdair, and went on to the breakfast-room. If Cuilean had been able to form the words, he doubtless would have said, in a joyful voice, *At last.*

Late at night, wide awake, in her bedchamber Fiona took out paper, ink, and a quill. She sat at her old escritoire, wearing not only her thick flannel nightgown but also two of her heaviest wool cloaks and four pairs of stockings. Logan Munro was right: the keep *was* atrociously cold.

Not that it was news to her.

Was she going to marry Logan?

She dipped her quill in the inkpot and slowly wrote:

Pros

Start a new life
Babies (hopefully)
Logan is very good-looking
His house is probably warmer

Cons

No real sense of humor; fond of puns (ugh)
Has a weak chin

She paused.

So what if Logan's chin was less than ideal? She herself, after all, was far from perfect. For example, she'd become so thin that the last time she'd gotten onto Gealag's back, he'd inquiringly turned his head around to see if it really *was* her, or perhaps a scarecrow from the field which someone had set on top of him.

Fiona looked down at the sheet of paper on which she'd begun her list.

Stared at it for a long time.

She thought again about the things Logan had said to her in the stillroom. Then she pushed aside her list, and began writing them down on a new sheet of paper.

The past is gone.
Start over again.
Second chances.
The future.

At this she also stared for a long time. Logan had said all the right things. He really had. Her mind moved and leaped, reversed itself and jumped ahead, looping over and over as she studied these eleven simple words.

Finally she slid aside the paper, revealing another blank sheet.

Slowly she began to write again.

He was dreaming that he'd been very far down in the water, where all was icy blackness.

He dreamed that he had at last figured out which way was up. Where the surface was. With powerful strokes of his arms, powerful kicks of his legs, he swam up, the water around him gradually brightening, until, his lungs seeming about to burst, he broke through and out into the air and light of the world. He breathed. A few gentle strokes of his arms kept him buoyant. Not for him another descent into the watery soundless gloom below. Radiance everywhere.

And then Alasdair woke up.

It was morning.

He turned from his side and lay on his back, looking around his bedchamber.

Another morning.

Hours ahead of him, to fill as best he could.

What next?

He remembered, suddenly, the time he, and Gavin, and a group of schoolfellows had been taken to a zoo in Glasgow, one of the very first built upon modern scientific principles. He remembered standing in front of an enclosure, inside which a bear had been confined. It was a very large enclosure. It had obviously been carefully designed so as to provide a comfortable setting for the bear; there were trees, shrubs, a spacious pool of water. Still, the bear wasn't free, and Alasdair had been almost unendurably sad to see it. Nonsense, said one of the masters, the bear is safe, it's got no predators or hunters, it's fed every day, what's there to be melancholy about?

But still he remembered wondering, at the age of ten, is it better to be safe or to be free?

It occurred to him now that safety was, perhaps, overrated. And in the wake of that thought, his being was flooded again with the essence of his dream.

Radiance everywhere.

It came to him, all at once, with the ease of an obvious idea, what he needed to do today.

It really was time to move forward.

Yes.

How simple it all was.

Simple, and yet risky.

The outcome was uncertain.

But he was going to try.

That's all he could do.

Alasdair got out of bed, pulled aside one of the heavy drapes, looked at the sky. There was snow in those low gray clouds. Well, it couldn't be helped. He wasn't about to let a little snow get in his way.

It had been a tedious morning. After nearly a week of mild sunshine, the weather had turned nasty. The oatmeal served at breakfast had been burnt, the tea tasted worse than usual, and Father had been grumpy. Mother was nursing a cold; Isobel had been solicitous until Father had snapped at her, reducing her to tremulous silence. Only Logan had been cheerful, relating amusing anecdotes about his tailor back home and regaling them with a few choice puns. Fiona had finally stopped listening to him, given up on the execrable oatmeal, and simply looked at how beautifully put together Logan's features were (aside from his chin). She had never before noticed that his eyelashes were so long and lush that they actually curled. A woman might envy them.

After breakfast the ladies had escaped to the solarium, where the weak gray light of a cold, windy day seemed to fill it with a kind of hopelessness that not even the pleasant and colorful chaos within could overcome. Wrapped in an enormous tartan shawl, Mother had dozed on a chaise longue drawn close to the fire, and Isobel valiantly attempted, once more, to untangle various skeins of unruly yarn. Logan poked his head in but, as if sensing the gloom pervading the solarium, had not come inside, only smiled intimately at Fiona before retreating.

As for Fiona, she only stayed long enough to complete the set of embroidered linen handkerchiefs which she had been making. Very absorbent they were; wonderful for mopping up tears. She smoothed them together into a neat little stack, then placed it carefully on the table at Isobel's side.

"For you, dear Isobel," she said. "May you have little need of them." Then she dropped a light kiss on the older woman's forehead, and went quickly to her bedchamber to change into a heavy, thick old gown, a long wool pelisse, and stout boots. On her head she tugged down a sturdy, close-fitting cap that was quite possibly the ugliest headgear she owned. But what did she care? It was warm, and outside it was freezing.

In the Great Hall she crossed paths with Father, who carried a musket in each hand.

"Cleaning your guns, Father?"

He nodded. "Aye. Where are you going?"

"The sheep pasture."

He nodded again, and so they parted in perfect harmony.

The wind whipped at her skirts, not playfully but in a grabby malevolent sort of way, as Fiona walked along a muddy track lined with trees stripped bare of their leaves. Winter was coming, that was for sure. Everyone said it was going to be a bad one this year.

She came to the pasture fence and leaned upon it for a while, thinking.

This past week had gone by so slowly.

More and more she had come to realize just how much she hated puns.

At breakfast Logan had said, *Why is it dreadful to have carrion near?*

And had answered himself:

Because it makes an offal smell.

He had laughed, and looked like he'd just thought

of another one, and that was when she'd left off listening.

Fiona straightened, then nimbly climbed over the fence and into the pasture. There were only some three dozen sheep contained here, and they eyed her placidly; she was well-known to them.

"Hello," she said, approaching them quietly, affably. A sharp gust of wind sent her skirts blowing wildly and doubtless revealed more of her legs than was seemly. Luckily there was no one out here to see it.

From behind her, however, someone said:

"Hello."

Fiona wanted to spin around, as fast as humanly possible, but through an immense act of will she schooled herself. She turned very slowly, very carefully, as if by so doing she would ensure that the owner of that deep, masculine voice — that voice like molten chocolate — would still be there when she was done pivoting her body.

He was.

Oh, he *was*.

"Hello," she said again, not to the sheep this time, but to Alasdair Penhallow, who stood just outside the fence in a dirty dark greatcoat. On his feet were tall, mud-spattered boots and his head was bare. He had an ugly gash on one cheek and his hair, longer than when she had last seen it, was a little rumpled. He was, without doubt, the most handsome, the most desirable man in all the great wide world. And his *chin*. So strong and so manly. She really could stare at it all day.

"So," said Alasdair, casually, "what are you doing out here?"

"Oh," she said, just as casually, "I had an idea the other day for treating bloody scours, so I tried it. I've come to see if it's working."

He looked interested. "What did you use?"

"I've been giving them a mixture of sodium carbonate in boiled water, with a pinch of salt and a little molasses."

"And?"

"So far so good."

"Excellent. I'll be sure and tell Shaw about your idea."

"Do." The wind whirled viciously at her skirts and this time she was able to clutch at them and keep them from flying up.

Alasdair squinted at the sky. "Blustery today," he remarked.

"Very," Fiona agreed. "By the way, how did you know I was here?"

"Your father told me."

"Oh? So you've met Father."

"Aye."

"And?"

"We had a pleasant conversation. He invited me to walk down to the bay with him, to see some fishing boats."

"What did you tell him?"

"I said I would. After I had found you."

"Do you know about fishing boats?"

"Quite a lot, actually."

She nodded. Then she said: "I'm surprised my letter arrived so quickly."

"What letter?"

"The letter I wrote to you."

"You wrote to me?"

"Yes."

He was silent for a moment. "You wrote to me," he repeated softly, as if he needed to hear it again.

"Yes. Isn't that why you've come? You got my letter, and you've traveled very fast to get here?"

"We did travel as fast as we could, but there was no letter from you before we left."

Now it was Fiona's turn to be briefly silent. "So . . . you came *without* hearing from me."

"Aye."

"Ah." She took this in, as might a parched land receive the sweet benediction of rain. Then: "You said 'we.'"

"Duff and I."

"Duff. Excellent. I'm so glad you had a traveling companion."

"He insisted on coming with me."

"Isobel will, I think, be very glad to see him."

"I hope so. *He* hopes so. What did you say in your letter?"

Fiona looked into those eyes, all amber and citrine, that were fixed so straitly upon her. "I asked if we could try again."

"Ah. May I tell you why I'm here?"

"Yes. Please."

Alasdair smiled. At last he smiled. And at once she felt an answering smile upon her own face as he said:

"Why, I've come to woo you, lass."

Fiona hoped she wouldn't explode, melt, dissolve into a dew, from the joy that was filling her to the brim. A gust of wind tried to blow her over, but she wouldn't let it. Slowly, unhurriedly, she walked over to meet him at the fence. "What do you mean, woo me?"

"You and I, Fiona Douglass, are starting over," he said. "If you'll have me."

"Yes," she replied instantly. "Yes, Alasdair Penhallow, I'll have you."

His face — his dear, beloved, familiar face — lit up. He looked so happy that even though she hadn't thought she could possibly feel more joyful, she did. *Don't explode*, she warned herself. *Today is the first day of the rest of your life.*

"Fiona."

"Yes, Alasdair?"

"Must I kiss you with this fence between us?"

"Nothing more between us, I say."

"I agree." He put one hand on the top rail, vaulted over the fence, and stood before her, the hem of his dark greatcoat rippling in the wind.

"You may get sheep dung on your boots."

"Think you I care about that?"

No, he wouldn't care. Of course he wouldn't care. Fiona lifted her face invitingly. Alasdair stepped close and gently set his big hands on her shoulders.

"You," he said softly, "are so very, very beautiful," and then his lips were on hers, and he was kissing her, in exactly the way a man might kiss a woman for the very first time, as if each sensation was new and wonderful, as if the taste of her was the most delicious thing in the universe and he was hungry, so hungry, but he didn't want to rush through the meal. He kissed her as if he never wanted to stop.

It was only when a strange sensation of being intently watched came upon Fiona that she finally drew back a little. She turned her head.

Said: "Dear me."

And laughed.

The entire flock of sheep had drifted near and together they had the rapt air of an audience at the theater for whom an enthralling performance was being enacted. But not, Fiona thought, *Romeo and Juliet*. Rather, a play in which the lovers are to live happily ever after.

Alasdair was laughing, too.

Then he turned to her and said, "I almost forgot."

"Forgot what?"

He reached into an inside pocket of his greatcoat. "To woo a maiden properly, gifts must be tendered."

"I like gifts as much as the next person, but they're really not necessary."

"Don't subvert the wooing process."

"I'll try not to."

"Good girl. Here." He gave her a small, tightly stoppered jar. In it was a thick golden substance. "This is from Monty. It's —"

"Honey!" she exclaimed. "From our hives?"

"Aye. From our hives. You and Monty have worked miracles." Smiling, he reached into his pocket again. "And this is from Sheila."

It was a sampler, not entirely clean, but clearly the product of concerted effort. Around the edges had been embroidered a simple, pretty floral pattern, which framed these words in black thread:

THY WOOD IS A LAMP UNTO MY FOOT.

"It's lovely. Absolutely lovely." Ignoring the misspellings, with great tenderness Fiona folded the grubby square of linen and put it, and the precious jar of honey, into a pocket of her pelisse. "What wonderful gifts. Did the whole clan know you were coming here?"

"Aye. The word spread quickly. Cook would have sent you entire meals had I not persuaded her of the impracticality of such a scheme."

"How kind," Fiona sighed happily.

"I've one last gift. I hope you like it. Give me your hand, please."

Fiona obeyed. Alasdair gently turned it until her palm was revealed, and upon it he placed a ring. It was made of gold and it was fashioned, without ostentation, around a sapphire — square-cut, beautifully faceted, of a blue so exquisite, so pure, it made Fiona's breath catch in her throat.

"Sometimes your eyes are that color," he said.

"Are they?"

"Aye."

"What color are they now, Alasdair?"

"Like that sapphire, lass."

She nodded. *My cup runneth over. I've never really understood that expression before. Now I do. Don't explode, you,* she told herself.

"Do you like it?"

"The ring?" she asked, a little dazedly.

"Aye, the ring."

"Yes. So very much."

"It was my mother's, given to her by my grandmother. Who had it from her mother. And so on. I should have presented to you, before, all the Penhallow jewels, as was your right. But somehow it never happened."

"There were distractions."

"Too many. Let's have a simpler life from now on."

"I'd like that. Alasdair, is this a betrothal ring?"

"What do you think?" He smiled warmly at her.

"I think — yes. But I need to know for sure."

"You can be sure."

"Will you say the words?"

"Of course. Will you marry me, Fiona? This time for real? For ever? No matter what that damned Tome might reveal tomorrow, next year, or fifty years from now?"

"Yes, Alasdair, I will."

"I'm glad, lass. Glad beyond words." With a reverence that brought a rush of happy tears to Fiona's eyes, Alasdair took the ring and slid it onto the fourth finger of her left hand.

"It fits," she said softly, admiring the sapphire's fiery sparkle.

"As we do."

He leaned his head down to kiss her again, and eagerly did she return his kiss. He pulled her close and she slid her arms tightly around his neck and they stood there in the sheep pasture, body to body, heart to heart, soul to soul. Despite the cold unfriendly winds buffeting them, Fiona was sure she'd never felt so warm before, so completely connected to another person. So safe.

When at length they pulled away a little, he said, "I love you, Fiona."

"I thought — I hoped you did," she answered, still a little breathless from that long, that delightfully long kiss.

"I'm sorry for my blindness, for my stubbornness, and my fear."

"I'm sorry for my own, and for my haste in leaving you. For running away. When Isobel and Duff found the second decree, I felt I *had* to go."

"Naturally you did. I'd hurt you. I was a fool."

"No. Not a fool. But — I think we both had to grow a little?"

"Aye. Do you still love me, Fiona?"

"Yes. I love you, Alasdair. More, I believe."

She could feel his arms tightening around her again, and she smiled at him. She reached up a finger and lightly traced the firm curve of his chin, and those delicious lines bracketing his mouth. "What happened to your cheek?"

"Oh, a mountain lion came at me near Golspie," he said, nonchalant.

"But how dreadful! Have you other injuries? Is Duff all right?"

"No other injuries, lass, and Duff is fine. Although he *did* get soaked to the bone when the bridge on which he was riding collapsed and he tumbled into a stream. I haven't seen him laugh so hard in years. He'll tell you, however, that he had more fun the day before last, when we were set upon by a pair of brigands in Brora, and that he whistled all the way through a snowstorm in the Grampian Pass."

"Gracious, what a journey," she said, twinkling up at him. "It's all *deeply* romantic, and Isobel will be so pleased to think of the travails you and Duff overcame on our behalf."

"Knights in shining armor, that's what we are!" Alasdair said, much struck. "I wonder I didn't think of that before. How I shall puff myself about. I suppose I'll be completely insufferable by dinnertime."

Fiona laughed. "Won't you come back to the keep, and let me put some of my salve on that wound?"

"If it will make you feel better, lass."

"It will."

Hand in hand, they strolled along the muddy path as if bathed in mild spring sunshine. Fiona told him about Nairna. Then, when her sadness lifted, she described her unavailing efforts to convince the cook to try some new recipes, and also about a harrowing birth in the stables at which Father had managed to save the lives of both the mare and her foal, now a healthy, promising colt for which Father had great hopes.

Alasdair in turn told her all about a fascinating book he'd been reading (the subject being an ingenious new plow he wanted to try in the spring), his suspicion that Cuilean had sired a large and thriving litter of pups by one of Shaw's retrievers (Shaw had offered to give her one), and also about the rumor going around the castle that Dr. Colquhoun had secretly proposed to Mrs. Allen. And of course he told her about the goldfinches.

"Oh, I can't *wait* to be home again," said Fiona fervently. "When can we, Alasdair?"

"Whenever you like, lass, although I must admit I'm keen to have you there sooner rather than later, and feed you Cook's good food myself if I have to. You need fattening up."

"Let's get married tomorrow, then."

"I brought your wedding ring. Just in case."

"A short betrothal."

"And a long marriage."

They laughed.

"Alasdair," Fiona said, "do you like puns?"

"You'd have to tie me to a chair to make me listen to them. Why?"

"I was just wondering." Fiona couldn't help it, she gave a little skip of joy, and together, hands still warmly clasped, they kept walking.

In the Great Hall they found a scene of genial confusion. Duff had wasted no time in gaining the hand of his Isobel (who, weeping happily, was successfully deploying one of her large new handkerchiefs), Mother was fluttering about still wrapped in her enormous shawl, Father had emerged from his gun room with one of the deadly-looking muskets grasped absentmindedly in one hand, his dogs were taking advantage of the disorder and boldly licking crumbs off the table, and Logan Munro stood close to the roaring fire, slavishly attended by two eager housemaids anxious to offer him tea or ale or whatever — whatever — he liked.

Alasdair was introduced, wedding plans put forth, Father's assent given, Mother joined Isobel in happy crying, and Logan, seeing that he was beaten, gave in with good grace, shook hands with Alasdair, congratulated him on his good fortune, and promptly made himself scarce, leaving the keep quietly the next morning and his absence mourned only by the maids — even Mother, the most good-natured person imaginable, privately confessing to Fiona that she'd gotten tired of having Logan lounging around the solarium, talking, and all too often interfering with her naps.

Chapter 17

And so the very next day, in the church where her sisters had been wed, Fiona and Alasdair were married. Rather to the disappointment of the local folk, there were no brawls, no sudden deaths, no ferrets dashing about, no spectacular leaks in the roof, or anything, really, to liven up what was, after all, just another wedding.

Of interest was only the fact that immediately after Fiona and her foreign laird were leg-shackled, *her* cousin and *his* uncle were also married, and although Dame Isobel twice sobbed loudly enough to drown out the groom's responses, nothing else untoward occurred.

The feast that followed was also sadly unremarkable. There was no shouting, no cursing, no overturned tables, no fights among the dogs for scraps.

Altogether a dull affair, said the locals.

Fiona, however, wasn't the least bit sorry everything had gone so smoothly. There were a few surprises here and there, but agreeable ones. Father, for one, was positively mellow. He had given a toast so eloquent and sentimental that she'd had to borrow Isobel's handkerchief with which to dry her cheeks.

And Mother had made a comment of stunning per-spicacity.

"I *told* you, Fiona dear, that you'd find someone you like!" she said complacently.

Further stunning those assembled, Father had nodded sagely, and then planted a loud kiss on Mother's lips.

Wonders *will* never cease, thought Fiona, and turned her gaze from Mother's astonished, but pleased countenance, to look across the table at Alasdair. They smiled at each other.

There was another surprise in store.

When the musicians began to play the lively, lilt-ing "Largo Fairy" — not well, but with enthusiasm — Alasdair came to her and said:

"Will you dance with me, lass? I've not yet had that pleasure."

Fiona demurred. "Oh, Alasdair, I don't — I haven't — the last time I tried was so long ago, and I tripped over my own feet, and forgot the steps, and really I was just terrible at it . . ." She trailed off, and for his ears alone she added softly, "I'm afraid."

He took her hand in his. "It seems to me that a woman who saved my life from the Dalwhinnies, and who kept herself alive and well when kidnapped by a band of desperate ruffians — to mention only two examples of your courage — need not fear a reel. But fear, I know, isn't always a rational thing." He lifted her hand to his lips, and kissed it. "If you wish, I'll teach you. If you trip, I'll catch you. And if you prefer not to, I won't persist."

Fiona took a deep breath. The fiddles and the flutes did sound awfully inviting. Plenty of other people were already dancing — among them Isobel and Duff, and he so light on his feet it was a gladsome thing to ob-serve. Everyone was having so much fun, and she —

She *had* been thinking about slipping away, to make sure Duff's things had all been moved into Isobel's bedchamber, and that Alasdair's had been brought into hers, and that a maid would be sure to bring up a hot cup of tea for Mother at bedtime, and also —

But no. She could do all that later, or not at all. Everything would work out just fine. And meanwhile, the dancing looked like so much fun. And wasn't it time that she allowed a little more fun into her life? Perhaps she and Alasdair could nip in there, inconspicuously —

"Yes," she said to him bravely. "Yes, I will."

And then he smiled, and led her into the dance.

They passed their first night together in her cold, draughty bedchamber. Her bed was really too small for them both. But Fiona and Alasdair noticed neither the cold nor the size of the bed. They were intent on each other, whether it was to rediscover, or to discover, each other it was impossible to tell. It didn't matter. A second chance had been given them — or perhaps it would be more accurate to say that together they had *created* this second chance — and they were both determined to make the most of it. Their lovemaking was by turns fierce and tender, raw and achingly sweet.

It wasn't until the deepest dark of night was just beginning to yield to soft intimations of morning that they lay at rest, entwined, at their ease, utterly content.

"Now that," said Fiona with a purr in her voice, "is what I call a proper wedding night."

He kissed her ear. "Aye. Better this time around."

"Indeed. It makes me wonder what our *third* wedding night would be like."

"I don't think we'd survive it."

She laughed, and snuggled her head a little more cozily into that wonderful hollow between Alasdair's shoulder and his neck. How good he felt, and smelled, and tasted. And how tired she was. But in a nice way. She yawned, and lifted a hand — happily conscious of the rings upon it — to cover her mouth.

"Alasdair."

"Aye, Fiona?"

"I've just had the strangest thought."

"Tell me it."

"It suddenly occurred to me that the discovery of that second decree, which seemed so dreadful at the time, actually helped bring us together again. Doesn't it seem that way?"

"Aye," he said, thoughtfully. "It was a kind of impetus, wasn't it? It helped each of us realize we wanted to fight. Fight to find each other again."

Lovingly she pressed her lips to the warm, faintly salty skin of his neck. "How wonderful, and how mysterious."

"Life is, I think, filled with mysteries."

"Yes," she agreed. "There's so much we can't know."

"How Isobel came to read the Tome in the first place."

"Why goldfinches arrived at Castle Tadgh," Fiona said.

"Is there really a mysterious Greyman roaming the summit of Ben Macdui."

"The reason dogs turn in a circle before lying down."

"Why people like bad poetry," said Alasdair.

"Will Monty let me have some roses in the spring."

"The spices your cook put into the mutton stew."

In the cozy dimness Fiona smiled. "That, I dare-say, we'll never know."

"And may be better off not knowing."

The edge of the thick wool blanket had slipped away from Fiona's shoulder, and Alasdair brought it up again, tucking it securely around her.

"Thank you, dear heart," said Fiona, drowsily, and yawned again. "Good night," she said to him, "sweet dreams," and then, as if it was the most natural thing in all the world, she gave a soft, happy sigh, closed her eyes, and fell deeply, deeply, asleep in his arms. And a minute or so after that, Alasdair had fallen asleep, too.

There were, in fact, so many things Alasdair and Fiona could not have known.

They didn't know that on this night they had conceived a child, who would grace them with his presence some nine months later. They would call him James Amhuinn Gavin Penhallow — *Amhuinn* being the masculine version of *Nairna*. James would have the dark-red hair of his father, the changeable blue-gray eyes of his mother, and a merry laugh so contagious that you couldn't help but laugh along with him.

They didn't know that James would be joined by a little brother approximately two years later: Archibald Stuart Bruce Penhallow, known at once and forever as Archie, much beloved by James — and vice-versa.

Nor could they know that Duff would become so outraged by how Isobel had been cheated of her modest fortune that he became a dedicated student of the law-books, and would successfully bring her case through the tangled morass of the Edinburgh courts. But they did not live in the city, preferring, instead, to set up house in a charming cottage not far from Castle Tadgh, which very soon became a favorite haunt of the local children, who could rely on Isobel for a doll or a treat, and on Duff for a toy he'd whittled or a fascinating story he would tell. James and Archie would spend a lot of time there.

Further afield, Logan Munro would eventually marry again, to an amiable, attractive young lady whose chief interest in life was dressing in the height of fashion. If he wasn't quite as good a husband to her as he was to Nairna, and if he thought of Fiona a little more often than he should, he at least managed to conceal this from his new wife reasonably well. And if he did kiss housemaids in the stairwell now and then — so fond of him as they were! — this too he did with admirable discretion.

Little Mairi MacIntyre, dainty, girlish, ethereally pretty, would receive several offers of matrimony, but confounded expectations by refusing them all. Instead she would become a passionate advocate for animal welfare in the Western Isles, spending most of her money on these endeavors, doing a great deal of good, and becoming yet more lovely as she aged.

Wynda Ramsay, who had run away from Castle Tadgh in the middle of the night, had gotten as far as Newcastle-upon-Tyne, England, where in due course she would marry a rich old shopkeeper who would then oblige her by dying within a year of their marriage, leaving her his entire fortune. Wynda would then — at last — betake herself to London. She would promptly wed an impoverished viscount, thus fulfilling her long-held ambition of entering the *ton*. If she hadn't quite made it to the upper echelons of Society, well, it was a beginning.

Her French never improved.

And what else lay in store for Fiona and Alasdair?

Immense happiness, and an appreciation for each other that would only continue to grow: love everlasting.

And in the meantime, some other things *would* become known to them.

For example, Shaw would give Fiona one of his retriever wolfhound puppies, who was, everyone agreed, the most engaging, the most adorable creature who ever lived (even with an incurable tendency to try and eat your shoes).

Alasdair, despite a lifetime of avowals to the contrary, would indeed go to England — with Fiona, of course — and to his surprise, he'd have a good time there on his visit. His Sassenach relatives, he would discover, weren't at all what he'd been expecting.

The goldfinches would return, year after year, to Castle Tadgh.

And Monty would indeed bring Fiona roses in the spring, and for as long as they grew and bloomed.

His *best* roses.

Keep reading for a sneak peek at

THE BRIDE TAKES A GROOM,

the third book in Lisa Berne's
irresistible Penhallow Dynasty series

Coming in Spring 2018!

The Basingstoke Select Academy for Young Ladies
Coventry, England
June 1805

A summer evening.

Overhead, a full, golden moon.

A soft, masculine voice murmuring in her ear, "*Ma chérie, je veux te toucher.*"

A hand, drawn across her bosom.

The faintest scent of lavender, carried ever so gently on the breeze that rustled leaves, caressed flowers.

Lavender, and . . . witch hazel?

A sudden, urgent warning sounded deep in Katherine Brooke's brain, but it was too late.

"Miss *Brooke!* Monsieur de la Motte! *What* is the meaning of this?" came the outraged voice of Miss Wolfe, headmistress of the very exclusive and even more expensive boarding school at which Katherine had been immured for two long, miserable years.

Germaine — Monsieur de la Motte — gave an audible gasp of horror, and before Katherine's equally horrified gaze the dashing music instructor who had

been so bold, so daring, so eloquent, seemed abruptly
to become a rather large pile of blancmange. He
released her and pulled away as if he had just been
holding in his arms a repulsive, bad-smelling troll
he'd found lurking under a bridge somewhere, and
gibbered:

"Oh, Mademoiselle Wolfe, forgive me — it was
nothing — without significance — a brotherly embrace
to comfort only — the poor *demoiselle* so lonely and
far from home — and but this one time, I do assure
you — it was that I felt so deeply sorry for her —"

"You lie, you — you *weasel*," interrupted Katherine
hotly. If she'd had her wits about her, she might have
gone along with his inane little story and maybe, just
maybe, mitigated this rapidly unfolding disaster, but
there was something about the way he was babbling
on, as if *she* was nothing, as if *she* was without significance, that made a crimson mist of rage rise up in front
of her eyes like a vengeful wraith.

She wrenched herself around to face Miss Wolfe.
"It's not the first time, we've been meeting in the
garden for *weeks,* and he's been *kissing* me!"

Germaine de la Motte, no doubt aware that his
days at the Basingstoke Select Academy for Young
Ladies had drawn to an immediate close, and that
within mere minutes he would be booted out onto
the street with only his hastily packed valise in hand,
gave Katherine a look of undisguised malice. "But
only, *mademoiselle,* because you sought me out."

Oh, splendid, now the cat was well and truly let
out of the bag, thus making things go instantly from
bad to worse. Katherine could feel her fury dissolv-
ing with almost ludicrous speed and giving way to
soul-shattering embarrassment and shame. So much
for the embraces, the kisses, the furtive touches here
and there, the intensely exciting feel of a man's body

pressed against her own. How wrong and awful she'd been, how *bad* —

And here, to emphasize just how bad, was Miss Wolfe again:

"I can hardly believe my ears! That a pupil of mine would stoop so low! To *solicit* such a thing! To sneak about, like a sordid criminal! And you but barely turned fifteen, Miss Brooke! Be sure that I shall inform your parents by express first thing tomorrow."

Katherine hung her head. She *was* a low, sneaking, criminal sort of girl. "Yes, Miss Wolfe," she muttered, resisting the impulse to kick at a stone which had somehow managed to crassly intrude itself on the otherwise immaculate path of the school's garden. If she was lucky, her parents would have her removed at once.

But as it turned out, she would stay on at the Basingstoke Academy for four more long, miserable years, her parents agreeing with Miss Wolfe's expert (and, ultimately, costly) assessment that Katherine — so unruly, so unpleasant, so unpopular with her fellow pupils — would need them in order to acquire even the most fundamental degree of polish, that essential and elusive *je ne sais quoi*, which would enable her to someday, one hoped, comport herself without committing further, dreadful gaffes.

Six years after the hushed-up incident at the
*   Basingstoke Select Academy for Young Ladies . . .*
Somewhere near the Canadian border
April 1811

It had been a perfectly good day, tramping along the St. Lawrence River and leading his men in a jolly little reconnaissance among the thickly clustered woods, until all at once there was a *crack* and a slight whistling noise.

Then there was a sharp pain six inches down and to the right of his heart.

"Damn it to hell," said Hugo Penhallow, whipping around and in a single rapid motion bringing up his own musket, sighting the French sharpshooter two hundred paces away, and targeting him rather more effectively. He watched with grim satisfaction as the other man crumpled like a puppet released from its string, then sat himself down hard on the ground. His hand, pressed against the front of his red jacket, came away equally red, but unfortunately with his own blood.

If he was lucky, the bullet that was now cozily resident inside him hadn't struck anything of particular importance. It occurred to him now that he was very fond of his internal organs, as they'd functioned beautifully all his life, and he'd love for them to keep on doing exactly that.

Carefully, Hugo allowed himself to slide down into a prone position. Everything was getting all hazy and woolly, and just before he closed his eyes he saw the concerned faces of his men hovering over him. Awfully nice bunch of chaps. He was fortunate to have a group like this under his command. Too bad for them they'd have to convey him all the way back to camp, but that, after all, was one of the hazards of military life, and he was sure they'd do a decent job of it.

The pain, he noticed vaguely, was getting decidedly worse. Well, this certainly was an annoyance. How he loathed those pesky Frenchmen, and wished they'd stay in their own country where they belonged, kowtowing to that blasted little egomaniac Bonaparte and also making brandy which was, admittedly, of excellent quality. In fact, he wouldn't object to a long swallow of that right now. But, he suspected, he was shortly to be losing consciousness, so all things considered, the brandy might well have been a waste.

His last sentient thought was gratitude for the fact that the reconnaissance had been a useful one. His men would be able to confirm that yes, of a surety, there were active enemies in the area, and here was their bloodied and insensate captain to prove it.

Chapter 1

Six months after the eventful reconnaissance
*   mission along the Canadian border . . .*
Brooke House, five miles inland from Whitehaven,
*   England*
October 1811

Many people would have considered Katherine Brooke to be an exceedingly fortunate young lady.

She was rich — rich beyond the wildest dreams of most. Her jewels were of a quality *and* a quantity even a queen would envy. Her gowns were made from the costliest fabrics. Her hats, gloves, shoes, stockings, shawls, pelisses, reticules, and parasols were delivered by the dozens. And her immense bedchamber had been modeled, without thought as to expense, after the neoclassical style currently made fashionable by no less a personage than the Prince Regent himself. It was a marvel of a room, with a high domed ceiling, large gilded mirrors, fireplaces artfully crafted so as to resemble the fronts of ancient Roman temples, pedimented window frames, half a dozen busts of eyeless long-dead emperors rendered in the purest of white marble, and walls painted Pompeiian red.

It was here that Katherine Brooke stood with her back against the closed door, looking at her maid Céleste. "Do you have it?"

"*Oui, mademoiselle.*"

"Give it to me, please."

"*Je suis désolée, mademoiselle,* but it cost more than expected." The maid's narrow face was impassive, her voice respectful, but her attitude was nonetheless imbued with every bit of her usual sly, self-satisfied insolence.

Here we go again, Katherine thought. "How much more?"

"It came all the way from London, *mademoiselle,* and as you know, secrecy is difficult to maintain across so many miles."

"I know it all too well. How much more?"

"*Le coût total* is one pound, eighteen shillings."

"That's absurd."

"*Mademoiselle* is concerned about *le coût?*" Céleste shrugged, glancing around the luxurious room as if she didn't, in fact, know exactly just how much pin-money Katherine received. "*Quel dommage.* Rest assured, I can easily dispose of it elsewhere."

"I'm sure you can." Katherine reached into the satin reticule hanging from her wrist, her fingers slipping past the downy, fragile marabout feathers with which it was lavishly ornamented, and extracted two golden guineas which she held out to Céleste. "Here."

Céleste didn't move. "Would *mademoiselle* like back *les trois shillings?*"

"Keep them." With effort, Katherine kept her face bland. Oh, tedious, tedious, this final extraction of money on top of what was most certainly an inflated fee. She added, insincerely: "By way of a thank-you."

"*Mademoiselle* is too kind." Without hurry, Céleste took the guineas, then slid her hand into the pocket-slit at her waist and produced from within it a small rectangular bundle wrapped in cheap, plain paper.

Katherine snatched it from her, and Céleste smiled.

"It is always a pleasure doing business with *mademoiselle*."

"You may leave."

"But you are expected downstairs, prior to the dinner hour, and your hair is sadly *ébouriffé*."

"Come back in twenty minutes, and fix it then."

"I shall come back in five."

"Ten." Her hands, Katherine noticed, were shaking a little with anticipation. But then, they always did at a moment like this.

"Five minutes, *mademoiselle*. Or *votre chère maman* will notice your absence, and she may well chide me for your lateness. I do not wish to be chided."

"Nor do I." A scanty patch of common ground between herself and Céleste. She said, "Have you ever wondered what would happen if Mother found out about our — ah — transactions?"

"I would doubtless be let go at once, and *sans reference*," replied Céleste coolly. "One can only speculate as to your punishment, *mademoiselle*. Too, you would lose my services as an *intermédiaire*, which would be a punishment in itself, would you not agree? It is not always so easy to find someone as resourceful, and as discreet, as I."

This complacent assertion Katherine could not dispute. It had been six years since that humiliating debacle at the Basingstoke Select Academy and the maid Céleste had been forced upon her; the two of them had lived alongside each other locked into this vile dynamic, in which their antipathy was mutual but each benefited from their clandestine dealings. Céleste had been magnificently feathering her nest with all the money Katherine gave her; and as for herself — she very nearly brought the little package to her nose, to sample its heady fragrance, but instead said:

"Which reminds me. Where are the books I asked for?"

"The volume of Shakespeare's plays is *en route*, I am told, *mademoiselle*, but the other — the Italian book —"

"*La Divina Commedia*."

"*Oui*. It is proving more difficult to locate in the original language. Rest assured, I have not forgotten." Céleste smiled again, with a knowing sort of glimmer that made Katherine feel as if her skin was prickling with shamed embarrassment. "Shall I leave you now, so that you might enjoy *votre petite gâterie?*"

"Yes. Do." Katherine stepped aside, and Céleste sauntered out of the room; the moment the door was shut Katherine leaned against it again and carefully, oh so carefully, unfolded the paper in her hands.

There. There they were. Saliva pooled in her mouth as she stared at the two dozen *diablotins*, the dark thin disks of chocolate covered densely with nonpareils, tiny, tasty white balls of sugar. For years Mother had forbidden her candy, insisting it made her hideously spotty, but still Katherine had found a way.

Diablotin.

It meant *imp* or *gremlin* in French.

A defiant little smile curved her lips and quickly she popped one of the disks into her mouth.

Oh, delicious. Delicious — exquisite — beguiling — magical — except that words couldn't even come close to describing it. She closed her eyes, savoring. The taste was both bitter and sweet, the chocolate smooth and rich on her tongue; the little nonpareils crunched between her teeth, yielding up a tantalizing contrast of textures.

But one wasn't enough. And time was short. Katherine opened her eyes and rapidly consumed three, four, five *diablotins,* waiting for the rush of pleasure that always came with eating chocolate. No wonder the ancient Aztecs believed that cacao seeds, from which chocolate was made, were a gift from the gods, or that they valued the seeds so greatly they used them as currency. She'd read that in one of her history books, at present hidden away in a locked box under her bed.

And speaking of books . . .

What excellent news that her contraband volume of Shakespeare's plays was on the way. At school they could only read the Bowdlers' version, *The Family Shakespeare,* edited — *dissected* was more like it — in a way that supposedly protected a maiden's delicate sensibilities. All the really good parts had been removed, the bits having to do with bad people using bad words, no doubt, and doing bad deeds. Katherine could barely wait to read them all.

She smiled, really smiled. She was feeling it now. For a few precious moments she would feel happy. Good. *Alive.*

Until Céleste came back, and did whatever she was going to do with her hair, and she would have to go downstairs. Ugh. Another excruciating evening spent with her parents and their — what was a good way to describe them?

"Guests" didn't quite do them justice. Katherine preferred "leeches in human form." Hovering a few rungs below Society's upper echelon, they doubtless had received no better invitations elsewhere, and so here they flocked, the best her parents could do. They

ate, they drank, they borrowed money, they expected
the Brooke servants to wait on them hand and foot,
and for all she knew they were smuggling the silver
into their trunks.

But their worst offense? Well, she'd be willing to
wager that none of them had ever read a book from
start to finish. And their conversation — if one could
call it that — reflected this sad fact. Mealtimes were
interminable.

But at least she would know, all throughout the
next several hours, that concealed in her armoire,
at the far end of a drawer underneath a pile of silk
stockings, were eighteen more *diablotins,* waiting for
her to come back.

At around the same time . . .
On the road to Whitehaven

Many people would have considered Captain Hugo
Penhallow to be a man in trouble.

He had almost no money, and no income to an-
ticipate; an old house was his only property. In addition, he had a large family to support: a widowed
mother, a younger sister, and three younger brothers.
His profession for the past eight years, in the Army,
was no longer a viable one, for he had recently sold
out. As the son of a gentleman, naturally he had no
training for any other occupation. And, finally, several months ago he had badly broken his left leg and
so now, when he was fatigued, he walked with an
unmistakable limp.

Yet here was Hugo, riding north along the Long-
town Road on this cool, cloudy afternoon, sitting

his horse with casual grace and whistling cheerfully, giving all the appearance of a person without a care in the world.

This was, in fact, largely how he was feeling.

For one thing, he was on his way home, and he'd soon be with his dear and delightful family, whom he hadn't seen once during those eight years, as he had been sent to the annoyingly obstreperous territory along the Canadian border. Letters had helped bridge the distance between himself and home, although he was fairly certain that not all of them were delivered or received, it being not uncommon to have placed in his hands a letter that looked as if it had been in a battle itself, so begrimed and bent was it.

As for the financial difficulties, Hugo wasn't ignoring just how dire they were, but he *was* taking action: he had decided to capitalize on his two chief assets, both intangible but clearly of significant value in certain circles.

One — he was a Penhallow. It was an old and illustrious name that loomed large, disproportionately large, among the *haut ton*. The first Penhallow, so it was said, had long ago come to England with the great Conqueror himself, and the Conqueror had humbly deferred to *him*. Hugo had gone straight from Eton into the Army, and so hadn't spent any time in Society; he'd therefore never personally observed the effect of his hoary surname upon even the loftiest dukes and earls. Nonetheless, he was fully aware of the cachet which enabled any Penhallow — even a straitened member of the cadet branch such as himself — to walk about trailing, as it were, clouds of glory. All rather comical, in his opinion, but there it was.

Two — the female sex evidently found him attractive, which would make his task easier. For years he had heard himself compared left and right to a Greek god which, as a modest fellow, he found extremely silly. He was one of those tall, fit sort of men, an attribute for which of course he was appreciative, but still, one couldn't help being born the way one was, and it was decidedly uncomfortable to be stared at as if one were an exotic beast on display.

Yet if his appearance assisted him in his quest, so much the better. And that quest was to marry into money. He had evaluated his limited options carefully, and all in all this seemed to be the best and most expeditious way to solve the problem.

He *could* have continued to accept assistance from his older cousin, Gabriel Penhallow, who several years ago had not only generously purchased his commission but had also provided him income in the form of an allowance (most of which he'd had diverted to his stalwart mama, holding the fort back in Whitehaven). No, that sort of thing — charity — was all well and good for a single-minded, Army-mad youth, but he was done with that now. That bullet in his midsection back in April had resulted in a serious, lingering infection, which ultimately had his kindly commander forcibly putting him onto a ship bound for home, and there was nothing like a long sea voyage when one was weak as a damned cat to inspire an extended period of introspection.

While Gabriel's assistance — which also included sending an additional cheque to Mama once or twice a year — was gratefully received by both himself and the mater, the plain truth was that it wasn't sufficient to see the children adequately established in life. With Gwendolyn now fourteen, the twins Percy and Francis thirteen, and Bertram twelve, the issue had become considerably more urgent. But he had no intention of asking Gabriel for anything more. Never in a million years could he imagine himself saying, *Thanks for all that you've done, Coz, and now could you give me many times that sum over again.*

It was, Hugo had concluded, a perfect time in which to take destiny by the shoulders and give it a good hard rattle.

And as luck would have it, a tremendous storm had blown up as the ship neared the western coast, forcing them to divert from Liverpool to Bude, where, his wound having reopened in spectacular style, he'd decided to hotfoot it to Gabriel's estate in Somerset, as it was much closer than Whitehaven and the last thing he'd wanted to do was horrify his family by staggering home as a moribund invalid.

Once he got to Surmont Hall, he had — in an embarrassingly dramatic fashion — toppled off his horse like a sack of turnips and nearly bled to death on Gabriel's enormous graveled carriage-sweep.

Some might have thought this a bad thing, but really, when you looked at it another way, it had all worked out beautifully. He'd been able to recuperate at his leisure, attended by a very capable doctor as well as by a veritable horde of servants offering a tempting array of food and drink multiple times a day. Too, it gave him the opportunity to thank Gabriel in person for his generosity and insist that he both accept repayment for the commission and terminate the allowance; to write home alerting them as to his arrival upon *terra firma;* and to receive in return a buoyant letter from his mother which contained along with her usual fond, rambling report of his siblings' health and activities a tidbit of neighborhood news which had instantly caught his eye.

According to Cook who had it from the butcher whose wife somehow seems to know

*everything that happens within a twenty-mile
radius of Whitehaven, Brooke House is packed
to capacity with guests along with, of course,
Mr. and Mrs. Brooke as well as Katherine —
your former playmate, you know, such a sweet,
lively little girl she was! — who had her first
Season and received many offers (highly understandable given the extent of her fortune)
but came home without, evidently, any of them
being accepted. Cook also says that the butcher's wife told her that one of the custom officer's
children very nearly drowned yesterday. Bertram says he knows the boy and that he'd been
told many times to stay away when the waves
are rough. How very frightening for his people.
Also Cook mentioned —*

Now here, to be sure, was another great piece of
luck. An unwed heiress practically on his doorstep!
What could be more convenient?

To own the truth, Hugo hadn't thought of Katherine in years. It was well over a decade since he'd
last seen her. He had been thirteen at the time, and
had come home from Eton for Father's funeral. The
Brookes, then, had lived next door, and more than
once had little Kate — six years younger than himself, yet even so they'd been good friends — slipped
between the line of bay trees separating their houses
and come to console him.

He'd been grateful for her visits, for a hard time
it was, very hard indeed: first the shock of Father's
sudden death, and then its painful aftermath, with
his three siblings so little, still in leading strings, and
Mama pregnant with Bertram.

Their man of business, Mr. Storridge, had laid it
out plain: the late Anthony Penhallow, always more

interested in science than in money, had left behind very little for his family aside from the modest sum of eight thousand pounds invested in the five percents and their big old house overlooking the wide sandy shore that gave way to the blue-green depths of the ocean.

If the remaining Penhallows practiced the strictest economy, Mr. Storridge had said in his dry, precise voice, they would manage to get by. Hugo had immediately declared his intention to withdraw from Eton and spare Mama the expense of his keeping there, but this she had, in her gentle way, forbidden.

Oh, my dear Hugo, she had said, smiling through the tears which seemed to flow almost continuously during those dark days, *it was your papa's dearest wish that you receive the same education he did. He was so very proud of you! And wasn't it clever of him to pay your fees in advance? Almost —* And here she had paused to hold back a pitiful sob — *almost as if he knew something would happen to him.*

Yes, Mama, he'd replied, *school's not a bad thing, but what about Gwennie, and the twins, and the baby? I'll make the headmaster give you back the money. And I'll find a job. I could become a sailor.*

And a marvelous one you'd be, too, darling Hugo. I can just picture you climbing a rigging like a monkey! But you're to keep on your path, go back to school, and not to worry about the children. Everything will be fine.

Somehow he had managed to swallow a great lump in his throat, and say, *How will it, Mama?*

It simply will, she had answered, confidently. *And look, I've just today received a letter from dear Anthony's cousin Henrietta Penhallow, with an invitation to spend the summer holiday with her and her grandson Gabriel in Bath. You and Gabriel will travel from school together. Isn't that kind?*

He would have infinitely rather have come home, but had only said, *If it will save money, Mama, I'll do it.*

That's my brave boy, she'd said, and at that moment he had felt that any sacrifice, large or small, was worth it, if it could but lighten her load. It was a feeling that had never left him, and now Hugo smiled a little, noticing with pleasure the familiar tang of salt air, and the faintest hint of the ocean's restless breeze.

Not much further now.

With luck, he'd be home by dinnertime.

Whistling again, gently he pressed his heels into his horse's sides, urging it to go just a little faster, and obligingly it picked up its pace.

Actually, by the time Katherine reluctantly made her way downstairs, there were only fifteen *diablotins* hidden in her armoire, as she had managed to quickly eat three more before Céleste had returned.

A light rain had begun to fall, and dusk was settling its mellow hand upon the streets, buildings, and gardens of Whitehaven, lingering softly upon the broad expanse of sand and sea, as Hugo came to the old stable that stood upon a corner of their property furthest from the beach. He dismounted and thrust the horse's reins into the hand of the aged groom who had cautiously emerged from the stable, and was now staring in evident amazement at the master upon whom he'd not set eyes in quite some time.

"Hullo, Hoyt!" said Hugo amiably, "you're looking exactly the same, I'm happy to see. Trust all is well?"

At the other's dumbstruck nod, Hugo went on, "Splendid! I say, take care of this nag, will you? She's held up wonderfully all the way here, bless her, and I'm no featherweight, am I? Well, I'm off to the house — hope I'm not too late for dinner. Good night, then."

He had already unstrapped from the saddle his neat leather rucksack, and so, after a friendly nod to the still-speechless Hoyt, walked with eager steps toward the large, rambling old house which looked, even to his own affectionate eyes, considerably more dilapidated than he remembered. The reddish clay bricks with which it was constructed were crumbling in places, the sloping slate roof looked extremely weather-beaten, and several windows on the upper-most story had been clumsily boarded up.

He took this in, and went lightly up the front steps onto the wide, welcoming portico.

He was home at last.

From inside he could hear dogs barking — they'd doubtless heard him come onto the portico, and he took a moment to wonder if he would know any of them after all this while — along with odd screech-ing noises and then, not waiting to bang the old iron knocker, Hugo opened the door and let himself in, into the chilly, ill-lit entry hall, large and high-ceilinged, shabby and familiar, and quite possibly the nicest place on earth. As he dropped his rucksack onto a bench, a pack of mongrels, all unfamiliar, surged down one of the halls toward him, barking fiercely, even as a maid-servant scuttled in from the kitchen passageway, look-ing alarmed and gasping out:

"Oh! Sir! Was you expected? I'll just get the mis-tress, if you'll wait here, please —"

"Not to worry, I'll go to her," answered Hugo over the cacophony of barks, yips, nails madly clicking on wood flooring, and loud hostile panting. "Are they all at dinner?"

"Yes, sir, but —"

"What's your name, then?"

"It's Eliza, sir, but —"

"Quiet!" said Hugo to the dogs who, recognizing the genial tone of authority, instantly subsided and sat on their haunches, wagging their tails and casting up at him looks of servile adoration. He counted them. There were only five, after all, although from their collective volume one would have thought there were at least a dozen, and altogether a motley lot — one was missing an ear, another seemed to have the head of a poodle set upon the body of a dachshund, and still another had eyes of a milky opacity which suggested severe vision problems if not actual blindness.

Hugo patted the biggest of them, an enormous white and brown Great Dane whose front legs were noticeably crooked, and said to Eliza:

"Tell Robinson to set another place for me, would you? I'll go in directly."

"Oh, sir, but Robinson's not here."

"Egad, not dead, is he?" Hugo hoped not, as he had been very fond of their old butler; he'd loyally stayed on after Father had died, despite having his wages drastically reduced.

"Oh no, sir, he's alive, but his palsy got so bad that the mistress pensioned him off, you see, and he's living with his daughter Nancy and her family, up on Roper Street. Very happy he is, sir. Takes a pint every day at the pub, and sings in the choir on Sundays."

Hugo was pulling off his greatcoat and hanging it on a peg. "Well, that's excellent news. I'll go see him later this week. See here, Eliza, I'm hungry as a bear. Can *you* set a place for me?"

"To be sure I can, sir! But — but — if you'll forgive me asking — who *are* you, sir?"

"Good God, didn't my mother tell any of you I was coming? No wonder poor old Hoyt looked as if he'd seen a ghost!" He laughed. "Never mind. I'm the prodigal son, Eliza! The eldest, you know — Hugo."

Eliza looked astonished. "Oh! Sir! *You're* Mr. Hugo? We was all afeared *you* was dead!"

"Dead! Why?"

"Because the mistress said you'd been shot by a Frenchy, Mr. Hugo, and that you was laid up in your cousin's house — and then there wasn't any more letters from you! Cook says them French bullets have a special poison in them, sir, that drains the life right out of a person!"

Blast it all, he'd deliberately trivialized the nature of his illness when writing home, not wishing to worry them — and why hadn't Mama received the letter he'd written from Gabriel's house a fortnight ago, informing her that he was fine, and would soon be on his way? Well, he could allay their anxieties right now.

"I *was* shot," he said to Eliza, "but it would take more than some beastly Frenchman to kill me, that's for certain! Go on, now, and bring me some supper, that's a good girl."

She bobbed a curtsy and Hugo, favoring his left leg ever so slightly, went down the long dim hallway to the dining-parlor, the dogs trotting behind with the same pliant obedience the children of Hamelin were said to have displayed while following the Pied Piper. The oak-framed double doors to the dining-parlor had been left open and so Hugo strolled right in and paused just inside the threshold. "I say, I'm home."

Five golden-blond heads swiveled in his direction, five pairs of wide blue eyes displayed shocked surprise, and then pandemonium erupted.

THE SMYTHE-SMITH QUARTET BY #1 *NEW YORK TIMES* BESTSELLING AUTHOR

JULIA QUINN

JUST LIKE HEAVEN
978-0-06-149190-0

Honoria Smythe-Smith is to play the violin (badly) in the annual musicale performed by the Smythe-Smith quartet. But first she's determined to marry by the end of the season. When her advances are spurned, can Marcus Holroyd, her brother Daniel's best friend, swoop in and steal her heart in time for the musicale?

A NIGHT LIKE THIS
978-0-06-207290-0

Anne Wynter is not who she says she is, but she's managing quite well as a governess to three highborn young ladies. Daniel Smythe-Smith might be in mortal danger, but that's not going to stop the young earl from falling in love. And when he spies a mysterious woman at his family's annual musicale, he vows to pursue her.

THE SUM OF ALL KISSES
978-0-06-207292-4

Hugh Prentice has never had patience for dramatic females, and Lady Sarah Pleinsworth has never been acquainted with the words *shy* or *retiring*. Besides, a reckless duel has left Hugh with a ruined leg, and now he could never court a woman like Sarah, much less dream of marrying her.

THE SECRETS OF SIR RICHARD KENWORTHY
978-0-06-207294-8

Sir Richard Kenworthy has less than a month to find a bride, and when he sees Iris Smythe-Smith hiding behind her cello at her family's infamous musicale, he thinks he might have struck gold. Iris is used to blending into the background, so when Richard courts her, she can't quite believe it's true.

JQ4 0916

At Avon Books, we know your passion for romance—once you finish one of our novels, you find yourself wanting more.

May we tempt you with . . .

- **Excerpts** from our upcoming releases.

- Entertaining **extras**, including authors' personal photo albums and book lists.

- Behind-the-scenes **scoop** on your favorite characters and series.

- **Sweepstakes** for the chance to win free books, romantic getaways, and other fun prizes.

- Writing **tips** from our authors and editors.

- **Blog** with our authors and find out why they love to write romance.

- **Exclusive content** that's not contained within the pages of our novels.

Join us at
www.avonbooks.com

AVON

An Imprint of HarperCollins*Publishers*
www.avonromance.com

*G*ive in to your Impulses!

These unforgettable stories only take a second to buy and give you hours of reading pleasure!

Go to *www.AvonImpulse.com* and see what we have to offer.

Available wherever e-books are sold.

AVONIMPULSE

IMP 0811